SOLDIER OF ARETE

Also by Gene Wolfe

Endangered Species
Free Live Free
Soldier of the Mist
There Are Doors
The Urth of the New Sun

GENE WOLFE

SOLDIER OF ARETE

NEW ENGLISH LIBRARY

British Library Cataloguing in Publication Data

Wolfe, Gene, *1931–*
Soldier of Arete.
I. Title
813.54 [F]

ISBN 0-450-51334-3

First published in USA by Tor Books,
published by Tom Doherty Associates, Inc.
First published in Great Britain 1990

Reproduced by arrangement with Tor Books,
Tom Doherty Associates, Inc.,
49 West 24 Street, New York, NY10010.

Published by New English Library,
a hardcover imprint of Hodder and Stoughton,
a division of Hodder and Stoughton Ltd,
Mill Road, Dunton Green, Sevenoaks, Kent TN13 2YA
Editorial Office: 47 Bedford Square, London WC1B 3DP

Printed in Great Britain by St Edmundsbury Press Ltd,
Bury St Edmunds, Suffolk

Bound by Hartnolls Ltd,
Bodmin, Cornwall

This book
is dedicated
to the old colonel,
the most underrated
of ancient authors
and the least heeded:
Xenophon the Athenian

And there came one to Xenophon as he was offering sacrifice, and said, "Gryllus is dead." And Xenophon took off the garland that was on his head, but ceased not his sacrifice. Then the messenger said, "His death was noble." And Xenophon returned the garland to his head again; and it is the tale that he shed no tears, but said, "I knew that I begat him mortal."

—Diogenes Laertius

Foreword

This scroll is in poor condition and contains various lacunae. "Latro" seems not to have written for a week or more following the departure of his party from Pactye. The Thracian winter may well have been the sole cause; although papyrus will endure for thousands of years, it falls to bits on being wet. Its fragile nature is only too well illustrated by this example, which has been severely damaged toward its center. By that, we have lost a considerable portion of the text, presumably dealing with the arrival of the *Europa* at Piraeus. A third hiatus, apparently resulting from morbid depression, follows his description of the ceremony of manumission at Sparta.

The horsemanship of the ancients has been much maligned by modern scholars unable to conceive of a rider retaining his seat without stirrups. They would be well advised to look into the history of the Plains Indians, who rode like ancient cavalrymen and like them employed lances, bows, and javelins. (The light, long-hafted axes used by the Persian cavalry would be instantly approved by Geronimo or Cochise.) In my opinion the Indian who fired his .45–70 Springfield from the back of his galloping pony—and this was done frequently—performed a feat more difficult than any demanded of ancient horsemen.

The reader should be aware that the horses of the ancient Greeks were unshod and were rarely gelded—never, if they were to be used in war. Though they were small by modern standards, the lack of stirrups made mounting difficult. (In fact, it may well be that stirrups were originally mounting devices, adopted when selective breeding had at last produced larger animals.) The cavalryman employed his lance or pair of javelins to vault onto his horse's back. Some horses were trained to advance their forelegs to render mounting easier.

As this account makes abundantly clear, modern historians are mistaken in rejecting the Amazons as legendary. Ancient writers record their invasion of central Greece in the time of Theseus (c. 1600 B.C.) in circumstantial detail, while the funeral mounds of fallen Amazon leaders dotted the route from Attica to Thrace. In any event, it should be obvious that among nomads a determined 120-pound woman might be a more valuable fighter than a man of half again her weight, equally effective with the bow while tiring her mount far less. It should not be necessary to point out that women warriors are found throughout history, or that our own age has more than most.

Pankration was the ancient equivalent of the martial arts. Only biting and gouging were forbidden, and the fight continued until the loser acknowledged his defeat. Students are cautioned that not every athlete shown striking another with his fists is a boxer. Boxers' hands were bound with leather thongs.

This scroll is of particular interest in that it contains the only known example of the prose of Pindar, after Homer the greatest Greek poet.

Part

1

1

I Will Make a New Beginning

On this fresh scroll, which the black man has found in the city. This morning Io showed me how I wrote in my old one and told me how valuable it had been to me. I read only the first sheet and the last, but I mean to read the rest before the sun sets. Now, however, I intend to write down all the things that will be most needful for me to know.

Latro is what these people call me, though I doubt that it is my name. The man in the lion's skin called me *Lucius,* or so I wrote in the first scroll. There also I wrote that I forget very quickly, and I believe it to be true. When I try to recall what took place yesterday, I find only confused impressions of walking, working, and talking, so that I am like a vessel lost in fog, from which the lookout sees, perhaps, looming shadows that may be rocks, or other vessels, or nothing—hears voices that may be those of men ashore, or of the tritons, or ghosts.

It is not so with Io, nor, I believe, with the black man.

Thus I have learned that this is the Thracian Chersonese, this captured city, Sestos. Here a battle was fought by the Men of Thought against the People from Parsa by which the chief men of the latter hoped to escape. Thus says Io, and when I objected that the city seems fit to stand a lengthy siege, she explained there was not food enough, so that the People from Parsa and the Hellenes, too (for it is a city of Hellenes), starved behind their walls. Io is a child, yet nearly a woman. Her hair is long and dark.

The governor of the place assembled all his forces before one of the chief gates and put his wives and female slaves (of whom he had many) in tented carts. There he harangued his men, saying he would lead them against the Men of Thought; but when the gates were unbarred, he and his ministers went swiftly and secretly to another part of the wall and let themselves down by straps, thinking to escape while the battle raged. It was for naught, and some are captives here.

As am I, for there is a man called Hypereides who speaks of me as his slave—the black man also. (His head, which is round and very bald, reaches to my nose; he stands straight and speaks quickly.) Nor is this all, for Io—who calls herself *my* slave though this morning I offered to free her—says King Pausanias of Rope claims us, too. He sent us here, and a hundred of his Rope Makers were here until just before the battle, when their leader was wounded and they (having little liking for sieges and expecting a long one) sailed for home.

It is winter. The wind blows hard and cold, and rain falls often; but we live in a fine house, one of those the People from Parsa took for their own use earlier. There are sandals beneath my bed, but we wear boots—Io says that Hypereides bought such boots for all of us when the city surrendered, and two pairs for himself. This Chersonese is a very rich land, and like all rich lands it turns to mud in the rain.

This morning I went to the market. The citizens of Sestos are Hellenes, as I said, and of the Aeolian race—the people of the winds. They asked anxiously whether we planned to stay all winter, and told me much of the danger of sailing to Hellas at this season; I believe this is because they fear that the People from Parsa will not delay in recapturing so fertile a country. When I returned, I asked Io if she thought we would stay. She said we would surely go, and soon; but that we might come back if the People from Parsa try to retake the city.

Something quite unusual happened this evening, and though it has been dark for a long while, I wish to make a note of it before I go out again. Here Hypereides writes his orders and keeps his accounts, so there is a fire and a fine bright lamp with four wicks.

He came while I was polishing his greaves and had me buckle on my sword and put on my cloak and my new patasos. Together we hurried through the city to the citadel, where the prisoners are kept. We climbed many steps to a room in a tower, in which the only prisoners were a man and a boy; there were two guards also, but Hypereides dismissed them. When they were gone, he seated himself and said, "Artaÿctes, my poor friend, it is in no easy position that you find yourself."

The man of Parsa nodded. He is a large man with cold eyes, and though his beard is nearly gray he looks strong; seeing him, I thought I understood why Hypereides had wanted me to accompany him.

"You know that I've done all I could for you," Hypereides continued. "Now I require that you do something for me—a very small thing."

"No doubt," replied Artaÿctes. "What is this small thing?" He speaks the tongue of Hellas worse even than I, I think.

"When your master crossed into our land, he did so upon a bridge of boats. Isn't that so?"

Artaÿctes nodded, as did the boy.

"I've heard that its deck was covered with earth for its entire length," Hypereides continued, wondering. "Some even assert that the earth was planted with trees."

The boy said, "It was—I saw it. There were saplings and bushes at the sides so our cavalry horses wouldn't be afraid of the water."

Hypereides whistled softly. "Amazing! Really amazing! I envy you—it must have been a wonderful sight." He turned back to the father, saying, "A most promising young lord. What's his name?"

"It is Artembares," Artaÿctes told him. "He's named for my grandfather, who was a friend to Cyrus."

At that Hypereides smiled slyly. "But wasn't all the world a friend to Cyrus? Conquerors have a great many friends."

Artaÿctes was not to be disturbed thus. "What you say is true," he said. "Yet all the world did not sit over wine with Cyrus."

Hypereides shook his head ruefully. "How sad to think that Artembares' descendant drinks no wine at all now. Or at least, I wouldn't think they give you any here."

"Water and gruel, mostly," Artaÿctes admitted.

"I don't know whether I can save your life and your son's," Hypereides told him. "The citizens want to see you dead, and Xanthippos, as always, seems to favor the side to which he is speaking at the moment. But while you still live I think I can promise you wine—good wine, too, for I'll furnish it myself—and better food if you'll answer one small question for me."

Artaÿctes glanced at me, then asked, "Why don't you beat me until I speak, Hypereides? You and this fellow could manage it, I imagine."

"I wouldn't do such a thing," Hypereides said virtuously. "Not to an old acquaintance. However, there are others. . . ."

"Of course. I have my honor to consider, Hypereides. But I am not unreasonable—nor am I so stupid that I do not guess that Xanthippos sent you. What is his question?"

Hypereides grinned, then grew serious once more, rubbing his hands as though about to sell something at a good price. "I—I, Artaÿctes—desire to know whether the noble Oeobazus was in your party when you let yourself down from the wall."

Artaÿctes glanced at his son, his hard eyes so swift I was not sure that I had seen them move. "I see no harm in telling you that—he will have made good his escape by now."

Hypereides rose, smiling. "Thank you, my friend! You may trust me for everything I have promised. And more, because I'll see to it that both your lives are spared, if I can. Latro, I must confer with some people here. I want you to go back to the place where we're staying and fetch a skin of the best wine for Artaÿctes and his son. I'll tell the guards to let you in with it when you return. Bring a torch, too; it will be dark before we go back, I think."

I nodded and unbarred the door for Hypereides; but before his foot had touched the threshold, he turned to put another question to Artaÿctes. "By the way, where did you plan to cross? At Aegospotami?"

Artaÿctes shook his head. "Helle's Sea was black with your ships. At Pactye, perhaps, or farther north. May I ask why you are so much interested in my friend Oeobazus?"

But Artaÿctes' own question came too late; Hypereides was already hurrying away. I followed him out, and the soldiers who guarded Artaÿctes (who had been waiting on the wall for us to leave) returned to their posts.

The wall of Sestos varies in height from place to place as it circles the city; this was one of the highest, where I think it must be a hundred cubits at least. It commanded a fine view of countryside and the sun setting over the western lands, and I paused there for a moment to look at it. Those who stare at the sun go blind, as I well know, and thus I kept my eyes upon the land and the sun-dyed clouds, which were indeed very beautiful; but as chance would have it, I glimpsed the sun itself from the corner of my eye and saw there, in place of the usual sphere of fire, a chariot of gold drawn by four horses. I knew then that I had glimpsed a god, just as—according to my old scroll—I had seen a goddess before the death of the man who called me Lucius. It frightened me, as I suppose the goddess must have also, and I hurried down the stairs and through the streets of Sestos (which are gloomy and very cramped, as no doubt those of all such walled cities must be) to this house. It was not until I had found a skin of excellent wine and bound together a handful of splents to make a torch, that I understood the full import of what I had seen.

For what I had seen was merely this: although the sun had nearly reached the horizon, the horses of the sun had been at a full gallop. It had seemed so natural that I had not paused to question it; but as I reflected upon the sight, I realized that no charioteer would drive at the gallop if he were close to the place at which he intended to halt—how could he stop his team without the gravest danger of wrecking his chariot? Indeed, though only two horses are hitched to the chariots used in war, all soldiers know that one of the chief advantages of cavalry is that horsemen may be halted and turned so much more readily than chariots.

Clearly then, the sun does not halt at the western limit of the world, as I have always supposed, to reappear next day at the eastern in the same way that fixed stars vanish in the west to reappear in the east. No, rather the sun continues at full career, passes beneath the world, and reappears in the east just as we should see a runner dash behind some building and reappear on the opposite side. I cannot help but wonder why. Are there those living beneath the world who have need of the sun, even as we? This is something I must consider at more length when I have the leisure to do so.

It would be a weary task to set down here all the thoughts—most half-formed and some very foolish—that filled my mind as I made my way through the streets again and mounted the stairs of the tower. Artaÿctes' guards let me in without caviling, and one even fetched a krater in which to mix water with the wine I had brought. While they were thus occupied, Artaÿctes drew me aside, saying softly, "There is no need for you to sleep badly, Latro. Help us and these fools will never learn you bore arms against them."

His words confirmed what I had already gathered from my old scroll—that I had once been in the service of the Great King of Parsa. I nodded and whispered that I would certainly free them if I could.

Just then Hypereides came in, all smiles, carrying six salt pilchards on a string. There was a charcoal brazier to warm the guardroom, and he laid the fish here and there upon the coals where they would not burn. "One for each of us, and they should be good eating. Not much fruit this time of year, or much food in Sestos yet after the siege; but Latro can go out and try to find us some apples when we've finished these, if you like. And some fresh bread, Latro. Didn't you tell me you'd seen a bakery open today?"

I nodded and reminded him that I had bought bread when I went to the market.

"Excellent!" Hypereides exclaimed. "It'll be closed now, I'm afraid, but perhaps you can rouse out the baker with a few thumps on his door." He winked at Artaÿctes. "Latro's a first-rate thumper, I assure you, and commands a voice like a bull's when he wants to. Now if—"

At that moment something so extraordinary occurred that I hesitate to write of it, for I feel quite certain that I will not believe it when I read this scroll in the days that are yet to come: one of Hypereides' salted pilchards moved.

His eyes must have been sharper than mine, because he fell silent to stare at it, while I merely assumed that one of the pieces of charcoal supporting it had shifted. A moment later, I saw it flip its tail just as a hooked fish does when it is cast onto the riverbank; and in a moment more all six were flopping about on the coals as though they had been thrown alive into the fire.

To give the guards credit, they did not run; if they had, I believe I would have run as well. As for Hypereides, his face went white, and he backed away from the brazier as if it were a dog with the running disease. Artaÿctes' young son cowered like the rest of us, but Artaÿctes himself went calmly to Hypereides and laid a hand upon his shoulder, saying, "This prodigy has no reference to you, my friend. It is meant for me—Protesilaos of Elaeus is telling me that though he is as dead as a dried fish, yet he has authority from the gods to punish the man who wronged him."

Hypereides gulped, and stammered, "Yes—that's—it's one of the chief reasons they insist that you—that you and your son— They say that you stole the offerings from his tomb and—and—plowed up his sacred soil."

Artaÿctes nodded and glanced toward the fish; by that time they had ceased to jump, but he shivered as if he were cold just the same. "Hear me now, Hypereides, and promise that you will report everything I say to Xanthippos. I will pay one hundred talents to restore the shrine of Protesilaos." He hesitated as though waiting for some further sign, but there was none. "And in addition I will give you soldiers from Thought two hundred talents if you will spare my son and me. The money is at Susa, but you can keep my boy here as a hostage until it is all paid. And it will *be* paid, I swear by Ahura Mazda, the god of the gods—paid in full and in gold."

Hypereides' eyes popped from their sockets at the magnitude of the sum. It is well known that the People of Parsa are rich beyond imagining, yet I think that few have dreamed that anyone other than the Great King himself could command such wealth as this offer of Artaÿctes' suggested. "I'll tell him. I'll— In the—no, tonight. If—"

"Good! Do so." Artaÿctes squeezed Hypereides' shoulder and stepped back.

Hypereides glanced at the guards. "But I'll have to tell him everything that's happened. Latro, I don't imagine you fancy any of those fish—I know I don't. I think it's time we went home."

I will return to the citadel now—perhaps something can be done to help Artaÿctes and Artembares.

2

Artaÿctes Dies

The herald's cry brought me from my bed this morning. I was pulling on my shoes when Hypereides rapped on the door of the room I share with Io. "Latro!" he called. "Are you awake?"

Io sat up and asked what the trouble was.

I told her, "Artaÿctes is to be executed this morning."

"Do you remember who he is?"

"Yes," I said. "I know I spoke with him last night, before Hypereides and I came home."

Just then Hypereides himself opened our door. "Ah, you're up. Want to come with me to see them killed?"

I asked him who was to die, other than Artaÿctes.

"His son, I'm afraid." Hypereides shook his head sadly. "You don't remember Artaÿctes' boy?"

I cast my mind back. "I have some recollection of seeing a child last night," I told him. "Yes, I think it was a boy, a bit older than Io."

Hypereides pointed a finger at her. "*You* are to stay here, young woman! Do you understand me? You've work to do, and this will be no sight for a girl."

I followed him out into the street, where the black man was waiting for us; and the three of us set off for the sand spit on which the Great King's bridge had ended. It was there, as half a dozen heralds were still bawling (and as half Sestos was busy telling the other half) that Artaÿctes was to die. The day was overcast and windy, with gray clouds scudding along Helle's Sea from the First Sea in the north.

"This weather reminds me," Hypereides muttered, "that we must all have new cloaks before we leave here—you particularly, Latro. That rag of yours is hardly fit for a beggar."

The black man touched Hypereides' shoulder, his eyes wide.

"For you, too? Yes, of course. I said so. For all of us, in fact, even little Io."

The black man shook his head and repeated his gesture.

"Oh, ah. You want to know about our voyage—I was about to tell you. Get us to where we can see what's going on, you two, and I'll give you all the details."

By that time the people from Sestos were crowding forward and Xanthippos' troops were pushing them back with the butts of their spears. Fortunately several of the soldiers recognized Hypereides, and we were able to claim a place in front without much trouble. There was nothing to see yet but a couple of men digging a hole, apparently for the end of a timber that they had carried to the spot.

"Xanthippos isn't here," Hypereides commented. "They won't be starting for a while yet."

I asked who Xanthippos was, and he said, "Our strategist. All these soldiers are under his command. Don't you remember Artaÿctes mentioning him last night?"

I admitted I did not. The name *Artaÿctes* seemed familiar, which was natural enough since the heralds had been shouting it as we came; then I remembered telling Io that I had spoken with someone called Artaÿctes the night before.

Hypereides looked at me speculatively. "You don't remember the fish?"

I shook my head.

"They were pilchards. Do you know what a pilchard is, Latro?"

I nodded, and so did the black man. I said, "A smallish silvery fish, rather plump. They're said to be delicious."

"That's true." (People in the crowd were shouting, "*Bring him!*" and "*Where is he?*" so that Hypereides was forced to raise his voice to make himself heard.) "But pilchards are oily fish—fatty fish even when salted. Now I know that both of you are sensible men. I want to put a question to you. It's of some importance, and I want you to consider it seriously."

Both of us nodded again.

Hypereides drew a deep breath. "If some dried and salted pilchards were cast onto the coals of a charcoal brazier—with a good fire going—don't you think that the sudden melting of all their fat might make them move? Or perhaps that oil dripping from the fish onto the coals might spatter violently and, so to speak, toss the fish about?"

I nodded and the black man shrugged.

"Ah," said Hypereides. "I'm of one mind with Latro, and Latro was there and saw them, even if he doesn't remember."

Just then a roar went up from the crowd.

The black man pointed with his chin as Hypereides

shouted, "Look! Here they come—worth a round hundred talents apiece, and about to be slaughtered like a couple of goats." He shook his head and appeared genuinely saddened.

The man must have been close to fifty, strongly built and of medium height, with a beard the color of iron. One saw at once, from his dress, that he was a Mede. His son appeared to be fourteen or so; his face was as unformed as the faces of most boys of that age, but he had fine, dark eyes. The man's wrists were tied in front of him.

With them was a tall, lean man in armor who bore neither a shield nor a spear. I saw no signal from him, but the heralds cried, *"Silence! Silence, everybody, for Xanthippos, the noble strategist of Thought,"* and when the chattering of the crowd had been muted a bit, he stepped forward.

"People of Sestos," he said. *"Aeolians! Hellenes!"* He spoke loudly, but as if this commanding voice were natural to him. *"Hear me! I do not come before you to speak for Hellas!"*

That surprised the crowd so much that it actually fell silent, so that the birds could be heard crying above Helle's Sea.

Xanthippos continued, *"I wish that I did—that we were come at last to a time when brother no longer warred against brother."*

That drew a resounding cheer. As it died away, Hypereides grinned at me. "They're hoping that we've forgotten they were fighting us not so long ago."

"Yet speak I do—and I am proud indeed to speak—as the representative of the Assembly of Thought. My city has returned to yours the greatest blessing that any people can possess—liberty."

Another cheer for that.

"For which we ask only your gratitude."

There were shouts of thanks.

"I said I could not speak for the Hellenes. Who knows what Tower Hill may do? Not I. Who knows the will of the wild folk of Bearland? Not I again, O citizens of Sestos. And not you. Those few Rope Makers who were here took ship before your city could be freed, as you know. And as for Hill, who does not know how savagely its spears seconded the barbarian?"

That brought a growl of anger from the crowd. Hypereides whispered, "Strike again, Xanthippos. They're still breathing."

"Many of my brave friends—and they were friends of yours, never forget that—lie in the great grave at Clay. They were sent there not by the arrows of the barbarians but by the horse of Asopodorus of Hill."

At this the crowd gave a little moan, as though a thousand women had felt the first pangs of labor. I reflected that it might well be true, that in years to come men might say that something new had been born today on this narrow finger of the west thrusting eastward into Helle's Sea.

"And yet my city has many more sons, men equally brave; and whenever you may have need of them, they shall come to you with all speed."

Wild cheering.

"Now to the business at hand. We stand here, you and I, as servants of the gods. I need not recount to you the many crimes of this man Artaÿctes. You know them better than I. Many have counseled me that he should be returned to his own country upon the payment of a rich ransom." It seemed to me that Xanthippos darted a glance at Hypereides here, although Hypereides appeared insensible of it. *"I have rejected that counsel."*

The crowd shouted its approval.

"But before justice is done to Artaÿctes, we will act as only free men can—we will hold an election. In my own city, where so many urns and serving dishes are made, we cast our votes on shards of broken pottery, each citizen

scratching the initial of the candidate he favors in the glaze. In Sestos, I am given to understand, your custom is to vote with stones—a white stone for yes, a black one for no, and so forth. This day, also, you shall cast your votes with stones. The boy you see beside him"—Xanthippos pointed to him—*"is the blasphemer's son."*

There was a mutter of anger at that, and a man on my left shook his fist.

"You of Sestos alone shall determine whether he lives or dies. If you will that he lives, move aside and let him flee. But if instead it is your will that he die, stop him, and cast a stone. The choice is yours!"

Xanthippos motioned to the soldiers standing with Artaÿctes and his son, and one whispered in the boy's ear and slapped his back. Xanthippos had assumed that the boy would try to dash to freedom through the crowd; but he ran away from it instead, down the narrowing finger of sand and shale toward the sea, I suppose with the thought of swimming when he reached the water.

He never did. Stones flew, and a score of men at least got past the soldiers and ran after him. I saw him fall, struck on the ear by a stone as big as my fist. He got up and staggered a few steps more before being struck by half a hundred. Although I hope he died quickly, I cannot say precisely when it was that his life ended; certainly many stoned his body long after he was dead.

As for his father, after he had watched his son die, he was laid on his back upon the timber and spikes were driven through both his ankles and both wrists into the wood; when it was done, the timber was set upright in the hole that had been dug for it and rocks and sand piled around it to keep it so. Some of the women present flung stones at him also, but the soldiers forced them to stop, fearing that their stones would strike the five soldiers Xanthippos had stationed to guard him.

"Come," said Hypereides. "The real action's over, and I've a good many things to see to. Latro, I want you to buy us those cloaks we were talking about. Can you manage that if I give you the money?"

I told him I would, if there were cloaks for sale in the city.

"I'm sure there must be. Take him and Io with you so that they can pick out their own. Nothing too grand, mind you; they would only get you into trouble. Get something bright for me, though. Not red, because that's what the Rope Makers wear—not that anybody would take me for a Rope Maker, I imagine. Not yellow, either; the yellow ones fade so quickly. Make it blue or green, rich looking if they have something like that, and suited to my height." He is half a head shorter than the black man and I. "And make certain it's thick and warm."

I nodded, and he handed me four silver drachmas. The black man touched his shoulder and pretended to tug at a rope of air.

"Ah, the voyage! You're right, I promised I'd tell you about that. Well, it's simple enough. Do both of you know about the Great King's bridge?"

I said, "I remember that the heralds said this was where it ended. I imagine that the Great King's army must have marched up the same road we came down to get here."

"Right you are. It was a bridge of boats, scores of them, I would think, all tied together by long cables, with planks laid over their decks to make a road. It was here for nearly a year, according to what I've heard, before a big storm finally broke the cables."

We nodded to show we understood.

"The People from Parsa didn't fix it, but they stored the cables here in Sestos. They must have been very costly, and of course they could be spliced if the Great King ever ordered the bridge rebuilt. Xanthippos wants to take them back to Thought to show off. They should cause quite a stir, because nobody at home has ever seen cables anything like their size." Hypereides held out his arms to indicate the circumference of the cables, and even if he was doubling their diameter, they are very large indeed.

"Well, as you can imagine," he continued, "the first thing that everybody's sure to ask is who made them and what happened to him. Xanthippos had me look into that, and I found out that the boss was a fellow called Oeobazus, one of the barbarians who let themselves down from the city wall with Artaÿctes. And last night, when you and I talked to him, Latro, Artaÿctes said that they had intended to go north, maybe as far as Miltiades' wall. Xanthippos would like to have this Oeobazus to trot out for the Assembly as well as the cables, so we're to go after him as soon as *Europa*'s ready."

I asked when that would be.

"Tomorrow afternoon, I hope." Hypereides sighed. "Which most likely means the day after. The men are touching up her caulking now, and they ought to be finished today. Then we'll have to load the stores. But there's still some to get, and I'm not getting them by standing here talking to you two. So go and see about those cloaks, like I told you. When you've done that, pack up everything—we may not come back here, I don't know."

He hurried off toward the docks after that, and the black man and I returned to Sestos and the house in which we had slept to fetch Io.

We found it empty, however.

3

The Mantis

Hegesistratus interrupted me, but now I write again. It is very late now, and all the others are asleep; but Io has told me that soon after the sun rises I will forget all that I have seen and heard today, and there are things that I must set down.

When the black man and I returned to this house and found Io gone, I was anxious about her; for though I cannot recall how it is I came to have such a slave, I know I love her. The black man laughed at my gloomy face and said by signs that he thought Io had followed us to see Artaÿctes killed, and I was forced to admit he was probably right.

Accordingly we left the house again and went to the market. Several of the shops fronting on it offered cloaks for sale. I bought rough, undyed ones for the black man, Io, and myself, new cloaks made without washing the oil out of the wool and woven so tightly they would shed rain. I knew that such a colored cloak as Hypereides wanted would be costly, so we bargained for a long time over ours, the black man (who is a better bargainer than I, I think) speaking much to the shopkeeper in a language I do not understand. I soon realized, however, that the shopkeeper knew something of it, though he feigned otherwise. And at length even I was able to catch a word or two—*zlh,* which I believe is "cheap," and *sel,* "jackal," a word the shopkeeper did not like.

While they were haggling, I was searching for a cloak for Hypereides. Most of the brightly dyed ones seemed too thin for winter to me. At last I found a thick, warm one of the right length, bright blue, woven of fine, soft wool. This I carried to the shopkeeper, who must have been very tired of arguing with the black man by then. I showed him our four silver drachmas and the four cloaks, and explained that the four drachmas were all the money we had.

(That was not strictly true, as I know the black man has some money of his own; but he would not have spent it for the cloaks, I feel sure, and he probably did not have it upon his person.)

If he would let us have all four cloaks for the drachmas, I said, well and good—we had a bargain; if he would not, we would have no choice but to trade elsewhere. He examined the drachmas and weighed them while the black man and I watched him to make certain he did not substitute worse ones. At last he said that he could not let all four cloaks go at such a price and that the blue one alone should bring him two drachmas at least, but that he would give us the gray cloaks we wanted for ourselves for a drachma apiece if we would buy it.

I told him we could not spare the smallest cloak, which we required for a child—after which we went to a different shop and started the entire process again. It was only then that I realized, from things that the second shopkeeper let drop, just how nervous such merchants here have become because they do not know whether the soldiers from Thought will go or stay. If they stay, these shops may hope for very good business indeed, since most of the soldiers have some plunder and there are a few who have a great deal. But if the soldiers go home and the People from Parsa return and lay siege to the city, the shops will have no business at all, because everyone saves his money to buy food during a siege. When I understood this, I contrived to mention to the black man that we would sail tomorrow, and the price of the green cloak I was examining dropped considerably.

Just then the keeper of the first shop we had visited came in (the owner of the second looking as though he hoped someday to murder him) and said he had reconsidered: we could have all four cloaks for the four drachmas. We returned to his shop with him, and he held out his hand for the money. But I thought that he deserved to be punished for making us bargain so long; thus I began examining the cloaks yet again, and while I was looking at the blue one I took care to ask the black man whether he felt it would do for Hypereides on the coming voyage.

The shopkeeper cleared his throat. "You're sailing, then? And your captain's Hypereides?"

"That's right," I told him, "but the other ships won't put out when we do. They'll be staying here for a few days more at least."

Now the shopkeeper surprised me, and the black man, too, I think. He said, "This Hypereides—is he bald? Rather a round face? Wait, he told me the name of his ship. *Europa*?"

"Yes," I said, "that's our captain."

"Oh. Ah. Well, perhaps I shouldn't tell you this, but if you're going to get that cloak for him, he'll have at least two new ones. He came in after you left and gave me three drachmas for a really choice scarlet one." The shopkeeper took the blue cloak from me and held it up. "That one was for a bigger man, though."

I looked at the black man and he at me, and it was plain that neither of us understood.

The shopkeeper got out a waxed tablet and a stylus. "I'm going to write out a bill of sale for you. You can put your mark on it. Tell your captain that if he wants to return the blue cloak, I'll show him the price and give back his money."

He scratched away at the tablet; and when he had finished, I wrote *Latro* alongside each line in the characters I am using now, keeping it close so it would be sure to blur if he held a heated basin near the tablet to erase it.

Then the black man and I carried the cloaks here and packed everything. I hoped from moment to moment that Io would return, but she did not.

When it was done, I asked the black man what he intended to do, and he made signs to show me that he was going to his room to sleep awhile. I told him I would do the same, and we parted. After a few moments, I opened the door of my room as quietly as I could and crept out just in time to see the black man slipping out his own with equal stealth. I smiled and shook my head, he grinned at me, and together we walked back to the sand spit where the Great King's bridge had ended, in the hope of finding Io.

That at least was the black man's only motive, I believe; as for me, I confess I went with a double purpose, for I meant to set Artaÿctes free should the opportunity present itself.

As we drew near the place, we met the last idlers from the crowd returning home; several told us that Artaÿctes was dead. One seemed a sensible enough fellow, so I stopped him and asked how he knew. He told us that the soldiers had pricked him with their spears without result, and at last one had driven the head of his spear into his belly to determine whether his blood would spurt; it had only leaked away like water from a sponge, so it was certain that the action of the heart had ceased.

The black man made signs then, urging me to inquire about Io. I did, and the man we were questioning said that only one child had stayed behind, a half-grown girl who was with a lame man. I did not think that Io could be considered half-grown (I remembered her well from having spoken to her this morning), and as we hurried along I asked the black man whether he knew of any such lame man. He shook his head.

Yet it was Io, and I recognized her at once. Only she, a boy, the soldiers, and the man the idler had mentioned remained with the corpse of Artaÿctes. The man with Io was leaning on a crutch, and I saw that he had lost his right foot; in its place was a wooden socket ending in a peg. This was tied to his calf with leather strips like the laces of a sandal. He was weeping while Io sought to comfort him. She waved and smiled, however, when she saw us.

I told her that she should not have disobeyed Hypereides, and though I would not beat her for it, Hypereides might. (I did not say this to her, but I feared that if he beat her too severely I might kill him. Then I myself might well be killed by the soldiers from Thought.) She explained that she had not meant to disobey, but had been sitting on the step when she had seen the lame man; he had seemed so weary and so sorrowful that she tried to comfort him, and he had asked her to go with him because both his crutch and the tip of his wooden foot sank in the sand. Thus, Io said, she had not gone to see Artaÿctes die—which was what Hypereides had forbidden—but to assist the lame man, a fellow Hellene, which Hypereides had certainly not ordered her not to do.

The black man grinned at all this, but I had to admit there was some justice in what she said. I told the lame man that she would have to return to the house with us now, but that we would help him if he, too, were ready to go back to Sestos.

He nodded and thanked me, and I let him lean upon my arm. I admit that I was curious about him, a Hellene who wept for a Mede; and so when we had gone some small distance, I asked what he knew of Artaÿctes, and whether he had been a good man.

"He was a good friend to me," the lame man answered. "The last friend I had in this part of the world."

I asked, "But weren't you Hellenes fighting the People from Parsa? I seem to recall that."

He shook his head, saying that only certain cities were at war with the Great King, some of them most unwisely. No one, he added, had fought more bravely at the Battle of Peace than Queen Artemisia, the ruler of a city of Hellenes allied with the Great King. At Clay, he said, the cavalry of Hill had been accounted the bravest of the brave, while Hill's Sacred Band had fought to the last man.

"I'm from Hill," Io told him proudly.

He smiled at her and wiped his eyes. "I knew that already, my dear; you have only to speak to tell everyone. I myself am from the Isle of Zakunthios. Do you know where that is?"

Io did not.

"It's a small island in the west, and perhaps it is because it's so small that it's so lovely, and so much loved by all its sons."

Io said politely, "I hope someday to see it, sir."

"So do I," the lame man told her. "That is, I hope to see it once more at a time when it will be safe for me to go home." Turning to me, he added, "Thank you for your help—I believe the road's firm enough for me now."

I was so busy with my own thoughts that I hardly heard him. If he had really been a friend of Artaÿctes' (and surely here no Hellene would lie about that) it seemed likely he knew Oeobazus, for whom we would soon be searching. Furthermore he might help me rescue him, if rescue were necessary. Crippled as he was, he could be of no great use in a fight; but I reflected that there is always more to a battle than fighting, and that if Artaÿctes had been his friend, Artaÿctes had perhaps found him of service.

With these thoughts in mind, I offered him the hospitality of the house Hypereides had commandeered, mentioning that we had plenty of food there and some good wine, and suggesting he might sleep there tonight if he wished, with Hypereides' permission.

He thanked me and explained that he was not short of

money, Artaÿctes having rewarded him generously on many occasions. He was staying with a well-to-do family, he said, where everything was comfortable enough. "My name is Hegesistratus," he added. "Hegesistratus, son of Tellias, though Hegesistratus of Elis is what I'm generally called now."

Io said, "Oh, we've been to Elis. It was on the way to—to a place up north where King Pausanias sacrificed. Latro doesn't remember it, but the black man and I do. Why do they say you're from Elis, if you're really from Zakunthios?"

"Because I'm from Elis, too," Hegesistratus told her, "and most recently. Our family has its roots there—but this is no story for a little maid. Not even a maid from Hill."

"I'm Latro," I told him. "You already know who Io is, I imagine. Neither of us knows our friend's name—we don't speak his language—but we vouch for his character."

Hegesistratus met the black man's eyes for a moment that seemed very long to me, then spoke to him in another tongue (I think in that which the black man had used to the shopkeeper); and the black man answered him in the same way. Soon he touched Hegesistratus' forehead, and Hegesistratus touched his.

"That is the speech of Aram," Hegesistratus told me. "In it, your friend is called Seven Lions."

We were nearing the city gate then, and he asked me whether the house I had mentioned was much farther. As it happened, it was on the next street after the wall, and I told him so.

"My lodgings are on the other side of the marketplace," he said. "Might I stop, then, and take that cup of wine with you? Walking makes my stump sore"—he gestured toward his crippled leg—"and I would be very grateful for the chance to rest it a bit."

I urged him to stay as long as he wished, and told him that I would like his opinion of my sword.

4

Favorable Auspices

Hegesistratus has been on the wall observing birds. He says our voyage will be fortunate, and he will come with us. Hypereides wanted to know whether we would find the man we seek, whether we would bring him to Xanthippos, and how the Assembly would reward us for it; but Hegesistratus would answer none of these questions, saying that telling more than one knows is a pit dug for such as he. He and I spoke together awhile, but he has left now.

An odd thing happened while the black man, Io, and I sat at wine with him; I do not understand it, so I shall record it here exactly as it took place, without comment, or at least with very little.

As we chatted, I became more and more curious concerning my sword. I had seen it lying in the chest this morning when I put on a clean chiton and again when the black man and I packed; but I had felt no curiosity about it at all. Now I could scarcely remain at my place. At one moment I feared it had been stolen. At the next, I felt certain it possessed some peculiarity upon which Hegesistratus' comments would be deeply enlightening.

As soon as he had mixed the wine and water, I rose, hurried to my room, and got out my sword. I was about to give it to him when he struck my wrist with his crutch and it fell from my hand; the black man jumped up brandishing his stool, and Io screamed.

Hegesistratus alone remained calm, never rising. He told me to pick up my sword and return it to the scabbard. (Its point had sunk so deeply into the floor that I had to use both hands to wrench it free.) I felt then as though I had wakened from a dream. The black man shouted at me, indicating the wine, then spoke loudly to Hegesistratus, pointing at me and toward the ceiling. Hegesistratus said, "He wishes me to remind you that a guest is sacred. The gods, he says, will punish one who, having invited a stranger, harms him without cause."

I nodded.

Io whispered, "Latro forgets. Sometimes—"

Hegesistratus silenced her with a gesture. "Latro, what were you going to do with that sword?"

I told him that I had wanted him to examine it.

"And do you still?"

I shook my head.

"Very well," he said, "in that case I will. Draw it again and put it on the table, please."

I did as he asked, and he laid both hands upon the flat of the blade and shut his eyes. So he sat for a long time—so long that I had rubbed my wrist and drained my wine before he opened them once more.

"What is it?" Io asked when he had withdrawn his hands.

He shivered a little, I think. "Are you—any of you—aware that divinity can be transmitted, like a disease?"

None of us spoke.

"It can. Touch a leper and you may discover that you have leprosy. The tips of your fingers whiten, or perhaps the spot appears on your chin or your cheek, because you scratched them with those fingers. So it is with divinity. One finds temples in Riverland in which the priests, when they have served their god, must wash and change their clothing before leaving; this though the god, in most cases, is not present." Hegesistratus sighed. "This has been handled by a minor deity, I think."

He looked his question at me, but I could only shake my head.

"Have you killed with it?"

I said, "I don't know. I suppose so."

Io told me, "You killed some of the Rope Makers'—" then covered her mouth with her hand.

Hegesistratus asked, "He killed Rope Makers? You may tell me—I assure you that I am no friend of theirs."

"Just some of their slaves," Io explained. "They caught us once, but Latro and the black man killed a lot of them first."

Hegesistratus sipped his wine. "That was far from here, I take it?"

"Yes, sir. Back in Cowland."

"That is well, for the dead may walk. Particularly those slain with this blade."

I looked around, for I had heard Hypereides' step. He was surprised to see Hegesistratus; but when I had introduced them, he greeted and welcomed him.

Hegesistratus said, "I hope that you will excuse me for not rising. I am lame."

"Of course, of course." The black man had brought a stool for Hypereides, and he sat down. "I'm not getting around very well myself. Been tramping my legs off all over the city."

Hegesistratus nodded. "And there is another matter about which I owe you an apology. A moment ago my friend Latro called me Hegesistratus of Zakunthios. That is true; I was born there and grew to manhood there. But I am properly Hegesistratus, son of Tellias—"

Hypereides started.

"And I am better known as Hegesistratus of Elis."

Hypereides said, "You were Mardonius' mantis at Clay. You told him not to advance—that's what I've heard."

Hegesistratus nodded again. "Does that make me a criminal in your eyes? If so, I am in your power. Both these men obey you, and one has a sword."

Hypereides drew a deep breath and let it out. "Mardonius is dead. I think we ought to let the dead lie."

"As do I, if they will."

"And if we're going after revenge, we'll have to enslave just about everyone in this city. Then who'd hold the place against the Great King? Xanthippos himself said that."

I had poured him a cup of wine, and he accepted it. "Do you know what the Assembly wanted to do to Hill?"

Hegesistratus shook his head.

"Level it! Sell the people of Cowland to the Crimson Men! I'm in leather—in peacetime, I mean. Can you imagine what that would have done to the leather trade?" Even though it was cold, Hypereides wiped his face with his hand as if he were sweating. "It was the Rope Makers who prevented it. Well, the gods know that I'm no friend to the Rope Makers—what are you snickering at, young woman?"

Io said, "You used the same words he did, sir. Just before you came in. That's lucky, they say."

"Why, so it is." Turning back to Hegesistratus, Hypereides asked, "Isn't it? You ought to know, if anybody does."

"It is," the mantis said. "It is always fortunate when men agree."

"You've got a point there," Hypereides conceded. "Now look here, I'm the skipper of the *Europa,* and we're close to sailing—we should cast off around midmorning tomorrow. How much would you charge me to see what the gods have to say about our voyage, and maybe give warning of any special dangers we may face?"

"Nothing," Hegesistratus replied.

"You mean you won't do it?"

"I mean no more than I say—that I will do it and charge you nothing. You intend to go up Helle's Sea after Oeobazus?"

Hypereides looked amazed, and so, I confess, did I. Hegesistratus smiled. "There is no mystery here, believe me. Before he died, Artaÿctes told me you had been asking about Oeobazus, as Io will verify."

I told Hypereides, "The black man and I went back when we were through packing. Artaÿctes was dead, and there was no one there but Hegesistratus and Io, a boy, and the soldiers. That was how we met Hegesistratus; he was mourning Artaÿctes."

"As I still am," Hegesistratus added. "And of course you thought that it might be useful to talk with someone who knew Oeobazus by sight. You revealed that quite clearly while Io was bringing our water and this really excellent wine. Very well. He is a Mede—not a man of Parsa, though we Hellenes often call them Medes, but a true Mede—of thirty-five or so, rather taller than most, a strong man and a superb horseman. There is a long scar on his right cheek, only partially concealed by his beard; he told me once that he got it as a boy when he tried to gallop through a thicket. Now may I ask Hypereides why he was trampling around Sestos? I would have thought that most of the things his ship requires would be easily found, or else clearly impossible to obtain. What is it that appears possible, and yet proves so elusive?"

Hypereides said, "Somebody who speaks the dialects of the northern tribes, knows their customs, and will come along with us. Either Oeobazus is safely back in the Empire and out of our reach, or he's being held in one of the civilized cities to the north—which ought to be easy—or he's in some barbarous kingdom on this side of the First Sea. So that's where we may run into trouble, and I'd like to be ready to deal with it."

Hegesistratus stroked his own beard, which is black, curly, and very thick, and said, "You may have found him."

He took leave of us then, and while the black man

prepared the second meal, Io drew me aside. "Master," she asked, "were you really going to kill him?"

"Of course not," I said.

"Well, you looked like it. You came in so fast with your sword, and you looked like you were going to split his head. I think you would have, if he hadn't been so quick."

I explained that I had merely wanted him to see it, but she looked unconvinced and asked me many questions about the things the black man and I did today. Describing them reminded me that I had not yet shown Hypereides the cloaks we bought, so when I had satisfied Io's curiosity, I got them and showed them to him. He seemed pleased with them, and most of all with his own; but he said nothing about the scarlet cloak, and I thought it would be unwise to inquire about it.

After we had eaten, Io brought me this scroll and urged me to write down everything that happened today; she said she felt sure that we would want to refer to it later. I have done so, giving everything of any importance that was said in detail and in the words the speakers used, as well as I can write them in my own tongue.

As I wrote before, Hegesistratus interrupted me. He wanted to know where Io and I had been when we had been captured by the Rope Makers, and when I could not tell him, he woke Io and spoke to her. Afterward he said he was going onto the wall to observe the flights of birds; it was dark, when birds seldom fly, though there are some kinds that do, I know. He was gone a long while, but when he returned he spoke with Hypereides, telling him that the word of the gods was favorable and that he would go with us if Hypereides wished it. Hypereides was delighted and asked him many questions, of which he answered only two or three—and even these in ways that told Hypereides very little.

At last, when Hypereides had returned to bed, Hegesistratus sat with me before this fire. He said he wished that he could read this scroll. I told him I would read it to him if he liked, and added I had another in my chest that was full of writing.

"Perhaps I will ask you to do that soon," he said. "Io tells me you do not remember, and I wonder how much you are aware of it."

"I know it," I said. "At least, I see that others remember the days that are gone. That seems strange to me, and yet there are certain things that I remember, too—my father and mother, and the house where we lived."

"I understand," he said. "But you do not remember how you were befriended by Pausanias of Rope?"

I told him I recalled Io's saying that we had been to Elis when we went with King Pausanias to sacrifice, and asked if this Pausanias was a real king.

Hegesistratus shook his head. "No, but he is often called that. The Rope Makers are accustomed to having a king as their leader; since he is their leader now, they call him a king. In reality he stands regent for King Pleistarchos, who is still a boy. Pausanias is his uncle."

I ventured that if Pausanias had befriended Io, the black man, and me, he must at least be a good man.

At that, Hegesistratus stared long into the flames, seeing more there (I think) than I did. At last he said, "If he were of any other nation, I would call him an evil one. Latro, if you do not remember Pausanias, do you perhaps recall a Tisamenus of Elis?"

I did not, but I asked Hegesistratus whether this Tisamenus was a relative of his, since both were said to be "of Elis."

"Only a very distant cousin," Hegesistratus told me. "Both our families are of the Iamidae; but they have been rivals since the Golden Age, when the gods dwelled among men."

"I wish this were the Golden Age," I said, "then I might go to some god, and he might make me as others are."

"You are less different from them than you believe, nor is it easy for men to earn the gratitude of the gods; and they are not much prone to it."

My heart told me he was right.

"Io has told me that you see the gods already. So do I, at times."

I confessed I had not known I did.

"Often I would be happier if I could forget what I have seen as quickly as you do." Hegesistratus paused. "Latro, I think it likely that Tisamenus, who hates me, has charmed you. Will you permit me to break his charm, if I can?" He swayed from side to side as he spoke, as a young tree may sway in a breeze that is strong yet gentle. He held up both his hands, their fingers splayed like the petals of two flowers.

Now, though I recall what he asked me, I do not remember my answer. He is gone, and the small knife I brought to sharpen my stylus is smeared with blood.

5

Our Ship

The *Europa* sailed from Sestos today, when the sun was already halfway down the sky. We could have gone much earlier. Our captain, Hypereides, found one thing wrong, then another, until at last the lame man who seems ill came aboard. Then there was no more such faultfinding.

We rowed out of the harbor. It was hard work, but pleasant, too. Once we were well into Helle's Sea, we hoisted sail; with this blustering wind in the west, there is no need to row. The sailors say the eastern bank is the

Great King's, and should the wind blow us too near it we will have to row again. As I began to write this, we passed three ships of the same kind as ours. They were returning to Sestos, or so it appeared, and had to row. With all their oars rising and falling, they seemed six-winged birds flying low over the wintery sea.

Io came to speak with the black man and me. She warned me many times that this scroll will fall to bits if it becomes wet; I promised as many times to put it away in my chest as soon as I have finished writing. I asked about the man with the crutch. She said that his name is Hegesistratus, that the black man and I know him (the black man nodded to this), and that she has been nursing him. They have laid him aft beneath the storming deck, where he is out of the wind—he is asleep now. I asked what his illness is, but she would not tell me.

The kybernetes has been going down the benches talking to the sailors. He is the oldest man aboard, older I think than the lame man or Hypereides, small and spare. Much of his hair is gone; what remains is gray. He came to our bench, smiled at Io, and said that it was good to have her on board again. She told me we once went around Redface Island on this ship, but I do not know where it lies. The kybernetes made the black man and me show him our hands. When he had felt them, he said they were not hard enough. Mine are very hard—I can see I have been doing a lot of manual work—but he said they must be harder than they are before I can row all day. We will have to row more, he said, so that we will be ready for it if ever we must row for our lives. Io told me he is an old sailor who knows more about ships and the sea than Hypereides, although Hypereides knows a great deal. Hypereides paid for this ship (because the Assembly of Thought made him); thus he is our captain. I said he seemed a clever man to me—perhaps too clever. She assured me that he is a very good man, though he knows a great deal about money.

I should say here that the black man and I have the upper bench on the port side. It is an upper bench, Io says, so that we can sit together, and it is near the prow because the best rowers are at the stern, where all the others can see them and take the beat from them. The black man, who sits nearer to the sea, is a thranite—a "bench-man." I am a zygite—a "thwart-man." This is because the black man rows against the parodos, which is like a balcony hung from the side of the ship. I row against the thwart, or rather against a thick peg in it. When the ship is under sail, men can be stationed on the parodos to keep the ship from heeling too much; but when we row, anyone who walks along it must step over the looms of the thranites' oars.

I should say also that the men below us are thalamites. It means "inside-men," I believe. Their oars pass through holes in the side of the ship, and there are greased-leather boots around their looms. One of the sailors was punished earlier (I do not know for what reason). The shieldmen bound him to a thalamite bench with his head out the oar hole. He must have felt as if a bucket of cold seawater were being thrown in his face each time he drew breath. He looked repentant enough, and cowed enough, when they untied him.

The black man was gone for a while. When he came back, I asked where he had been, but he would only shake his head. Now he sits staring at the waves. There are leather curtains along the railing to keep out spray, but they do not come as high as our heads.

We came to shore to spend the night here, hauling our ship onto the beach. We built fires to warm ourselves and to cook on—there is plenty of driftwood—and I am writing by the light of one now, while everyone else is asleep. This fire was nearly dead, but I have collected more wood. A moment ago one of the sailors woke, thanked me, and went back to sleep.

There is a tent for Hypereides, the kybernetes, Acetes, and Hegesistratus. If it rains, we will make more from the sail and the battle sail; but now we sleep beside these fires, rolled in our cloaks and huddled together for warmth. When I asked where we were going, Io said to Pactye, where the wall is.

I woke and saw a woman watching our camp. The new moon was high and bright, so that I could see her quite clearly, standing just beyond the shadows of the pines. Two of Acetes' shieldmen were on guard, but they did not see her, or at least did not pay heed to her. I got up and walked toward her, thinking that she would vanish into the shadows when I came too close, but she did not. I cannot have lain with a woman in a long time; there was a tremor in my loins like the shaking of the sail when we tried to steer too near the wind. There are no women on our ship save for Io.

This woman was small and grave and very lovely. I greeted her and asked how I might serve her.

"I am the bride of this tree," she said, and pointed to the tallest pine. "Most who come to my wood sacrifice to me, and I wondered why you—who are so many—did not."

I thought I understood then that she was the priestess of some rural shrine. I explained that I was not the leader of the men she saw sleeping on the beach, but that I supposed they had not sacrificed because we had no victim.

"I need not have a lamb or a kid," she told me. "A cake and a little honey will be sufficient."

I returned to the camp. Tonight the black man, Io, and I ate with the four in the tent, the black man having prepared our food; thus I knew that Hypereides had honey among his stores. I found a pot sealed with beeswax, kneaded some of the honey with meal, water, salt, and sesame, and baked the dough in the embers of the fire. When both sides of the cake were brown, I carried it to her, with the honey and a skin of wine.

She led me to the foot of the pine, where there was a flat stone. I asked her what I should say when I laid our offerings there. She said, "There are rhymes men use, and others favored by their wives and daughters; but all of them have forgotten the true way, which is to present what is offered without speaking a word."

I set the cake on the stone, poured a little honey on it, and set down the pot of honey beside it. Opening the wineskin, I poured some on the ground.

She smiled and sat down before the stone with her back to the bole of the tree, broke off a piece of the cake, dipped it into the honey, and ate it. Bowing, I offered her the skin of wine; she took it from me and drank deeply of the unmixed wine, wiped her mouth on the back of her hand, and motioned for me to sit across from her.

I did, believing I knew what would soon come, but unsure how I might bring it about, since the altar stone lay between us. She returned the skin to me, and I swallowed the hot wine.

"You may speak now," she said. "What is it you wish?"

A moment before I had known; now I knew only confusion.

"Fertility for your fields?" She smiled again.

"Have I fields?" I asked her. "I do not know."

"Rest, perhaps? We give that as well. And cool shade, but you will not want that now."

I shook my head and tried to speak.

"I cannot take you to your fields," she told me, "that lies beyond my power. But I can show them to you, if you like."

I nodded and sprang up, extending my hand to her.

She rose, too, the wineskin upon her shoulder, and took it.

At once bright sunshine covered the world. The trees, the beach, the ship, and the sleeping men all vanished. We walked over furrows of new-turned earth in which the worms yet writhed. Before us went a man with grizzled hair, one hand on the plow, an ox goad in the other. Over his bent back, I saw a garden, a vineyard, and a low white house. "You may speak to him if you like," the young woman said, "but he will not hear you." She took another swallow from the skin.

"Then I will not speak." I wanted to ask her then whether these fields were indeed mine, and if so why the old man plowed them; yet I knew they were, and that the garden, vineyard, and house were mine as well. I even guessed that it was my father who plowed.

"It will be a good harvest," she told me. "Because I am here."

I asked her, "How did you do this? Why can't I stay?"

She pointed to the sun, and I saw that it was almost at the horizon; already the shadows were long. "Do you wish to see the house?"

I nodded and we went there, passing through the vineyard on the way. She plucked some grapes and ate them, putting one into my mouth. It tasted sweeter than I had thought any grape could, and I told her so, adding that the sweetness must have come from her fingers.

"It is not so," she told me. "These grapes taste sweet to you because they are your own." In the thick shadows under the vines I could see stars reflected in water.

Something that was neither ape nor bear crouched beside the doorstep, hairy and uncouth, yet possessing an air of friendship and goodwill, like an old dog that greets its master. Its eyes held golden sparks, and when I saw them I remembered (just as I remember now) how I had seen them dance about the room once when I was small. This hairy being did not move as we approached it, though its golden eyes followed us as we passed.

The door stood open, so that we entered without difficulty, though I felt we would have passed through it just as easily if it had been barred. Inside a kettle bubbled on the fire, and an old woman sat with her arms upon an old table and her head upon her arms.

"Mother!" I said. "Oh, Mother!" It seemed to me that the words had been snatched from my throat.

"Lucius!" She rose at the sound of my voice and embraced me. Her face was aged now, lined, and streaked with tears; yet I would have known it at once anywhere. She clasped me to her, weeping and repeating, *"Lucius, you're back. You're back! We thought you were dead. We thought you were dead!"*

And all that time, although my mother held me in her arms as she had when I was a child, I could see across her shoulder that she slept still, her head cradled in her arms.

At last she kissed me and turned to the young woman saying, *"Welcome, my dear! No, you must welcome me if you will, and not me you. This is my son's house, not mine. Am I—are my husband and I—welcome here?"*

The young woman, who had been drinking from the skin while my mother and I embraced, swayed a trifle but nodded and smiled.

My mother rushed to the door, calling, *"He's back! Lucius is home!"*

The plowman did not turn, guiding his plow and thrusting at one of his oxen with the long, iron-tipped goad he carried. The sun had touched the muddy fields; I could see our beached ship in the darkness at the bottom of the furrows, so that it seemed that this farm, lit by the dying rays of the sun, hovered over a benighted world that the toe of the plow had reached.

"We're going now," the young woman said thickly. "Aren't we going to make love?"

I shook my head, one arm around my mother and my other hand clutching the frame of the kitchen door. They melted as clotted honey does, warmed in one's mouth.

"Well, I do," she said.

The last glimmer of sunshine faded, and the air grew cold. Through dark boughs I saw the sea, our dying fires, and the ship lying on the beach. The young woman pressed her lips to mine; I felt then that I drank old wine out of a cup of new-turned wood. Together we sank to pine needles and fern.

Twice I lay with her, weeping the first and laughing the second time. We drank more wine. I told her that I loved her while she vowed she would never leave me, each laughing at the other because both knew we lied and that our lies were without harm and without malice. A rabbit blundered into the moonlight, fixed us with one bright eye, exclaimed, *"Elata!"* and fled. I asked if that was her name, and she nodded while drinking deep from the skin, then kissed me again.

Far off at first, then nearer and nearer, I heard the sound of dogs coursing deer. Vaguely I recalled that many who by some ill stroke of fortune have found themselves in the path of such a hunt have been torn to bits by the hounds. I wished then that I had put on my sword before I carried our offering to the tree. Elata was sleeping with her head in my lap, but I rose—nearly falling—with her in my arms, intending to carry her to one of the fires on the beach.

Before I could take a step, there was a crash of splintering limbs. A stag bounded from the shelter of the shadows, saw the fires (or perhaps only winded the smoke), and sprang back, nearly knocking me down. I could hear its labored breathing, like the bellows of a forge, smell its fear.

Elata stirred sleepily in my arms as the stag dashed away, and the baying of the hounds sounded closer than before; I set her on her feet, intending to lead her to the fires. She kissed me and pointed, announcing with drunken solemnity, "'Nother man coming to see me from your ship."

6

The Nymph

Elata returned a moment ago, pleading with me to extinguish this fire. I would not, though the rest are only embers. I know she has lain with Hegesistratus, and after that, I believe, with one of Acetes' shieldmen. Now she has washed in the stream where we draw our water; but when I suggested that she dry herself at my fire, she seemed afraid and asked me to put it out, kissing and begging while one hand crept under my chiton.

I am very tired; if Elata wishes to lie with a man again, she will have to choose another one. Yet before I sleep, I must write about the woman (Hegesistratus calls her a goddess) with the piebald hounds. What she said and what Hegesistratus said may be important tomorrow.

The goddess was young, less voluptuous than Elata and more beautiful—I feel certain she has never know a man. There were others with her, beautiful women also. Them I could not see as well, because they shunned the brilliant moonlight in which the Huntress shone so boldly.

But first I should tell of her hounds; we saw them before the Huntress and her retinue. Having no sword, I had snatched up a stick. When I saw those hounds, I understood how foolish that had been—a reed would have been of equal service. Each was as big as a calf, and there were twenty at least. Leaning heavily upon my arm (and in truth I do not think she could have stood alone) Elata saved me. The fierce hounds fawned on her, snuffling her scent and licking her fingers with their great, rough tongues when she stroked their heads. I did not venture any familiarity with them, but they did not harm me.

Soon the Huntress appeared with her silver bow. She smiled at us, but her smile was without friendship; if her hounds had brought the stag to bay, her smile would have been the same, or so it seemed to me. Yet how delicate she was! How lovely!

"The man who forgets." Thus she named me; her voice was a girl's, but there was the shout of a hunting horn in it, high and clear. "You will not have forgotten me." Then she touched me with her bow. At once I remembered how I had met her at the crossroads, though at first, and at the last, she had been both older and smaller, flanked by huge black dogs of another breed. I recalled, too, that she was a queen, though she looked so young; and I bowed to her as I had before.

"I see that you've debauched my maid." Half-smiling, she pointed.

I replied, "If you say it, Dark Mother."

She shook her head. "Call me Huntress."

"Yes, Huntress, if that is what you wish."

"You would furnish my pets some sport, perhaps. Would you like a running start? I might permit you a stade or two." Her nymphs were clustering in the darkness behind her; I could hear the silver chimes of their laughter.

I said, "As you wish, Huntress. The end will be the same." Yet the fires on the beach were not much more than a stade away, and I wondered whether I might not snatch up a brand. With fire in my hands and the sleeping sailors roused, the hunt might take a different turn.

A new voice, a man's, called, *"Latro?"*

"Over here," I said, hardly raising my voice.

"Is there someone with you?"

I nearly smiled at that. The Huntress answered, "Surely you know us, mantis."

Hegesistratus was nearer now, so that it seemed to me that he must certainly have seen the Huntress in the moonlight; but he said, "Is that a woman by the tree?" Though he had the help of his crutch, he could walk only with difficulty over the dark, uneven ground. I dropped my stick and extended my hand to him; he took it, and at once bowed his head before the Huntress. The Hellenes do not kneel as we do, nor prostrate themselves like the peoples of the East; yet it seems to me that there is more honor for the gods in the bent heads of men who will not kiss the dust for anyone.

"Whom do you serve, Hegesistratus?"

He murmured, "You, Cynthia, should you wish it."

"And you, Latro? Will you serve me again, if I ask it?"

My bowels had turned as milk does in a churn, and the arm with which I supported Elata shook; but I reminded myself that this uncanny woman had given one memory at least back to me—that of my earlier meeting with her. (I have forgotten it now, though I recall that I remembered it not long ago; and I recall still what I thought and said of it.) "You're a queen," I told her humbly. "Even if I wished to, how could I refuse?"

"Others have sometimes managed it. Now listen, both of you. No, by my virginity! Hear me, all three of you."

The girls in the shadows gasped.

"Latro named me a queen. Soon you'll meet another—you may rely upon me for that. She has a strong protector, and I intend to make use of him to flush a boar; all of you must aid, and not oppose, her. But when the moment comes, the slut must lose. It will be at my brother's house—you know it, mantis—and thus you should be on friendly soil. Press on, north and west, until you meet her. The queen will save you, if you don't turn south."

Hegesistratus bowed and I assured her we would do our best, although I did not understand anything she had told us. One of her huge hounds was snuffling Hegesistratus' feet. She glanced at it and said, "Yes, take that scent well."

She told Hegesistratus, "Latro has all the qualities of a hero save one—he forgets instructions. You must see to those. My queen must win in order that the prince may be destroyed—and thus this queen must not win."

He bowed lower still.

"You bring victory, Latro, so you must drive for my prince. If you succeed you'll be rewarded. What is it you wish?"

"My home," I told her, for my heart was still bursting from the sight of it.

"What? Barley fields, pigpens, and cowsheds? They aren't mine to give. I have it—do you remember what it was you asked of Kore?"

I shook my head.

"It was to be reunited with your friends. She granted your wish, sending you to some of them at least. They were dead or dying, as was only to be expected since Kore is the Queen of the Shades. I shall return you to your friends also—but to living ones, for I have no interest in the dead."

Hegesistratus whispered, "Yet you are she who brings sudden death to women."

I was so happy I scarcely heard him. Releasing Elata, I fell to my knees. "Huntress, you are too good!"

She smiled bitterly. "So many have said. You are content, then, with your reward?"

"More than content!"

"I'm delighted to hear it. You shall be punished as well, for what you've done tonight to my maid, losing for a while at least what you're pleased to call your manhood." She advanced toward Hegesistratus; though she was hardly taller than he, she appeared to tower above him. "As for you, you shall not choose your reward. Your filthy longings are known to me, so there is no need of it—that soiled child shall be yours for the present, though Latro has been there before you."

Hegesistratus was already supporting Elata as I had a few moments before; he murmured his thanks.

"But you may have her only until you come this way again," the Huntress warned him. "Whenever you do, she shall be free to reoccupy her home."

At her final word, all were gone—the Huntress herself, her pack, and the maidens of her train; only the mantis, Elata, and I remained in the darkness beneath the largest pine. For a long moment I thought I heard the wild baying of the hounds, far and faint; but even that faded.

Hegesistratus was too lame to walk well over the stones and the slippery carpet of fallen pine needles, and Elata was still too drunk. In the end I carried her down to the beach while he held on to my arm. As we went, I begged him to explain what had taken place—to tell me who the Huntress was and just what power she wielded. He promised he would; but he would not do so then, leading Elata far away from the fires instead. Near the water, where the sand was moist and packed by the waves, he could walk well enough.

Thus I wrote as I did, beginning with the time I noticed Elata watching us. When I had finished writing of the stag, Hegesistratus returned and spoke with me as he had promised. While we talked, Elata returned as well, and washed herself in the stream.

I asked Hegesistratus who the Huntress was, and added that he seemed to know her.

"Only by reputation," he told me. "I had never seen her before. You have, obviously."

I could no longer remember the time, but I felt that was correct and told him so.

"She is a goddess," he told me. "Could you think her an ordinary woman when you spoke to her?"

"I thought her a woman," I said, "because that was

how she appeared to me—but certainly not an ordinary one. Is her name Cynthia?"

"That is one of them," Hegesistratus told me. "She has a great many. Do you know of the Destroyer?"

I shook my head and said that from the sound of his name I did not wish to.

"You are sadly mistaken, forgetting how many things should be destroyed—wolves and lions, for example. Why, he even kills mice."

At that, some memory called through the mist that seems to fill the back of my head, and I said that though there might be no harm and even some good in the destruction of mice, I was far from sure I would wish to see all the wolves and lions dead.

"You would if you kept sheep or goats," Hegesistratus told me practically, "or even cattle. Do you have many cattle? The goddess implied you did."

I said that I owned a yoke of oxen at least, if the vision Elata had shown me was true. After that I had to tell him all about it—how she had returned me to a place she had said (and I had truly felt) was my home, and all that we had seen and done there. When I asked how she had accomplished it, he admitted he did not know and wondered aloud if such things were still in her power. I asked whether she was a witch.

"No," he said, "that is a very different thing, believe me. She is a dryad, a kind of nymph."

I said, "I thought that only meant a bride, a marriageable young woman."

Hegesistratus nodded. "Since you are a foreigner, that is easy to understand. Of all the unseen beings, the nymphs are nearest us; they are not even immortals, although they are very long-lived. Our country people both fear and love them, and as a compliment to a girl, her swain may pretend to believe her a nymph in disguise. From such frivolity, 'nymph' has become a commonplace compliment."

I said, "I see. It would seem that another way in which they are much like us is that they, too, must obey the Huntress, whom you say is a goddess."

"She is," Hegesistratus affirmed. "She is the sister—in fact more than a sister, the twin—of the Destroyer, of whom we just were speaking. He is one of the best of the Twelve, a true friend to men, the patron of divination, of healing, and of all the other arts. His sister . . ."

Seeing his expression I said, "Is not quite so friendly, I take it."

Just then Io came to sit with us, rubbing her eyes but full of curiosity. "Who's that woman?" she asked Hegesistratus. "I woke up, and she was lying next to me. She says she belongs to you."

Hegesistratus told her that was true.

"Then you'd better find her some clothes, or there may be trouble when the sailors wake up."

I sent Io to bring Elata's gown, which had been left under the pine.

Half to himself, Hegesistratus said, "I wish there were a place on the ship where she would be out of sight. I hate the thought of them ogling her." I pointed out that he need only put her forward of the first bench, at which he chuckled. "You are right, of course, when the men are rowing; but most of the time they are not."

I said, "Even when they're not, only those nearest her will be able to see her clearly, because the ship's so long and slender. But is what the sailors are going to want from her so different from what you want?"

"My filthy desires, you mean. That was what the goddess called them."

I nodded.

"She also indicated that you had the nymph before me."

I forbore telling him that I had her twice, and apologized, mentioning that the Huntress had not yet given him Elata when we had lain together.

He sighed. "Nor would I have her now if you had not. As for those filthy desires of mine, only a woman would call them that, and not very many of them. I lost my wife, you see, some years ago; and it is not easy for a lame man far from home to find a new one. Or for any man alive to find as good a one, for that matter."

I asked, "Doesn't the Huntress have lovers of her own?"

Hegesistratus shook his head. "She has had a few—or at least men or gods who wanted to be. But they all came to bad ends, and quickly. There is a story . . . I don't know whether it's true."

I urged him to tell it anyway, for though I am so tired, I know how important it may be to learn as much as possible about the Huntress.

"All right. She is the daughter of the Thunderer—I don't think I've mentioned that—and according to this legend, at the age of three she came to him and asked for as many names as her brother, a bow and silver arrows, to be queen of the nymphs, and a great many other things; and when he promised to grant all her wishes, she asked that she might be full-grown at once, like her parthenogenetic sister the Lady of Thought, who was of age when she sprang from her father's head. That, too, was granted her, and it is sometimes said that because of it she has never grown up in truth."

I suggested that the same thing could be said of this Lady of Thought, and Hegesistratus agreed. "Neither one has ever had a real lover, as far as anybody knows. But the Lady of Thought, at least, does not insist upon virginity in others. It may be that she is not a whole woman, just as certain men are not whole men, because of the way she was born."

Io returned then to report that she had found Elata's gown and covered her with it. She said also that there was a large animal moving among the trees; it had frightened her so much she had snatched up the gown and run. Hegesistratus and I agreed it was probably a cow, but she seemed doubtful. He asked for her help in protecting Elata, to which she readily consented after receiving my permission. I suggested that the boy might help as well, but they both insist that there is no boy on our ship.

Now I see the first faint light of dawn.

7

Oeobazus Is Among the Apsinthians

Hegesistratus said, "It is both bad news for us, and good. But I confess that I would not change it if I could. The news might so easily be worse."

Our captain nodded, rubbing his bald head, as I believe he must often do when he wants to think.

Io, who had gone with Hegesistratus to watch Elata, asked them, "Who are the Apsinthians?"

But before I write the rest of the things that were said today in the cookshop, I should write here who these people are and so forth, though perhaps something about them is written elsewhere in this book already. (I have been looking, but have found only a little.)

This town is called Pactye; it is on Helle's Sea. When I was unrolling my old book—because I wished to find how I came to own a slave—I found a passage recounting an oracle of the Shining God in which he told me: *But you must cross the narrow sea.* A short time ago I asked Lyson (he is one of the sailors) whether Helle's Sea was narrow. He says it is very narrow. I asked then if there was a sea narrower still somewhere, but he does not think so. He said also that we have never crossed it, but only sailed up its western coast. He says that the eastern shore is governed by a satrap of the Great King's, and we would be captured or killed if we crossed.

Nevertheless, I think that this is the sea I must cross if I am to be healed as the Shining God seems to have promised me. Here is something else I wrote (I know the hand is mine) in that book: *Look under the sun if you would see!* Since I am not blind and have no wish to be a mantis like Hegesistratus, it must mean to see the past. That is the thing I cannot do; yesterday and all the days behind it seem wrapped in mist. I asked Io whether she, too, was blinded by mist when she tried to look back. She said that the mist was there only when she tried to remember the years when she was small; that seems strange to me, for they are the only ones I have not lost.

Hegesistratus the mantis is forty or a little younger; he limps and has a curly beard. His wife, Elata, is very lovely—wanton, too, I think. He never leaves her unless he must, and then my slave watches her for him. Since I have no need of her now, I have no reason to object.

It was Io who told me most of the things I know about these people. She is my slave, of eleven or twelve, I would guess. I should ask her how old she is; surely she must know. I think she must be somewhat tall for her age, and her little face is lovely; her long brown hair looks almost black.

There is a black man, too. He is my friend, I think, but I have not seen him since we tied up. He spoke with

Hegesistratus in a foreign tongue and went to the market with the others. But when Hegesistratus returned, with Elata and Io, this man was not with them. He is tall and strong, his hair curls more even than Hegesistratus' beard, and his teeth are large and very white; he is about my own age, I would say.

Our trierarch is Hypereides. He is a hand's breadth below my height, bald (as I said), and exceedingly lively, talking and hurrying here and there. I polished his armor before we docked, and he wore it when we landed. It is very good armor, if I am any judge; and perhaps possesses a spirit, for when I polished it, it seemed a tall woman with a shining face stood behind me, though when I looked, she was not there.

I should mention also that I have a sword. Hypereides had me wear her when we went ashore. I did not know where she was, but Io showed me this chest (I am sitting on it) and my sword was in it. She is a fine one with a leather grip and a bronze guard, and hangs from a bronze belt such as men wear. FALCATA is written on her blade in the characters I use. It was while I was getting her that I found my old scroll in this chest.

Hypereides told us the Apsinthians' land lies north and west of the Chersonese. That is good, because it is farther from the Empire; but bad, too, since we cannot reach it in our ship without sailing back down Helle's Sea in the direction we have come and rounding the tip of the peninsula.

Little Io wanted to know what Oeobazus was doing among the barbarians. Hegesistratus shrugged and said, "He may not have gone there freely. If you force me to guess, my guess is that he was captured and carried there—the barbarians in this part of the world are forever fighting, raiding, and murdering each other, and robbing and enslaving anyone who ventures too near their territory without an army the size of the Great King's. But all I actually know is that I came across a barbarian who swears that another barbarian—a man he knows well and trusts—told him the Apsinthians have such a captive."

Our captain pushed away his greasy trencher. "But you can learn more, can't you? Can't you consult the gods?"

"I can consult the gods indeed," the mantis acknowledged. "How much the gods will tell me . . ." He completed his sentence with another shrug.

"Just the same, we shouldn't make any definite plans until you do. What'll you require?"

While they talked about that, Elata showed me the bracelet that Hegesistratus had bought her. It is Thracian work, or so she said. The gold is crudely yet cleverly shaped into bunches of grapes and grape leaves, from which peep two eyes with blue stones at their centers; and the whole is bound together by the twining grape tendrils. Io says it reminds her of the big tree half-smothered under wild vines at the place where Hegesistratus found Elata, though I could not remember the place even when I studied the bracelet.

Hypereides said, "Go with them, Latro. Do as Hegesistratus tells you."

I was surprised, not having paid a great deal of attention to their talk; but I stood up when Hegesistratus did. Smiling as she drained her wine, Elata asked, "Are we to come, too?"

Hegesistratus nodded. "There is a sacred grove near the city; we will use that." To Hypereides he added, "Are you sure you do not want to be present?"

"I wish I could—not that I'd be of much help, but because I'd like to know as much as possible as soon as I can. But if we're going to sail around Cape Mastursia, there's a lot I have to attend to first."

"Your absence may affect the result," the mantis warned him.

Hypereides rose. "All right, I'll join you later if I can. A sacred grove, you said? Who's it sacred to?"

"Itys," Hegesistratus told him.

As we left the cookshop for the wet streets of Pactye, Io asked, "What did you and Hypereides do, master?" I described our morning (we had visited officials and haggled with chandlers, mostly, and on several occasions I had run back to the ship with messages), and asked about hers. She told me she and Elata had gone shopping while Hegesistratus talked with various barbarians around the marketplace. "There are Crimson Men here," she said, "the first ones I've seen since we left the Great King's army. Hegesistratus says they're waiting for the ships from Thought to leave Helle's Sea so they can sail home." Her bright black eyes discovered an open door, and she pointed. "There's some right there. See them?"

I did, four swarthy men in embroidered caps and beautifully dyed crimson robes arguing with a cobbler. One of them noticed that I was looking at him and waved. *"Bahut!"*

I answered, *"Uhuya!"* and waved in return.

"What did you say to him?" Io asked.

"My brother," I told her. "It's just a friendly greeting you give someone you're on good terms with, particularly if you're in the same trade, or both foreigners in the same place."

She looked up at me intently. "Master, can you speak the language of the Crimson Men?"

Hegesistratus halted momentarily and glanced back at us.

I told Io that I did not know.

"Well, think about it. Pretend I'm a Crimson Man—one of their daughters."

"All right," I said.

"Over there, see that big animal? What is it?"

I told her, *"Sisuw."*

"Sisuw." Io was delighted. "And—and him back there. What do they call him, master?"

"The boy in the colored cloak? *Bun* or—let's see—*nucir.*"

Io shook her head. "No, I meant the old man. I didn't even see the boy. Where is he?"

"He's seen that we see him," I explained. "But he's still watching us around the corner of that cart. He's probably just curious."

"I think that you really can talk the way the Crimson Men do, master. At least a little bit, and maybe pretty well. I know you can't remember, but one time you told me that *Salamis* means *peace.*"

I confirmed that it does.

"So I ought to have known already from that," Io said, "and it's something I'm going to have to find out a lot more about." Despite what she said, she has not asked me any more questions concerning that language; nor did she even speak again, I think, while the four of us walked the ten stades or so to the sacred grove, contenting herself with silently chewing a lock of her hair and often looking behind her.

At the city gate Hegesistratus bought a little wine and a pair of pigeons in a wicker cage, remarking that they would make us a good meal after our sacrifice. I asked him how one read the entrails of such birds. He explained that it is really not much different from reading the corresponding organs of a heifer or a lamb, save that the shoulder bones are not consulted; but that he did not intend to divine in that fashion today. I then asked how he would question the gods, and he said that I would do it for him. After that I asked nothing more, because the girl who sold us the pigeons was still near enough to overhear us.

The leaves of the grove have turned to gold, and most have fallen. It must be a lovely spot in spring, but today it seemed forlorn. Nor do I think that Itys receives frequent sacrifices from the people of Pactye—surely they would build him a temple, if he did. When I poked among the ashes of the last fire before his altar, I found them soaked to mud by the autumn rains.

"But we must have fire," Hegesistratus declared. He gave me a coin and sent me to a house from which smoke rose to buy a torch.

"Don't many people come between now and the good weather," the untidy old woman I found cooking there declared as she tied a double handful of dirty straw around a long stick of kindling for me. "And mostly them that does come wants me to give their fire to them for nothing."

I assured her that she would be rewarded by the gods for such a pious act, and mentioned that having given her money, I expected my straw to be well doused with oil.

"You mean lamp oil?" The old woman stared at me as though it were a foreign commodity practically unheard of in this part of the Chersonese. "No use wasting *lamp oil* on this—why, I've got you some nice grease here that will burn every bit as good. Well, I don't give away much fire for nothing, I might as well tell you. Not unless they're kin to me." She paused, brushing back her straggling gray hair. "Once I did last year, though, because of how the poor mother was all by herself and crying so. Are you the one that's lost your child, young man? How old was it?"

I shook my head and told her that I did not think any of us was missing a son or daughter.

"That's what everybody comes for, mostly—children strayed or dead. Dead, mostly, I suppose. When there's lots of people, they get their fire from each other, naturally."

Her grease was old enough to stink, but it took fire with a roar when she thrust the end of the torch into the flames under her pot. I inquired about Itys, whose name was not familiar to me, and she told me that he had been eaten by his father.

The sailors are talking excitedly among themselves—I am going over to ask them what has happened.

8

The *Europa* Sails at Dawn

The kybernetes told all the sailors that he will cast off as soon as it is light enough to see, and Hypereides sent Acetes and his shieldmen into Pactye to collect those who have not yet returned. When the ship puts out, I do not think that Io and I will be aboard—or the black man, either. I should ask about that when I have finished writing.

The sailors say the Crimson Men's ship has slipped out of the harbor. Earlier this year Pactye was ruled by the Empire, and Crimson Men traded here freely, they having been subdued in the same fashion. Now the Great King's armies have withdrawn, and the citizens of Pactye do not know whether their city is to be independent (as it once was), or subject to Parsa or another place. When Hypereides and I conferred with the councillors, they warned us that there must be no fighting with any of the people of the Empire while we were here, for fear Pactye would suffer for it later. Hypereides promised there would not be; but now that the Crimson Men have left the harbor, they are fair game; and since they spent the summer trading around the First Sea and the Euxine, they should be carrying a rich cargo. The sailors say that if the Crimson Men merely cross Helle's Sea to some port still in the hands of the Great King (Paesus being the most probable place), we can do nothing. But if they try to run down Helle's Sea and along the coast to return to their homes in Byblos, there is a good chance that the *Europa* will catch them. A trading vessel such as theirs can sail by night as well as by day, while *Europa* will have to anchor almost every evening to take on fresh water. But a trireme like *Europa* is a much faster sailer; and when a fair wind is lacking, it can be rowed faster than any trader can sail.

Now I must write about the boy. Hegesistratus, Elata, and Io had laid a small fire while I was gone, using the driest wood they could find. I lit it, and as soon as it was burning well Hegesistratus told us the legend of Itys, son of Tereus, who was a king of Thrace.

This King Tereus was a son of the War God and an enemy of Hill. Thus when Hill went to war with Thought in his time, he came with an army to the support of Thought. There he wooed and won Princess Procne, the daughter of King Pandion. When the war was over and her husband returned to Thrace, she accompanied him and there bore him Prince Itys. All went well until her sister, Princess Philomela, visited the court; Tereus fell madly in love with her and, after picking a quarrel with Queen Procne, banished her to a remote part of his kingdom.

When Princess Philomela resisted his advances, he arranged that it should be reported that Queen Procne had lost her life during an incursion by a neighboring tribe. Believing that she would become his queen, Philomela submitted; but in the morning Tereus cut out her tongue to prevent her from revealing what had taken place, for he did not wish the succession of Prince Itys, whom he loved as dearly as a bad man can love a son who bears his face, endangered by a son borne by Philomela.

The maimed princess was then sent home to her native city. Although this occurred before the age of letters, it does not seem to me that the loss of speech alone can have kept her from telling others what had been done to her, for such things might readily have been communicated by gestures, as the black man talks with me; and surely her father and many others must have wondered to find she could no longer speak. But how many women who have tongues, similarly wronged, have held their peace from shame! Doubtless Philomela, cruelly forced to silence, felt as they did.

Soon, however, she learned that her sister was still alive and living once more with King Tereus as his wife; and that was too much. Many months she spent in making a royal robe for her sister of the finest stuffs, and into it wove pictures relating her sad story.

With the most admirable courage she returned to Tereus' court, and there displayed her robe to him before presenting it to her sister. No doubt she had held it some distance from the king's eyes, so that the pictures could not be seen clearly; but when Procne examined it in her chamber, she understood at once all that had happened, and with her own hands she murdered their son, Itys. Together the sisters butchered the unfortunate boy, roasted his flesh, and served it to his father that night. Gluttonous and unsuspecting, Tereus emptied the dish; and when he had pronounced it good, they revealed to him that he (like the Time God, Kronos, said Hegesistratus) had devoured his heir.

With drawn sword Tereus pursued the sisters. But Cynthia, who avenges the wrongs of virgins as her own, changed him to a black vulture, Procne to a nightingale, and pretty Philomela to a swallow, a bird whose tail has been cut away in the same way that Philomela's tongue was; thus it is that the one sings only when it cannot be seen, while the other flies too swiftly to be caught; for their foe pursues them always.

And so it is also that Itys, slain by his mother to avenge the crime of his father, brings help to children, who suffer for reasons they are too young to understand.

When Itys' history was finished, Hegesistratus had me stand between the altar and the fire. Murmuring invocations, he cut the necks of the pigeons, scattered their blood upon the flames, poured a libation of wine, and fed the fire with fragrant herbs. When these things had been done, he sang the paean of Itys, with Io and Elata for his chorus.

The fumes of the fire made me want to sneeze and sleep; as if in a dream, I saw the youth Io had pointed out, a boy coming into manhood, with the first sproutings of his beard apparent on his face. His cloak was costly and of the east, his black hair elaborately dressed. There were rings of gold in his ears, yet his manner was furtive; and he appeared surprised when I pointed at him and asked why he had come to our sacrifice without taking part.

Just then Hegesistratus asked if I remembered who he was, and I replied that he was Hegesistratus, the mantis. He asked whether I could run as fast as he; when I declared I could, he asked whether I might not run faster, and I acknowledged it was so. He asked if I also recalled the kybernetes, and whether I thought he could outrun him. I answered that he could not, and he asked me why.

I said, "Surely you know."

"Yes," he told me. "But I must discover if you do."

"Because you're lame. You were wounded by the Rope Makers, or so you told me once." When I said this, Io looked surprised; I do not know why.

Hegesistratus asked, "And where was I wounded?"

"In the thigh."

He nodded. "What do you think of my new winter boots? Are they well suited to running? Both of them?"

I glanced at them and assured him that they appeared to be of excellent quality (which they did). "But like all footwear they're better for walking than for running. Every man runs his fastest in bare feet."

"That is well said," Hegesistratus admitted. "Now,

Latro, do you still see the boy you spoke to a moment ago?"

Elata winked and pointed him out to me, though that was not necessary. I told Hegesistratus that I indeed saw him still.

"Ask him how Oeobazus fares."

I cannot say how the boy came to have word of Oeobazus, nor how Hegesistratus came to learn of it, unless someone mentioned the boy to him this morning in the market. But I called, "Boy! Stand nearer our fire. What can you tell us about Oeobazus, the Rope Maker who rove the cables of the Great King's bridge?" I knew who this Oeobazus was because the mantis had talked of him with our captain in the cookshop.

"Oeobazus is not a Rope Maker," the boy replied. "He is a Mede."

"But you know him," I insisted.

He shrugged. "He is a Mede. We can't trust them as we do our own people."

Hegesistratus told me, "You must repeat everything that he says, Latro." And so I did. When I had finished, Hegesistratus said, "Ask where Oeobazus is now."

It was not needed, for the boy could hear him as well as I. He shut his eyes for a moment. "He is on a horse."

"He rides," I told Hegesistratus.

The mantis stroked his jaw. "Is he alone?"

"No," the boy replied, addressing me. "Many ride with him, tall warriors with lances. A hairless man who looks very strong holds the noose about his neck." Seeing that Hegesistratus had not heard him, I repeated all this.

"His hands are bound?"

The boy nodded. "The cord is passed through the girth of his horse."

"Latro!"

Startled, I looked around and saw our captain, Hypereides, who had just come up. He waved, and I waved in return, getting my chest full of smoke in the process. I fell to coughing, and had to leave the fire.

Hegesistratus called a greeting and moved to a place from which Hypereides could see him. I do not know what happened to the boy; I have not spoken to him since. When Hypereides drew nearer, he asked how our sacrifice had gone and whether the omens had been favorable.

"Very much so," said Hegesistratus, "provided we follow the advice of Itys."

"Wonderful!" Hypereides crouched before the fire to warm his hands. "And that is . . . ?"

"You and your crew must round Helle's Cape to rendezvous with us on the Thracian coast. We—Itys specifically indicated the four of us here, and your black slave—must track Oeobazus in Thrace."

Hypereides winced. "I'll be sorry to lose you."

Smiling, Elata said, "Let us hope the separation will not be a long one."

He nodded gloomily at that and stared into the fire. "As regards myself—and *Europa* and the crew—I can understand Itys' advice well enough. We certainly can't abandon the ship, and if Oeobazus is in Thrace—"

"He is," Hegesistratus told him. "Itys confirmed it."

"Then the only thing we can do is report it to Xanthippos and get there as fast as we can. But the five of you will be running a terrible risk." He glanced over at Io. "The child must go, too?"

Io said, "If Latro's going, I have to go with him."

Hegesistratus nodded. "Yes. She must."

"All right, she can go. She and Elata won't actually be in as much danger as you and Latro and the black man." Hypereides sighed. "They'll give you two fighters, at least. They're both good—at least I've seen the black man fight myself, and a poet, Pindaros was his name, told me one time that he meant to compose some of his verses about Latro. You won't be able to do much in the way of fighting yourself, I'm afraid, with that wooden foot and your wound only half-healed."

(It was only then that I saw that Hegesistratus' right foot, which I had supposed booted, was indeed no more than a wooden peg; and I resolved to kill him when I can.)

He would not agree. "My wound's closing fast, and though I might not be of much use in a phalanx or on the storming deck of your warship, put me on horseback and I'm as good as any other man."

Hypereides stood up, rubbing his hands. "Horses cost a lot of money. You'll need at least—"

Hegesistratus waved the offer away, saying that he would pay for them. But after we returned to Sestos, the black man drew him aside and took him to see five horses. This I know because I followed them, though they did not see me. Surely it was to buy these horses that Hegesistratus sent the black man away, and that was long before we went to the grove of Itys. Besides, the boy with whom I spoke was not Itys, or so I think, but merely a common, living boy, perhaps from some foreign ship. Nor did he say the things that Hegesistratus told Hypereides he did.

Hegesistratus is betraying us, and for it I shall kill him when the ship has gone.

Io came to me just as I lay down to sleep, saying that she was cold. I wrapped us both in my cloak and laid hers over us. When I asked her age, I heard her hesitate before answering as she pondered the greatest age I might accept. I will not write here the age she gave me, for I know it to be false. It was not long before I discovered what she wished, and I would not give it to her, though many would, I think. I asked whether she was glad we were going to Thrace with Hegesistratus and Elata, and she said she was. When I asked why, she said that Thrace is on the road to Hill, and Pindaros is probably in Hill, and that the best thing for me would be to find Pindaros, who might take me to some place where I would be cured. When I heard that, I was happy that I had written so carefully all that was said of this Pindaros.

Then I slept for a time. When I woke, Io was weeping. I asked why she wept, and she said it was because she had been a temple slave in Hill, and if she returned, she would surely be punished very severely. I asked her whether my own home was in Hill, though I did not think it was. She confirmed that it was not, only hers. If that is so, I have no desire to go there. I will travel the world until I find a place where the people know me and tell me I am of their blood.

Nor will I put Io in more danger than I must.

Part

2

9

Elata Says

I must read this each morning when I rise, and write each day before it is too dark; thus it will become a habit. Though I forget that I am to do it, I will do it still.

This morning, when I saw the three women, I did not know their names, nor why they danced. The others were still asleep when Elata returned to our camp. I did not know then that she was one of our party; but she told me that she was, and after I had counted our horses I knew that it was true. Besides, the others accept her as I have seen since. She told me that she danced alone because she loves to dance, and riding leaves her stiff and sore.

But I had seen the other dancers. I praised their grace and asked her where they had gone. She said then that they are the river's daughters, and that their home is in the river—she offered to take me there if I wished so that I might see it for myself. One who wears the belt of manhood, as I do, should not be afraid; but I was as frightened as a child when she said it, and I would not come with her.

She laughed at me and kissed me; and even though she is so small, it seemed when I held her in my arms that she was larger than I. She says this river is the Melas, the boundary of the country of the Apsinthians.

I asked then why they danced, and she said it was because the rains had come. "You don't remember how much wine I drank the night I met you, Latro. I drank because I was burning with thirst." She smiled at me, her head to one side. "Now the rain has returned, and it is the season of growth. Would you like to lie with me again?"

I was still frightened, but I nodded. Just then one of the sleepers stirred, and she laughed and backed away. Perhaps she was only teasing me, and I have never lain with her. Yet I feel it is not so.

The sleeper sat up, rubbed his eyes, and said, "Good morning, Latro. I am Hegesistratus. Will you help me with my boots?" I said I would if he required my help; and he told me he did, that they were very difficult to pull on, and that I helped him every morning. I feel sure this is true, though I do not remember it and his boots slipped onto his feet easily enough. He said that he would be happy when the warm weather returned and we can wear sandals again. So will I; boots are very uncomfortable whether one walks or rides.

The girl woke then. She says her name is Io, and she told me something of the rest and where we are going. She said that we hope to take prisoner a Mede called Oeobazus for the city of Thought. I nodded at all she said; but I know that there is not much love for Thought in my heart, and a great deal of sympathy for this man Oeobazus.

The black man rose and went to wash in the river. Because I was afraid for him, I went with him and washed, too. Elata came with us, perhaps because she feared I would tell him of the other dancers, for she held her finger to her lips when he was not looking. She let her gown fall to the ground and dove into the rushing waters, but the black man and I only waded in up to our waists, and Io (who had come with us, too) merely washed her hands and feet.

Last of all, Hegesistratus came, I think because he feared for Elata; but because he had come, he had to take off his boots and wash his feet. When he had dried them, he put on his boots again without my help. I do not know what this may mean. Can it be a sign of submission to assist a comrade, a man older than myself, in pulling on his boots? I cannot believe it—those who submit walk beneath a yoke.

I, too, was afraid that I would mention the dancing women, and so I told the black man and the rest about the rider I had seen, a big man with a lance on a big horse.

"That will be an Apsinthian," Hegesistratus said. "He may even be a scout of their king's, though it's more likely he was just a petty aristocrat out hunting. When we ford the river, we will be in their country." He smiled sourly and added, "I would imagine that a few of them will welcome us to it before the day is over." I asked him then whether the Apsinthians hunted with lions as other men do with dogs, and he assured me that they do not. The beast that ran beside the rider's horse seemed a lion to me, but I did not speak of it then.

The sun that had shone so brightly at dawn soon hid behind clouds, and a thin rain fell. We had to ride a long way upriver to find a ford; and though hoofprints proved it a ford indeed, its water was higher than the horses' bellies. The rain stopped soon after we had crossed, but the sun did not return. In the cities, the market must have been full by the time we reached a place from which we could see the ashes of our fire across the noisy river.

The black man had been leading us, but when we halted for a moment to look at the thicket where we had slept, he turned back and spoke long to Hegesistratus in a tongue I do not understand. Hegesistratus explained that he had urged that we ride west from each ford in future instead of returning to the coast as we have been doing.

"It would save a great deal of weary riding," Hegesistratus conceded, "and it is certainly true that we are beginning to run short of food; but it would also greatly increase our likelihood of becoming lost, and we might even wander out of Apsinthia and into the country of the Paetians to the north. We can steer by the sun and the stars whenever the god grants us clear weather, but we are not apt to see much of that for some time to come."

The black man pointed to the sky to show that he knew where the sun was, though its face was veiled.

Hegesistratus said, "Until now, we have tried to stay near the coast so we can meet the *Europa* at the queen's great temple at the mouth of the Hebrus. Yet we must locate Oeobazus first; and should we reach the Hebrus, we can follow it to the temple. So let us vote upon this matter. Those who wish to do as Seven Lions has suggested, raise your hands."

The black man's hand shot up, and I raised mine as well, because I feel that he is my friend. Io held up hers, too, I think out of loyalty to me; and thus it was decided.

When we rode on, I looked for hoof marks where I had seen the rider, for near them I hoped to discover the footprints of the animal that had bounded beside his horse as well, and from them to decide whether it had been a dog, as Hegesistratus had said, or a lion, as I had thought it. It is not safe to try to distinguish between these by size alone, for the great hounds of Molossis leave imprints as big as a small lion's; but the claws can be seen in front of the toes in the track of a dog, while in the pug mark of a lion they are not to be found. The hoofprints of the rider's steed were equally invisible, though I discovered the pug marks of a lion.

Here the shoreline is low, almost flat, and often muddy, so that we did not always ride within sight of the sea; when we did there were no islands in view, though I cannot say what a summer day might have shown. We ate the first meal without dismounting; but we halted here where there is good water, hobbled the horses, and built a fire to cook the second. We had finished our bread and olives and were deciding whether to set up our tent when Io saw the riders.

She shouted and pointed. It was dark enough by then that they could not be seen at once if one had been looking into the fire; but after a moment I made them out against the trees that grow beside the stream—nine men on horseback armed with lances. Hegesistratus rose and greeted them in the Thracian tongue while I made sure my sword was free in the scabbard and the black man groped for his javelins. I should write here that Hegesistratus and I, as well as the black man, each have a pair of well-made javelins; Io says Hegesistratus bought them for us in Pactye, a city to the east and south. Hegesistratus has one of the light, long-hafted war axes of the Medes also, inlaid and footed with gold. The black man has a knife with two edges; it, too, appears to me of their making, though its fittings are only bronze like those of my sword.

When Hegesistratus spoke again, he raised his cup, so that I knew he was offering to share our wine. One of the Thracians replied. I could not understand him, but his tone told me that he had refused. I whispered to Io that she could be of no help to us and instructed her to go to the sea. She nodded as if she intended to obey and left the circle of firelight, although I do not think she went far.

Soon the Thracian horsemen trotted over to us. The one who had spoken to Hegesistratus spoke again.

Hegesistratus hung the wineskin on his lance, and he lifted it until the skin slid into his hands. He drank the unmixed wine and passed the skin to the man beside him. Hegesistratus gestured toward our small pile of possessions, I think to show that we had no more wine.

The Thracian pointed toward the black man with his lance and spoke again.

"You must put down your weapons," Hegesistratus told him, and he did, sticking their heads into the soft earth. I thought then how simple it would be to kill the Thracian with a single cast, for my own javelins were not far from my hand. With their leader dead, the rest might ride away, or thus it seemed to me. Yet I did not act.

He rode to where Elata watched us, and indicated by a sign that he wished her to stand nearer to the fire where he could see her better. When she only shook her head and trembled, he managed his big horse very skillfully, so that its broad chest crowded her closer and closer to it.

At last her foot touched one of the burning sticks, making its end move in the flames and sending up a cloud of red sparks. She screamed, Hegesistratus shouted at him, and another Thracian urged his mount forward and thrust at Hegesistratus. The black man's javelin struck him below the eye. The point seemed to sprout behind his ear like a horn. I should have cast my own then; but I stabbed the leader—up and beneath the ribs—instead, and severed his head as he fell. This I wondered to see, for I had not known my blade was so good.

At this the other Thracians galloped off and wheeled with leveled lances. I ran for my horse, hoping there would be time to take off the hobble before their charge. I found him freed already, and bridled; Io held his reins. As I sprang onto his back, the thunder of the charge began.

It was not the Thracian lancers who charged. All in an instant, as a storm roars out of the night, long-haired riders boiled around us, one galloping through our fire and scattering its coals, so that she seemed to leave a trail of flame, as a torch does when it is thrown.

I rode after them and had a singing arrow sting my ear for my pains; nor did I shed any other blood, for all the Thracians who were not dead had run by the time I reached the point where they had received the charge. A woman (whom I believed a man) writhed beside a corpse, blood bubbling from her mouth as she gasped for breath. (Even before I dismounted, I could hear the sucking of the wound in her chest—a horrible sound.) I tore her tunic to bandage her and bound the wad of wool with strips of rag. It was while I did this that I found she was a woman, for my fingers brushed her breast. Her friends returned before the last knot was tight, but when they saw that I was trying to help her, they did not interfere.

We tied her cloak to the shafts of two lances and carried her to the fire. Hegesistratus has sewed her wound with sinew wet with wine. I know that he does not think she will live, nor do I. Elata says that she will surely live, however.

Elata has smeared my ear with warm pitch to stanch the blood; and now Io weeps for me, which I do not like. I have told her it is not blood from a nick that kills a man but the will of the gods. The black man laughs at us both and stands very straight with his chest thrown out because these women have never seen such a man as he.

Now everyone is asleep, save for Hegesistratus and one of the women, with whom he speaks. The horses stamp and nicker, frightened by the smell of so much blood. Surely the Thracians will return and bring with them others—but not before dawn, I think.

10

The Amazons

The warrior women burn their dead. This and a great many other things I have learned about them from Hegesistratus, who speaks their tongue. He says it is not the same as Thracian. I asked how many he speaks—for it seems to me that I have only this one in which I am writing and the one I speak to Io and the others, though she says I have at least one more. He answered that he speaks all tongues, and perhaps it is so; Io calls him a mantis and does not wish to tell me more about him. The warrior women think the black man uncanny; and I know that Io thinks the same of the lovely Elata; yet I think that Hegesistratus is stranger even than the warrior women.

He names them breastless* ones, and so do Io and Elata, so I will call them that as well. Io says that we were told of them last summer by a wicked woman called Drakaina, though I cannot remember it.

If Pharetra dies, the others will halt and build a pyre for her. We need not halt, too, unless we choose, Hegesistratus says; but it seems to me that it would be foolish to leave them. We are sure to encounter more Thracians, and it would be better to fight them together if we must fight. I have spoken about this with the black man, and he agrees. Hegesistratus and Elata will certainly not go without us.

---

*In Greek *amazos,* "without a breast."—GW

The other Amazons have made a litter for Pharetra and slung it between two of the captured horses. This morning when I rode beside her, she smiled and spoke to me. When I shook my head to tell her I did not understand, she showed me by signs that she wanted me to help her out of her litter; but I would not. Her hair is nearly the color of my own, though I think more touched with red. Her wound has made her face white and thin, so that it seems that the high bones beneath push through her cheeks, as stones rise in a plowed field after rain.

All these Amazons are tall and strong. They have only the left breast, and a flat white scar where the right breast should be; their tunics have a single strap, worn so that it covers the scar. I asked Pharetra about this. She made many signs until I said, "You need only one to nurse a single child?" She nodded to that, so she must know at least a few words in the language of the Hellenes.

I asked her name. She spoke it for me, but I cannot say it as she does. Pharetra, "bowcase," is as like it as any word I know, though she laughed at me when I called her that. Now we are going to move on.

We have ridden through the Thracian town and camped here, in this muddy field beside the river. Everyone is angry about it—I, too. We met the Thracians after the first meal; Io says most of them look like those we killed last night. I have read all I wrote about that but learned only a little. I must write less about what has taken place and more about the things I see.

The highest Thracians have tattooed cheeks and gold rings, and so much gold on their bridles that their mounts are burdened by it. There were at least a hundred. We could not have fought them with three men and a few women, but Hegesistratus and the queen spoke to them and made peace. He says he is not certain it would have been possible if the Thracians had not wanted to show the women to their king. He says also that some know the speech we use, though they feign otherwise; we must be careful of what we say. He asked permission for us to gather wood for a fire, but they say there is none here (a lie) and some will be brought us. Thus I must write quickly, while the light lasts.

It is young rye we trample here, and plainly not all these Thracians are horsemen, for we have seen many peasants on foot. The horsemen are the landowners, perhaps, and their attendants. Certainly many are rich.

The lance seems their chief weapon. Their lances are half again as tall as a man and no thicker than a spear; I would find them awkward, but they handle them very well. The swords I have seen have only one edge, like Falcata, and long tapering points. Some have bows, but theirs do not look as good to me as the bows of the Amazons. The Thracians wear cuirasses of linked rings or quilted linen, however, and some have helmets, while the Amazons wear no armor at all.

The Amazons' bows are made of layers of horn and wood bound with leather. Each keeps a lump of black beeswax in her bowcase with which she rubs her bow to keep it dry; they wax the bowcase also, and all have beautifully made bowcases of boiled leather. Pharetra let me look at hers. There was a compartment for the bow, a hollow bone to hold strings, and a quiver for her arrows. A griffin on the front of her bowcase has slain a man—not drawn or painted, as I would have thought such a picture would be, but molded into the leather. I would guess that the images were cut into wood, and the boiled leather hammered into the depressions while it was still hot and soft. Each arrow is as long as my forearm from the end of the longest finger to the elbow—a cubit and two fingers. The tips are iron and seem too slender to me.

Her sword looks very odd. It is crooked like mine, but

sharp along the outer edge. If someone were to take a leaf-shaped sword and cut away half the metal down the blade, what remained would be something like the swords of the Amazons. I can see, however, that such long, light blades might be useful on horseback.

A peasant has brought firewood in a cart. With a fire on which to cook the second meal, all of us feel better, I think. Hegesistratus paid for the wood—two obols, which seems very dear to me. He told Elata that the peasant promised to bring wine and a young goat, so we may have meat later. Io says it has been a long time now since we have had a good meal. Some meat will be good for Pharetra, too.

Hegesistratus has told me that the Thracian town is Cobrys, and the king's name is Kotys. Some of the people we passed in Cobrys looked like Hellenes to me, though no doubt most of them were Thracians. A dozen horsemen guard us, sometimes gathering in twos and threes to talk until their commander scatters them again. I will eat with the others and pretend to sleep; later I will see how watchful these Thracians are.

Not wishing to reveal what I planned, but anxious to learn how dangerous it might be, I asked Hegesistratus to tell me what Fate has in store for me. He smiled and agreed that was perhaps as good a means of passing the evening as we would find. Io was eager then to have her future foretold as well, and he promised he would do that also, provided that she would assist him with mine.

When she agreed readily, he got a small mirror from his bag and polished it with salt, poured out a libation to the Goddess of Love (mirrors are under her care, as he explained), and had Io take a brand from the fire. Sitting with his back to the fire, he watched the stars in his mirror for a time, or so it appeared to me. It is not clear tonight, but not wholly clouded either; wisps of cloud come and go, sometimes passing across the face of the moon, and often across the face of her who holds it.

When he was satisfied that everything was correct, he taught Io a simple prayer and had her walk in circles around him as she recited it, holding high the brand and matching her steps to the words. Elata crooned a different invocation, a sighing, nearly inaudible sound that seemed to fill the night, like the soughing of the wind. Soon four of the Amazons were clapping to keep the time, while a fifth strung her bow and plucked the bowstring, sliding one finger up and down. The black man tapped a stick of firewood with two others.

"Swords," Hegesistratus muttered. "I see swords. You are in great danger that will become greater yet, many swords, long and sharp."

I asked whether I would die.

"Perhaps. Yet I see gods about you, many smiling. Nike accompanies you always. The Destroyer smiles upon you—" He dropped the mirror. Io halted her march, and the others fell silent. Elata hurried to his side.

"What did you see?" I asked him.

He shivered, picked up the mirror, and turned it so that its polished side lay face down. "My death," he replied. "All that is mortal dies—I should not have let it master me."

It was clear that he did not wish to say more, and I said nothing to force him to.

At length he continued, "Nike is with you, as I said. You see the gods, or so Io has often assured me."

I told him I did not know.

"You do not see her because she stands behind you. Perhaps if you were to look into a mirror, as I just have, you would see her then. But you may not look into mine."

I said, "I don't want to."

"Good." He wiped his brow with his finger, flinging

the sweat onto the ground before him. "Let me see—what else was there? You will travel far. I saw the Boundary Stone beckon, and he is the patron of travelers. The Lady of Thought and the Huntress were playing draughts, which means that each will use you in the game if she can."

The queen, who had been listening as though she understood most or all that Hegesistratus said, now asked a question in her own tongue. She is no taller than the others, and I think not much older than I; but she has eyes like cold seas, and all the rest hurry whenever she speaks to them. Hegesistratus calls her Hippephode, the cavalry charge.

Now he shook his head. "No, I did not see the War God." To me he added, "She said that you possess his virtues—*arete,* as we would say. She felt he might be inclined to defend you, and it may well be true; I did not see everything."

Io said, "But you said the Destroyer smiled at him. That's good, isn't it? The Destroyer gave him good advice the time he came to our oracle in Hill. I used to remember what it was, but I'm afraid I'd get it wrong."

The mantis nodded slowly. "He is often a friend to men. I have sometimes wished that his twin were more like him, although she is occasionally friendly toward women, and especially toward girls like you. And certainly she has been a good friend to me—a very generous friend indeed." He clasped Elata's hand as he spoke.

I asked what advice he had for me, based upon what he had seen.

He shrugged. "Like all who are in great danger, you must be bold, yet not overbold. It is those who are daring but not rash who live through dangers. If possible, you should go to Dolphins. The greatest of all the Destroyer's oracles is there, and if you consult it and make the right sacrifices, he may have something very useful to tell you. Will you write that in your book? And read it, too?"

I assured him I would.

"Beware of women, and of the learned, whether women or men. They will advise you in their own interests, not yours, if you allow it. But that is a warning such as I might give every man."

I nodded, for I understand very well what he meant, though he is a learned man himself.

"Be careful not to offend those who favor you, and do what you can to gain the goodwill of those who do not. Hunting may please the Huntress, for example, and study the Lady of Thought, or favoring her city. Or sacrifices of the proper kind—though nothing is sure."

Io asked, "Now will you do me?"

"No," Hegesistratus told her. "Or not this evening, at least."

Just then the peasant who had brought us firewood returned leading a young he-goat and carrying a jar of wine. The mantis poured out a few drops of the new wine to the Destroyer; and the black man (who was very clever about it) dispatched the goat, skinned it, and cut it up for us more quickly than I would have believed it could be done. With his fingers he told us that he wished to keep the skin to make a drum; everyone agreed that he should have it.

Pharetra sat up to eat and drink with us; surely that is a good sign. When I asked when she had been hurt, Io said it was last night when we fought these Thracians. Io and Elata take good care of her, and the Amazons seem happy to let them.

After we had eaten, the Amazons sang; only Hegesistratus understood their words, I think, but they have wonderful voices—so fine that our guards drew nearer to hear. (They wear foxskin caps; their cloaks are divided and cover their heels.) At last everyone except Elata and I lay down to sleep. The fire is nearly dead, and though it is so cold, I will not add more wood; that would only frighten Elata and make it easier for our guards to see me.

When I wrote of the Amazons, I should have said that they lack bronze bits for their horses. Theirs are of rawhide, and though I cannot remember, it surprised me very much; thus I do not believe I have seen such bits before. Their reins, too, are rawhide, their saddle pads of sheepskin, not greatly different from ours.

Hegesistratus is lame and has a curly beard, very black; Elata is smaller than the Amazons and very beautiful, and Io is still a child. It is written here that we are to find Oeobazus. Hypereides the Trierarch sent us. I asked Hegesistratus and Io before they slept, and both confirm it. This land is Apsinthia, in Thrace.

I have tried to write until Elata slept as well, but I am tired and this fire is almost out. Perhaps she will not sleep tonight at all. Another rider has joined our guards, a larger man than the rest. That is bad, the dog very bad, perhaps. I am going to lie down, but stay awake till Elata sleeps and the fire is out.

11

Ares and Others

King Kotys, Oeobazus, and Cleton—I must remember them all, or at least remember them when I read this, and remember to read it frequently.

I had not meant to sleep, but sleep overpowered me. When I woke, the moon was low, and only the glow of embers showed where our fire had been. Elata was gone; Io, Hegesistratus, the black man, and the Amazons sleeping. I could not see our guards, but I heard their horses snort.

Though I can no longer recall yesterday morning, I know we were not prisoners of the Thracians then. I remember how I saw them riding across the plain. Perhaps we should have fled, but they would surely have pursued us, and it seemed better to fight on unwinded horses if we had to fight, and to make peace if we could; thus we are here.

There is little cover near our camp, so I waited until the moon was down, then crept over the new rye toward the Thracian city, keeping low in the furrows. They surely expect us to try to flee it, thus that seemed the best way. Once a rider passed close, but he did not see me. I took my sword, but left my two javelins behind. All this time I wondered about Elata, thinking that perhaps the guards had lured her away from our camp, raped, and killed her.

There are few stone buildings in the city, and its wall is toward the sea. The houses closest to us were humble, built of wood and wattle and roofed with straw. In several streets, not one showed a light.

Thinking that such poor people would not be likely to sound the alarm unless their own lives and property were threatened, I called softly at a door; and when no one came, I thumped it with the pommel of my sword. At last an angry man answered. I could not understand him, but using the speech of the Hellenes, I told him that I was a Hellene and a traveler; and I asked him to take me to the house of someone of my own nation, where I could find lodging.

I do not believe he understood anything I said, but perhaps he recognized the tongue I spoke. In any event, he unbarred the door. He had a club, but let it fall when he saw Falcata. He led me almost to the docks, where there was a house—Cleton's—larger than most; then he pointed to the door and ran away.

A woman opened when I called. I do not know her name, but she is a servant of Cleton's, I think, a Thracian. She did not want to let me in. She was frightened, but once she understood that I could not speak Thracian, she woke her master.

Cleton is short and fat and gray of beard, but not lacking in courage, I think, for when he came, it was with an angry face and a heavy staff; nor did he lay it down when he saw my sword. His hours of business, he told me, were from the opening of the market until nightfall. If I wished to speak with him, I could do it at his warehouse, and now I must go.

"I cannot see you then, noble Cleton," I replied (for his servant had mentioned his name), "because I am guarded. Do you think I always go about in a dirty chiton, with muddy knees? I had to creep like a lizard to visit you here."

He stared at me, then ordered the woman to go back to bed. "You don't have to worry about her," he assured me. "She only knows three words: come, go, and spread your legs. You're no Ionian, though you talk like somebody from Thought. Where are you really from?"

"I can't remember," I said.

He laughed. "Well, there's many another lad that's had his troubles. You don't have to give me your name, son. What is it you want from me?"

"Nothing but information," I told him. "Where is Oeobazos the Mede?"

"That's common knowledge," he said thoughtfully.

"Not to me. I don't speak Thracian."

Cleton shrugged. "It's a barbarous language. I used to think I didn't know it very well myself, because I had so much trouble with shades of meaning. Later I realized they couldn't do much that way either—it's a language for yelling at people. Would you like some wine?"

I nodded, for it seemed clear that Cleton's friendship was worth having. He leaned his staff in a corner and led me to a larger room where there were benches and a table.

"We eat inside a lot here," he said. "The weather's awful. So's the wine, but because of the war it's all I've got. Do you know if the Great King's coming back?"

I said, "I have no idea."

"I hope so—the army bought everything I had, last time. Paid well, too. Have a seat, won't you? If you'll excuse me for leaving you, I'll fetch the wine."

It occurred to me, of course, that he had gone to get help; but there was nothing I could do about it except listen, which I did. He was soon back with wine, water, a mixing bowl, and two cups.

I said, "If Oeobazos' whereabouts are known to everyone, there's no reason you shouldn't tell me."

"Yes, there is," he explained as he handed me my cup. "So far I've had nothing in return. What have you of value to tell me?"

I thanked him and asked what might be of value to him.

He shrugged again. "You could start by telling me where they're keeping you, and what you've done."

"Nothing that I know of," I said. "We're being held in a field, inland, not too far from the city."

"There's more than one of you, then. There must be—they wouldn't hold one man in a field. How many are there?"

"Thirteen."

"That's an unlucky number, don't you know that? There are twelve Olympians, and they never permit a thirteenth. When the wine god came, the hearth goddess resigned to make room for him. It's not pleasing to him to make a face at your host's wine, by the way. It may be bad, but it's the best I've got."

I said, "It isn't the wine—what we drank tonight was far worse. It's that I read tonight that I see the gods, and yet I know nothing about them."

"Neither does anyone else, son—don't let them fool you. Who are the other twelve they're guarding, and what brings you to Cobrys?"

I explained that we were not a single group, but two that had been traveling together. "My companions and I were sent by a captain from Thought," I told him. "His name is Hypereides. Besides myself, there are Hypereides' mantis and his wife—"

"Wait a moment." Cleton held up his hand. "Did you say Hypereides? What does he look like?"

I did not know, but I sensed that if I confessed it, I would learn nothing more. I said, "A thousand people must have seen Hypereides—he's a very well-known man. What would it prove if I were to describe him?"

Cleton said, "You prove to me that Hypereides sent you, and I'll tell you where the Mede is. What does Hypereides want with him?"

"He's been ordered to find this Oeobazus and bring him to Thought," I told him. "I can't tell you more than that. As for proving that Hypereides sent me, his ship's to meet us at the mouth of the Hebrus. You might send someone there and ask him. I'm called Latro, and his mantis is Hegesistratus."

Cleton's eyes flew wide. "Hegesistratus of Elis? The man with the wooden foot?" I was too stunned to reply, but he took my silence for assent. "You're traveling in fast company, son. Very fast indeed. Do you know who Hegesistratus of Elis is?"

I said, "He's Hypereides' mantis, as I told you."

"And that's all you know. Yes, of course. Well, when the Great King's army came through here, he was Mardonius' mantis. I never actually saw him myself, but I heard quite a bit about him. The Great King held the supreme command, as you'd expect, but Mardonius was his strategist—some sort of relation, too—his son-in-law, I believe. So Mardonius' old mantis is working for Hypereides now?"

Having need of wine, I drained my cup. "If you say it."

"Hypereides does a little business with me once in a while. Horsehides, mostly. Maybe a bit of amber if the price is right. Say hello to him for me."

I promised I would.

"Is that all you want? Where Oeobazus is?"

"If you could procure our release, we would all be very grateful," I told him.

Cleton nodded. "I'll come out tomorrow and have a talk with Hegesistratus; then I'll see what I can do. Do you know where the temple of Pleistorus is?"

I shook my head.

"Northwest of the city, up on the hill. These Thracians put all their temples on hilltops, and Pleistorus' is the big one, because he's their war god. We call him Ares."

I asked how far it was.

Cleton fingered his beard. "I haven't been up that way all that often, son. I'd say maybe ten stades or a little bit less. There's a processional road that'll lead you out from town—you know, smoothed down and everything. You can't miss it once you get on that."

Yet I did, and I doubt whether Cleton himself has ever gone that way by night without a lantern. The processional road he had told me of began at the marketplace, as I expected, and gave me a smooth, well-marked path out of the city, for it had gotten plenty of attention from the spade, and there was a carved post on one side or the other every ten or fifteen cubits.

The night was nearing that moment at which one feels that dawn must come (though in fact it does not come) as I left the city behind me; and as the processional way rose, lifted by the first low hill, I could see the scarlet spark of our fire to my right. Someone had been cold enough to wake up and put on more wood, obviously; I wondered who it had been, and whether he had noticed that I was gone.

Then the processional way divided into two, equally wide as well as I could judge in the dark, and without any indication as to which led to the temple of Pleistorus. Thinking it would be prudent to stay as near our camp as I could (for I hoped to get back before dawn), I chose the one to the right. I had not gone far when I heard music, and not much farther before my eyes caught the glare of torches.

I had scarcely time to take a step before the dancing girls came whirling down the processional road. There were five, two clashing cymbals and two thumping tympana, followed by a larger group that included flutes and carried torches. The fifth girl, who bore no instrument, halted her wild dance to embrace me. I cannot imagine that I have ever been more surprised than I was then.

"Don't you recognize me, Latro? I know you forget, but is it as quickly as that? Come dance with us. Can you move your feet the way I do?" She took my hand, and in a moment more I found I was prancing along beside her, greatly handicapped by my boots.

"Step to your left, step to the right—turn and turn about. Left, right, right. You're getting it. Why, you're doing very well!" The others were dancing backward to watch, and though I could not see their smiles, I did not need to.

"You were sitting by the fire trying to write, not so long ago, and you couldn't keep your eyes off me. Don't you want to dance with me now?"

Between gasps I tried to explain that I had urgent business at the temple of Pleistorus.

"You're lost, then, poor boy. This goes to the temple of the Mother of the Gods—we're coming back from there."

Someone I at first took for one of the Amazons caught up with us then to tell us we could not dance at the head of the procession, and must wait until the king had passed.

Very happy to wait, I nodded and moved to one side of the road; but Elata laughed at him and said that she and her friends had been dancing at the head of the procession all the way from the temple. "Oh!" he exclaimed (his tones were like those of a deep-voiced woman). "Are there many more of you?" She said that there were, and he ran on to find them—but passed all four as if blind.

Before he was swallowed by the night, the larger group was upon us. Its dancers and musicians were mostly men and sensibly barefoot, clustered around a file of riders. Though it has been only a short time since I saw them, I cannot remember much about those who rode in the train of the first; his eyes caught mine, and I could not look away. Nor, I think, could he.

He was youthful and tall, broad of shoulder, mounted upon a milk-white stallion. Mail that shone like gold covered him from neck to sole, save for a breastplate in the likeness of a lion, and greaves terminating in the features of a woman, tranquil and grave; but it is his own face that I remember most clearly, its thick brows, piercing eyes, and heavy jaw. It was the face of such a man, I think, as might lead entire armies to the edge of the world and beyond.

After him, the other riders, and the strange dancers, came a rabble singing and carrying torches. I suppose that they were from the city, though I do not know. When the last of them had passed, I asked Elata whether the first rider had been the war god. She laughed at me just as she had at the womanish priest, assured me he was not, and told me that her friends had called him King Kotys.

By that time Dawn's rose-tinted fingers barred the eastern sky, and though I had hoped to visit the temple of the Thracian War God before daylight, I wanted far more to return to our camp while Hegesistratus still slept. Together Elata and I left the road, descended the sheep-nibbled hillside, and crossed fields and jumped water-filled ditches, guided now and then by glimpses of the fading fire, and at last by the towering white column of its smoke. Hegesistratus was still in this tent, rolled in his cloak. I plunged Falcata into his back.

At first I did not understand what I had done, and it was while I stood staring at his body that Hippephode and the black man overpowered me, seizing me from behind and wrenching Falcata from my hand. Hegesistratus has told them to keep me here, and not allow me to go outside; and though the black man has kindly brought me this book, with my stylus of slingstone metal pushed through its cords, he has also made it clear by many signs that he and the Amazons stand ready to kill me should I try to leave.

When I think back upon the night, I cannot understand why I desired so greatly to take the life of Hegesistratus the mantis. It was out of friendship for him, and not from any regard for Hypereides, the captain from Thought, that I sought Oeobazus—for I do not remember the captain save as a name in this book. Yet I wished with all my heart for the death of Hegesistratus, and I saw no contradiction in that.

Although I no longer desire the life of Hegesistratus, it seems to me that what I learned concerning Oeobazus, King Kotys, Ares, and the others may be of importance in the future. Thus I have written everything here, and I will try to remember to read it tonight.

12

We Will Fight

When everyone had spoken, only Elata voted to do as the king has demanded. We have eaten the second meal as usual; when the fire dies, Hippephode will give the signal. We will have to leave the tent behind, with a few other things; but that cannot be helped. I will take this book and my old book, thrusting them through my belt.

Though I have read my own account of all I did at dawn, the only things I recall are seeing Hegesistratus asleep before me, and stabbing him. Hippephode and the black man must have been watching, for one held each arm before I knew they were upon me. If I had fought, I think I might have freed myself; but I could only stand and wonder at what I had become, someone who murdered a friend and found himself prisoner of two others.

Then Hegesistratus himself came into the tent, and only a blanket lay at my feet, a blanket that had been pierced by my sword.

The black man brought this book, as I said. Hegesistratus would have come sooner to speak with me, I think; but a fat old man drew him aside. They talked long in voices too low for me to hear. The old man was Cleton. I cannot recall going to his house in Cobrys now; but I know I did, because I wrote about it here. And when I saw him with Hegesistratus, I recognized him and whispered his name.

When Cleton left at last, Hegesistratus and Elata entered the tent; Io followed, tiptoeing to escape their notice (though I doubt she did) and sitting silent in a corner for a long while before she spoke. Once I saw the tent wall move, so I knew that the black man listened, too, though doubtless Hegesistratus had spoken to him and the Amazon queen before Elata and I came back this morning.

When Hegesistratus had seated himself on the ground before me, he asked whether I were not surprised to see him alive and well, and I acknowledged that I was indeed.

"Do you understand," he asked, "that I am no ghost? Nor a phantom born of your imagination, nor any other such thing?"

I said I did, and added that I did not think myself much inclined toward either imagination or phantoms.

"But you saw a phantom this morning," the mantis told me. "And in fact you killed it, insofar as such a phantom can be killed."

When I said nothing, he continued, "Do you see me clearly now, Latro? I, having stepped in here from the bright sunshine outside, cannot see very well yet. Have your own eyes adapted to these shadows?"

I told him that I could see him perfectly, that I had been writing in this book earlier and had thought the light entirely adequate.

"Then as I entered, you will have noticed that I possess a physical peculiarity that is rather rare." He gestured toward his wooden foot.

"I saw that you're lame," I said, "but I don't consider it well mannered to speak of it."

Her face very serious, Elata told me, "Yet there are times when such things must be spoken of. Then it is inoffensive to do so. Hegesistratus has been mutilated; as I have told him, I love him all the more for that. What exactly is the nature of his mutilation, Latro?"

"He has lost his right foot," I said. "It has been cut off at the ankle. Did I do that?"

Hegesistratus shook his head. "You did not, but the person who did it is indeed present. I will speak of that in a moment. But first, what would you call this?" He tapped his peg.

"A wooden foot," I said. "A device to permit you to walk."

"Then I am a man with a wooden foot?"

"Yes," I acknowledged, "I would say so."

"You cannot tell me, of course, whether you have ever seen another foot like mine. But do you think such feet common?"

I said that I did not.

"In that case, I am *the* man with the wooden foot, am I not? I might be called that?"

"Certainly," I said.

"Do you hate me? On that account or any other?"

I shook my head. "Of course not, why should I?"

Hegesistratus held out his hands. "Touch me," he said, and I did. "I am real, you see. I can be felt as well as seen and heard. Now I want you to consider our situation. You are young and strong. I am twenty years your senior, and lame. You have no weapon, but you should hardly need one. By the time Elata's cries bring the others, I will be dead."

I told him that I had no desire to harm him—that I was sure he was my friend.

"Then let me tell you how I came to have this." He tapped his foot again. "I was born on the lovely Isle of Zakunthios; but my family originated in the city of Elis, on Redface Island. That is the southernmost part of the mainland of Hellas."

I nodded to show that I understood.

"Our family has always been closer than most to the unseen. For some of us it seems very close indeed; for others no nearer than for other men. Or other women, I should say as well, for the gift is given to them at least as often as to us men, though we men have gained greater fame from it. In me it has been very marked since childhood."

I nodded again.

"As my reputation grew, I was invited several times to come to Elis, our ancestral home. Year after year these invitations came, each more cordial than the last. I consulted the Fates, and each time I was warned not to go.

"After more than a decade of this, a message arrived that came not from the Assembly of Elis, as the previous letters had, but from Iamus, the head of our family. In it he said that no less a god than the Destroyer had thrust aside the veil of the years for him and shown him in such a manner as to inspire his complete confidence that I would one day succeed him, that our family would thrive with me at its head, and that I myself would be rich, and respected throughout Hellas. That being the case—and as I said, he had received such guarantees that there could be no doubt of it—Iamus urged me to visit him in Elis without delay. He is an elderly man, as I ought to have told you. His health is poor, and there were matters concerning certain family properties, and to be honest certain ingrained family quarrels, with which he was eager to acquaint me before Death came to him. He wished to give me his blessing also, and indeed the blessing of such a man is not to be despised."

Hegesistratus fell silent, as men often do when they try to speak of the decisions that have shaped their lives; and at last I asked, "Did you go?"

"No, not at first. I made a pilgrimage to the navel of the world instead, to Dolphins, where—as I told you yesterday—the Destroyer has the greatest of all his oracles. For three days I prayed and sacrificed, and at last, escorted by six priests, I entered the sanctuary of the pythia. My question was: 'If I go to Elis, as it appears that my duty demands, will I escape the danger awaiting me there?' The responses of the god are often cryptic, but this one was as straightforward as any petitioner could desire:

> "Though those most feared lay hold of thee,
> Thy own strong hand shall set thee free."

Hegesistratus smiled bitterly. "What would you have done in my position, Latro?"

"Gone to Elis, I suppose, and been as careful as I could."

He nodded. "That is what I did. The god's words could be interpreted in only one way, as my own good sense, as well as the priests, assured me: I would be beset by enemies of whom others were mortally afraid—in my foolish pride I supposed that these would be from some disaffected group within our family, for not a few are heartily afraid of us, although their fear is seldom warranted—but I would escape by my own efforts.

"And so this prophecy appeared fully reconcilable with the one Iamus had been given, while justifying the many warnings I had received. I went, met with the leading members of all the various branches of our family, and sensed no deadly hostility in any.

"Soon the Assembly invited me to officiate at the Italoan sacrifice, and to foretell, as the custom is, the future of the city from my scrutiny of the victims. So signal an honor could hardly be refused, and in fact I could see no reasons to refuse it, although I warned the magistrates that they might be sorry to hear all that I would tell them—this because I already had some notion of the future of that part of Hellas. They absolved me in advance from any blame and repeated their invitation.

"I performed the sacrifice, and the presages were as urgent and as unambiguous as any I have ever seen—the freedom of Elis was menaced from the south; only by the exercise of the greatest courage and prudence could it hope to preserve even a modicum of its ancient independence. I confess that in conveying this to its citizens I drew somewhat upon previous revelations that had been vouchsafed me; but the portents were so clear that I felt entirely justified in doing it. I left little doubt in anyone's mind as to whom these despots might be, for there was little in my own; and I stressed the urgency of my warning.

"If only I had listened to my own words, I would have fled Elis that night; as it was, I remained until the celebration was complete, spent the following day in thanking Iamus and various other members of our family, and in saying good-bye to everyone, and went to bed resolved to depart next morning.

"And so I did. A dozen Rope Makers reached our wall before dawn, the feebleness of their force a measure of the contempt of Rope for my ancestral city. Few though they were, Elis did not dare to resist them, knowing that the finest army in the world stood behind them. Our gates were flung wide; they marched into our city, hailed me from my bed, and carried me to Rope."

Seeing my wonder, Hegesistratus said, "Oh, there was nothing supernatural about it, I'm sure. Some spy had repeated my words to them, and they had acted at once, as they frequently do. Are you at all familiar with the place?"

Io spoke then for the first time. "We've been there, but I'm sure Latro's forgotten it. It's not much anyway."

Hegesistratus nodded. "There was a pretense—a very thin one—that I was merely the guest of one of their judges; thus I was detained in a private house. My legs were clamped in stocks of iron, and I was questioned for several days. The Rope Makers seemed to believe that someone had bribed me to divine as I had, and they were understandably anxious to learn the identity of my corrupter. When at last I convinced them that I had only spoken the truth, I was informed that I would be publicly disgraced, tortured, and ultimately killed, the following morning.

"That night one of my captors, feigning kindness, provided me with a dagger. Do you know that dishonorable custom of the Rope Makers?"

I shook my head; but I could see the dagger as if I held it in my hand, and I felt I knew what was coming.

"The doomed captive is permitted to take his own life, thus sparing Rope the opprobrium of having done away with some well-regarded person; afterward their judges can swear by every god on the Mountain that he died by his own hand. Some unfortunate slave is accused of having provided the weapon and duly executed—they killed one of their own kings, Cleomenes, in that fashion about ten years ago. I will never forget the sound of the door shutting and the heavy bar outside being set in place, nor the sharpness of the blade as I sat testing it with my thumb."

Io said, "But what about the oracle? Didn't you remember that the Destroyer had promised you'd be able to free yourself?"

"Oh, yes, of course." The bitter smile came again. "And I also recalled how often I had been warned against going to Elis, and how I had continued to ask, by this means and that, until I so wearied all the gods that I received a response that could be twisted into a favorable one, then hurried off. That is what we mortals do, you see; and subsequently we wonder to discover that our gods mock us. I grew up that night, child, and I hope your own maturation is a great deal easier.

"For a long time I simply sat there with the dagger in my hand, listening to the house go to bed. The Destroyer had been correct, of course, as he nearly always is: my own strong hand could free me, and in a very short time, too. All I had to do was plunge that dagger into my chest. But it is hard, terribly hard, for a man to end his own life; King Cleomenes could never strike deep, they say, though eventually he made so many shallow cuts that he bled to death.

"I thought of him sitting in stocks like mine—possibly the very same stocks, and in that very room—striking at himself and flinching, and in a few moments striking and flinching again; it started my thoughts down a fresh path, for I remembered how many animals I had sacrificed in my life, everything from small birds to bulls, always without flinching. And I recalled how slippery their blood had made the handle of my knife, particularly when I had dispatched three or four large animals at a time, as I just had at Elis. Leaning forward, I nicked both feet until my ankles were slick with my own blood; then I wrenched and pulled as hard as I could.

"In that way I was able to get my left foot out, but not my right. Perhaps it was a little larger; or perhaps that opening was a trifle smaller—I cannot say. By now you know, of course, what I did next; I began to cut away that foot, one small slice at a time. Twice I fainted. Each time I awoke I cut away more, until at last I could draw out what had once been my right foot. So many sacrifices and the examination of so many victims have taught me something about the way an animal is put together; and despite all our boasts, man is only a featherless animal on two legs—if you have ever seen the skinned carcass of a bear, you know how like it is to a human body. I tied off the major blood vessels, trimmed away flesh I knew could not live, and bandaged the stump as well as I could with my filthy chiton."

Io asked, "Could you climb out the window then? I would've thought you'd be too weak."

Hegesistratus shook his head. "There were no windows, but the wall was only mud brick, as the walls of most houses in Rope are. With the dagger, I was able to pry out a few bricks. Rope itself has no city wall; one of its greatest boasts is that its shieldmen are its walls. Late at night, there was nothing and no one to prevent me from hobbling into the countryside, though every step was agony. In the morning I was found by a slave girl milking cows. She and a few of her fellow slaves concealed me in the cowshed until my stump was half-healed; then I made my way to Tegea, and from Tegea, home."

At this point in Hegesistratus' story, three Thracian lords galloped into our camp, all of them finely mounted, with gleaming armor and many gold ornaments on their bridles and their persons. They spoke for some time with Hegesistratus while he interpreted for Hippephode.

After they had gone, she called the Amazons together, and Elata came for Io and me. Hippephode addressed her women while Hegesistratus repeated the message the Thracians had carried to us from their king.

They had begun, he said, by affirming King Kotys' goodwill and offering various proofs of it: he had not killed us, though he had thousands of warriors at his disposal; he had permitted us to camp here close to his capital, had allowed us to buy food and firewood, and so forth. Now, they said, it was time for us to prove our own goodwill toward him and his people. We were to surrender our horses and our arms; and when we had done that, we would be taken before the king, who would listen to whatever requests we might make of him with a gracious ear.

After repeating this to Hippephode, Hegesistratus had asked for time in which to consider the matter, and had been told that if we had not turned over both our horses and all our weapons by tomorrow morning, we would be overwhelmed and killed.

When Hegesistratus had reported this, the black man spoke, and Hegesistratus translated his words for the rest of us, first in the tongue of the Amazons, then in that of the Hellenes. "If this king is indeed our friend," the black man had said, "why should he wish to take away our horses and our weapons? Every king wants his friends well equipped and his foes disarmed. So let us do this. Let us assure this king of our friendship, just as he has assured us. Let us swear to him that if there is any task he requires of us, we will do it—we will slay his enemies, and bring him anything he wishes, though it lies at the edge of the world. But he in turn must allow us to keep our horses and the weapons his service will require, tell us where Oeobazus is, let us take Oeobazus to Thought if Oeobazus is in his kingdom, and give the Amazons the horses they have come so far to get."

If I had known before why the Amazons had come to Thrace, I had forgotten it; but I do not think Io knew, because she looked as surprised as I felt.

Queen Hippephode spoke next; all the Amazons cheered her lustily when she was through, and Hegesistratus interpreted for us: "I agree with everything that Seven Lions has said, but I have one thing more to add. We Amazons are the daughters of the War God; and though we love him, he is a strict father, laying upon us laws we dare not break. One is that we never lay down our arms, lest we become as the daughters of men. We may make peace, but only with one who trusts our pledge; and if he will not trust it and demands that we break our bows, we must fight until we die. To the present day, no Amazon has ever violated this law, which was not made by women or by men, but by the god who is our father. King Kotys must be made to understand that we will not violate it either."

13

We Await the Attack

Cleton came back to warn us. This time I talked with him, as well as Hegesistratus, and I must tell about that here; if we live, it is something I may require. But first I will set down everything I had intended to write before Hegesistratus came to speak to me again.

When Hippephode had finished, he asked whether anyone else wished to be heard, and I said we need not ask King Kotys where Oeobazus was; he was in the temple of Pleistorus, the War God. I added that since this god was the father of the Amazons, they could ask him to let Oeobazus come with us. Hippephode promised they would, and I recounted what I had seen and heard the night before. Hegesistratus confirmed that Cleton had come as he had told me he would, and questioned him about Hypereides. Then we voted, with the result I have already recorded.

After that, Hegesistratus talked with Hippephode and the black man; that was when I wrote what stands above, laying it aside when he returned to speak with me again.

"We have been discussing tactics," he asid. "When morning comes, we will send the king a fresh message, offering to give him a hostage as a guarantee of our good behavior. That should at least postpone any attack."

I agreed that seemed an excellent plan, and asked who the hostage would be.

"We will offer to let him choose—any single individual he selects."

"Then he'll choose you," I told Hegesistratus, "if he's not a complete fool. Losing you would cripple us more than losing anyone else."

Hegesistratus nodded. "That is what we hope he will do. If I can meet him face-to-face, I may be able to accomplish a great deal—which brings me to the matter I wanted to tell you about, Latro. And you, Io." She had followed him to the door of the tent, where I was sitting.

"Before the Thracians arrived, I recounted something of my history to you. If I bored you, I am sorry; but I thought that you ought to know why the Rope Makers hate me, and why I hate them."

Io said, "I can certainly understand now why you hate them. But if you were just telling those people in Elis what the gods had told you to tell them, why should they hate you?"

Hegesistratus smiled. "If only everyone were as reasonable as you, there would be fewer quarrels. Unfortunately, men hate anyone who opposes them for any reason. And not only did I warn the Eleans against the Rope Makers, but I have warned many other cities since then—warned anyone who would listen whenever I had the opportunity, in fact. Furthermore, they were humiliated by my escape, and they know that I served Mardonius to the best of my ability.

"I said that the Rope Makers hate me; but there is someone else, a man who is not truly one of them, who hates me far more. Tisamenus of Elis is his name, and this Tisamenus is the mantis of Prince Pausanias, the Regent of Rope."

Io's expression when Hegesistratus pronounced these names was such that I asked her if we had encountered these people. She nodded without speaking.

Hegesistratus said, "Io has already told me that you

have met them, although you do not remember it. She has told me, in fact, that Pausanias calls you his slave."

I think I looked angry at that, because he added hastily, "Without any right to do so. Io also told me that she believed you had written a good deal about your interview with Tisamenus in your other book—more, or so she thought, than you had told her. Would you be willing to read it to me?"

"Of course," I said. "But you called him Tisamenus of Elis and said that he was this prince's mantis. Is he a relative of yours?"

Hegesistratus sighed and nodded. "He is—a rather remote one, but of our blood nonetheless. I told you that there were family quarrels. Do you remember that?"

"Yes," I told him. "Certainly."

"The most ancient of all is that between the Telliadae and the Clytiadae—the sons of Tellias and the sons of Clytias, who betrayed him. I am of the Telliadae, as you know; Tisamenus is of the Clytiadae. He is of about my own age. Should I recount a little of his background?"

Io said, "I wish you would. I'd like to know more about him."

"Very well then. Although the Clytiadae are descended from the first Iamus just as we Telliadae are, they lack something of our reputation, and I have heard that the young Tisamenus showed few of the early signs that mark an authentic mantis. Instead, his chief ambition was to gain honor as a victor in the games—for he possesses extraordinary swiftness of both body and mind, and great strength for a man of no great size.

"Though he had married sooner than most, his wife bore him no children; and with that as an excuse, he borrowed sufficient funds from his wife's family to take him to Dolphins to consult the Destroyer. Once there, however, he took the opportunity to question the god about his whole future, and was assured that he should win five glorious victories."

Io asked, "You mean running races and so on?"

Hegesistratus shook his head. "No, though that is what he believed. As you perhaps know, the great games in honor of the Destroyer take place at Olympia, which is near Elis, every four years. Tisamenus enrolled himself as a contestant in no fewer than five events.

"It was the talk of Elis, as you may imagine, and word of it reached us on Zakunthios very quickly. An uncle of mine, my mother's brother Polycletos, asked that I look into the matter. I consulted the gods by half a dozen methods; the results were uniformly negative, and I reported that Tisamenus would win none of the events he had entered, which proved correct.

"But enough of this—I know I am taxing your patience. Let me say briefly that after the games Tisamenus soon discerned his true vocation and was taken into Pausanias' service, and that he has never forgiven me. Presumably the battles of Peace and Clay were two of the victories the god promised him, for Eurybiades, who commanded the combined fleets at Peace, is a subordinate of Pausanias', while the regent himself directed the allied armies at Clay."

Hegesistratus fell silent for moment, his piercing eyes fixed on mine. "Here you must accept my word for what I tell you. It is possible for a mantis—if he is both skilled and powerful—to cast a spell that will force another to work his will. Are you aware of that?"

We both nodded.

"The magi, as the sorcerers of Parsa are called, are adept at it. I learned it from one of them while I was in Mardonius' service. Where Tisamenus has learned it, I cannot say; perhaps from a magus taken prisoner at Peace, though that is conjecture. But I feel sure that he *has* learned it; and if you, Latro, will read the applicable passage from your book aloud, I may discover something of interest."

Accordingly I untied the cords of my other scroll,

searched it for the name of Tisamenus, and read aloud everything I found, beginning with the words, "In the regent's tent there was no one to meet me." One section Hegesistratus asked me to read twice. I give here precisely as it is in the older scroll:

> "There is one more thing to tell, though I hesitate to write of it. A moment ago, as I was about to enter this tent Io and I share with Drakaina and Pasicrates, I heard the strange, sly voice of Tisamenus at my ear: *'Kill the man with the wooden foot!'* When I looked around for him, there was no one in sight."

Hegesistratus nodded as if to himself. "There it is. When I mentioned these spells, I ought to have told you also that the caster can—and often does—steal the memory of the event. I do not mean it is lost after a single day, as you ordinarily forget everything; rather it is forgotten at once, as soon as the event itself is past. In this case it appears that my cousin was not quite so skillful as he perhaps thought himself, for in you, who forget everything, some fragment of memory remained for you to record, though it seemed to you nothing more than a voice in the wind. Perhaps knowledge of your condition made him careless, or perhaps the very flaw that makes you forget everything permitted you to remember this."

Io said, "Tisamenus was really there, even if Latro didn't remember him being there as soon as he left—is that what you're telling us? Like you can't touch a ghost?" She shivered.

Hegesistratus said, "Latro's memory of him was killed, if you will allow it; its ghost vanished, as ghosts frequently do. When Latro, with Prince Pausanias and a shieldman of Pausanias' bodyguard, returned from the cliff after viewing the ship that would take you both to Sestos, my cousin must have called Latro aside. I would guess that he took him to his own tent, though it is barely possible that the whole thing was done elsewhere, in some other place where he could feel certain he would not be interrupted. There he cast the spell, and as it happens we can be fairly sure of the very words he used: 'Kill the man with the wooden foot.' But there was a second spell as well; one to make Latro forget the first. It was intended, at least, to make him forget that he had spoken to Tisamenus without Pausanias present. I doubt that the regent would have appreciated having the man he was sending to the Chersonese employed for a private purpose by my crafty cousin, so the second spell—the spell of oblivion—would have been absolutely necessary."

Io had been chewing a lock of her hair; she spat it out to speak. "But I remember when Latro and the black man found us at that place outside the city. He didn't try to kill you then."

"Yes, he did," Hegesistratus told her. "Although you must understand that he himself did not realize what he was doing; he did not plan these acts. He brought me to the house Hypereides had commandeered, where his sword was. He saw to it that I was seated and relaxed, and he got his sword."

"But you hit it with your crutch! I remember. Latro, you looked like somebody who'd been woken up with a kick."

Hegesistratus told her, "That is a very good way to think about it. Under such a spell the charmed person moves as though in a dream, and scarcely seems to know that he walks and strikes in the waking world.

"There were a couple of oddities involved, by the way—one that helped my cousin, one that opposed him. It is difficult to force any man to act against his essential nature, you see. For example, if I were to cast such a spell on you, ordering you to pat your horse's nose, there would be no difficulty—it would be something you would have no rooted objection to doing, and you would do it. But if I were to tell you to kill someone instead, that might be another matter. I doubt that you have ever done such a thing."

Io shook her head. "I haven't."

"Latro, however, has been a soldier, and indeed from what you and the black man have told me, he was in the Great King's army when it marched down from Horseland. It is probable that he has killed a good many sons of Hellen; I was only one more."

I asked him, "What was it that worked against the spell? I'd rather hear about that."

"*Lingua tua,*" Hegesistratus said, using the very words that I write here. "Your tongue. Tisamenus did not know it, and so he had to cast his spell in one not your own, which is extremely difficult; I was surprised to find that he had succeeded as well as he clearly had.

"After I had reviewed everything I knew of the subject, and consulted with a certain friend who was hiding in Sestos—do not speak about this man to others, please—I returned, intending to remove the spell if I could. I found Latro writing; he had put his sword away again, but he had that little bone-handled knife he uses to sharpen his stylus, and when I attempted to take off Tisamenus' spell, he stabbed me with it." Hegesistratus touched his side. "The wound is still not quite healed, and perhaps it will always give me a twinge at times. But to continue, seeing how hazardous that was, I cast several spells of my own—one to make him overlook my wooden foot, for instance. Of course you know what happened to that."

"No," Io said. "I don't. What was it?"

"Then you were not listening when Latro spoke to all of us a short while ago. He recounted his conversation with Cleton, the merchant from Hundred-Eyed he discovered in Cobrys. He had mentioned my name to him, and Cleton, suspecting nothing, called me 'the man with the wooden foot.'"

I nodded. "And that made me want to return here and kill you. I practically forgot about Oeobazus."

"Exactly. But there are powers in the four worlds that are far greater than my wicked cousin, and one chose to protect me. Or perhaps chose to protect us both, for if you had killed me as you tried to, it is more than probable that either the Amazons or the black man would have killed you—people generally do not take kindly to someone, even another friend, who kills a friend while he is asleep. But as I started to say, I am protected by certain spells and charms, and it is most probable that one of the gods they invoke stepped in to save me."

Io said, "Then maybe they'll save us tomorrow."

I saw how frightened she was and hugged her, telling her that only those of us who fight are liable to be killed, and the worst thing that can happen to her is having to sweep the floors of some Thracian house.

14

In the Cave of the Mother of the Gods

This is written by the light of our fire. Cedar is stored here for the sacred fire, and the embers were still smouldering from a sacrifice. Io found the wood and puffed the embers while the rest of us fought at the mouth. Three Amazons are missing, and two more are wounded badly. The black man's cheek was laid open by a thrust; Hegesistratus sews it shut. No one knows what has happened to Elata.

It is raining outside.

I have just read what I wrote before sunset, and there is much more I must write down. Cleton returned. Hegesistratus, Queen Hippephode, the black man, Io, and I spoke with him, and he told us about the prophecy.

"I went to the palace," he said. "I've done some trading for King Kotys—very profitable for him—and I like to believe I've got some influence. I had to wait quite awhile, but they brought me in to see him at last.

"He was sitting at table with three noblemen, with his best gold rhyton in front of him. Those drinking horns they have are symbols of power, did you know that? If you've got one, you'd better be ready to back it up. Well, I could see that he was a little drunk, which is unusual for him. All the barbarians are pretty hard drinkers, but Kotys usually carries it better than most of them. The way you reason with a king (this is what I've found myself) is you tell him he's got a problem and offer to take care of it for him—so that's what I did. I said I knew he had all of you outside his city, some of you barbarians from the east (because you always tell barbarians it's the other fellows) and who knows what the tribe might do if there was real trouble? And some of you my own countrymen that had just beat the Great King and all his Medes, and were liable to have an army on his doorstep any day.

"I said right away that I'd gone out here to talk to you, because it's always better to tell them yourself before somebody else does. I said what I'd heard was that you were traders, so I'd got my wagon and my best mules and come out here hoping to do a little business. I told him, too, that Egbeo's doing a fine job. Egbeo's in charge of your guards, see? I bribed him—not much—so I didn't want him to get into trouble.

"Then I said I'd found out you weren't really traders, but pilgrims and ambassadors from Thought, because Kotys knows all about Thought, it and Hundred-Eyed being just about the biggest trading cities up this way. I told him it looked to me like the whole thing could be wrapped up without hard feelings, so if he'd just have his key people cooperate with me, I'd try to take care of everything for him.

"Then he grinned and said, 'When the moon's high,' and all the nobles went *haw, haw!* I knew right then there was something up, so I said, no, I'd really been planning to go out here again and see about it this afternoon.

"He shook his head. 'Cleton, my friend, don't you trouble yourself about them anymore today. Go tomorrow. Then you'll have my permission to act in whatever way you think best.'

"I bowed three times and backed out, saying how happy I was to be of service, got the wagon again, drove up to the temple of Pleistorus, and asked to see Oeobazus. Kotys is high priest, but there's always somebody there, and they're priests, too. I knew a couple of them, and when I said I'd just come from the palace and was supposed to set some things up for tomorrow, they let me talk to him. Have any of you seen the place?"

None of us had, and we told him so.

"Well, don't expect a nice marble building like one of our big temples back home. It's pretty big, all right, but built out of this local stone—limestone, I guess—and it's pretty narrow, because the boys up here don't trust themselves with long spans. You have to go in at the front where there's a hall so that the most important ones can get out of the weather. Then the altar and so forth, and a great big wooden statue. In back of it is a nice curtain I got them from Sidon. Some of the nobles' wives have embroidered it with the god riding his horse. His lion's running alongside, and he's got his lance in one hand and his wine horn in the other. They wanted to do Zalmoxis as a boar down in one corner, but there wasn't room enough for that, and besides, it would be mostly in back of the statue down there. So I told them just to do his front, his forequarters, if you follow me. His head—"

Hegesistratus held up one hand. "Were you able to speak to Oeobazus?"

Cleton nodded. "They've got him in a room in back. It's got a window, but it's way too small for anybody to get through, and there's a couple of bars in it. Kotys is going to sacrifice him."

I do not believe Hegesistratus is often surprised, but he was surprised by that; I saw him blink. Hippophode touched his shoulder and he translated for her, using a tenth as many words as Cleton had. I told Cleton I had not known that these people practiced human sacrifice.

"Only the kings do it." Looking important, Cleton clasped his hands behind his back and threw out his chest. "The king's sacrifice can't be like an ordinary man's, so the difference is that commoners and even nobles sacrifice animals like we do, but the kings sacrifice people. Usually they're captives from their raids. You've got to take into account that the king isn't just a regular man." He winked. "The king's descended from Tereus—lots of them are named for him—and *he* was the son of Pleistorus himself. Pleistorus is the son of Kotytto—that's our Rhea—and sometimes he's her lover, too. So when the king stands up there at the altar with his sacred regalia on and chops the head off a *human being,* you know he's something more. It's one of the ways he proves it, see?"

"When?" Hegesistratus asked.

"Tomorrow," Cleton told him. Hippephode knew that word; I saw the shock on her face even as I felt it on my own. No one said anything until Cleton added, "He moved it up—they weren't supposed to do it until next month."

There was another silence, and at last Io asked, "Does he know about it?"

Cleton nodded. "He was the one that told me, then I talked to the priests, told them I wanted to see it and so on. There's no secret about it, and in fact the priests have been trying to get the news out—sending out heralds and so forth—ever since Kotys ordered it. If you ask me, he's got this spring's oracle on his mind."

Hegesistratus grunted. "Then perhaps you had better tell us about that in some detail."

"Well, every year whoever's king up here sends an embassy to Lesbos, where they keep Orpheus' head in a vault underneath the temple of Bromios. You know about that? The head's still alive, or anyhow it's supposed to be. And in the way of thanks for the gifts the ambassadors brought it, it gives the king some good advice for the year that's starting. Generally it doesn't amount to much, stuff that boils down to beware of strangers but trust your friends and so forth. Only sometimes it'll make your hair dance across your head, and then pretty often the king will cut the throats of a few of his dear relations because of it."

Hegesistratus said, "I assume that this was one of those years. What was the oracle?"

"The exact words?" Cleton asked.

"That would be best, if you remember them."

"I couldn't forget them if I wanted to," Cleton told him. "It's announced every year at the festival, and this year half Cobrys reeled it off to you until you were sick to death of it." He recited something in singsong Thracian.

Hegesistratus pulled at his beard, his eyes half-shut, and addressed Hippephode in the speech of the Amazons. She stared at him, I noticed, before touching herself just below the neck. He shrugged and turned to us. "I am not sure I can render it in acceptable verse, but I will try.

"Ill fare the strong when god, god smites,
Then howl the hounds and wheel the kites.
Doves stoop like hawks, and oxen gore,
The child rides armed, and maids to war.
Then Bendis seeks to halt the sun,
But see how swift the lions run!
The Lord of Battles, battle brings,
And battle drinks the blood of kings."

When Hegesistratus was finished, I glanced at the black man and he at me so that when I spoke it was for both. "I don't see that it has anything to do with Oeobazus."

Io added, "Or with us. Aren't you going to explain it to us, Hegesistratus?"

"Later, possibly." To Cleton he muttered, "All this sounds extremely serious, my friend. Have you more bad news for us?"

"I think so," Cleton said. "But I'll let you judge it for yourselves. After I left the temple—this wasn't long ago, you understand—I had to go back to the city to catch the road that comes here. Well, I ran into Egbeo and thought they'd let you go, so I stopped him and asked. He said no, his orders had been to get everybody onto fresh horses, so he'd sent them off one at a time and gone last himself."

I told Hegesistratus, "They plan to attack us when the moon is high—it will give light enough for them to use their lances. There will be many more than our present guards, I imagine; and this King Kotys may very well lead them in person."

Hegesistratus shook his head. "Do you really think

they may? I would have said that we could trust the king's word."

Cleton declared frankly, "Well, I wouldn't."

When all of us had thanked him for his information and good offices, and watched his mule-drawn waggon rattle down the road, Hegesistratus told me, "You are quite correct, Latro, I am sure. But although I do not believe our friend Cleton is a spy for the king, he may very well repeat what he has heard here to someone in the city. If he does, it may reach the king's ears, or those of one of his officers. We must get away tonight, if we can."

Seeing the questions in my eyes, he added, "I would like to consult the gods before I say anything further, and the Amazons have yet to beseech the father of their race."

He spoke briefly with their queen, then said, "Hippephode agrees that a horse would make a suitable sacrifice. Certainly it must be the worst we have, for under these circumstances we cannot spare the best. I believe the god—this god particularly—will understand. Perhaps one of the horses we took from the Thracians at our first encounter. Then I will leave it to you two"—he meant the black man and me—"to devise a plan for our escape, with Hippephode. You must be our strategists, and I shall be your mantis—though I will have to translate for you, I fear."

The Amazons built an altar of wood and earth and plunged a short sword into it. Meanwhile, the black man and I had washed the worst of the horses (which I thought still a very good horse indeed) and decorated it with such finery as Io and Elata could contrive. Hippephode performed the actual rite, slitting the horse's throat after what I assume were appropriate prayers and a hymn sung by all the Amazons. Hippostizein, the tallest, caught the blood in a basin, smeared some on the sacred sword, and threw the rest into the fire. Then the queen and Hegesistratus opened the paunch, and cast the heart and liver, with other organs and certain bones, into the flames. Hegesistratus watched them and the smoke with care, and scrutinized both shoulder blades before telling us what he had learned.

"There is bad news," he said, "but good news, too. We will not escape every danger threatening us unscathed; but it appears that in the end we shall obtain what we wish."

The black man gestured quickly toward Elata, Io, himself, and me, and then toward Hippephode and her Amazons.

"Yes," Hegesistratus said. "Both groups, not immediately—not tonight, I believe—but soon. Ares, at least, is pleased to grant his daughters' request."

The black man crept past the sentries as soon as the sun had set so that he might watch the road. We assumed that the Thracian leader would ride at the head; and though it would be well if he were the king, if he were not he would nevertheless be the best hostage. Io and Elata were to remain behind in our tent. The rest of us mounted as soon as we could be certain we would not be seen, hoping to attack before the moon rose—even the wounded Amazon sat a horse, insisting (so it seemed) that she was well enough to fight, when Hippephode ordered her into the tent with Io and Elata. Someone kissed me in the darkness, and I think it was she. Certainly it was a woman larger and stronger than Elata.

15

I Would Go Now

Hegesistratus will not agree to it, and I have promised to defer to him. We spoke in private and agreed that if something is to be done, it must be done quickly, and I am the one to do it. I told him I planned to go as soon as I finished; but he insists I rest first and sleep if I can.

This is because of the events he foresaw in the flames of our sacrifice—that though we would indeed secure Oeobazus, it would not be tonight. If we wait for dawn, he says, it will be easier to discover the other exit from the cave, if one exists. I had planned to leave through the mouth, for which night would be the best time and in fact the only possible time. Perhaps I should not have agreed, though there is as he says a wind from the mouth. I can see it carrying away the smoke.

I have just reread what I wrote before Hegesistratus came, and I find that I passed over something that should be set down before I forget. After our sacrifice, Io asked Hegesistratus about the spring oracle again.

He said, "I suppose that nothing less than a full, line-by-line exegesis will satisfy you; very well, I will attempt one. But you must realize that the king will have a sage of his own; and that this sage, having a sizable body of the pronouncements of this oracle to study, will understand it far better than I.

"'Ill fare the strong when god, god smites' is the initial line, and the sole questions involved are the identities of 'the strong' and of the gods. It is not at all uncommon for oracles such as this to set a riddle in the first which is solved in the final line, and I believe that to be the case here; 'the strong' are the kings referred to in the last line. Do you follow that?"

Io nodded, and so did the black man and I.

"At least three gods are mentioned, though there well may be more. Those we can be certain of are 'the Lord of Battles,' that is, the War God; 'Bendis,' which is the Thracian name for the Huntress; and 'the sun,' which can only be her twin. Those three we can feel certain are involved.

"The second line runs 'Then howl the hounds and wheel the kites.' The wheeling kites would appear to indicate that many will die; kites feed upon carrion and wheel over battlefields. The question is whether 'hounds' refers to the many-headed dog who protects the principal entrance to the Lands of the Dead. Because Bendis is referred to so openly, I think them hunting dogs instead, and if I am right, the line means, 'There will be pursuit, and many will die.'"

Io said, "What does it mean about the child?"

"Be patient," Hegesistratus told her. "We shall reach that soon enough. The next line is 'Doves stoop like hawks, and oxen gore.' I believe this line may bear two meanings; the first and certainly the most obvious is simply that the orderly operations of nature will be suspended—there will be prodigies. Doves do not swoop down upon their prey like falcons in the normal course of things, and oxen are the most docile of beasts. But I think that we are being told here as well that specific individuals or groups whom we do not expect to fight will do so. Doves are of course birds sacred to the Goddess of Love, and when they appear in prophecy they most frequently represent fair young women—you will recall that when we sacrificed at the grove of Itys outside Pactye I told you about two princesses who were transformed into similar birds. The 'oxen' mentioned in the second half of this line are presumably peasants, though in this country, as in our own, the peasants are far from docile and often accompany their lords on their raids."

I told Hegesistratus, "The next line's the one that Io's so interested in: 'The child rides armed, and maids to war.'"

"Correct," he said. "Latro, you have an excellent memory when you have one at all. That is indeed the line as I gave it, but unfortunately there is very little I can tell you about it. 'The child' may possibly be the God of Love, the goddess's son; but as he habitually goes armed, and flies rather than rides, I have little confidence in that interpretation. The Huntress is another weak possibility—passing at once to womanhood, she has remained a child in some respects; and it is true that she often rides, particularly here in Thrace. But she, too, habitually goes armed, so that this interpretation is open to the same objection as the first one. Worse, she is named outright in the line that follows: 'Then Bendis seeks to halt the sun.' She will act when 'the child rides armed,' and thus she herself is unlikely to be the child referred to. What would be the point in saying that she will act when she acts? I would guess that this 'child' is someone with whom we are unfamiliar, possibly a prince of this or a neighboring state.

"The 'maids' are in all probability the persons referred to as 'doves' in the line above, and if that is correct, these two lines with the 'doves-maids' pair constitute a smaller cycle of riddle and solution set within the greater one. If 'the child' is indeed the Huntress, then the 'maids' Orpheus has said will ride to war may well be the nymphs of her train—but a far more probable solution has already occurred to all three of you; I can see it in your faces."

The black man pointed emphatically toward the Amazons, and Io and I named them.

Hegesistratus nodded. "And that, we can say with virtual certainty, is the interpretation the king and his adviser have settled on. Consider King Kotys' situation; he received this oracle in spring, nearly a year ago, and it hints strongly that he himself may be killed, warning that 'when god, god smites . . . battle drinks the blood of kings.' Summer finds the mighty forces of the Great King streaming through Apsinthia in full retreat. Can this be what the oracle foretold? But the Great King was not even wounded, and in any case Orpheus' oracle was given to him, Kotys, and not to Xerxes, as we call him.

"Now, so near the year's end, warrior maidens—perhaps to Kotys an unheard-of thing—appear in his kingdom. From what Cleton has told us, we may be certain that the first party of Apsinthians we encountered knew of the oracle. They molested us and found themselves attacked by maids riding to war; thus the second party, which agreed to a truce and conducted us to Cobrys. Latro, you are King Kotys. What will you do next?"

"Come here, I suppose," I said, "and see the warrior maids for myself."

"You would be running a grave risk," Hegesistratus told me. "As your adviser in all such matters, it is my duty to warn you that the events foretold may not occur until you yourself have encountered one—or perhaps all—of the portents. If you do as you plan, King Kotys, you may yourself bring about the very results you fear."

I nodded. "I think I understand. What do you advise me to do, Lord Hegesistratus?"

"First, send three trustworthy men to verify that these are indeed warrior maidens, as specified by Orpheus. Second, disarm them. If you attempt to destroy them, they are sure to resist; and their resistance may itself begin the war spoken of. But if you deprive them of their weapons and horses, they cannot 'ride to war.'"

Io shouted, "Wait a moment! I know he sent those lords who wore so much gold, and he wants us to give him our weapons and horses. But he gave us until tomorrow morning, and now you and Latro say he's really going to attack tonight."

Hegesistratus sighed. "Yes, I'm afraid he is. Cleton and the gods brought the same warning; thus we can be as sure of it as of anything. Although we did not say outright that we would not surrender our horses and weapons, we were playing for time, and he knew it. Now he means to take the wolf by its ears if he can. Kings may bleed, but a wound may be all that is meant, or the oracle may refer to other kings, not to him. Or the oracle itself may be false; the Bright God is said to spoil the oracles of Orpheus from time to time, and as we have already seen, he is certainly involved in all this, acting in opposition to his twin sister."

Io jumped up, too excited to sit still. "So was that why he moved up sacrificing Oeobazus? Because he wanted to get on the good side of the Lord of Battles?"

"Precisely. Let us consider the four final lines as one: 'Then Bendis seeks to halt the sun,/But see how swift the lions run!/The Lord of Battles, battle brings,/And battle drinks the blood of kings.' Bendis and the sun we have spoken of already. I would guess that 'the lions' are strategists or perhaps mighty warriors; they rush to battle. The Lord of Battles is of course Ares—or Pleistorus, as he is called here. All right, he is to bring battle, but someone will presumably be victorious. May it not be Kotys himself? The divine favor of Pleistorus is thus to be sought at once, and fortunately a suitable victim is at hand. Kotys will destroy the warrior maidens if he can, then urgently petition Pleistorus' favor."

That was all Hegesistratus said then, or if there was more, I do not remember it now. But when we spoke here in the temple—apart from the others and in the tongue I write, so that they could not understand us—he gave me a warning that may be of the greatest importance.

"You do not remember our conversation with the

Huntress," he said, "but perhaps you have read of it in your book today?"

"I didn't," I told him, "but at the moment whatever she may have said to us is of no interest to me. You speak my tongue—tell me where my land lies."

Hegesistratus shook his head. "I would if I could, but I do not know. If we live through this night, I can consult the gods for you. Do you wish it?"

"How can you speak my tongue and yet not know where it's spoken?"

Hegesistratus seated himself beside me; this was before we talked about my going to the temple. "Because I am the man I am. Do you know of Megistias?"

That name signified nothing to me.

"He was the mantis of King Leonidas of Rope, and died with him. It was given to him to know the speech of every bird and beast, and thus he learned of many faraway things, though once he told me that most beasts, and all birds, concern themselves little with the doings of our kind."

I asked, "Could a bird tell me where my home lies?"

"I doubt it. In any case, I—who sometimes talk with gods—cannot converse with birds. Yet another power of tongues has been given me as that was given him; I know the speech of every man I meet, and of every woman. I cannot explain how I do it. Mardonius often used to ask me, but I could only ask in reply how it was that he could not. It is possible I never learned, as other children do, to speak our own tongue at all."

I believe that at that moment I could have fallen upon my sword. "It seems to be the will of the gods," I said, "that I never find my home."

"If that is indeed their will, you must bow to it," he counseled me. "Will you read the words of the Huntress?"

I shook my head.

"Then I will tell you. She promised you that you

should be returned to your friends. I did not speak of it earlier because your slave girl was listening; but I tell you now. I advise you to read that part of your book, and also to read again that part which you read aloud this afternoon in the tongue of the sons of Hellen."

Here I will write of the battle. The moon was low in the east when we heard the black man's cry. At once we broke the circle of our guards, Hippephode leading her Amazons at my left, Hegesistratus at my right. Two were before us, but the Amazons' bows sang; though I forget everything else, I will never forget the whiz of the arrows. The bones of the Thracians broke under our horses' hooves.

The king's hand was upon his sword, but before it cleared the scabbard I was upon him; I pinned his arms to his sides and wrenched him from his saddle. A Thracian charged me—I recall the gleam of the moonlight on his lance head. I swung my horse about so that the king's body would receive the lance, and the Thracian raised it and galloped past. The king is very strong; he freed an arm and struck me in the face, so that it seemed to me that all the stars of heaven had rushed into my eyes; but I got one hand around his throat and choked him until he no longer tried to pull my arm away.

All this time I was riding north by west as we had agreed, driving my heels again and again into my horse's sides. He is a fine horse, but he could not outrun the Thracian horses with two heavy men upon his back. The black man, Hegesistratus, and some of the women reined in until they rode beside or behind me. The black man held a javelin still, and with it he killed the first Thracian who would have overtaken us, turning in the saddle and casting it hard and well when the Thracian was very near. The arrows of the Amazons rid us of more, the men tumbling off their horses, or their horses falling under them; but there were too many.

Suddenly I felt that we were flying. I looked down and

saw the silver bow of the moon below us, so that it appeared we had leaped above the sky. It was only one of the ditches with which the Thracian farmers drain their fields, and my horse had jumped it before I knew it was there. He stumbled on the farther side; I almost fell, and nearly dropped the king.

In a moment more, I knew that I must, or die. The man on my right was not Hegesistratus but a Thracian, his lance poised high for a thrust. I would have thrown his king at his head if I could; but though I lifted him well, I could not make such a throw from horseback. The king fell between us, and the lancer pulled up, as I knew he would. I could cast my javelins then. One I killed, I think; one I missed.

I do not know how we found this sacred cave. We rode into the hills, then along a road, because it was only there that our horses could gallop. I heard a voice: "*Latro! Latro!*" It was the black man, and though it seems that he seldom speaks, he was shouting. The road ended at the mouth; it glowed crimson in the night, lit by the embers of its altar fire. It is too low to ride through, even if the rider lies on the neck of his horse, though the chamber is much loftier a short way in.

When I reached the black man and the others gathered at the mouth, the black man dismounted and led his horse inside, waving for the rest of us to follow. A young priest rushed at him with a sword; the priest's thrust would surely have killed him had it been a finger's width to the right, but the black man caught his wrist and cut his throat.

Elata is no longer with us; we left her behind in the tent. I believed that Io was there as well until I saw her among the Amazons (this was before she built the new fire for us). I told her she would have been killed had she met one of the Thracians face-to-face.

"I did, and on foot he would have been nearly as big as you, but on our horses we were about the same. I stuck him in the neck."

Several Thracians rushed into the cave on foot, but Amazons killed two with arrows, and the rest fled back out the mouth.

I asked Io where she had found her sword.

"The queen gave it to me," she said. "Queen Hippephode."

I told her, "She shouldn't have, Io, and you shouldn't have taken it."

She had finished wiping the blade (far more thoroughly than it required, and on the hem of her own peplos) and had knelt to blow on the embers, pretending to pay very little attention to what I was saying. "I asked her. I told her I couldn't shoot a bow, but I can ride as good as anybody, and you'd need everybody to protect you if you were going to steal King Kotys. She asked me if I knew what it meant, going into a battle, and I said I'd seen lots of fighting, I'd just never done it. Then she looked through her things and gave me this sword."

"She wouldn't give you her own sword, surely."

"It belonged to an Amazon who got killed before they met us. That's what she said."

I wanted to take it from her, but how could I disarm her when I knew we might be fighting for our lives again very soon?

"I guess she still feels bad about her friend that died," Io said, "because she was crying when she gave it to me. I didn't think they cried."

And that is all I will write now. I must sleep a little—Hegesistratus has promised to wake me at dawn. Except that Io told me she had taken the young priest's robe, thinking that she might make a chiton from the unstained part. "He's been cut," she told me. "Like they do with yearling bulls." She pointed to her own groin.

16

The Horses of the Sun

The white horses Pharetra and I stole are stabled with our own; and indeed (like the sun itself) they seem to wash every shadow. Queen Hippephode says that we must not slaughter them, no matter what happens, and Hegesistratus agrees; but the Thracians do not know that.

I had been asleep. I believe this was the sleep I spoke of when I last wrote on this scroll, saying, "I must sleep a little—Hegesistratus has promised to wake me at dawn." But it was not Hegesistratus (he is the mantis, and has a wooden foot) who woke me, but the Men of Thrace.

No, not even them in truth, but the sentry in the mouth of the cave. She shouted that they were coming, and I woke at the sound of her voice. I saw her draw her bow and let fly before she ran back toward the sacred fire. She nocked another shaft, turned, and shot again without ever breaking step; I would have thought such bowmanship beyond the reach of mortals, but I saw it and write only what I saw.

The Thracians ran in through the narrow mouth, but by that time I was on my feet, and this sword—FALCATA is written on the blade—was in my hand. Those in the van were highborn, or so I should guess. They had fine helmets, well-painted shields, and costly armor, of scales sewn to leather. Behind them were many peltasts; some had helmets, and each two javelins.

I believe that the Thracians would have been wiser to form a phalanx with their lances, but they had left them outside and came raggedly, sword in hand. I myself killed only two of the Thracian lords. After the fight, I would have claimed the mail shirt of one; but Falcata had spoiled both, cleaving the bronze with the flesh. There was a third with an arrow through his eye, however; Queen Hippephode and her Amazons presented me with his mail. I am wearing it now.

I cannot tell how many peltasts I killed. There were many dead; but the black man fought with the priest's sword, it would be difficult to distinguish wounds left by Falcata from those of Hegesistratus' ax, and some of the Amazons used their swords, I think. Hippephode fears all may exhaust their arrows, but those shot in this battle they reclaimed, or most of them.

In the cave's gullet, three peltasts could front me, and no more; I cut down several, while the bows of the Amazons thrummed like lyres. When the peltasts fell back to cast their javelins, the Amazons slew many more with arrows, and the javelins grazed the stone, which is so low in places that I must stoop to walk there. We laughed at them.

When the fighting was over, and the Amazons had honored me with this armor, we decided that Hegesistratus should approach the Thracians crying a truce, for we had not wood enough to burn all the bodies. Besides, we agreed that if Hegesistratus could meet with King Kotys, he might make some agreement that would be to our benefit, since the War God was plainly on our side, and had in fact favored his daughters so greatly in the battle that not one had received a serious wound.

Hegesistratus talked with the king, and afterward everyone began dragging the bodies of the dead Thracians to the mouth of the cave, where the living Thracians were to claim them. That was when I stole away, though it was not yet dawn.

A hundred steps from the sacred hearth, the cave was darker than the blackest night. I very much regretted that I had not brought a torch, though I knew I could not have made one without drawing attention to myself; the black man would have insisted on coming, though his cheek pains him so much, and perhaps the queen would have wanted to send some of her Amazons as well. So many, I felt certain (and Hegesistratus had agreed), would only weaken the rest by their absence, and could accomplish no more than one; if Oeobazus were to be rescued, it would have to be by stealth, for we had not force enough.

Yet as I crept along, I feared that I might forget; and in this, too, Hegesistratus had concurred. At his suggestion, I had thrust this scroll through my belt. I had promised him that if I discovered another way out of the cave, I would stop and read it as soon as there was light enough.

As I have written already, I wore the armor the Amazons had given me; I should write also that I had Falcata, the helmet of one of the lords I had killed, a pair of javelins, and a pelta; for I had thought it would be well for me to look as much like a patrician of Thrace as I could. Of the helmet and javelins, I was soon exceedingly glad, because the first saved my head from many a knock, and I probed the uneven stones before my feet with the iron heads of the second; but I had to cast the pelta aside, for twice I had to climb in order to keep the faint draft I felt full on my face. I was counting my strides and had counted one thousand two hundred seventeen when I heard the roaring of a lion and the snarl of another.

To meet such a beast in that blackness would mean my death, I knew—and yet I was not willing to go back, and tried to turn aside instead; but though I left what seemed the larger passage, I heard the lions before me still. Many times I wondered what had brought them so deep into the hill; though I knew they often slept in caves by day, I had not thought they would willingly enter one so far.

When I had counted more than two thousand steps, I glimpsed light. Then I felt myself a fool indeed, because the answer to the riddle seemed plain: the lions had not gone so far into the dark, but rather had made their den in the very place I sought, the opening through which the draft blew. And though I had no liking for lions even by day, it seemed likely that a few stones and a shout or two might permit me to slip past them. Not many wild beasts will face an armed man by choice.

As the light grew brighter, and the rocks and slippery mud over which I had groped my way so long appeared, I recalled the promise I had made Hegesistratus; but though I took this scroll from my belt and untied the cords, I could not distinguish the words, and had to walk farther before I could sit down upon a stone and read everything I wrote yesterday, beginning with "I would go now." And even then, I was not actually within sight of the mouth.

At last I read of the oracles of the ox and the child and how each had been fulfilled, all of which I believe I recalled at that time, as well as my writing about them, although I have forgotten those things now. After that it was time to face the lions in earnest. I rolled this scroll up again, put it in my belt as before, and advanced with a javelin in each hand.

Soon I met with an illusion so extraordinary that it ought to have forewarned me of what was to come, though in fact it did not. To my left there rose a pillar of the kind sometimes found in caves, lofty and damp. Stretching from the stone beneath my boots to the stone over my head, it glistened like pearl; but I am not sure I would have paid much heed to it if it had not at first appeared otherwise to me. For when upon approaching it, I had merely glimpsed it from the corner of one eye, it had seemed to me not natural object at all, but rather just such a column as is often seen in the houses men build for the gods, columns of white marble or wood painted white.

When I took my gaze from it and walked on, it again seemed to me a thing made by hands, so that I stopped, turned back, and stared.

After that, I felt I traveled not in the cave but through a broken and tempestuous landscape, where rock and mud alternated with smooth walls and floors, and they with sallow grass and the bright blue skies of droughty summer. The sharp stone teeth of the cave seemed simultaneously a forest of columns and a thicket of spears, all echoing to the roaring of the lions who waited for me outside.

For they were outside, beyond even this new, smaller, and more circular mouth. For a moment or two, when I had seen that they were not in the cave at all, I had come to doubt their very existence. Was it not more likely that the sounds I had heard were nothing more than the rage of rushing water? The roar that of a waterfall? That I, who saw a portico where none stood, who felt that there were a hundred men at his back, then looked to find himself alone, had dreamed the lions as I had so much else?

Then a lion stalked before the mouth of the cave, snarling, tawny in level sunshine, with a mane as black as his exaggerated shadow. One javelin poised above my head, I hurried forward.

The sun had just risen over the hill I left. Before me lay a narrow and rocky defile with a stream running along its lowest point; what I saw there was like—and yet utterly unlike—what I had anticipated. I had expected to find several lions, the sons and daughters of the black-maned beast that I had caught sight of through the mouth of the cave, and a mature lioness, perhaps with cubs. I indeed counted no fewer than four lions; but all were huge males, as large as that I had first glimpsed—and in fact the four were so much alike I could not have said which I had seen first.

And though there was a lioness as well, she wore a woman's shape. Tall and strong, more massive of limb than the largest of Hippephode's Amazons, she regarded the stony lips of the cave from the elevation of a silver chariot no horses drew. Her face showed unmistakably her strength and her unswerving purpose; her large eyes burned yellow and fierce—eyes that might adore, thus they seemed to me, or thirst for blood. All of which was august enough; yet there was something more extraordinary still (while still more beautiful) about her appearance, a thing that in the whole time I spent with her I never dared to ask about and never fathomed: it appeared that a second sun rose behind her, between her broad back and the rugged wall of the defile, splendid light enfolding her in a mantle brighter than the purest gold.

"Come." She motioned to me. "I have need of you." In her hand was a large tambour, and though her fingers did not appear to brush its head, its taut skin shook with each thudding of my pulse.

I hesitated.

"You fear my lions." She whistled, and all four bounded to her. She stroked their muzzles, scratching their chins and ears as if they were so many puppies; but when their amber stare fell upon me, I recalled that they were truly lions.

"Much better." She nodded as I edged nearer her. "Do you know who I am?"

I shook my head again.

"My name is Cybele—to you, here, at this time. My priests would tell you that I am the greatest of all gods." She smiled; and seeing her smile I knew I loved her. "But their priests say that of most gods."

"Do you hear my thoughts?" I asked her, for it seemed that she had read them.

"When they are written upon your face? Certainly. Do you not kneel even to a goddess?"

"Not when there are lions present, Cybele."

"They are less than kittens to me—and to you, for as long as I protect you. Do you remember driving such a cart as this? Tell me what you are doing here."

"No," I said, "I don't. The Thracians—King Kotys holds a Mede called Oeobazus. He will be sacrificed to Pleistorus, and I must find the temple and save him if I can."

"You are children," Cybele told me, "you and that foolish seer with the crutch. He thinks to fancy the immortal gods as bettors fancy horses. Your black friend owes me a blood price, by the way. He slew one of my priests, a most promising young man."

I said, "I didn't see everything, but I've been told that your priest was promising to kill him at the time."

"He will not be permitted to pay in jests, although his are somewhat more amusing than yours." Cybele waved a hand, and her lions bounded away, scrambling up the sides of the defile until they had gained the hilltops; she rose and stepped down to stand beside one of the chariot's tall, slender wheels. "Get in," she instructed me. "Take up the reins."

Slowly, I advanced and did as she bid. The chariot seemed higher than I had thought and lighter than I would have believed possible, as if its gleaming sides weighed nothing. There were four pairs of reins, a set for each horse; I looped them through my fingers in the proper way. And though only empty harness lay upon the ground before me, in those trembling strips of leather I touched the fire of four mighty hearts. "Yes," I told Cybele. "I've done this."

"Then listen to me."

I put the reins down and turned to face her, discovering that her eyes were now at the level of my own.

"If you do as you've planned, you will be killed. Not

by me, directly or otherwise; but you will die. I can show it to you if you like—how you'll be found out near my son's temple, your flight, the lance through your back, and all the rest. It will seem as real as this to you. Do you wish to see it?"

I shook my head.

"You're wise. All deaths before death are for cowards—let them have them. Very well. You do not recall your meeting with the usurper, and that is my doing, though you do not recall that either."

"She promised to reunite me with living friends," I said. "Hegesistratus and I were talking of it not long ago."

"But he did not tell you her price, although he knows it." With an expression of contempt, Cybele waved that price aside, whatever it had been. "It does not matter; she would only cheat you in the end. And the end, you may be sure, would be long in coming. I can be cruel as well as kind, but my pledge is a pledge, even as my punishment is punishment. I have saved your life today, for you would have done as you planned and died for it if I had not been here. Now I ask *you* to reward *me.* Will you do it?"

"Of course," I said. "And willingly."

"Good. The Mede will be your reward—do as I tell you, and he will drop into your hand like ripe fruit. The usurper warned you that you would soon meet a queen. Have you met one?"

"Yes, I have—Hippephode, Queen of the Amazons." I blurted out a sudden realization: "Why, they must be your granddaughters! They're the children of the War God, and he's your son."

"And what does Queen Hippephode want? Do you know what has brought her to this land?"

"Sacred horses from the Temple of the Sun. She has brought precious gems and gold—so Hegesistratus told me—with which to buy them."

"This king will no more sell them than free your Mede—but we will force him to both. Do you know where the temple lies?"

I was not sure which temple she meant, but since I knew the location of neither, I shook my head.

Cybele smiled again, the smile of one who laughs inwardly. "The sun will show it to you. When you're clear of this gorge, look toward it. The temple will be directly beneath it. Look under the sun."

I said, "I understand."

"That is well—so does he.* His sacred herd grazes in the Meadow of the Sun; it lies between us and the temple. You must drive the horses around the temple. There you will strike the processional road. Turn right at every forking, and you should reach the entrance of my own temple. Lead the sacred herd into it and hand them over to the queen, and you shall have the Mede, living and whole. That I promise you."

"Aren't the Horses of the Sun guarded?" I asked, and added, "Surely you must know there are armed Thracians at the entrance to your temple."

I wish I could describe her look as she replied; there was love and sorrow in it—rage as well, and towering pride and many other things, too, perhaps. "Why do you imagine I have chosen you?" she asked me. "If a child might do it, would I not send a child? Nor shall you be without assistance. The three whom you will meet first will be your auxiliaries, worthy of your trust because they come from me. Go now."

---

*Latro appears to have spoken Greek to the gods he encountered. If so, the word he used may have been μανθάνω, whose literal meaning is "I learn." The god of the sun was also the patron of learning and prophecy.—GW

17

Sworn Before All the Gods

King Kotys' oath will surely bring destruction upon him and his nation, should he break it. One of the Amazons' best horses was our sacrifice, a red heifer the sacrifice of the Thracians. The terms: Hippephode may choose four, for which she must pay the price agreed. We must bring the rest, unharmed, to the temple of the War God, where Oeobazus the Mede will be handed over to us, also unharmed. We will leave Apsinthia, with the Mede and the four sacred horses, unmolested.

The exchanges are to take place tomorrow, then we will go. Meanwhile, food and wine are to be brought to us. We have no need of water—there are many pools in the depths of this cave, which Hegesistratus has told me the Thracians say is a path to the Country of the Dead. The Amazons and I watered the horses from one such pool. Io helped us.

I asked Hegesistratus about Cybele before I wrote of her. She is surely a mighty goddess—she saved me and will save the Mede. Hegesistratus says she is numbered among the friends of men, and was once accounted the greatest goddess, mistress of all the beasts, though Cynthia contests it with her as she does other things. The Queen of the Dead is Cybele's daughter, and I made sure both were among the gods to whom the oath was sworn.

Yet I distrust King Kotys. There was fury in his eyes when he looked at me. There was triumph in my own, I think, for it was I who brought the Horses of the Sun here as Cybele commanded me, with the aid of Pharetra and the lion. There is a boy with us called Polos, who says that he helped us, too, and certainly he ran in behind the last horse, and may well have been driving it before him. Hegesistratus thinks Polos may be a spy for the Thracians; but he wishes to let him stay so that the Thracians will know that we do not violate our oath.

It was the ceremony that interrupted my writing, but just now I read what I had written; I still recall all those things. Certainly my encounter with Cybele was more important than the capture of the sacred horses—but were not the horses captured at her command? Meeting her was more important to me, but to her it was our taking of the White Horses of the Sun, for if she had not desired it, she would not have appeared to me as she did, perhaps. Thus I should write of that, too, before I sleep.

I have been watching the women walk to and fro before the fire, when I should have been writing. We have a big fire now, because some peasants came with more firewood, and hay and grain for the horses, and the cave is cold. One of the Amazons found iron spits in a small chamber not very far back, and she and two others are building supports for a spit so that we can roast our meat that way. Her name is Badizoe.

Their limbs are round—how gracefully they walk!

The lion was the first; I had not gone more than two stades from the defile where I had spoken with Cybele when he stood in my path. I knew the goddess had sent him—he was one of hers—but it was very difficult to approach him without fear. I said, "Come with me," and he walked at my heels like a dog, though I did not dare touch him. At that time I could not see the Temple of the Sun because of the trees.

Pharetra was the second; we found her just where the trees ended and one could see the white horses on the hillside, nearer the temple. Although I did not know her name, I knew her for an Amazon by her fine bowcase and bowman's eyes. She embraced me, and I her, but she released me and backed away very quickly when she saw the lion. It was some time before I could convince her that the lion would not harm her; but I knew it would not, since both had been sent by the goddess.

We crouched behind bushes, the lion on my left, Pharetra on my right; I asked how she came to be there, but though it seemed she understood my whispered questions, I could not always follow her replies. The mantis spoke with her when we returned, and he says that she fell from her mount in the battle and hid from the Thracians.

She pointed to the sacred horses and sucked in her cheeks like Hippephode's, counting four fingers.

I asked, "Your queen requires four of those white horses?" I said it because Cybele had told me that the horses were to be Hippephode's.

Pharetra nodded, pointing to herself and me.

I said, "You suggest that we take four and bring them to her." I spoke slowly, and when I had held up fingers to make the word "four" clear, Pharetra nodded enthusiastically.

I shook my head, pointed to the horses, and drew a circle in the air to show that I had been instructed to bring *all* the horses to her queen. When Pharetra did not seem to comprehend, I counted them—twenty-five. I opened and closed my hand five times, then drew the circle again.

She stared at me and shook her head, then shrugged.

I was looking at the herdsmen. There were five, all noble Thracians whose bridles and persons flamed with gold. They had swords and lances, but no helmets; and only one wore armor. The question was whether to proceed against them at once or wait for the third helper

Cybele had promised. I know that even the best of gods do not mean all that they say, and we were three now; it seemed possible that the third who was to help us was myself. I was going to suggest that we approach a couple of Thracian lords who appeared deep in conversation when we heard the quick triple drum taps of a cantering horse.

It was Elata, though I did not know her then; she was the third. She rode up to us on a handsome bay colt, and the noble herdsmen saw her. Everyone rides in Thrace, so I would not have imagined that the sight of one slender girl on horseback would have alarmed them, and perhaps it did not. But one rode toward us as if to learn what she wanted.

It might have been wiser to wait, and attack him while he suspected nothing—or even to have mounted Pharetra on the colt. Surely she would have been a lighter burden, one better suited to such a young animal. As it was, I did neither. Elata slid from the colt's back, and I leaped onto it and jabbed the colt's sides with my heels. It was foaled for a charger (I wish it were here with us now), and though it was so young and carried a man in armor, it shot toward the Thracian like a dagger from the hand; only then did I realize that Elata had been riding without reins.

That did not really matter; the bay colt knew its business. The roaring of the lion behind it would have terrified any other horse, and perhaps the colt did not seem frightened only because it was already galloping as hard as it could. My first javelin struck the noble herdsman square in the chest and tumbled him from his saddle. The lion raced past, easily avoided the second Thracian's lance, and pulled him down.

Pharetra was sprinting toward the sacred horses. My knees and my hand on its neck directed the colt after her; the three remaining Thracians were on the other side of the herd. Neither of us had to fight them, as it turned out. They dropped their lances and galloped away as fast as cowards can.

I saw Pharetra mounting a milk-white mare and followed her example—exchanging the bay colt (who was slackening then) for a white stallion, the biggest of the sacred horses. For a moment I feared he might throw me off, for I did not know whether the sacred horses were ever ridden, and it would be no easy task to break a full-grown stallion of such great size; but though he was as fiery as the storm, he wished to run, not to buck. Off he flew, and the rest of the herd after him just as I had hoped. We had the last stabled here in Cybele's holy cavern long before the Thracians arrived to demand them back.

Thus our situation is as I described when I began; we are eleven—twelve, if Polos is counted among us. Of those fit for battle, there are only seven—Hippephode, Pharetra, and two more Amazons; Hegesistratus, the black man, and me. Two other Amazons are badly wounded; Elata and Io tend them, but I do not believe either could be of service in a battle. Elata would not fight, though perhaps Io would. The boy has a sling and a little bag of stones for it; he promises to teach her the art.

When the Thracians came, Hegesistratus discovered that the noble herdsmen who fled reported that Pleistorus took the sacred herd. (I wish we had Cybele's lion still so we could deceive them in the same way again.) Hegesistratus told them he did it because he desires that Oeobazus be given to us, and that he is angered with King Kotys because the king wants to sacrifice him to overawe the people, and not for the glory of Pleistorus. I asked Hegesistratus whether the Thracians had believed it, and he told me he thought they had.

Just now when Io got more wood for the fire, she discovered a bundle of arrows concealed among the logs. There was a letter in the bundle, which she read aloud to us: "May the Stone favor him who does this! These cost-two owls. Europa's man may repay me. I send him greetings."

Hippephode says that they are not very good arrows, but ten thousand times better than no arrows. All the Amazons have full bowcases now. The black man says he can use a bow; he wants to borrow that of one of the wounded Amazons; but she will not let him take it. Hegesistratus says these arrows were hidden in the wood by Cleton, a friend in Cobrys. I think that Cobrys is the chief town in this part of the world.

I am sitting near the mouth so I can write by daylight, but not so near as to give some Thracian bowman a clear shot at me, I hope. It is time for the first meal—Io and the black man are preparing meat. Hegesistratus begs information from the gods; he fears that the king may have sacrificed Oeobazus despite his oath.

Io came here to speak with me a few moments ago. She began by telling me that she was my slave and that she had been a most faithful servant to me for nearly a year. She told me that she understood that I forget this between the setting and the rising of the sun, but she assured me that it is so.

I told her that though I may forget, as she said and indeed as I myself sense, I knew that she was a good child and a true friend, for my heart warms whenever I see her; but that I could not believe she was my slave, because I love her too much not to have freed her.

Then Io asked me about Elata, and from her tone I knew that she had come to the matter that truly concerned her. I thought she was afraid Elata might betray us to the king, so I said that I was certain she would not. Cybele, I explained, had promised me the help of three trustworthy allies, and these had been the lion, Pharetra, and Elata. Since Cybele wished Queen Hippephode to have the sacred horses, it was hardly likely that she would send someone who would betray us.

"Have you asked Pharetra about Cybele's sending her? Did the goddess appear to her or anything?"

"No," I admitted. "But Pharetra didn't mention anything of that sort when Hegesistratus asked how she had become separated from us in the battle—or if she did, Hegesistratus didn't tell me. Besides, suppose that Cybele had told her not to speak of it. We'd be putting Pharetra in an awkward position if we asked her about it."

Io shrugged. "I guess so. What do you think about Elata otherwise? Is she an ordinary girl?"

"Certainly not," I said. "She's much more lovely than most women. I may forget things quickly, Io, but I know that."

"Do you want to lie with her?"

I considered my answer. It seemed certain that a truthful reply would give Io pain; and yet I could not help feeling that lies, though told from the kindest motives, do more harm than truth. At last I said, "I suppose I'd have her if she wished it; but she's shown no sign of wanting me to, and Hegesistratus told me this morning that she's his."

"The black man has had her," Io said.

"If that's true, it lies between him and Hegesistratus," I told her. "I only hope it can be settled without bloodshed."

"I don't think Hegesistratus knows. I didn't tell him."

"Do you want me to do it?" I asked. "I wouldn't tell any man such a thing unless I'd seen it myself."

Io shook her head.

"Then what's the point of our talking about it? Besides, if Hegesistratus is a mantis, he has no doubt discovered it for himself. It would be very difficult to conceal unfaithfulness from a mantis."

"I don't think he's tried to find out about that. I think he's afraid of what he might learn—like that time when you and Elata came back together in the morning."

It had begun to rain, a light drizzle that dripped from the lips of the cave, a few steps from where we were sitting. I rolled up this scroll and tied it with the cords as I considered my reply. "Hegesistratus is a wise man, Io. He makes mistakes, no doubt, as even wise men do. But he is wise nevertheless, and I think his wisdom shows in what you have just said."

"But do you think Elata's just a common girl? Except for being so pretty?"

"What do *you* think her, Io?"

"I don't know," Io answered.

"Why are you so concerned about her?"

"Because of Pharetra. You like Pharetra—I know you do."

I admitted it. "But that doesn't mean that I don't love you, Io."

"Well, just a few days ago, Pharetra was nearly dead. One of these barbarians had put his lance right here"—Io touched her own ribs—"and you could even see the big cut in back where the point came out. She was spitting up lots of blood, and she could hardly breathe."

I said that I found that very hard to believe.

"So do I," Io declared. "So do the rest of the Amazons, I think. She was hurt the first night we fought the barbarians. Then they brought us to that field where they made us camp, and we spent the next night there. The night after that was when we fought them again and you tried to steal their king."

I shook my head to show that I had forgotten it, as I have.

"And Hippephode didn't want Pharetra to fight, but she did. And today she was well enough to help you steal all those white horses." Io paused, her eyes upon my face.

"Master, you were with Hegesistratus when he got Elata. I want you to look in your book and find the place. It was one night between Sestos and Pactye. Will you open your book again, and read me what you wrote then?"

I read it to myself first, however; and when I had finished, I told Io that I wanted to consider the entire matter further. This woman Elata is a nymph, or so I wrote. If the rest do not know it, she would surely be angry if I revealed it.

Hegesistratus says the Mede is still alive; he caught sight of him in his mirror, staring at our hill from the narrow window of the room where he is confined. Hegesistratus thinks someone has told him we are bargaining for his life. He says Cleton may have smuggled a letter to him.

I wish that I could smuggle such a letter to Pharetra, but I write no tongue but this. If it were not winter, I would at least send Io with a flower, though I had to face down a hundred Thracians to get it.

18

Pharetra Is Dead

She lay beside me when Hippostizein woke me. I could just see her face in the firelight. I kissed her cheek before I rose, though she slept on.

I think I remembered her, though I did not remember where I was, or who the people I saw sleeping nearer the fire were. The tall woman who had awakened me picked up this sword, whispering, *"Guard, guard."* Thus I knew that this sword is mine. I buckled it on and followed her. She led me away from the fire, through the darkness to the cave mouth, where a sentinel darker than the night stood guard. He had a long sword and a pair of javelins; when he grinned at me, I knew that we were friends. He embraced me and I him, and we wrestled for a moment.

I asked them whether we had enemies who might try to come into the cave, first in this tongue, then in the one the woman had used. Neither understood this one, as well as I can judge, but both clearly understood the second, nodding vigorously and pointing down the road that begins at the entrance to the cave. I said that if anyone tried to enter, I would shout and wake the rest, and that seemed to satisfy them. They went back into the cave.

I went outside and watched awhile from there, for though the night was cold, the cave was colder. It had been raining not long before; the ground was still wet, and water chuckled here and there down the rocks. When I had been outside for a long time (or at least so it seemed to me) a dog began to howl far away. Surely a man with a sword should not be afraid of a howling dog, yet I was frightened, feeling that a horrid thing stirred in the darkness. That was when I returned to the cave, wrapping myself in my cloak and standing well inside where the howling sounded very faint. Though I smelled the smoke of the fire, I was cold. I paced up and down to warm myself.

Soon there was another step—the harsh tramp of a leather boot followed by taps that made me think of a blind man feeling his way with his staff. The man who came to the mouth was not blind, however, but crippled; he has lost a foot and walks with a crutch. He is called Hegesistratus, "Leader of the Host," but I did not know that then. He greeted me, calling me *Latro,* as all these people do, then went outside as I had. I did not see him again for a long time.

At length the night covering was drawn from the world. The howling ceased, and the tall woman came again, and the woman who had slept by me with her. I touched my chest and said, "Latro?" They nodded and told me their names, Pharetra and Hippostizein, though they did not say them precisely as I have set them down. I write them as Hegesistratus and the girl say them, not having letters for the other.

The tall woman and I went into the cave, where the children were bringing water from the depths and the lame man mixing wine in a krater. The black man handed me a cup; I recall that very well, and how I dropped the cup when Pharetra cried out, so that it smashed on the stone, splashing my boots with wine.

She was dead when I reached her, lying beneath the bodies of peltasts. I fell on my knees, letting the Amazons and the black man rush by me while I lifted them from her; an arrow had gone through her throat. I picked her up and carried her back into the cave, though it was filled with smoke; the image of the Mother had fallen over onto the sacred hearth, its ancient, dry, paint-daubed wood burning fiercely and making too much smoke for the wind from the earth to carry away. Deeper in the cave, the horses were stamping and whinnying.

Falcata is my sword; she split the old image like kindling. I heaped the pieces on the fire until the flames whipped in the wind and licked the stone ceiling. I took away Pharetra's sword and bowcase and laid her on the fire.

The Thracian lords came calling for a truce; we allowed two into the cave. Hegesistratus spoke for us, telling them that we could take their lives without incurring the displeasure of the gods, because they had broken the peace made yesterday. (When I have written, I must read this and learn of that.)

They said they had not broken it, that it still stood. The peltasts who killed Pharetra this morning did so without a lord, they said, out of the hate they feel for us;

they also said that their king will punish those who live, and that he has appointed riders to protect us.

Then they accused us of burning the holy image of Kotytto. Hegesistratus said that we did not destroy it intentionally, we having no wish to give offense to any god and having sufficient wood—no doubt it was knocked over in the excitement following the attack. He offered them silver to pay for the carving of a new image, which they accepted.

The leader of the women spoke through Hegesistratus, saying that the sacred horses had been frightened in their dark stalls beyond the fire. Two ran and fell, as she said, and we have had to kill them.

When they heard that, the lords of Thrace looked grave and declared that we had violated our oath. Hippephode (that is her name) became extremely angry, shouting at them in the tongue of Amazons. Hegesistratus wanted to let both return in safety to their people; but Hippephode's women seized them, putting swords to their backs.

After that, Hegesistratus and Hippephode spoke together for a long time, and only a moment ago it was decided that we shall let one leave but keep the other. If the king of Thrace honors his agreement today, we will return the lord to him. But if he does not, we will kill him.

While I was reading about the sacrifice and oath yesterday, the children came to speak to me. The girl is Io Thabaikos; the boy, Polos. The girl is my slave, she says, though she kissed my cheek like a daughter and I held her on my lap. She is the "Io" who helped water the horses yesterday, as I just read. I asked if Polos was my slave, too.

She laughed. "No! He's mine—I'm teaching him to talk."

The boy grinned.

"Isn't he the son of one of these women?"

Io shook her head. "They don't keep them. If they have a boy, they take him to his father. Usually the fathers are Sons of Scoloti. You don't remember the Sons of Scoloti, master, but there were some on Hypereides' ship. They have long beards, and one had blue eyes. They're very good bowmen."

I said, "I don't care about the Sons of Scoloti right now, Io. Tell me about Polos."

"Well, he knows more about horses than anybody else in the world. If Polos had been back there with the horses, those two wouldn't have fallen over the ledge."

The boy seemed to understand her; he nodded solemnly.

"He can't be Hegesistratus' son even if that young woman's Hegesistratus' second wife," I said. "Hegesistratus speaks the way we do. Who does he belong to?"

"Me," Io said. "I told you, master."

I shook a finger at her and made her leave my lap. "Don't answer me with jokes. Where are his father and mother?"

Io shrugged. "Northwest of here someplace—that's the way he points. I don't think he lives with them anymore."

The boy shook his head. *"Enkilin."*

"They live in the hills," Io translated. "Show him what you found, Polos."

Shyly, the boy groped in the ragged sheepskin he wore and produced a small leather sack. When I held out my hand for it, he loosened the thong and poured a tinkling flood of little gold coins into my palm.

I whistled. "This is a considerable sum of money, Polos. Where did you get it?"

He looked at Io as though seeking permission to answer, or perhaps only to speak as Hellenes do. "From a dead man."

Io said, "One of those you killed, master. He thinks

that because you killed him, you should have the money."

I considered that for a moment. "Perhaps we could share it? Half for you, Polos, and half for me?"

The boy nodded enthusiastically.

"But Io must keep my half for me—otherwise I'll forget it, as she knows very well. And neither of you should show how much you have in any civilized place, or you'll get your throats slit for it. Understand?"

We counted the coins into two piles. There were eighteen, each about the size of the end of my smallest finger. Io ran to fetch a rag, into which she knotted my nine. Polos returned his to the sack and gave that to her as well.

I asked, "How many peltasts would you say attacked us this morning, Io?"

"A lot. They had a lot more than we did."

I nodded. "But how many is a lot?"

"Twenty or thirty, maybe."

"Could there have been eighteen? We might guess better if we knew the number of their dead—did you and Polos count them?"

Io said, "I suppose there could have been. I counted the ones you killed. Seven."

We went to look at them; there were eleven dead altogether. The man who had carried the coins wore a helmet, and had worn a ring until someone took it. He saw me, even as I saw him, but there was no hatred in his stare. "Io," I said, "Hegesistratus thinks Polos may be a Thracian spy. What do you think? Can he be trusted?"

Before she could answer, Polos lifted both hands, shook his head violently, and dashed toward the back of the cave. Io told me, "He doesn't want to hear any secrets. I suppose it's because you might think he told if somebody found out."

"If he doesn't want to hear secrets, we can take it he's no spy. But who can we trust? Trust absolutely?"

"The black man."

"All right. What about Hegesistratus and his wife? The queen?"

Io shook her head.

"Why not?"

"Well, the queen has her own people to look after. And she has to do what her god told her—bring the Shining God's sacred horses to his big temple in the south, and all the rest of it. She'd have to put those things ahead of us."

"Very good. And Hegesistratus?"

Io looked uncomfortable. "To start with, he cares a whole lot more about Elata than I've ever seen any man care about any woman. When you read about her in your book, you wouldn't tell me what it said. Do you remember it now, master?"

"No, but I'll read it again when I have the chance. That was to start with. What's the rest?"

"He worked magic for the barbarians—I mean the People from Parsa, not these barbarians here—and you fought for their Great King, master, and so did my city."

"And the black man?" I asked.

Io nodded.

"Then we were all on the same side; that's not a very good reason to distrust someone, Io."

"But now he's working for Hypereides, and so are we. And Hypereides fought *against* the Great King. That's an awful lot of changing around."

"Perhaps," I said.

"Besides Hegesistratus hates the Rope Makers as much as he loves Elata. I don't like them myself, but they're the friends of Hypereides' city."

"All right," I told her, "that's quite enough. Go and get the black man."

"Can I say something first, master? I promised Polos that I would."

"Certainly," I said, "if it's important. What is it?"

"Well, master, Hegesistratus and Queen Hippephode have been deciding what we're going to do, just about always. But you're the one who really ought to. That's what Polos says and I think so, too. The Amazons are all good fighters—I didn't know women *could* fight like that till I saw them. The black man's really wonderful, and Hegesistratus is like a wounded lion. But it's not any of them that the Thracians are afraid of. It's you. I was in back of you this morning with my sword, and I could see their faces. Polos says they call you 'the hero,' and it means Pleistorus is inside you even if you don't know it."

When she fell silent, I asked, "Is that all?"

"You see the gods sometimes, master. You really do. Once you saw the King of Nysa and touched him, and then I could see him, too. He was old and he looked like the black man—but . . ."

"Go on."

"One time before the Shining God gave me to you, I went to the theater back in Hill. It costs a lot, but sometimes a rich man will buy seats for poor people, and that time my old master did and let us in first. The actors wore masks, but the people in the play didn't know."

"You aren't making a lot of sense, Io," I said. "I think perhaps you'd better bring the black man now."

Suddenly defiant, she stood up very straight, her eyes on mine. "You can beat me if you want to—only I know you won't. How long do you think we could stay in this cave if you weren't in here with us? I know Apsinthia's just a little hole-in-the-corner barbarian kingdom, but the king's still got hundreds and hundreds of soldiers, and maybe thousands."

Then she was gone, before I could order her to go. I have written this while I wait for her to return with the black man.

19

My Duel with the King

Oeobazus the Mede, the battle at the temple, the strategist from Rope and Cleton's other news—I must set down all of these, for we will soon sleep and I will forget them.

When I cast back my thoughts to morning, I see the women's heads on the lances, their long, dark hair dripping in the rain. Lordly horsemen in gilt ring mail flanked us, and the first pair bore the heads on their lances. Yet though we were few, and our equipment not so fine, I soon saw they feared us.

Hippephode rode in front on the Destroyer's white stallion—that was how we started, I think. Hegesistratus came after her, and Elata close behind him. Then the black man and I, and the children, with Polos on a white colt; then the white horses without riders, and last, the rest of the Amazons, driving the horses ahead of them.

But the women's heads made me angry; and so when I saw that the Thracians were afraid, I rode past Queen Hippephode and the rest until I was between the Thracian lords who held the lances, and asked in the tongue of the Hellenes where they had found the heads and whose they were. The lords would have had me believe that they could not understand my words, but I saw clearly that they did, for they flushed with anger.

"We thought you warriors," I told them, "but warriors

would never boast of killing women—warriors kill men, and bring their women home to warm their own beds. Do you trim your lances with infants' heads, also? Or do you believe it more manly to impale the whole infant upon the lance head?"

They said nothing and looked to right and left, unwilling to meet my gaze. "When a boy hunts," I told them, "he kills a bear cub and says he has killed a bear, never thinking that the day will come when he will meet a bear. Then he will have need of his little spear."

Hegesistratus called to me to be silent.

"I will be silent," I said, "if they will give us the heads of these women so that we may burn them honorably."

At that one of the Thracian lords spoke with Hegesistratus in their own tongue, and Hegesistratus told me they had agreed to give us the heads when we reached the temple of the War God and permit us to burn them on the sacred hearth. Thereafter I kept silent, but I urged my horse forward so that I rode before the Thracian lords who held those lances.

At the temple, it seemed at first that the Thracians' word was good. The king waited for us there, dressed in golden mail and a rich cloak; behind him rode an old man with a white beard, also richly dressed, and many glittering lords of Thrace. All of them sat excellent horses. When the king saw me, he looked angry, and when he saw the boy riding one of the sacred horses, he looked angrier still; but the Thracian lords spoke with him, and both he and the old man nodded. Then the women's heads were taken from the lances, and though the Thracians held them by the hair, the Amazons who received them cradled them in their arms. There was already a fire in the sacred hearth. Queen Hippephode spoke to the Amazons as Amazons speak, lifted her arms in prayer to the War God, and conversed for a brief time with him. After that the heads were set upright in the fire, and fragrant wood heaped upon them.

When they were consumed, the king addressed the Thracian lords who had come into the temple with him. In a low voice, Hegesistratus repeated what he said to the Amazons; and Polos did the same for the black man, Elata, Io, and me, though he speaks the tongue of Hellenes worse even than I.

"Listen to me! You know what we promised. Who has ever called our vows worthless?"

The king had a fine, deep voice and piercing eyes. It was strange to listen to Polos' halting speech instead.

"We have sworn that they shall go in peace. No one shall so much as offer them insult—though our charge would scatter them like chaff. There shall be no war!"

Then all the Thracian lords repeated his words.

"The gold they give us for the Sun's sacred horses shall go to the temple of the Sun. Thamyris shall receive it." Here he glanced at the old man. *"And they shall go in peace!"*

Again all the Thracian lords echoed his words. After that, the old man and some of the lords went behind the curtain at the back of the temple and led out Oeobazus the Mede. Hegesistratus and the black man sighed, and Io said, "Well, finally!" He is tall and strong, with a scar that rises out of his black beard; his face is darker than Hegesistratus', but not so dark as the black man's.

Then the king spoke again, but Polos did not translate his words for us because he had run to look at Oeobazus' sword and bow, which had been brought forth. Nor did Hegesistratus repeat to the Amazons anything that the king had said, because he and Oeobazus were embracing. When he spoke to Oeobazus, it was, I suppose, as the Medes speak; but I understood a few words, and from those and his manner knew he was telling Oeobazus that he would present us when there was time for it.

Oeobazus took up the weapons that had been returned to him, and we deserted the temple's fire for the chill drizzle outside. There Queen Hippephode pointed out the sacred horses she wished to take, choosing the stallion she had ridden and three others, all of them fine animals; an Amazon slipped a bridle onto each. Hippephode counted gold into the old man's hands—a great deal of it, or so it appeared to me. The king questioned several of the pieces, biting them to test the goodness of the metal; when the last was passed, a peltast brought the old man scales with which he weighed the gold. I could not understand what he said, but it seemed clear that he had announced himself satisfied.

Here was the crisis, and all of us must have known it. The black man sprang onto his horse. Hegesistratus was no more than a moment behind him, vaulting into the saddle with his crutch as I think he always must. But in the tongue of the Hellenes, and almost as a Hellene might have said it, the king told us, "*Wait!* We have promised you shall go in peace. However, if one of you should choose battle instead, in that there can be no violation of our pledge."

I knew then that many of the lords of Thrace understood the tongue of Hellenes, for they stirred at his words and some laid their hands upon their swords.

Hegesistratus said loudly, "We do *not* choose to fight. Let us leave in peace as you swore."

The old man spoke to the king as Thracians speak, his voice low and urgent. It seemed to me that he, too, called for peace; but the king shook his head angrily.

"This does not concern you," he said to Hegesistratus, "nor any of your party save one." Although he spoke to Hegesistratus, he looked at me. "The rest of you may begin your journey, if you like. He, too, may go in peace, if he wishes. We have said it. But if he desires instead to meet us with arms—as one hero meets another—he need only tell us."

Hegesistratus called sharply, "He does not desire it. Mount, Latro!"

"Yes," the king told me. "Mount! You will need a lance. Someone bring him one—a good one."

Though I do not believe that the king had confided his plan to his counselor, one of the Thracian lords at least must have known what he intended to do; without an instant's delay, he was at my side holding a new lance.

I would not take it. "You have called yourself a hero," I told the king, "and I know that what you said is nothing more than the truth. Only a fool fights a hero, unless he must." I went to my horse to mount; but one of the Thracians pricked its flank with his dagger, so that it cried out and danced away from me, its eyes rolling with pain and fear. The Thracian who held the lance thrust it in my face.

Hippephode confronted the king then, a woman taller even than he; anger flamed in her cheeks and blue ice flashed from her eyes. I do not know what she said, but she pointed toward the lowering sky, then to the temple, and at last to sky again, and her voice was like the snarl of a panther. The black man urged his horse forward as though to join her, but many hands tore him from the saddle and threw him to the ground. The king turned away from the Amazon queen again and again; always his eyes were upon me.

I said, "What sort of fool are you, who tell your people that we are to go in peace, and break your word with the next breath? Don't you know that it is thus that kings lose their thrones?"

"Take it if you can!" he shouted, and spat in my face. At that moment, the lance was thrust at me again, and I did as he said.

At once everyone fell silent. Those who had held the black man released him; he stood, wiping mud from his clothing and his person, his wounded face a mask of rage.

Hegesistratus rode to where we stood, and no one

stopped him. The king said, "If you would speak to us before we fight, dismount!"

Hegesistratus nodded. "Out of the respect I have for Your Majesty." He slid from his horse, keeping hold of his saddle until he could brace himself with his crutch. "King Kotys," he said, "you have sworn before your gods and ours that you would let us go in peace. Do so now, before battle drinks the blood of a king. It may be they will forgive you."

"If that is all you have to say," the king told him, "be silent or we will stuff your mouth with dung."

Hegesistratus turned to me, his voice so soft that I could scarcely hear him. "Do you know how to use a lance, Latro?"

I said, "I don't know, but I doubt that there's a great deal to learn." The Thracian lords grinned at that, pulling their beards and elbowing one another.

"He has a helmet. You had one yesterday, but you seem to have left it behind. Do you want one now?"

I shook my head.

The king said, "You have your lance. Mount!"

I asked him whether we would fight on the hillside.

"No." He pointed. "Ride to that thicket, turn, and meet my charge."

Hippephode had been speaking swiftly to Hegesistratus; now he said, "The queen asks a favor of you: she wishes you to take her horse. Your own is badly unsettled and is, as she says, too small."

I thanked Hippephode and mounted her white stallion, still the holy steed of the Sun. A disordered mob, we streamed to the base of the hill; there some of the Thracian lords made the rest stay back, with Hegesistratus, the Amazons, the black man, and the others. The king reined up perhaps ten cubits before them. "No quarter will be given," he told me. "Do you understand?"

I said that I did not think I could kill a man who

begged me for his life, but I would try. Then I rode down the misty valley to the trees he had pointed out. They were half a stade from the bottom of the hill, perhaps.

A lion roared as I wheeled the stallion. At the sound of his challenge, other lions roared to my left and right, hardly a bowshot from us.

The stallion reared, pawing air. Afraid the king's charge would find us unprepared, I shouted into the stallion's ear, digging heels into his sides and flourishing the lance overhead to make it clear we had to fight whether lions roared or not—though their terrifying voices rose behind us like the tumult of an army.

He sprang forward. I felt the earth quiver beneath us; the roaring of the lions and the thunder of his hoofbeats filled all the world.

I glimpsed the king at that moment, I know. He was urging his mount forward, his lance poised. Rain more violent than any we had seen that day intervened, washing the king, the throng of riders behind him, even the hill of the War God's temple from my sight. It cleared almost at once; and when it was gone, the king had turned from me as if charging the lords of his own court, or perhaps the Amazons. There was a swirl of men and horses, and a shriek that pierced the rain and freezing mist with astonishing immediacy, as though we were already in the midst of that wild melee.

Swords flashed; there was a confused shouting.

A moment more, and we were part of the fight indeed. I do not know whether I could have halted the stallion with a rawhide bit; I was so stunned by what I had seen that I scarcely tried. I could have killed half a dozen lords of Thrace then if I had wished, but I did not, lifting my lance instead and leaving them unscathed.

Yet a battle had begun. Before me two Thracians struggled knee to knee—a third stabbed one from behind. The black man rode past like a whirlwind, his pelta cut nearly through and his sword red with blood. Hippephode called her Amazons to her, her voice a trumpet. I tried to rein the white stallion toward them, ducked a thrust from a Thracian whose squealing mount was pinned between two others, and hacked wildly at the lance shaft; it was only then, with Falcata already in my hand, that I realized I had dropped my own lance and drawn her.

Someone shook my shoulder. It was Hegesistratus, with the Mede at his elbow. *"Run!"* he shouted. *"Get clear!"* Then they were gone. Before I could cleave a Thracian's helmet, the man threw down his sword and raised his hands. As I passed him I caught sight of Io and Polos, galloping off into the mist. I rode after them.

There is not much more to tell, and in any event our supper is ready. After what seemed a very long ride, I overtook Io, who explained that she and Polos had become separated. We rode on until even the stallion was exhausted and at last, long after this short day had grown dark, halted at this farmhouse. Io has money that she says belongs to me. She offered the man and his wife a small gold coin—at which their eyes grew large indeed—if they would feed us well, let us pass the night here in safety, and say nothing. Soon after that Polos joined us, leading three riderless horses. One is mine, and it had my scrolls and stylus still in its saddlebags. Io showed them to me and told me about the record I must keep.

I was reading how the mantis escaped from Rope when a wagon driven by a fat old man rattled into the farmyard. The farmer—who seems just such a man as the peltasts who came to the temple with their lords—swore he had seen no strangers today; but Io called, "Cleton!" and brought him in to share our wine. He says the king is dead; the old man, Prince Thamyris, rules the city. A strategist from Rope has come in a warship with many soldiers, demanding news of Oeobazus and of us.

20

Raskos

The wounded man came before sunrise; we three were sleeping on the floor. I sat up at his knock, and the girl, Io, sat up, too. I told the boy—his name is Polos—to unbar the door. He would not and looked frightened. I did not want to leave the warmth of my blankets; I tossed fresh wood upon the fire and asked who was there.

"Raskos!" he replied.

Then the farmer came out of the room where he had slept with his wife and opened the door.

Raskos came in. He had a pelta and javelins; I threw off the blankets at once, thinking that I might have to fight. He spoke to the farmer, who laughed, made a fist, and tossed his thumb into his mouth. He waved toward a stool by the fire, and though I could not understand what he said, it seemed that he was inviting Raskos to sit down.

Speaking in the way the Hellenes do, Polos whispered, "He's not drunk." He was shaking so much I put my arm about him, at which he breathed violently through his nose, which I think must be a habit of his. He is ten, I would say, or perhaps a year or two older. He has reddish hair and dark eyes.

Raskos spoke more, mumbling and looking around as though he had never seen the house before, often repeating the same words. Io asked what he was saying, and Polos told her, "He says he was lost in the snow."

I went to a window and opened the shutter. It had

indeed snowed during the night; snow a little thicker than my thumb lay over everything, so that all the bushes and trees appeared to be covered with white blossoms, bathed now in moonlight.

Raskos was beseeching the farmer, whose name was Olepys, or something of the sort. I was about to close the shutter when I saw people walking up the road. Three of them were carrying a long and apparently heavy bundle upon their shoulders, and when one pointed toward the house, it was plain that they intended to stop.

But I was too full of my own thoughts to pay much attention to these travelers then. As I latched the shutter, I asked Io, "Do you remember what Cleton told us? I've been considering it, and since we're all awake, I think it would be best if we got an early start."

She said, "Do you want to send Polos into the city to talk to this Rope Maker?"

I shook my head, for I knew that no strategist was apt to tell the truth to a ragged boy. "The first thing is to locate Hegesistratus and warn him that the Rope Makers are here. We know that they've learned about him, and they probably want to kill him."

"Maybe they have already," Io speculated gloomily. "I know you don't remember it, master, but a few days ago Hegesistratus was trying to read the future for you and saw his own death. It sounded as if it was pretty close."

I was about to tell her that we ought to warn Hegesistratus just the same, if we could, when someone tapped at the door.

It was a weeping woman in a dark cloak. Straggling hair, loose and disordered, hung about her shoulders, and her cheeks were streaked with tears; with her was another, younger woman. The three men who carried the bundle waited a few steps behind them, looking uncomfortable. Two were hardly more than boys.

Io jabbed Polos with her elbow, and he told us, "She says her husband's dead. They're going to the burning. They want this man to come."

"This man" was the farmer, who smiled at the woman, shook his head, and pointed to the stool beside the fire, though there was no one there.

The woman only sobbed the louder, at which the farmer's wife came out of the room to comfort her. *"Ai Raskos!"* the weeping woman cried. *"Ai Raskos!"*

The farmer shouted at her then, and when she paid no heed to him, at the three with the bundle, who shook their heads and would not meet his eyes. In a moment they laid the heavy bundle in the snow and removed some of the cloths; it was a man's body, and though it was too dark there upon the moonlit snow to be sure, it seemed to me that he looked very much like the one who had awakened us.

The farmer got a brand from the fire and held it above the dead man. His beard was marked with two gray streaks. His nose looked as if it had been broken. An eye stared at us from under a half-open lid; although I wished someone would close it, I did not try to do it myself. An ax or heavy sword had severed his left shoulder, cutting through almost to the final rib.

After a great many whispered instructions to his wife, the farmer replaced one of the youths who had carried the body, and all six trudged away. I made certain the children cleaned their teeth and washed their faces and hands, then went out to saddle our horses, who had passed a comfortable night in the shed with the cows; we had a big white stallion, a white mare, and four others. "Thanks be to whatever god governs horses," I said to Polos, who had come to help, "that this mare's not in season."

He grinned. "Oh, if we let them cover her a few times, it would be all right. It's the Earth Shaker, the Sea God. He's the Horse God, too."

The white stallion had been rolling his eyes and baring his teeth at me, but Polos calmed him with a touch. "Which one are you going to ride?"

"My own." I pointed to the one who had worn my saddlebags the night before.

"How do you know that he's yours?" Polos asked. "Io says you forget from day to day."

"This isn't from day to day," I explained. "It was late when you brought these horses, and the sun isn't properly up yet."

Polos thought about that for a moment as he saddled Io's small, docile chestnut. "Do you remember fighting King Kotys yesterday?"

I admitted that I did not know I had ever fought a king, and added that since I was still alive I appeared to have won.

"You didn't really fight. He ran away, and then his people killed him for running. Should I call you Latro, or can I call you master like Io does?" Polos paused. "Io's your slave, did you remember about it?"

I shook my head. "I'll free her, then, so that she can go home to her father and mother. If you're not my slave, Polos, you shouldn't call me master. I'm sorry to hear that this king was a coward; I suppose some kings are, but one doesn't like to think of them like that."

"I don't think he was," Polos told me, "but it's not the kind of thing I know much about."

I laughed at his solemn little face and mussed his hair. "What is?"

"Oh, horses and goats and dogs—all kinds of animals. And the weather. I'm a wonderful weather prophet."

"Really, Polos? What will today be like?"

"Sunny and windy, at first. The sun will melt this snow, so that the ground gets all muddy. But after that thick clouds will come, and the day will end too soon."

I sighed, reflecting that he might have been speaking of me, though it did not seem that he intended it.

"Master—Latro—I'll do anything you say."

"All right," I said, "but why are you telling me? Have you disobeyed me? Did I beat you?"

"No," Polos told me. "I've always done everything you told me, although you haven't told me much. But I wanted to say that I thought you were wrong about some things, and I don't want you to be angry with me."

I said we would see about that when I knew our disagreement.

"I think I ought to call you master. If I don't, lots of people will ask why I'm with you. But if I do, they'll think I'm your slave, like Io."

I led him back into the house so that we could toast our stiff fingers at the fire; it gave me an opportunity to consider what he had suggested. "Suppose I were to die, Polos. You say I fought a king yesterday, and if it's true, I may very well die today. Won't my heirs—if I've got any—claim you? You might have to spend the rest of your life as somebody's slave."

Polos shook his head, a little mule. "If the king couldn't kill you yesterday, master, who's going to kill you today? And besides, if you have heirs, they're probably nice people. There are lots of people—not very nice people at all—who catch boys and girls that don't belong to anybody."

Io came in, and I asked her whether she had given the woman the money she had promised her after the farmer left.

"Not yet," Io said. "Not until we're ready to go, because we might need something else. Do you remember why we're going, master?"

"To find a man called Hegesistratus, if we can."

Polos asked me, "Do you remember him? What he looks like?"

I shook my head.

"Or why we want to find him?" Polos persisted.

"Because the Rope Makers want to kill him." I asked

Io, "Hegesistratus is a friend, isn't he? When I pronounced his name, it seemed a friend's in my mouth."

There was a knock at the door. From the other room, the woman shouted something.

"Raskos!"

Io told me, "Don't open it!" as I drew my sword.

I had to, if I wanted to go on calling myself a man; but I had not time enough to explain that to Io. Sword high, I opened wide the door with my left hand.

There was no one there. The sun had just risen, and long purple shadows fled from every little ridge of wind-driven snow. The footprints of those who had carried the body to the door—and carried it away—were half-filled with snow already; so was the formless depression where the body had lain. There were no newer, fresher tracks.

"Io," I said, "you can speak the way these people do, can't you? A little?"

Io nodded. "It's Thracian, master—we're in Thrace. I've picked up a bit, and Polos knows it."

I said, "Then, Polos, you must warn the woman that Raskos may come back. Do you understand me? If he does, she mustn't open the door. She must tell him, through the door, that he is dead."

Polos nodded solemnly.

"The snow's fallen since he died, I think, and changed the landmarks he knew. Snow's something one usually finds only high up on mountains, so if he comes again before it melts, she must tell him—without opening the door—exactly how he can reach the spot where his body will be burned."

When Polos had spoken with the woman as I told him and Io had given her a coin, we rode off. "Just before that happened"—Polos jerked his head to indicate the farmhouse—"I was going to tell you I thought you ought to ride the white one. You rode him when you fought King Kotys, and I don't believe he'll give you any more trouble."

I shook my head. "He had a hard day, yesterday, I imagine. Didn't I ride him a long way, Io?"

She nodded. "A very long way, master. We were both really tired when we stopped here, and so were the horses." Each of us was riding one and leading another.

Polos asked, "What if somebody wants to fight with us?"

"Then I'll get on him," I promised. "And he'll be better rested for not being ridden now."

Polos looked from me to the big white stallion, considering. "You *are* heavy."

"Of course I am, and I'm wearing a sword and mail."

"Oeobazus has a sword with a gold hilt, but I think yours must be better."

I asked who Oeobazus was.

Io told me, "The Mede we made the king free. Really, you made him, mostly. You've been keeping up your new book really well, so there ought to be a lot about it there. But probably you shouldn't try to read it while we're riding, especially in this wind."

"All right," I said, "I won't."

Polos asked, "Sometime will you show me how to fight with a sword?"

"You've seen him," Io said. "I know you were watching us the last time. You saw what my master did."

"I was watching," Polos admitted, looking at me. "I saw what he did, but I don't know how he did it. Four men came at him together, and I thought he'd be killed, but he killed them, one after another. There can't be many swordsmen like him."

I had to confess that I no longer recalled the incident he described.

"But you know how to do it. What would you do if you were faced with four together?"

"Get away," I told him, "if I could."

"But if you couldn't?"

I turned the problem over in my mind, seeing soldiers with spears and swords who were not actually there, but who had once, perhaps, stood before me in that way. "Determine which is the leader, if you can," I told Polos. "One is always the leader when there are four, the one the rest would be ashamed to have see them run. It's very likely that there aren't really four trying to kill you. One is trying to kill you, and three are trying to help him. Disable him at once, if you can. Killing him is good, of course; but a deep cut in his sword arm or his leg may be just as good."

We stopped at a solitary house; Polos talked to the people there and told me that they said they had seen no strangers, and that he felt they were telling the truth. I spoke loudly: "They haven't seen Hegesistratus?" I did it hoping that Hegesistratus would hear me and know my voice, but no one answered.

On the road again, I said, "Your sword must be a part of you, Polos. Do you understand that?"

He nodded. "But when I held your sword last night, it didn't want to be."

"Falcata's too heavy for you," I told him, "and you haven't handled her nearly enough. It's good to have a good sword, but it's better to know the sword you have and keep it sharp. Some scabbards dull the blade, because they're lined with hard wood; some of them even have bronze where it rubs the sharp part of the blade. If you've got a scabbard like that, sell it and get another—only leather or wool should touch the edge."

Polos nodded; I could see he was thinking about what I had said.

"And yet you must always remember that it isn't the best sword that wins, but the best swordsman."

A man carrying two javelins was walking some distance ahead of us—a man who, as nearly as I could judge, left behind him no tracks. I asked Polos about horses, knowing them a subject that would occupy Io as well, and learned much.

21

The Strategist from Rope

A leader of the invincible armies of the Silent Country demands that the Apsinthians hand over to him any foreigners they hold—so the wounded peltast told Badizoe, and the villagers beg us to go before it becomes known in Cobrys that we are here. They beg us, I say; but they dare not make us go. They fear us too much, though we are only myself, the two women, and the children. All their fighting men are gone, having been summoned to the city a few days ago.

Badizoe came to tell me that she had made use of their fear to get news as well as this food; I asked what she had learned, and called Io here to hear it. Io says it is more than we found out from Cleton, but not very much different. We asked Badizoe how the villagers came to know these things, and she said that a man wounded in yesterday's fighting has been permitted to return to the village. When she heard of it, she made these women take her to him. Elata goes with her, speaking first as one nation, then as the other. Here is what she says he said.

King Kotys is dead. He challenged a Hellene but fled him. When his nobles saw it, they cut him down, though others sought to save him. Thamyris and those who tried to save the king have barricaded the palace.

While the rest planned their assault, the strategist

from Rope made port. He has the lambda of Rope upon his hoplon and wears a scarlet cloak. With him are shieldmen from Pylos. He told the lords that if they do not do as he says, it will not matter who is king in Cobrys—he will return with an army and burn the city. He spoke with the Thracian lords outside, where the wounded peltast overheard him, then went into the palace.

We are going now. Badizoe wants to find her queen and the rest of the Amazons, and Elata to find Hegesistratus the mantis. Io thinks it would be best for us to go with them, and so do I.

Everyone is asleep save for the boy from Susa. All fire is holy to him; often he prays to this one, but at times he wanders beyond the firelight searching for a place to rest. There is surely something wrong with him; I doubt that I have ever met a boy before—or anyone not wounded—who could not rest. I think that Polos knows what is wrong, but Polos will not tell me. The boy's name is Artembares.

I have been reading in this how a litter was constructed for Pharetra and slung between two horses. I cannot remember Pharetra, but when I read her name, I seem to feel her hand touch mine; surely she was lithe and lovely beneath her fiery hair. I know I loved her, even though I have forgotten her.

The gods own this world, not we. We are but landless men, even the most powerful king. The gods permit us to till their fields, then take our crop. We meet and love, someone builds a tomb for us, perhaps. It does not matter—someone else will rob it, and the winds puff away our dust; then we shall be forgotten. For me it is no different, only faster; but I have written in my scroll how Pharetra smiled at me. For as long as the papyrus is preserved she will be here, though even little Io is only brown dust sobbing down the night wind with all the rest.

But having read it, I know that for my own sake tomorrow I must write what I recall now: how we came to the new village and took their wine and the pig, then camped here, far away, because we feared their numbers, though we could not let them see that. I was tired and cold, and drank deeper than I should, perhaps; and Elata more deeply still. Then Badizoe and Io were afraid I would violate her while she slept—as I would have, if only they had not been there, and Polos watching. As things were, I was extremely angry with them both. I could have killed them, but I was neither so angry nor so drunk as that, and if I had struck Io, Badizoe would have drawn her sword; then I would certainly have killed her. I lay down, pretending to sleep; but the pretense was quickly real.

When I woke, Io and Badizoe slept, too. I tried to awaken Elata by kissing her, and with such caresses as men give women; but each time she stirred it made the hills uneasy. I heard our horses speaking as one man speaks to another; and though I lose so much, I have not forgotten that horses cannot speak; and so I let Elata sleep on, and began to read, as I have said.

But first I heaped what wood we had left on the coals and, discovering a dead tree, lopped its limbs with my sword and moved Elata away from the fire so that she would not be scorched while she slept.

It may have been the brightness of the flames that brought the boy. He asked if he might warm himself, and I, seeing that he was alone and harmless, said he might. When he had watched me reading for some time, he said, "I know you don't worship the way we do—you say that Hephaistos is the god of fire, and he's not even one of your greatest gods. But do you object if other people believe something else?"

I said, "That depends on what they believe, I suppose." We were both keeping our voices low so as not to awaken those who slept. "You're from Parsa, aren't you? I know that you people pray to Ahura Mazda by building fires on your mountaintops, and I have no objection to that."

He smiled; it was not until he did that I saw how sad his face was. Then he abased himself before the fire in the eastern way and spoke to his god in a tongue I do not know.

By the time he had finished, my eyes were smarting. I laid down this scroll and asked if he was lost.

He nodded. "That was why I got on the ship. You were on it, then Hegesistratus came aboard, too, so I thought perhaps it would take me to Susa. You must have visited our country. Have you ever been to Susa?"

"I can't remember," I told him. "I forget a great deal."

He moved closer, fearful, it seemed, that he would wake Io, although she slept on. "So do I. No, I can remember a lot, but I can never remember anything important. Is that how it is with you?"

"No," I said. "I can remember only a few things—how Polos and Io drove the pig, for example; that's Io beside you, and him on the other side of her. He gathered those pine boughs to make them a bed. Nothing important, as you say. I've been reading this to find out how I came to be here, and I've learned that I came to find Oeobazus, a Mede; but he's not with us now. Do you know him?"

"Certainly I know him," the boy said. "You asked me about him once before, and you and the other barbarian asked my father about him when we were in the tower. Have you forgotten that?"

"Yes," I admitted. "I'm afraid I have."

"You didn't ask my father that time, really. It was the other barbarian, the short one. Do you remember how you tried to free us?"

I told him I was sorry to learn I had not succeeded.

"There were guards with us in that room in the tower. One heard a noise and went to see what it was. He never came back, and when the other went to look for him, you came in. You had cloaks and helmets, and you wanted us to put them on. You said that once we were outside the citadel we could hide in the city till the barbarians sailed away. But my father said the people there—I don't remember the name of that city."

"Neither do I," I told him. "Go on."

"That they might—would hurt us if they found us. And he said Yellow Horse would look everywhere for us because he had promised him so much for our freedom. He thought Yellow Horse was going to accept the money and let us go. My father's very rich." The boy tried to look modest. "He'll reward you, I'm sure, if you take me to him."

"So you wouldn't come with me? What happened then?"

"Nothing." The boy fell silent, staring into the flames. "You left, more soldiers came, and we went to sleep. Will you come back to the ship with me?"

"What ship?" I asked.

"The one you were on before—you and the little girl and the peri."

I do not know what that word means, but he glanced toward Elata when he said it. I said that I did not think I could go back to the ship with him until we had found Oeobazus.

"He's over there," the boy said, and pointed.

"How do you know?" I asked.

"The same way I knew where he was when you asked me before. Don't you remember? You wanted to know where he was, and I told you he was riding a horse, with his hands tied."

Polos sat up then. I told him I was sorry we had awakened him, that we had tried to talk quietly.

He said politely, "You didn't wake me up. I was thirsty."

I began, "This is—"

"Artembares the son of Artaÿctes," the boy from Susa told me. He is older than Polos, and at least a head taller, I would think.

"Artembares," I repeated.

Polos would not look at him, though I saw his eyes roll. "When did he come? Did you call him?"

"Certainly not," I said. "He was cold and saw the fire; he asked if he could sit here until he got warm, and I said that he could."

"He spoke to you first?"

"Of course," I said. "What is it that's bothering you so much, Polos?"

Artembares said, "I spoke first here at your fire, but you had spoken to me already at another fire, when you asked about Oeobazus. I don't like to speak to people who haven't talked to me first." He hesitated. "It doesn't seem right."

Polos announced, "I'm going to the stream to get a drink," and I gave him some wine to mix with the water so that he would not become ill. I asked whether he had met Artembares before, and he shook his head and ran away.

Now I am going back to sleep.

I have been talking with Oeobazus, who speaks the tongue of Hellenes better even than Artembares. He came to me while I was sharpening Falcata with the farmer's stone and told me his name, saying that though he knew that all of us had fought to save his life, he also knew that I had done the most, and that he wished to thank me for it.

"It's not our custom," he said, "to spend many words—not even on great matters. But for as long as I live, you've only to call on me whenever you need my help."

"You may spend few words," I told him, "but no man could have said more."

He smiled at that and held out his hand, and I took it. I believe we were both somewhat ill at ease; after a moment he chuckled, indicating the whetstone. "I see you've blunted your sword on the necks of our enemies."

"No," I said. "I did it last night, chopping firewood. I thought I'd find her edge wrecked this morning, but it's hardly worse than it was—this is a very good blade." That reminded me of Artembares, who had come to our fire just after I split the last of the deadwood. I said, "There's somebody of your nation with us, a boy from Susa. Have you met him?"

Oeobazus looked mystified and shook his head.

Io had been listening; she said, "My master forgets. You said the mantis told you about him before we got here."

"Yes, he and I had a long talk yesterday. Your master may forget me, and I'll understand if he does; but I'll never forget him."

"Did he tell you, too, that sometimes he sees things other people don't?"

Oeobazus nodded.

"Sometimes people think they're not real, but once I saw the same thing he saw. I think it depends on what each person means by real."

Oeobazus smiled at her. "Spoken like a true Hellene! I've listened to your wise men argue such things all night—and never reach any conclusion. For us, there are only truths. And lies. We don't trouble ourselves about unreality."

"That's good. Just after we woke up, my master said he'd found a boy from Parsa who knew where you were, and he was going to guide us. Badizoe and I wanted to know where he was, and my master said he'd already gone as far as the next hilltop, and he pointed. We could see a young stallion there, kind of red brown and about half-grown, only we couldn't see anybody riding him.

And when we asked Elata, she just laughed. But that horse led us right to you."

Oeobazus fingered his beard, which is black and very thick. "Perhaps you should ask Hegesistratus."

"I have," Io told him, "only when he was through answering I didn't know what he'd said."

"Or Seven Lions. He tells me he knows your master better even than you do."

Just then the black man himself dashed into the shed where we were talking, pointing with his chin and talking very fast to Oeobazus, who appears to understand his tongue; Oeobazus told us, "He says that there's a chariot coming, and the rest of the Amazons are following it."

We all ran out to look. Hegesistratus and the lovely Elata were already there, and Badizoe galloping off to meet her queen. A Thracian was driving the chariot, but the man who rode beside him looked like a Rope Maker, a tall soldier in a scarlet cloak. As they drew nearer he waved and shouted, "Noble Hegesistratus! Latro! By every god, it's good to see you both!"

22

There's Where We Camped

Io told me, "I'll bet if we went over and hunted around for it, we could see exactly where we built our fire. Look, our altar's still there."

I admitted the place seemed familiar, though I could not actually recall having been there.

"The Amazons were with us then," Io said.

They left after the first meal, half a dozen strong women, of whom two are badly hurt. They took all the white horses, and they have a guard of Thracians sworn to ride with them as far as the fords of the Hebrus. Hegesistratus says the Hebrus is the western border of Apsinthia. They bear tokens from three lords here to other lords, their kinsmen in Cicones. Besides these, their queen has a letter written with this stylus upon a strip of white lambskin by the strategist from Rope; it declares them to be under the aegis of King Leotychides and Prince Pausanias the Agid Regent.

"I'll miss them," Io told me. "You won't, master, but I will. And I miss Polos—I miss him a lot. Do you remember him?"

I shook my head, for I did not.

"He was just a boy—a Thracian, I guess. Anyhow the way he talked sounded a lot like Thracian. He was younger than me, but it was nice to have somebody around who was about my age."

I told her I hoped we would someday live in a place where there were other children, and a wise woman who could teach her all the things that women must know.

"I learned a lot, just watching the Amazons," Io declared. "Queen Hippephode liked me, and Hippostizein and Pharetra tried to be nice to me because they liked you. I didn't like Pharetra because you looked so silly every time you saw her—then she got killed, and I felt so bad. I still do. You don't remember her now, do you, master?"

"I do, a bit," I answered, because I sensed the knowledge in me, though the mists hid it. "What did she look like, Io?"

"She was almost as tall as you, with great big cheekbones." Io pulled up her own cheeks to show me. "She had red hair and lots of freckles, and her legs weren't quite straight, I think from riding so much."

I sighed, as I sigh now. "She sounds very beautiful."

"Well, I wasn't trying to *make* her sound like that!"

"No," I said, "but you couldn't hide it." Then I leaned from my horse to Io and kissed her cheek.

"Anyway"—she wiped her face—"that reminds me that I have to talk to you as soon as we're by ourselves. About him"—she gestured swiftly toward the chariot—"and Hegesistratus, too."

"All right," I said. I decided then to write down all that we had said, and I now have.

We are in a fine big house in Cobrys, the property of one of the lords who have sided with Thamyris. There are servants, though I doubt that they are to be trusted. When we had given our horses over to them to be watered, fed, and stabled, Acetes drew Oeobazus aside, and me with him, and told us that he was not truly a strategist from Rope, as he has told the Thracians. All the others had recognized him, of course, and would have smiled at our amazement. I am glad they did not see it.

Oeobazus said, "I wondered why Hegesistratus was so cordial. He hates the Rope Makers."

"I'm not very fond of them myself," Acetes admitted, "but I understand them better now. It's great sport to be one."

At the second meal, we had to act as though he were a Rope Maker for the benefit of the servants; but when it was finished, he sent them off and we gathered before the fire to drink the harsh wine of the country and crack nuts.

"Hypereides is staying here, too," he told us. "He has the room next to mine. The rest of you will have to sleep in here, but I daresay you've slept in worse places."

Everyone laughed and agreed we had.

Oeobazus voiced the question that was on my own lips: "Who is Hypereides?"

"The captain of our ship," Acetes told him. "He's the

one Xanthippos told to fetch you. The rest of us are just working for him, one way or another."

Io said, "Well, I wish he were back here now. I'd like to see him, and he shouldn't be out so late."

"He's bargaining about food and wine for the voyage home," Acetes explained, "and doing a bit of trading on his own account on the side, if I know Hypereides. Don't worry your head about him—he can take care of himself."

Oeobazus asked, "He sent out Hegesistratus with Elata, and Seven Lions—the black man—and Latro with Io, is that correct?"

Acetes and Hegesistratus nodded. Hegesistratus added, "We met the Amazons by the favor of a certain goddess. They were on an errand for the War God, but we could have accomplished nothing without them."

Oeobazus nodded, mostly to himself, I think. "I ran across a tribe years ago who believe that the War God's none other than Ahura Mazda—Ahura Mazda incognito, as it were. Perhaps they're right. How did you know where to look for me?"

Acetes grinned. "Hegesistratus here sniffed you out, or so Hypereides says. What I don't understand is what you were doing here. You can't have been heading for Media or Parsa."

Oeobazus shook his head. "I was going to Thought."

"To Thought!"

"Yes." The Mede seemed to hesitate, looking around at our faces. "Hegesistratus, you're the only person present who knows me at all well. What do you know about me? Tell them, and me."

"You are a brave soldier, a superb horseman, and a skilled technician.* You were Artaÿctes' adviser on fortifications and siege engines."

---

*I assume "Latro's" abbreviation *TC* indicates Lat. *technicus*. Presumably the word Oeobazus employed was Gk. τεχνίτης, which would have been immediately recognized by a speaker of Latin. In translating such terms, it is often impossible to escape the appearance of anachronism.—GW

"And nothing else?" Oeobazus pressed him.

Hegesistratus fingered his beard. "Let me see. You are a Mede, and though you told me once that you have an estate near Ecbatana and a wife, you also told me—on a different occasion—that you have no heir. And there is this: you were practically the only man at Artaÿctes' court who never asked me to read his fate."

"We once had three sons." Oeobazus' expression had grown sad. "Fine young men, all of them. They entered the Imperial Army. Noblemen of my nation, you must understand, go into the king's service as a matter of course; anyone who did not do so would be highly suspect."

Hegesistratus said, "Certainly."

"The king—Xerxes, the Great King, as you call him—planned an expedition against the barbarians of the north. You have all met their warrior women now, so you know what they're like—wild horsemen who follow their herds. One may defend oneself against them, but to attack them is like attacking smoke; they fight and flee, then circle back, having neither cities nor crops to lose. The expedition was bound to be a travesty, and everyone realized it save the king. But Susa was crammed with supplies that would be sent north to the army at need."

No one spoke. I glanced around at the boy from Parsa, who was sitting beside Elata well back from the fire. He seemed to be listening attentively, though I could not see his expression.

"Spring came, and the army camped about the city wall," the Mede continued. "My sons were with it, cavalrymen all of them; and so was the king. Artaÿctes presented me to him, praising me as the man who had contrived so much storage for his supplies. The king was pleased; he smiled and offered to grant me a boon, as a reward for my service. Greatly daring, I asked that one of my sons be permitted to remain with me."

Oeobazus fell silent until Io asked, "Didn't he do it?"

"Yes, he did. He nodded and smiled again, and promised me that all three would be left behind in Susa. Next morning, when the army marched north, my sons lay beside the road with their throats cut, so that every soldier who passed might see with his own eyes what happened to those whose—" Oeobazus stood up, and seemed for a moment to wash his face in his hands. "I apologize. You asked why I was trying to get to Thought, and instead of the straightforward reply to which you were entitled, I've inflicted this rigmarole on you. If you'll excuse me now, I think a quiet ride around the city might help me sleep."

When the door had shut behind him, Acetes cleared his throat and spat into the fire. "He really ought to have somebody with him, but you can put me down for an idiot if I see how we can do it."

A boy's voice from the back of the room called, "I'll go, sir. He won't see me."

I turned around to look, as did everyone else. It was not the richly clad youth from Parsa (as I had expected), but a boy a good deal younger, clothed in a ragged sheepskin.

Io shouted, *"Polos!"* as he slipped out the door; a moment later we heard the clatter of hooves as he galloped away. Io was on her feet. "Master—"

"Absolutely not!" I caught her arm and forced her down again.

"I just wanted to ask him where he'd been," Io explained. "I haven't seen him since last night."

"He was with us before?"

Hegesistratus told me, "Yes, in the Great Mother's sacred cave. This morning you said he had been talking with you beside your fire last night, but had gone for water and never returned. I suppose he must have followed us."

Elata, who I think must seldom speak to more than one, now said, "He makes himself useful whenever he can and bears a happy heart—I'm glad that he's decided to stay with us. But, Io, your master's right. The night streets of this troubled city are no place for a young girl."

The black man nodded emphatically.

Hegesistratus refilled his cup. "They will be back soon, I think; if either was going into danger, I did not sense it. Io, this seems to me a good time for sharing nuts and telling ghost stories, not worrying about absent friends. You told me a fine one on the ship—how your master was present when a necromancer raised a dead woman, remember? I know he cannot recall it, and I doubt that the others have heard it; so why not tell it again?"

Acetes exclaimed, "That! By the Maiden, I've never been so frightened in my life. Io wasn't there. I suppose she got it from the poet—he was from Hill, too. You don't do that sort of thing, do you, Hegesistratus?"

"Necromancy?" The mantis shook his head. "I have laid a ghost or two, and I questioned one once." He swirled the wine in his cup and peered into it, seeing more in the flickers of firelight reflected there than I would have, I think. At last he said, "Our ghosts are becoming worse, have you noticed? It used to be they were no more than lost souls who had wandered away from the Lands of the Dead, or perhaps never reached them, spirits no worse dead than they had been alive, and frequently better. Such were the ghosts of which my masters told me when I was younger; such, indeed, were those I myself encountered as a young man. Now something evil is moving among them." He paused again. "Have any of you heard about the things that happened to Captain Hubrias? Do you know about the White Isle?"

Acetes shook his head; so did the black man, Io, and I.

"It was two years before the war, so he told me. His ship was off the mouth of the Ister, becalmed in fog, when the man at the masthead called down that he heard music and the beating of many wings. They had been talking on deck, I imagine, but after that they listened, and they heard the same sounds. Soon they realized that what they had taken for a thicker bank of fog was in fact an island with white stone cliffs and a beach of white sand. Hubrias told me he had sailed those waters since he was a child, and he knew perfectly well that there was no such place—but there it was."

Io asked, "What did he do?"

"Nothing, really," Hegesistratus continued, "until a man in armor appeared upon the beach. He waved and shouted for them to send a boat; Hubrias assumed he wanted to be taken off, so being curious about the island, he had four of his crew row him over. He soon realized, however, that this man was more than a common soldier; he was as handsome as a god, Hubrias said, and looked as strong as a bull. As soon as they had sand under the bottom, Hubrias jumped out and saluted him, assuring him that he and his ship were ready to serve him in any way he wished.

"'I am Achilles,' the ghost informed him, 'and I require a favor from you.' As you may imagine, Hubrias told him that he needed only to name it. 'Then go to the temple of Athena Ilias,' the ghost told him. 'There you will find a slave called Chryse. Buy her from the priests and bring her to me.'

"Hubrias swore he would, naturally, and jumped back in the boat as quickly as he dared. Just as they were putting out, the ghost told him, 'She is the last of Priam's line—treat her with honor!'

"They sailed to the Troad with fair winds all the way, and Hubrias located this girl; she was about fourteen, he said, and had been keeping house for one of the priests. He paid a stiff price for her and lodged her on his ship in as much comfort as a ship permits, requiring her to do no work. He told her that she was intended as a gift for the king of an island in the Euxine, and she promised quite willingly always to speak well of him to this king."

Acetes asked, "What happened when he got back to the island?" I myself was wondering whether Hubrias would be able to find it a second time.

"Off the mouth of the Ister they met with fog again." The mantis shook himself and emptied his cup, tossing the lees into the flames. "But this time there was a good wind. Hubrias said they had to reef their sail again and again; even so they nearly ran aground on the White Isle. The ghost was there, waiting for them on the sand; and standing beside him was the most beautiful woman that Hubrias had ever seen. It had been over a year when I talked with him, yet his eyes lit up still each time he tried to describe her to me. There was something in her that beckoned to you, he told me. You knew she was the proudest woman in the world—and the most humble. There was not a man alive, he said, who would not have laid down his life for her, and been happy to do it.

"He had tricked out this Chryse in amber beads and so on, and they put her in the boat and rowed her over. She knelt to the ghost and the woman—who was a ghost as well, no doubt—and they clasped hands when they saw her.

"'My friend,' the ghost told Hubrias, 'you have served me well. Go in peace, and I promise you will not go unrewarded.' Hubrias said that after that he could not seem to make an error in navigation, or even do a bad trade. He paid silver and was repaid in gold, as the saying goes. If he wanted to go south, the wind was in the north; and when he was ready to come back, it was in the south. He was already a local magnate when I spoke with him. He owned an estate near Tower Hill and was thinking of buying another."

"Well, that doesn't sound like such a bad ghost to me," Io said. "I don't think I'd have minded meeting that one."

Hegesistratus shrugged. "Perhaps not. But as Hubrias was sailing away, he heard a scream. He turned then, he said, and looked behind him. The ghost was holding Chryse above his head by an arm and a leg, while the beautiful woman watched. Chryse screamed again, calling Hubrias by name, begging him to return and save her. Then the ghost tore her apart."

I heard the long *O-o-o-h!* of Io's indrawn breath before Elata laughed. "Is that really true?" I asked Hegesistratus. "Did it actually happen?"

He shrugged. "I did not see it. But I myself talked with Hubrias, and I believed him. No player from Thespiae could have looked as he did when he described the woman, or sweated as he did when he described the death of the slave girl. Acetes, tell us about the raising of the dead woman in Thought. Was that as bad?"

Acetes had just crushed a walnut between the heels of his hands; he picked at the meat as he spoke. "Worse. I've seen a man killed by a bear, and I don't think that what your ghost did to the slave girl could have been much worse than that. This was. We'd all gone to a hetaera's—Hypereides, the kybernetes, the poet, a couple of other fellows, and me. Latro belonged to this hetaera then, and he was on hand to keep us in line. There was lots of good wine and some of the best food I ever ate, and the girls were real lookers—"

Someone—I suppose that it must have been the black man—had barred the door after Oeobazus and the boy had left. Now someone pounded on it, and I heard the boy shout, *"Let us in!"* The black man and I hurried over, lifted the bar, and pulled open the heavy door. Oeobazus and Polos stumbled into the firelight, half-carrying a fat old man with blood streaming down his face.

23

At This, My Zygite Bench

I must finish what I began writing last night. I have just now reread it all, and I confess that I think myself rather foolish for having recorded Hegesistratus' story in as much detail as I did; but the time we spent about the fire, between the time the Mede left and the moment when he and Polos returned with Cleton, seems very precious to me; I think that Io and I cannot have had many such moments, times of comfort, free from danger. Perhaps that is why Io speaks of Kalleos' house in Thought as she does. Kalleos was the hetaera Actes mentioned, she says.

The old man was nearly unconscious when Oeobazus and Polos carried him in. While Hegesistratus and Elata saw to his wound, Acetes, the black man, and I questioned Oeobazus. He said that he knew Cleton because Cleton had come to see him while he was a prisoner in the temple of Pleistorus. He had seen him standing in the street arguing with half a dozen Thracians. There had been a woman servant beside him holding a lamp—its light had attracted his eye. He had just recognized Cleton when one of the Thracians cut at him with a sword. The woman had dropped her lamp and fled; and the boy—Oeobazus had not known his name—had dashed up to help. Together they had lifted Cleton onto Oeobazus' mount and brought him here.

"He'd said he was a friend of your master's," Oeobazus told me, "and I know he was a friend to me while I was imprisoned—the only person who offered me any hope."

"He was," Hegesistratus confirmed, glancing up from binding Cleton's wounds. "Or rather, I should have said he is. I don't think this is going to kill him."

Elata nodded, and winked at me.

"The sword was not heavy enough or the arm strong enough—whichever way you care to put it. The blade bit into the bone, and deeply, too; but a skull is thick this high above the ear."

Cleton (whose name I had heard by that time from Oeobazus) muttered, and Elata held a wine cup to his lips. "He's dry—it's how I often feel as the vine laps my roots. He must have water to make new blood."

He drank all the cup held, and we laid him before the fire. That is when I wrote what I did, starting when Io showed me our old camp; for she had said (this as we whispered among ourselves and listened for the old man's rasping breath) that he had come to see us there, speaking to me as well as to Hegesistratus. I asked her whether I had written of that and whether she thought I should read it now, but she said she had overheard everything that had been said and would tell me at need.

After a long time, Cleton spoke to Hegesistratus and the black man, who helped him sit up. That was when I ceased to write. They set him beside the hearth, with his back to its warm stones.

"They took Hypereides," he told us. This was the captain mentioned earlier.

"Who did?" Acetes demanded.

"Nessibur and Deloptes."

Hegesistratus said, "Do not excite yourself—that can only do harm. Do you know where they have taken him?"

"To the palace."

"I see. Oeobazus has indicated that there were more than two Thracians confronting you when he caught sight of you—six at least. I take it that the rest were retainers of these two?"

Cleton nodded wearily.

Hegesistratus turned to Acetes. "In that case, those he names are certainly two of the aristocrats who sought to protect King Kotys. Presumably they slipped out of the palace through a side entrance."

Cleton nodded again.

Acetes said, "They got him from your house, fellow? How'd they know he was in there?"

Cleton's clouded eyes went from his face to Hegesistratus', from Hegesistratus' to mine, from mine to the black man's, and at last to Elata's. I thought then what a terrible thing life is, in which a man grown old and weak may find that some ill-considered act of his has doomed a friend. "I told them," he said. "I told Thamyris. He sent them . . . they said so."

Acetes cursed and asked Hegesistratus, "Do you understand the political situation here?"

"Not as well as he does," Hegesistratus told him. "Perhaps not even as well as you do yourself. You've been to the palace and talked with Thamyris, I know. I never have."

"And I'm going back, as soon as I can get my men together. Will you come with us?"

"Certainly," Hegesistratus told him. Oeobazus, the black man, and I nodded together.

Io had squeezed between the black man and me; now she asked Cleton, "You were a spy for this Thamyris, weren't you? Besides for Hypereides—and you seemed so nice!"

At that Cleton managed a smile and took one of her hands in his. "I've tried to be," he assured her. "Honestly, I have. I sent you more arrows. Did you know that?"

Io nodded.

"Do you think I could have done that without friends among the Thracians? That I could live and trade here at all?" His hand left hers to grope for his cup. Elata held it for him.

When he had drunk he said, "I gave you good advice, child. I did. Kotys was a hothead, but Thamyris had his ear—sometimes anyway. Didn't want the Mede killed, afraid the Amazons might kill Kotys, wanted to let everyone go."

Hegesistratus said, "The other aristocrats must hate him, if he was so near the throne—most of them at least. I would guess that those standing with him now are family connections, sons and cousins and so on."

Cleton nodded again. "Nessibur's his grandson. Deloptes is a nephew."

Hegesistratus pursed his lips. "And who do the others want crowned? A younger brother of Kotys?"

"His son. He's only three."

Oeobazus told us, "But now Thamyris has my unknown friend to bargain with. He'll threaten the rest with phantom armies from Hellas—make them appoint him regent for the young prince, perhaps."

Cleton spoke to Io and me. "Hypereides came to see me this afternoon. We're old friends, done business together for years. This time he needed wine, I had it. We struck our bargain, and I told my people to take the wine to his ship. He promised he'd bring the money tonight."

Acetes said, "So when he left, you told Thamyris he'd be coming back."

"Sent word to him," Cleton whispered. "Told him the Rope Maker's man of business would be in my house. Maybe . . . trading rights. Keep the others out."

I said, "But Thamyris didn't come. He sent the two lords."

Cleton sighed, and sipped from his cup again. "I didn't expect him to—just send somebody who could bargain for him. But they wanted to take Hypereides back to the palace, and he wouldn't go. Said he'd come in the morning and bring the Rope Maker. I think they thought he was lying. Maybe he was, maybe he felt they couldn't win."

I nodded.

"They got him and bent his arms back. I followed them out into the street, tried to explain to them that he was my guest, my customer."

Io said, "And they tried to kill you."

Under his breath Acetes added, "And probably believe they have—that they've killed their own agent. They're desperate. These are players who have to win the next throw."

Io asked, "What are we going to do?"

Acetes straightened up. "Get the men together, go there, and get him out."

I asked how many he had.

"Shieldmen? Five, and two bowmen."

"Cleton, do you have hoplons and breastplates among your goods? Helmets and so forth?"

His head moved less than a finger's width. "Yes, four."

"Four of everything?"

Again the feeble motion.

"Good. Acetes, find out where they're stored, arm the four largest sailors, and teach them how to behave like shieldmen—they probably know already. Take Hegesistratus, this Mede, and the black man with you. When you reach the palace, insist that they let everyone inside."

Acetes nodded. "You're right—that's just what a real Rope Maker would do."

"I'll join you if I can't get in. What's it like?"

I felt Io's grasp tighten on my hand.

"You'll have to slip past the Thracians outside first," Acetes warned me.

"I know, but how is the palace laid out? Where might they keep Hypereides?"

Cleton gasped for breath. "Square. Hear me, son. I've been in it many times. . . . A wall, not too high. No towers. Inside's courtyard, stable in back. Palace square, too. Hall and kitchen . . . ground. Sleeping rooms up steps . . . captives down. Underground. Turn right, five streets."

Hegesistratus tried to remonstrate with me, but I brushed him aside and got out the door before even the black man could halt me.

The streets were dark and oozing with filty mud, so that I had to walk slowly. I had not gone far before I nearly collided with a woman, but it was not until she spoke that I realized she was Elata.

"Latro," she said, "stop, and listen to me. Do you know I cure?"

"Of course," I told her. "I saw you helping Hegesistratus with Cleton tonight."

"And I would cure you, Latro, if I could. I can't, but I do understand how utterly you forget. I think I'm the only one who does, even now, though Io knows better than the rest. You don't remember who Hypereides is, nor do you care. Nor should you. My tree is old already, yet it and I will live for a great many seasons after Hypereides is dead and forgotten. You must guard your seed, Latro. Tonight you're risking it for nothing. Why?"

I did not understand what she meant by her tree, for women do not have that; but I told her, "I am doing it so that I will never be as Cleton is tonight. Let that be enough for you." I kissed her and ordered her to go back before someone harmed her. I, too, had drunk a good deal of wine; yet though she had chewed resin to sweeten it, her breath tasted of more.

A man rode past. He stared, and I saw he wore a helmet and bore a lance; I was glad that he did not stop. I hurried on and had nearly reached the palace when Io overtook me.

"Master!" she called, and caught at my cloak.

I spun around, my fist up. "Have I ever struck you, Io?"

"I don't remember," she said. Then, when I lifted my fist higher, "Yes, master, once or twice. It doesn't matter."

"I should strike you again now. You could have been killed, and now I have to take you back."

"Good." She sounded happy. We turned and began to retrace our steps. "You're the one who would have been killed, master, don't you know that? I'll bet there are a thousand Thracians in there with this Lord Thamyris, and your being dead wouldn't help Hypereides one single bit."

I told her, "If you follow me again, Io, I won't bring you back; I'll take you with me. That will be safer, I think, than leaving you in the streets of this barbarian town alone."

"You ought to stay in the house with me, master, or go with the black man and Acetes."

"I can't do that."

"Why not?" she asked. "Nobody'd blame you."

"But they'd know, Io, what I had set out to do, and that I had not done it—had not actually tried. While I myself would not know. I would see how they pitied me, as at times I've seen it today; and I would not know why." Quite suddenly there was a rush of moisture to my eyes, as if some veering wind had carried smoke to them. I did not weep, since men do not do such things; yet my eyes streamed, no matter how quickly I blinked. Today I must guard myself against this self-love, for surely it and wine were what unmanned me.

I believe a tear may have struck Io; she looked up quickly and said, "I can go the rest of the way alone, master. I'll be all right."

"No," I said, and shook my head, though perhaps she could not see the gesture.

When we reached the house, I had to pound on the door with the pommel of my sword before Elata lifted down the bar for us. Io threw her small body into my arms, and I kissed her as I had kissed Elata, knowing her a woman, however young, though I had thought her only a child before. "I won't run after you again," she promised. I nodded and did not tell her how much I hoped she would—how frightened I was.

Recalling the man with the lance, I chose not to follow the dark street I had walked down before, this time turning right at the first corner, then left at the next turning. When I did, I saw that a fire had been built in the middle of this new street, almost to the palace. Several men were standing around it, and it seemed to me that they were warming their hands.

24

The Boar

The great beast in the shadows was what struck everyone's fancy—so much is clear. I have listened to Hypereides, the mantis, the Mede, Acetes, and the shieldmen; and every one of them spoke of it. The mantis wanted to know how I had entered the palace. I had simply climbed the wall, which had not been difficult, and I told him so.

But first I described how the black man had saved me when I circled the watchfire. That made Hypereides happy and the black man, too. He showed us how he had snapped the Thracian's neck before he could draw his sword. I did not tell anyone that he had run ahead of me hoping to stop me; it would make Hypereides like him less. Nor did I say anything at all concerning Elata or Io. I told him instead of the other things that I did before pulling off my boots and making my dash for the wall. They are lost now, no doubt, with our horses and a great many other good things that we left behind us in the house. I remember that I considered discarding my cloak as well; now I am glad I did not, but I could not have climbed the wall wearing my boots.

Polos desires me to tell him many things about swords; I have explained that I must write this first. I will strive to be brief.

The black man had warned me I might be killed, pointing at the dead Thracian and to me, and opening and shutting his hands to indicate how many Thracians he felt might be within the wall, which was a very great number indeed. I did not dare answer him aloud for fear the other Thracians would overhear me, and so I spoke as he, with my fingers, saying it might also be that they were few and I would kill them all. He grinned at that—I saw his teeth flash in the darkness. Then he went away; he is my brother.

Though my hands had spoken so boldly, they trembled when I crouched in the shadow of a house to take off my boots. Because they stood against a cold sky bright with stars, I could see the Thracians upon the wall, the black outlines of their helmets and the sharp heads of their javelins. If I were to talk to Polos of swords and fighting now, as he wishes, I would tell him how important it is to stand for a time in the place of your enemy; I do not believe any man can win who does not do that, save by the favor of a god. Thus I supposed myself Thamyris and penned within the palace wall.

The lords siding with me I could not station upon the wall, because they would not consent to it; they would mount the wall only if there was an attack. On the other hand, I would require a force of picked men who would rush to counter any such attack. Very well—the lords would be that force. Peltasts could guard the wall through the tedious watches of the night, and sound the alarm.

But I, Latro, knew that peltasts are simple men, however hardy—just as I myself am a simple man. Simple men would keep their eyes on the men around the fires.

Thus I needed a distraction that would draw their eyes to a fire some distance from me. If the black man had remained with me, I would have asked him to provide it. As it was, there was no one to help me except the dead Thracian. Crouching very low, I dragged him to the back of the wood piled for the fire I had been skirting when he discovered me; there I stood a log upright and drove his knife into it. I was afraid someone would hear me, but the men around the fire were talking and the fire crackling. It was not easy to make his flaccid hand grasp the hilt, but by slipping the pommel into his sleeve I managed it.

Then I went quickly to the other side of the palace, not by shunning the light of each watchfire in turn, as I had before, but by going a short distance into the city (so that I kept well away from all the fires) and returning to the wall again. Soon, I knew, someone would go for wood and discover my dead man, and he would be filled with amazement when he saw that this man had (as it would appear) fought with a log and died. He would want the others to see everything that he had seen—and the peltasts upon the wall would hear him.

I had expected to wait for some time; but though everything happened, I think, as I had anticipated, I had scarcely reached a house near the palace wall before I heard shouts. Hesitation would have doomed my plan, for the peltasts would quickly return to their posts. I dashed to the wall and began to climb.

The top was the most hazardous point; I leaped as soon as I saw a roof below me, though I had no means of knowing how strong it might be. When I struck the thatch, I heard a pole snap under me, and the thatch sagged; but it muffled the sharp crack, save for the horses beneath. I slid down the roof and dropped to the ground, and though that distance was considerable, the courtyard was muddy and soft; I knew I was safe for a time then, since the men upon the wall were certain to look outward.

The palace stood dark before me. Hidden by the shadows of its broad eaves, I traced its wall, my fingers groping the rough ashlars. Soon they discovered a deep-set doorway, and within it a low and narrow door, of wood bound with bronze. Softly I put my shoulder to it, pushing with all my strength. It budged less than a hair's width; but when I relaxed, it seemed to me that it swung toward me, though only very slightly. Groping, I found a ring at one side. I pulled; the creaking of the hinges startled me so much that it has not been until this present moment, while I sat writing this, that I realized how foolish I had been.

Not long ago, I wrote that one must stand in one's enemy's place; but I myself had failed to do it when I hoped (as I had) to enter by some window. Thamyris would have been a fool to bar his doors—it would only have impeded his lords as they hurried to defend the wall. In the same way, the king who had built the palace would not have had its doors open inward; such doors only obstruct those who would rush out, and they are easily broken by rams.

I found myself in a smoky corridor lit here and there with cressets. Halfway along its length, there was a door on either side, and I saw that a wide chamber, more brightly illuminated, awaited me at the end.

One of the doors was barred within. The other gave access to a dark room where bundled lances, spears, and javelins leaned in corners, and wooden figures wore helmets, swords, and leather shirts much like my own, heavy with scales and plates. From one I borrowed an oval shield faced with bronze, and after stumbling over a sheaf of javelins, I severed the thongs with my sword and selected two. I understood then that the gods intended I should fight for my life—why else would they thus equip me? I took a helmet as well (I have it still), a high one with an august crest like the spread fingers of a webbed hand.

When I left the storeroom, Thamyris was standing at the end of the corridor as though waiting for me. "Come," he said, and motioned to me.

I did not know who he was, for if I had seen him before I had forgotten it; but I did as he asked. He vanished from the end of the corridor as soon as he saw I obeyed him; and when I entered the megaron, he was seated upon his throne. Though the megaron reeked of smoke, another scent underlay it. Some time passed before I recognized that second odor.

"Come closer," he said. "Have you come to kill me?"

I told him that I certainly had not—that I did not even know who he was.

"I am Thamyris, son of Sithon," he said. He was old, his long beard faded to a solemn white, though his glance still held a spark. Something huge twitched, though only very slightly, in the shadows behind him.

"I'm called Latro," I told him, "and I've come here to kill no one—only to free your captive, the Hellene. Give him to me and allow us to leave unmolested, and I swear we will do no one here the least harm."

"You are called Pleistorus in this land," he told me. "By many other names in others. As for your Hellene, I care nothing for him—he was the bait that hooked you, nothing more." He clapped his hands, and two armed men stepped from the shadows. When I saw them, I thought that it had been one of them I had seen move.

"Bring in your foreigner," he told one. "He may be of further use."

The man addressed hurried away; the other waited beside the throne with sword drawn.

"This is my grandson Nessibur," the old man on the throne said, nodding toward him. "He will succeed me as King of Thrace."

I congratulated him.

"Are you not going to say that I am not yet so much as king of Apsinthia? Or that Apsinthia is only one small kingdom among fifty?"

I shook my head and told him I knew nothing of the matter. The truth was that I was not thinking of it at all, but of the name he had given me. I have since asked Io, who says that it is only the name of some Thracian god.

"Latro!"

It was the prisoner, a bald, round-faced man whose hands were bound behind his back. Seeing that, and thinking it best to act boldly, I shouldered the lord who had brought him aside and cut him free.

"Thank you," he said. He shook his hands and slapped one against the other. "I'd like to have one of those javelins of yours, but I'm afraid I couldn't hold on to it."

The man who had brought him asked whether his sword should be returned to him.

Thamyris laughed. The laughter of old men is often shrill cackling, I know; yet there was something worse in his, the wild mirth of those who have felt the hand of a god. "Why not," he asked, "when he cannot grasp it? Pleistorus, were you not about to tell me that Thrace—and even the Apsinthian throne"—here he struck its armrest loudly with his open hand—"is beyond *my* grasp?"

I shook my head again, adding, "I've no desire to be rude, Thamyris, and don't know whether Apsinthia, or Thrace, is beyond your grasp or within it. If they are what you wish, then I wish you well in them."

The captive said, "You're Lord Thamyris, sir? My own name is Hypereides. I hail from Thought, but I've been assisting the noble Acetes, the strategist appointed by Prince Pausanias, the regent of Rope—the Rope Makers are our allies, as I imagine you know already. I assure you I'm not a spy or troublemaker of any kind, and I have friends here who'll be happy to vouch for me."

Thamyris spoke as if he had not heard him. "We Thracians could be masters of the world. Do you know that?"

I said, "I'm sure you breed many valiant men."

"None but the Indians are more numerous"—he leaned toward me—"none but the Rope Makers more warlike. Were we united—as we shall be—no nation on earth could resist us!"

Hypereides said quickly, "But you'll need allies, Thamyris. What you have here is cavalry and light infantry. It's good, I know. It's very good. But you're going to need heavy infantry, too, and a navy. Now the best phalanxes are the Rope Makers', as everybody knows. And the best ships are ours, as we proved at Peace."

Thamyris leaned back as old men do, staring at the smoke-blackened ceiling. At last he sighed. "You are still here. I shall have you gutted with your own weapon as soon as Deloptes returns with it. Disemboweled by Pleistorus, if I can arrange that, and I imagine I can." He rose with these words and came down from the throne to stand before me.

"You are reputed to be overlord of every battlefield. You are not. After so many years, I—we—have found him." Briefly, fingers like claws caressed my jaw below the cheekpieces of my helmet, before coming to rest upon my shoulders. "If you were what you say, you would slay this foreigner for me with his own sword, the moment that it was brought to your hand. You know *he* would, but you do not know I know it. Learn that I do."

He seemed strange to me—not like a man, but rather a doll manipulated by another. I said, "Very well, I am the master of all battlefields, if you say it. In the person of that master, I tell you no strategist worthy of his command kills those who might readily be brought to fight for him."

That was all Thamyris said and all I said, because at that moment the wide door at the head of the megaron was thrown back. A peltast ran in and knelt to him, still grasping his javelins; he spoke in a tongue I do not understand, and Thamyris replied in the same way.

The peltast objected, and indicated the door through which he had come, expostulating. He was somewhat younger than I, and I could see that though he did not wish to disagree with the old man, he felt he must.

Thamyris shouted at him; then Nessibur spoke, stepping down from the dais. There came a guttural grunt from the shadows, at which Thamyris trembled, though he did not seem to know it. He called loudly and clapped his hands, and half a dozen well-armed men filed in to stand at either side of him. Nessibur left with the young peltast, I suppose to arrange whatever difficulty had brought him.

Just then Deloptes returned, carrying Hypereides' sword, a bag of coins, and some other things. Hypereides tied the bag to his belt by the thongs and slung his sword about his neck in the fashion of the Hellenes, who seldom wear the sword at the belt.

"Your master is at our gate," Thamyris informed Hypereides. "Nessibur will admit him; and if you die before his eyes as a man ought to, you will have the satisfaction of showing him that his nation is not alone in its boasted courage."

"And if I live," Hypereides replied, "I shall show that mine is without peer—as it is—in overcoming adversity."

Thamyris turned to me. "Take his sword, Pleistorus, and take his life. Or lose your own."

I exclaimed, *"It's a boar!"*

I did not intend to speak thus aloud, but the words

escaped my lips before I could shut them in. Although Hypereides stared at me as if I had suddenly gone mad, what had actually happened was that I had at last identified the pervasive odor underlying the smoke of the megaron: it was not the stench of a pigsty but a deeper, harsher smell, ripe with musk—the smell a hunter may catch when one of those great brutes is brought to bay.

25

Farewell to Thrace

Io called me aft to watch its coastline vanish behind us. When I told her I had been writing, she wanted me to return to it at once; but I stayed with her until nothing could be seen save the wake of our ship and the gray sea. It is winter and the season for storms, the kybernetes says; but I do not think we will have one today. The sun rose in bright gold at dawn; and though the wind is chill, it serves us well, and the sun is golden still.

As soon as I had placed the boar's scent (so I was upon the point of writing when Io called to me) I could also make out the beast itself, huge and black as night, where it lay in the dusky area behind the dais; its chin rested flat upon the stone floor, but it watched our every movement with eyes that shone as red as embers.

When I said I smelled a boar, several of the men protecting Thamyris spoke; and though I could not understand their words, I sensed that they had understood mine.

"Is it chained?" I asked. "They can be dangerous."

If he replied, I did not hear him. I went to examine the boar more closely, and the Thracians who had come at his order stepped aside to let me pass.

The boar rose as I approached it, and I saw at once that it was not chained. For an instant its eyes left me for Thamyris, and he shouted an order. My attention was upon the boar, not on him or the men beside him; but I spun about when I heard a sword drawn. Hypereides had pinned the Thracian's arm—another's hand was on his hilt.

I cast both javelins, and the distance was so short that I could not miss. If the remaining four had come at us as one, we would have been killed immediately; as it was, I had to shelter Hypereides with my shield as much as I dared, for he had none of his own. We were driven back, as was to be expected; but to be driven back from the place where we were, was to be driven toward the boar.

"Run!" I told him, and together we fled along the wall of the megaron, for I hoped to put the boar between our attackers and ourselves. It turned toward us, as I had feared it would. Falcata stabbed deep—but in the side of the neck, not over the eyes as I had intended; and for that bad thrust we might have died.

We lived instead, as Hypereides had foretold. The enormous boar recoiled from my blade, scattering the remaining Thracians like so many birds and opening one from groin to throat with its fearsome tusks. (Its shoulders were higher than theirs—this I saw.) Thamyris drew his sword and rushed upon us like a madman, and Hypereides ducked beneath his cut to kill him.

What would have happened next had we, the three remaining Thracians, and the boar remained pent in the megaron, I cannot say; the great door opened once again, and through it dashed a pack of piebald hounds. For an instant, they foamed like the sea about the boar, so that it seemed to me they would surely drag it down and tear it to bits; but it shook them aside and fled through the open door. Outside I heard the shouts and shrieks of those in the courtyard, and the baying of the hounds.

Then boar and hounds were gone.

Of the rest of the battle I write but a little, for though many a wound must still bleed, all I recall of it is scattered and confused. Acetes had come, and (so he explained to us a few moments ago) had persuaded Nessibur to admit his shieldmen and Hegesistratus, Oeobazus, and the black man, as well as himself; but before he had called for a truce and advanced to the wall, he had given a pledge to the Thracians besieging the palace that he would open its gates for them if he could. He did this, as he himself conceded, upon the advice of Hegesistratus, who had pointed out to him that he could not lose by it, for he need not unbar the gates unless he wished the aid of the Thracians outside them.

It would seem that when the boar dashed into the courtyard, someone there—whether a Thracian or a Hellene no one can say—threw wide both gates, perhaps merely in the hope that it would run out; at this the Thracians outside rushed in, believing that Acetes had fulfilled his pledge.

Nessibur is dead, they say, and with him all who sided with Thamyris except a few peltasts. With much gold, Acetes received the daughter of a noble Thracian, who offered to buy a girl from him in addition. The gold has been divided, the greater portion among our crew, but much also to Hypereides, Hegesistratus, the kybernetes, Oeobazus, the black man, and me. Mine I have hidden in my chest. Some was in coins of many sorts, most in ornaments, rings, buckles, and the like; thus the division was by weight.

We might have had much more gold, I think, had we remained in Thrace; but all of us were eager to go. It was for Oeobazus that we came, Io says, and we have him.

We sailed in such hurry that many useful articles were left behind. In justice to Io, I must add that I do not think anything can have been left by her. She brought a sword she says the Amazons gave her, a sling Polos made for her, my clothing as well as her own, this scroll and my old one, and other things. I still have the helmet I took from the palace, though my shield was so deeply cut I left it behind.

I was talking to Polos, who asked many questions about the boar; all the Hellenes have been chattering about it. I brought him to Hegesistratus, who told us that in Thracian art a boar is the foe of Pleistorus; this foe is called Zalmoxis, and is often shown as a bear instead. Hegesistratus and Polos say Pleistorus is the god to whom Oeobazus was to be sacrificed. Hegesistratus could not explain why Thamyris had a boar in the megaron, except by saying what everyone says: that besieged men are unlikely to turn out any animal that can be eaten at need.

Polos wanted to know whether Hegesistratus had seen the boar, and whether it was as big as everyone is saying. "I did," Hegesistratus told him, "and it was as large as they are saying now. However, it was not as large as they will say it was when we reach Thought."

I think that a very good answer indeed.

Perhaps I should not trouble myself with such trivialities, but I have nothing better to do than write, though some of our crew are bailing or shifting the supplies in the hold to better the trim of the ship. Thus I will set down that we who were in the battle at the palace are the envy of the rest. Hypereides has told the four sailors to whom Acetes gave helmets, hoplons, and breastplates that they may keep them as the reward of their valor. These represent a great deal of money, but Acetes told Cleton we would pay for—rather than return—them. Hypereides plans to bill the priests on the high city for the full amount; because he is bringing Oeobazus, they will not refuse him.

After I wrote last I went privately to Hegesistratus to ask him about the hounds; it puzzled me that no one mentions them. He said he did not see them; he heard their baying, but thought himself the only one who had. I assured him I had heard them, and seen them. He says they are Cynthia's; she is a goddess to whom both of us are indebted. He was fervent in her praises—even more so when I described to him how her hounds had chivied the boar.

Elata challenged us to swim, though the sea looks so cold. (This is the one these Hellenes call the Water.) The kybernetes had a sailor tie a long line to the sternpost, letting it trail after the ship so that swimmers could catch hold of it, should it appear they might be left behind. When Hegesistratus took off his clothing, I saw that he had been wounded several times, some very fresh; he says he received those when he and I fought alongside the Amazons. (Io says these women gave her the sword. It seems very strange to me that women should also be soldiers.)

Hegesistratus pointed to the oldest wound and asked whether I remembered it. When I admitted I did not, he told me that he received it from an assassin in Sestos. I cannot recall Sestos, though I know that there is such a city on Helle's Sea.

Everyone stared at Elata when she took off her gown. She did not seem to mind, but soon grew chilled and dove into the sea; Hegesistratus untied the thongs that hold his wooden foot and dove after her. They called for me to join them, but I do not think Hegesistratus truly wished it; though no one swam with them, they swam together for a long time. When they returned to the ship, they sat very close together and wrapped themselves in both their cloaks, saying that though the sea is cold, the wind is colder.

The kybernetes says that this island is Sign-of-Thrace; it is called so because it is a day's sail from the Thracian coast. Everyone says we have been in Thrace, though I cannot recall that either. Io tells me I have written much about it in this book.

There are fine ports on this island, Hypereides says, but this is only a fishing village. We do not wish to dock at one of the ports because no one knows whether these Hellenes remain loyal to the Empire; here we count two men for each villager. Besides, these poor people care nothing for the Empire, and it nothing for them. Hypereides, Io, and I are going to sleep here tonight; this is the largest house in the village. It is good we have a house to sleep in. We would be very uncomfortable, I think, if we slept outside, even if we slept around a fire built in a sheltered spot.

As things are, we have been roasting fresh thrushes, which is very pleasant. Kroxinas, whose house this is, netted them a few days before; his wife plucks them for us, and we roast them on green sticks.

Kroxinas has as many questions as Polos, it seems, but he asks them mostly with his eyes. When he can no longer hold one back, he asks Io. Hypereides answers, usually. Kroxinas asked what had brought our ship to Thrace so late in the season, and Hypereides told him we came to set the son of King Kotys firmly upon the throne of Apsinthia.

Kroxinas had heard of Kotys, but had not known he was dead. (All this was greatly complicated by the fact that Kotys' son is named for his father.) Hypereides said that now that the Empire is crumbling, it is the task of Thought to bring the rule of law to the islands of the Water and the lands along its coasts. His talk has made me think that the Great King must need me now more than ever.

Io added, "There was a big battle—my master and Hypereides were right in the thick of it."

Kroxinas and his wife were as eager to hear about it as I, and Hypereides obliged us. I will set down here only the meat of what he said, omitting a good deal.

"After King Kotys was murdered by his nobles, his mother's brother, Thamyris, tried to take the throne. He was getting on in years and had been chief adviser to his nephew—a good one, from all I heard—but now he wanted to be king himself. We had been patrolling Helle's Sea against the Great King, but as soon as Xanthippos got word of it, he sent us off to Apsinthia right away. The Thracians are afraid of the Rope Makers; so since we didn't have any with us, I bought a scarlet cloak for Acetes in Sestos. When we got to Thrace, he pretended he was a strategist from Rope and the rest of us were allies and auxiliaries from their league. That got the nobles supporting the prince on our side pretty quickly, and I was able to find out what was going on, even though the whole situation was still badly confused at that point.

"With Thamyris surrounded and the other Thracians afraid of us, I didn't think anything of going around Cobrys alone. I had my sword for footpads—which a man isn't allowed to wear back in Thought—and like I said, the city was friendly. I didn't even wear armor. What I should have done is taken Latro and the black man with me; they're my bodyguards, but I didn't think I needed them.

"Well, I got quite a surprise. I was sitting around in the house of a friend of mine, telling a few jokes and talking about business, when in comes a couple of high noblemen. Their faces were practically blue with tattoos, and by the stone I'm glad I won't have to look at those again for a while! Each had half a dozen henchmen with him, every one of them armed to the teeth. 'King Thamyris wants to talk to you,' they said. 'We've come to escort you to the palace.'

"I know what barbarians are like, and I could see I wasn't going to get out of that palace until I bought my way out, so I said I'd come tomorrow and pretended to be drunk. They weren't buying any, though. 'Our orders are to bring you,' they told me. They threw me down and tied my hands behind my back, and off we went.

"Latro here found out about it and came to the palace to try to get me out. They brought me in and told me they were going to make Latro kill me; it was just a threat to bring us around, of course, but I didn't like it and neither did he.

"Thamyris had a pet boar. It's one of the shapes Zalmoxis is supposed to take, so I imagine it was a sacred animal of some kind. I don't suppose you've ever been to Riverland, Kroxinas, but believe me, the country's full of them. Then, too, we've got owls in Thought, as you likely know; they're the sacred birds of our goddess, and her priests feed them.

"So to change the subject, Latro said, 'That's a lovely pig you've got there,' and went over to have a look at it. Thamyris must have thought he meant to harm it, so then everything turned upside down. He had half a dozen retainers with him, thinking that was enough to hold us, I suppose; but we killed a couple as quick as you could snap your fingers and were getting the upper hand of the rest when Latro saw that the boar was set to charge. 'Run,' he yelled to me, and believe me, we ran! That was the biggest boar you ever saw in your life, and it went for those Thracians like we went for the Great King's ships at the Battle of Peace."

Io asked, "Isn't that when Acetes came?"

Hypereides nodded. "That's right. Acetes had heard about what had happened to me, too, and he led the loyal Thracians' attack. If he hadn't, they probably would've killed Latro and me sooner or later. We had the wildest battle you ever saw; no formations and 'each man stand shield to shield for his city' stuff—this was the kind of real knock-down fighting old Homer tells about. I haven't had so much fun since Fennel Field."

Kroxinas, who had listened openmouthed, asked Io, "What became of Thamyris? Did they cut off his head?"

"Yes, as a matter of fact that's exactly what they did," Hypereides told him. "Cut it off, stuck it on the point of a lance, and put it up at the palace gate for everybody to see. But only after I'd killed him with my own hand."

Io nudged me as though to say, "I bet it was you, master."

I said, "I've been talking to Hegesistratus about the boar. No one ever killed it, he says."

Hypereides shook his head. "A hundred people have asked me what became of it, but I don't know."

Kroxinas' wife murmured, "Don't you think the boar might have been Zalmoxis himself? We're Hellenes, but we have people who worship Zalmoxis here." She shivered. "I don't think the baby prince's uncle would've tried to be king if he hadn't been promised it by some god."

Io told Hypereides, "Pleistorus doesn't like Zalmoxis. In Thrace we saw pictures of him sticking Zalmoxis with his spear."

Hypereides laughed. "Well, Pleistorus didn't come around to help us. I wish he had—we could have used him."

Part

3

26

In Cimon's Garden

Comfortably seated in the shade of an apple tree, the great men received us. Hypereides had described them to me already; thus I knew that the tough-looking, round-headed, blunt-featured man was Themistocles, and the tall, fine-looking, younger man Cimon, our host. Xanthippos we have met previously, so Io says, though I do not recall him. At any rate he greeted us as friends, and Cimon's servants brought stools for us.

"We've asked you here to discuss the death of Oeobazus," Themistocles began. I saw that he watched Oeobazus himself for his reaction, and so did I. There was none.

After a moment, Xanthippos chuckled. "Not many dead men have borne the news of their own demise with such equanimity, Oeobazus. You are to be congratulated."

The Mede's white teeth flashed like a sword in the thicket of his beard. "If you mean you're going to kill me, I've heard that in other places."

Themistocles shook his head. "I said only that you were here to talk about it. It took place quite some time ago. You were sacrificed by the Thracian barbarians to—what is it they call him?"

"Pleistorus," Hegesistratus prompted him.

Themistocles cocked an eyebrow. "He's one of their major gods? In that part of Thrace?"

Hegesistratus nodded. "Very much so."

"Good. That was the end of you, Oeobazus. Most certainly you never came to Thought or any other part of the Long Coast. Since we can clearly no longer call you Oeobazus, what would you like us to call you instead? Not by one of your family names, please."

The Mede thought quickly, or perhaps had been warned that some such question would be asked. "Why not Zihrun? I believe I'm entitled to that."

Xanthippos smiled, as did Hegesistratus and the black man. Seeing that no one else understood, Xanthippos explained, "It's 'Life chose me.' Certainly that's a good name for you, Zihrun. You're not unwilling to return to the Empire?"

At that Cimon spoke for the first time. There is nothing extraordinary about his clear, pleasant voice, and yet there is something very extraordinary about being spoken to by Cimon; I think it must come from the level gaze of those gray eyes. He said, "We won't tell you how dangerous this is for him. You're not children."

I looked around for Io, for she is indeed a child still, though she might say otherwise; but she and Elata had wandered away among the trees, perhaps feeling it more decent to leave men's talk to men. Polos was helping in the stable.

"Well put." Themistocles nodded. "We'll have to talk more about this in private, Zihrun—who you're to see and what you're to tell them, everything we need to learn. I'm going to impress the importance of your death in Thrace on everyone here in just a moment. But first we owe you more of an explanation, and more in the way of assurance, than you've had yet. What do you know of our politics?"

"That your people are themselves your king," the Mede said. "That you're their war leader, their highest-ranking strategist, called the polemarch. Beyond those, nothing."

"And you, Hegesistratus?"

"A foreigner's knowledge, and out of date at that. I am eager to learn."

"Then I'll explain to both of you, as quickly and simply as I can. If I show any prejudice for my own party or my friends, my colleagues here will correct me, you may be sure. I ask you to notice—to begin with—that I'm outnumbered."

Xanthippos shook his head and cleared his throat. "Hardly. Hypereides is your man, and a speaker of considerable eloquence, as I've several times been forced to admit."

Themistocles grinned; it made me like him. "There you see it—that's how we do it here. Among you Medes, I'm told, there are many men so honorable that everyone trusts them. We're not like that at all—we never trust one another. So what we do instead is make sure that each side's represented, so that every rascal's got two worse looking over his shoulder. Hegesistratus knows all this, of course. We Hellenes are all the same.

"The Rope Makers—we'll be talking about them soon—would tell you they have two kings so each can keep the other honest. We have two political groups instead—the shieldmen's party and the naval mob. I'm head of the naval mob. Xanthippos and Cimon are leaders of the shieldmen's party. That means that when we say we're behind you, you've got the pledges of both sides."

The Mede nodded.

"We have our differences," Themistocles continued,

"serious and profound differences. You said earlier that our people rule themselves. It's actually the case only when my own party's in power."

Cimon shot him a glance both censorious and humorous.

"I represent the working poor, who make up the majority in our city just as in every other. My people want jobs as seamen, stevedores, and dockyard workers. They make our pottery and so on, and they know that for them to eat, Thought must trade. That means we get the shipowners—like Hypereides here—and most of the merchants and manufacturers, too."

Cimon glanced at Xanthippos and said, "Allow me to speak for our side, Themistocles. I'll begin by warning Zihrun and the rest that not everything you've said is true. And, Zihrun, you're not to suppose that because we're shieldmen, we think that Thought could live without ships, although Themistocles and his friends sometimes talk as if it could live without soldiers. Nor does Themistocles, as he tried to imply, represent all poor men who work. Wholly untrue! No men work harder than those who must plow and sow, tend and guard the herds and flocks, harvest and thresh the grain, prune and manure the vines, and trample the grapes. If you were to go into our Assembly, Zihrun, you would find that those vital workers, without whom we would all starve, support our party to a man. And should Themistocles challenge that, I will show you two score of them here and let you speak with them yourself.

"Although we are proud to champion the interests of these hardworking citizens, and their wives and children, they're by no means our only supporters. You yourself, Zihrun, and you, noble Hegesistratus, are yourselves far from their lowly, though absolutely necessary and valuable, class; nor would anyone count either of you among the naval mob's surly loiterers. You're men of breeding and learning, and it is we and not Themistocles, who is a man of mean birth and small education (though I scruple to say it), who represent the best families in Thought."

Themistocles fidgeted upon the stone bench in a way that showed him eager to speak, and Cimon rose as if to make sure he retained the floor.

"Nor are those all. The virtue of a city does not reside in its best families; however excellent their stock, they are too few. Nor does it lie in the poor, who cannot fight unless some other feeds them. No, it is in the craftsmen, the skilled artisans, the worthy merchants, and the independent freeholders that true *arete* is found. *They* are the defenders of the city, and even Themistocles cannot deny that they are ours."

Themistocles applauded derisively.

"You will say now that it was not defended when the Great King came, and you will be right. Our sheep and our goats and our cattle were driven off, our horses stolen, our poultry and swine devoured, our crops destroyed, the tombs of our ancestors and the temples of our gods desecrated, and our city burned to the ground. All that is perfectly true. All that took place because the resources of our city were unwisely diverted from its army to the ships. And none of it can be permitted to take place again, or we shall be ruined utterly. The land *must* be defended! If the Long Coast were an island, you would hear me speaking in support of Themistocles. It is not."

Themistocles rolled his eyes. "Are you through at last, young man?"

"Why, no." Cimon sat down again. "My career has scarcely begun, and I intend to be polemarch myself before I'm through. But I've said what I had to say for the present, if that's what you mean."

"Good." Themistocles leaned toward us with the look of a man never more in earnest. "Then let me say that you spoke the truth when you said I was of humble birth—I am. My grandfather was a silver miner, and my father also worked in the mines for a time. As for learning, isn't it a matter of what a man learns? What do you Medes learn, Zihrun? You're an educated Mede, as my young friend pointed out. What does a Mede's education consist of?"

"One learns how to honor the gods," the man we had called Oeobazus told him, "most of all, how to honor Ahura Mazda, who is the god of gods; and to ride, to shoot with the bow, and to tell the truth."

Themistocles nodded as though what he had heard had merely confirmed what he had already known. "A very good education, I would say. Cimon here can play the lyre quite well, and he's a fine singer. You'll hear him tonight, I feel sure. As for me, I know how to make a city great."

Hegesistratus began, "You spoke of the Rope Makers—"

Themistocles silenced him with an upraised hand. "And I shall have much more to say about them soon. But before I do, I must make certain that our friend from the east understands one thing. It's that though we differ, we are alike in our devotion to Thought. As you may know, we have the custom of ostracizing politicians—Xanthippos, Cimon, and I are all politicians, you understand—who are considered too divisive. We send them away, without dishonor, for a specified number of years. But when the Great King's army came, I called all those who'd been ostracized home and gave them commands. They served the city well, as I knew they would.

"Xanthippos, Cimon, are you with me in everything we're doing today? Do you agree that all of us shall work for the good of Thought?"

Both nodded, and Cimon added, "We do."

"Do you pledge yourselves to hold in strictest confidence everything we say here today, provided I share whatever I can learn with you? To do everything in your power for Zihrun and the rest? And particularly for—" Themistocles glanced toward Hypereides.

"Latro," Hypereides supplied.

"For Latro?"

Both nodded again. Xanthippos said, "You have our hands on it, all of you."

"And mine." Themistocles paused; the warm breath of spring sighed in the newly green boughs, and though birds trilled there, it was so quiet I could hear the men taking down the wall beside the road talking at their work.

"I'm afraid that's as much assurance as we can provide you, Zihrun," Themistocles said, "but it's better than the word of a king. If I fall from power—and I will eventually, you can be sure—Xanthippos or Aristides will become polemarch. Aristides couldn't be here in person—Cimon's his representative. But I swear there isn't a man who walks on earth less likely to betray somebody it's his duty to look out for than Aristides. There're a few of us who're just as honorable as any Mede, and he's their chief. Notice that it's me, his enemy, who says that. I think he's wrong about a lot of things. I believe he's misguided, and the whole Twelve know he's pigheaded. But if the shieldmen have sworn to protect you, and they have, Aristides would die to save you.

"Now listen to me, all of you. I'm not going to threaten you—I know free men can't be checked long by threats. But if this were the Empire or any other tyranny, you might very well be strangled tonight to keep Zihrun safe. Hypereides, didn't you say Latro's got a bad memory?"

Hypereides nodded. "He forgets everything in a day or so."

"Then he must learn to forget faster. Any of you who still remember what Zihrun used to be called must forget it at once." Themistocles pointed toward the black man. "Hypereides says you don't speak our tongue, but you seem to have understood what I've been saying. What's the name of that man beside you, the one with the beard?"

"Zihrun," the black man told him.

"Hegesistratus, why did Hypereides send you to Thrace?"

Hegesistratus answered smoothly, "To assure King Kotys and his people of the continued friendship of Thought. King Kotys—that particular King Kotys—is now deceased, alas. But his son, a child dear to the gods, has his crown. And his son's advisers have sent many tokens of their goodwill."

Themistocles nodded, satisfied. "What about you, Latro? Why were you sent to Thrace?"

I told him quite honestly that I had not known I had ever been there.

Hypereides said, "Don't any of you forget. If anybody asks you about Oeobazus, we heard he was sacrificed to Pleistorus. We didn't see it ourselves because we weren't there at the time. It's just what we were told."

Xanthippos glanced at the sun, as a man does who wishes to judge just how much of the day remains. "I think we can get on with it, Themistocles. Latro, are you and your friend aware of your legal status here?"

I told him I could speak only for myself, but that I had assumed we were foreign visitors. I knew we were no Hellenes.

27

Io Weeps

While I was writing what stands above this, Polos came wanting to talk of chariots and horses. I made him wash, then spoke with him as he wished.

Io has brought a bouquet of apple blossoms. Not many

have opened yet, she says, but she found a few; and some of them that Elata broke in the bud opened while she held them, which seems strange. I explained to them that we are going to Rope tomorrow with Themistocles, and that has made Io very unhappy. She says the Rope Makers are cruel men who cannot be trusted, and indeed Hegesistratus says the same; thus it may be wise to record here everything else we said under the tree.

Xanthippos and Hypereides explained to the black man and me that under the laws of Thought we are Hypereides' slaves, having been given to him as prisoners of war by the city of Tower Hill. (I must ask Io about this.)

"I was planning to sell you to Kalleos," Hypereides said, "and I wrote her a bill of sale. I was to get five parties in return, with up to ten guests. But since I've only had one so far, you haven't actually changed hands, understand?"

I nodded, and so did the black man.

"I can see you don't like the idea of being slaves, and I don't blame you for that, I wouldn't myself. What we've worked out here—Xanthippos, Themistocles, Cimon, and me—is a legal mechanism for freeing you both. It's simple for the black man, but for you things get complicated because Prince Pausanias is claiming you."

He glanced at Themistocles for confirmation; Themistocles nodded.

"Some of Pausanias' men took you away from Kalleos, see? And while we were in Sestos, she applied to him for compensation and got it. You can understand the prince's position—he paid for you in good faith, and we've got you. He feels we ought to return you to him."

On behalf of the black man and myself, I told Hypereides that he would have neither of us long.

"That won't be necessary. I said we'd worked something out—weren't you listening? I got word of this the day we landed, and I talked to Xanthippos about it as soon as I'd let him know about—about our trip to Thrace."

Xanthippos smiled. "You see, Latro, I believe strongly in assisting those who have assisted me, and Hypereides had a great deal to say about what happened in the palace, though perhaps we shouldn't speak of that here. I enlisted Cimon in your cause—he has some useful connections in Rope—and Hypereides enlisted Themistocles. You mustn't imagine that Pausanias is an ordinary Rope Maker. He represents the old Lacedaemonian aristocracy, or what's left of it, and he's both a reasonable and a magnanimous man."

Seeing that Xanthippos had finished, Hypereides said, "So here's where we stand. I'll free the black man for two minas, the money to be paid whenever he has it. Is that all right?"

The black man hesitated, then nodded.

"And I renounce any claim on you, Latro. So does Kalleos—I talked to her about it today and paid her a little something. Themistocles is going to Rope, where they want to honor him for what he's done in the war. You'll go with him—Io, too. When you get there, Pausanias will free you and declare you a resident of Rope—not an actual Rope Maker, you understand, but an alien living there and a free man. You'll be his subject, of course; he's the Agid Regent. But you'll be nobody's slave."

I asked if I would be permitted to leave Rope to search for my home.

Cimon said, "Certainly, at any time. It's only the Equals* who can't leave without the permission of the judges. As an alien resident, you'll be able to travel and even to trade; and if anyone anywhere tries to harm you, you'll be able to claim the protection of your city."

---

*The *Homoioi,* who could vote in the assembly and hold office. Latro seems to have been declared a *perioikos,* a "neighbor."—GW

The polemarch, who had been watching me narrowly, asked, "Will you do it? Come to Rope with me?"

I shrugged. "Would you, in my place?"

He actually seemed to consider it for a moment, rubbing his heavy jaw, then nodded.

"Hegesistratus? Will you advise me?"

"Reluctantly. I know you don't remember it, but you read a fairly lengthy passage from your old book to me once. In it the regent told you that you were no longer to be his slave but his friend."

I felt then as though a heavy burden had been lifted from my shoulders.

"He sounded sincere, or at least it seemed you thought he did," Hegesistratus continued, "and it is only fair for me to tell you that. Nevertheless, my advice is that you should not go."

Then I wished to ask Io, but I—a grown man taking counsel with others—was ashamed to ask the advice of a child. I asked the black man instead, and he spoke to Hegesistratus.

"Seven Lions wishes to learn whether he is now free," the mantis said.

Hypereides nodded. "I have to give you a paper, and you have to sign one. But those are just formalities."

The black man spoke again, and Hegesistratus said, "Then he advises Latro to go, provided Themistocles permits him to go as well. Themistocles?"

The polemarch nodded. "Certainly. Will you come, Latro?"

"Yes," I said. "You have my word on it."

Cimon, particularly, appeared to relax after I had spoken. He smiled and gave me his hand.

"Which leaves no one but Elata and me to be disposed of," Hegesistratus said, "and we should not be much trouble."

Just then one of Cimon's household slaves came and spoke briefly to Cimon, who said to Themistocles, "Simonides is here, with the others. He says they've brought everything."

"Good. We'll start in the morning. Hegesistratus, I hope you understand that my party can't make further use of you here. You were with the Great King, so we'd be handing Xanthippos and Aristides a weapon. Your connection with Hypereides is ended."

"I understand, and I regret it," the mantis said. "It has been a fortunate connection for me."

"And for me," Hypereides put in. "I regret it, too."

Themistocles asked, "Any bad feelings? Do you think you've been misused in any way?"

"No, I do not," Hegesistratus assured him. "Precisely the contrary."

"Hypereides says you have sufficient funds. If that's not the case, I can arrange something."

Hegesistratus waved the offer away. "Doubtless you would tell Zihrun that no Hellene can refuse money, but the truth is that we are quite comfortable. We will take passage on a ship bound for Zakunthios as soon as I can find a decent one; I have a house there. After that, to Dolphins, perhaps."

Cimon came here to speak with me. He began by asking the children the name of the Mede. I had already told them about that, and both answered, "Zihrun, sir." He asked whether they were certain, and they repeated, "Zihrun," after which he sent them away, saying we wished to be alone.

When they had gone, he began by thanking me for agreeing to go to Rope as Prince Pausanias had asked. "It would have put me in a very embarrassing position if you hadn't," he told me. "We had men standing by to overpower you if necessary—Themistocles insisted on it—but how would it have looked, when I'd persuaded the prince to free you? And Themistocles' gang might have used the entire business against me; they were my men. If he were to report that we had stolen the slave of a citizen, that slippery trader would back him to the hilt."

I said that if his men had succeeded in overpowering me, I would certainly have been grateful to Hypereides for anything he did to free me.

"I suppose so. There's actually a fairly strong argument for holding that you're a free man already, do you know that?"

"No," I told him. "But I'd like very much to hear it."

"You two were captured by the Rope Makers after the Battle of Clay," he explained. "Nobody disputes that. The Rope Makers handed you over to Tower Hill for some reason, and their people gave you to Hypereides. You were mercenaries, weren't you? You and the black man?"

I said that I thought so.

"All right. But a couple from Hill were captured with you; and you have that little slave from Cowland. It turns out that the man was Pindaros, son of Pagondas, a member of one of their leading families who's been making a name for himself as a poet. He's claiming that at the time you were captured you were not employed by the barbarians directly, but by him on behalf of his city. If that view were accepted, we'd have to send you back to Hill under the terms of the peace Rope forced upon us."

I jumped up, I confess, when he said this, and strode back and forth exulting. I did not feel myself a slave even when we met under the tree, and now that feeling has been vindicated.

"The question was how much pressure this Pindaros could get the oligarchs of Hill to bring on behalf of a mercenary," Cimon continued, "though no matter how much they brought, we couldn't have given in to it. Their city's unpopular here, and it would have severely damaged our relations with Rope. As things stand now, I've chalked up a minor diplomatic triumph. Aristides and Xanthippos acknowledge it. Xanthippos and his son are staying over for dinner, by the way; so are Hegesistratus and his wife."

I said that I was glad of that, for I am by no means eager to be parted from Hegesistratus, and Io and the black man like him, I know.

"Themistocles and his retinue will be there, too, of course. We'll eat in the courtyard; I think we've seen the end of the rains for another year. Then tomorrow you'll be traveling with Themistocles. I wish I could come along with you—I like Rope—but it wouldn't look right. I came here, really, to caution you about Themistocles."

I said that I realized he was a powerful man here.

"He is, and a crafty one. Do you remember how he asked the mantis about the Thracian god?"

I nodded. Though I know I forget, I have not yet forgotten that.

"His mother was a Thracian, just as mine was. He knows the country backward and forward; he even speaks a little Thracian to the ambassadors sent by their kings. If you lie to him about Thrace, or try to hide anything, he'll know it."

That did not seem to be the right moment to explain that I have forgotten Thrace, so I held my peace.

"And I wanted to give you this letter. Do you read our tongue? You speak it well."

I shook my head.

"Then I'll read it to you. It's to one of the judges—his name's Cyklos." Cimon took the letter from his chiton and read: *"To Cyklos son of Anthes, Cimon the son of Miltiades sends his greetings. Latro, who bears this, deserves well of you and of us. Shield him from every harm, good Cyklos, lest we are both disgraced."*

I thanked Cimon for this introduction and asked him to add a request that the judge help me return to my home, which Cimon has promised to do. He will have a servant bring me the letter again, and I intend to roll it up in my old scroll.

That is all of importance that has happened today, though I might add that this farm of Cimon's is indeed a beautiful place. The house is a double square, with many rooms. There are three large barns besides the stables, all limed as white as the house and in excellent repair. The garden I described earlier I think very lovely, but the meadows beyond it are at least equally so. Over their rich grass the foals romp as joyfully, and almost as awkwardly, as Polos himself. When I talked with the laborers taking down the wall, they said that Cimon's father had been a great man; there was no need to tell me—I had seen it already. The stones from the wall are to be carted to Thought and cast into the marsh between Thought and Tieup, where Themistocles and Cimon wish to build a long wall to defend the city. I asked how Cimon intended to keep travelers from stealing his fruit. The laborers said that he will allow them to take it.

28

Mnemosyne

The mistress of memory has given me what is surely the strangest adventure any man ever had. It has not returned to me the time I so much wish to recall; but Simonides thinks that through it I may retain the day just past, and many of those to come.

We dined in the larger court—a great throng. Cimon, our host, reclined at the head of the table, Themistocles to his right and Xanthippos on his left. With Xanthippos were his son, a good-looking youth who wore a cap throughout the meal, and his son's tutor, Damon, a quarrelsome old man. With Themistocles was the white-bearded Simonides of Ceos, whom Hypereides calls the greatest poet alive. Hypereides may say that if he wishes, but I have not forgotten what Cimon said of the poet Pindaros, who declares me a free man; and it seems to me that no poet can be greater than the one who announces to a man that freedom is his right.

Hegesistratus reclined next to Simonides, I should say, and Hypereides next to him. I was next to Damon and thought it bad luck when I heard how he contradicted everyone, but soon noticed that he argued with no one who did not speak. I kept silent and was safe. The black man was at my left—I could not wish better company.

Hegesistratus, as I saw, soon fell into conversation with the poet, so that the two of them seldom spoke to anyone else, though many times they glanced across the table at me. Little Polos helped serve and ate at the foot of the table, but came trotting up so often to tell me something he felt I might wish to know or to ask me some question or other, that everyone was soon laughing at him and he became a general favorite, Pericles swearing that on one occasion he had galloped around the table in both directions and bumped into himself.

A fine lyre was brought after the meal, as Themistocles had predicted. Hegesistratus played and sang beautifully, at which the black man spoke to me with his fingers of another time, when we had sung with many women; he struck his chest and flourished an imagined spear, so that was certainly a great day. Simonides played very well, chanting his own verse. Pericles played and sang nearly as well as Hegesistratus. His tutor would not sing, though Xanthippos says his voice was once very fine. He played the lyre, however, better than anyone else. Cimon sang last and with the best voice; when he had finished, all of us shouted his praises and pounded the table with our cups.

Servants came and took away most of the dishes. As soon as the table was clear, the dancers entered and performed upon it. There was one who brought five daggers she made stand upright on their pommels. She danced among them with great skill, and when we thought she could do no more, leaped from the center of the circle into the air, turning backward so that she landed on her hands with her feet high above her head. Everyone shouted, and she rolled off the table like the wheel of a cart.

Hegesistratus touched my shoulder then, whispering that he wished to speak to me. I left the table and went with him into a small room where Simonides sat. He asked whether I recalled Cimon's saying that it was here, upon his own estate, that the Thunderer had fathered the muses. I assured him I did—it had been said just before the singing began—but I knew neither the Thunderer nor the muses.

"The Thunderer is the father of gods," Simonides told me, "Zeus Maimaktes." I understood then that he is the god my own father called the bright-sky father.

I asked about the muses, but Hegesistratus waved it aside. "The important thing," he said, "is that it was here—at least, according to Cimon, that the god found Mnemosyne, the Lady of Memory. Simonides is a sophist and a famous teacher as well as a poet. Did you know that?"

I shook my head.

"One of the skills he offers to teach his students is that of memory. His own is perhaps the most famous of all time; it is said that he forgets nothing."

"Which is not true," Simonides told me, "although it brings me many students, of whom you may be one. What I've proposed to Hegesistratus is no more than that we visit the spot tonight and offer a sacrifice to Mnemosyne. Afterward I'll give you a lesson in the art of memory, and I can teach you more on the journey to

Rope. It's possible that with training you may come to remember a good many things that you've forgotten. Or if not, you may at least cease to forget so much. Will you do it?"

I agreed gladly—this has surely been a fortunate day—and Hegesistratus spoke to Cimon regarding what we planned and got a kid to sacrifice, a donkey on which he rode (for he has lost one foot), and a servant to guide us. The place was nearby, though it did not seem so because we soon left Cimon's fields and woods behind and climbed a rocky hillside by a winding path. From the cleft rock where the small altar top lay upon three half-embedded stones as though by chance, Cimon's big house had dwindled to a few golden sparks.

The servant had brought wood for a fire and a fire box full of embers. Simonides recited the invocation, and I held the kid while he cut its throat. Afterward we skinned it and burned the heart and liver; when Hegesistratus had poured the libation, we roasted a few pieces of flesh over the fire.

"Now, Latro," said Simonides, "tell me truthfully. Do you really wish to remember?"

"Very much," I told him.

"Then close your eyes. Do you desire to remember so much that you would perform a great deal of work in order to do it?"

"Oh, yes," I said.

"Then you must think of a very large building. We're going to erect this building in your mind. We will not merely look at it as we looked back at Cimon's house while this man kindled the fire, but come to know it as only men who build may. Each stone and ornament must stand distinct in your mind."

I felt the hill tremble beneath me, as if a creature larger than any wild ox had risen to its feet. Opening my eyes, I saw a huge woman, twice the size of any man, emerge from the depths of the narrowing cleft, which seemed too small to have contained her. Her long, fair hair was braided, and the braids, as thick as my arm, were entwined and bound with gem-heavy cords of many colors. Her face was racked with grief, her gaze upon far-off things.

"No, Latro," Simonides said, "I want you to keep your eyes closed."

Feeling certain that the giantess meant us no harm, I shut them again.

"We must have a site for the palace we are going to build," he continued. "You must imagine this place. Think about it." After a long time he asked, "Have you done so?"

I nodded.

"Describe it to me."

"It's where the desert begins," I told him, "at the margins of the last fields."

"Look to the north," he instructed me. "What do you see?"

"Desert. Yellow sand and red stones."

"Is that all? Look to the horizon."

"I see a low line of rock. It seems darker than the stones nearby."

"Very good. You're facing north, are you not? That's the direction in which I told you to face?"

I nodded.

"Since you're facing north, east is toward your right; turn your head and tell me what you see."

"More desert. Rocky hills like this that climb higher and higher. The sun peeping above them."

"Excellent. Since you're facing north, south lies behind you. Look south, over your shoulder, and tell me what you see there."

"Sand," I said. "Yellow sand lying in waves like the sea. A man is leading three camels, but they are very far away."

"Better and better. Look to the west now, along your left arm."

I did as he told me. "Fields of barley and millet, and the mud huts of peasants. Beyond is the river, and beyond the river the setting sun."

"How many huts do you see?"

There were four, and I told him so.

"Do people live in these huts?"

"Yes," I said. "The men who till the fields live in them with their families."

"Good. It may be that we'll meet some of these people by and by. Look now toward the spot where your palace is to stand. What's the first thing you will do when you begin to build your palace?"

"Clear away this sand," I told him, "so that my palace may rest upon rock."

"Good. We'll clear it now. I've sent a thousand men with spades and baskets, and they've taken away all the sand. Do you see the naked rock?"

I nodded.

"It must stretch very far—as far as the hills you saw. If it does not, we'll have to bring back the men with spades. Does it stretch very far?"

"Yes," I said, "very far indeed." I felt the warm wind on my face and wondered to behold such a mighty work.

"Now you must lay your foundation. These blocks may be of rough-hewed stone, but they must fit well. Lay this foundation now. Does it extend across a great distance?"

"Very great."

"Then you're ready to lay the floor. It must be of smooth marble, white, but veined brown and black. Into each slab some glyph has been cut, and no glyph is like any other. The first four have a circle, a triangle, a square, and a cross. Do you see them?"

I nodded again.

"And there are many, many other shapes, too. Some

are like the heads of animals. Some depict the whole creature. Some are like the footprints of men or birds, while some resemble leaves. There are many straight lines, but also many lines that waver or bend. Walk slowly across them—a long way—studying each glyph. Have you seen two that are the same?"

"No," I told him.

"That's well. Now we're going to approach the palace, but in order to approach it we must leave it. Look toward the west. Do you still see the river there? Is it a wide river?"

"Very wide. I can scarcely glimpse the trees on the other bank."

"Good. Walk west to the river, please. All the way to the river, until the water laps your feet. Is the riverbank clothed with grass?"

It was not, but covered with thick black mud.

"Good. Turn now. Face the east; lift your eyes and look back at your palace. It's very high, isn't it?"

It was, with a hundred lofty arches and airy galleries, and course upon course of pillars, each towering colonnade thrusting a hundred carved capitals above the last.

"Walk toward it. Now stop and look to your left and right. What do you see?"

There were fields of grain rippling in the wind.

"And before you?"

An avenue lined with statues.

"What are these statues? Describe them."

Lions with the faces of men.

"No. Only the one nearest you is a lion with a man's face—that's what's deceived you. If you look more closely, you'll see the rest are somewhat different. Describe the statue facing the one you've already described."

A winged lion, with the head and breasts of a woman.

"That's correct. Walk forward a little, just a couple of

steps, and describe the statue beyond the lion with the woman's head."

I did as he directed. It was a winged bull with the head of a bearded man. Facing it across the avenue stood the image of a powerful man with the head of a bull.

"Good."

It seemed to me that I heard the tones of old Simonides in the sobbing wind; for a moment I marveled, knowing as I did that he was not where I was but north of the sea. I decided that he was surely dead now, and it was only his ghost I heard, somehow separated from his tomb and searching for it.

"Look back now toward the lion with a man's face. Study it carefully. It shall be the conservator of your name. The stone is soft. Take out your knife and carve your name, Latro, in the right foreleg of this statue."

I did as the ghost had said, though I feared some guardian might appear to kill me for it. As I fashioned each careful letter, I wondered how I had come to this place from far Hellas. Long ago I had eaten a good dinner there, listened to music, and climbed a hill. After that, everything was wrapped in mist.

"Turn around, so that you face the lion with a woman's head and breasts. . . ."

I did. She rose, spreading mighty pinions that would have outreached the yard of a trireme. "Surely you know *me,* Latro." Her voice was the purring of a huge cat.

I shook my head.

"I am your mother, and your mother's mother. For me and by me you stole the horses of the sun, that they might be returned to him. I am she who asks what walks upon four legs at sunrise, upon two at noon, and upon three at evening. And all who cannot answer me, at evening die."

29

The Palace Walls

Its thousand columns, its thronging statues and pictures, still rise around me—I have never remembered anything so vividly. So I told Simonides when he asked, a few moments since, what I was writing. He asked me several trifling questions, some of which I answered, and some of which I could not. Overall, he appeared pleased.

To tell the truth, I feared I would forget the palace when he interrupted me; that has not occurred, however. Thus I will take a few moments more to write that this is a lovely morning. Hegesistratus and his wife, and Zihrun the Mede, set out a short while ago. The black man and I, with Cimon, Hypereides, Io, and some others, walked a few stades along the road with them to say our goodbyes. Io and the boys lagged behind as we returned to Cimon's house; and I, seeing she wished to speak to me, lingered also and fell into step with her.

"Master," Io said, "there's something I've got to tell you. You've probably written this in your book already, but maybe you ought to write it again. And if what the old man's teaching you will really help you remember, remember it."

I said that I would certainly try, if she thought I should.

"We were all in Thrace—I know you don't remember, but it's true. We were in Kotytto's sacred cave, where there was the big painted statue of her that got burned up later the same day. A lot of Thracians were outside, and you were guarding the way in for us. You told me you heard a dog outside, and Hegesistratus went out, and the Thracians didn't try and stop him. You and me and the black man talked about that, but we didn't really decide anything. I don't know if you asked him about it later."

"Nor do I," I told her.

"I know, but I thought I ought to remind you. Did you hear the dogs last night?"

I had not, and I shook my head.

"I did, and so I thought you should know and write it down, just in case you should meet Hegesistratus again when I'm not with you."

"Aren't you coming to Rope?" I asked. To which she replied that she was, but that the Rope Makers are not nice people.

I could not recall the taller boy's name, but I remembered Polos from the second meal the night before, so I asked whether he would come with Io and me. He nodded, and so did the older boy.

We have a cart drawn by mules to carry our food. My chest is in it, and so are some things of Io's. Simonides drives the cart because he is too old to walk far. Themistocles has said that anyone who becomes tired may ride on the cart as well, but it sways and jolts. Only the Median boy rode this morning; Io and Polos walked with me. Now we have stopped at a farm for the first meal. I should add here that two of Themistocles' slaves are with us—their names are Diallos and Tillon. I am wearing my sword, though my helmet and the other things are in the cart. The road will be safe enough, Themistocles says, until we get to Bearland.

I have just read what I wrote this morning; I should finish it, though I do not believe I could ever forget the winged lion-woman.

When she asked me her question, I remembered Hegesistratus and how he had ridden the donkey—but at other times walks with a crutch. So I said, "It is a traveler, Gaea. When he begins his journey he rides a horse, but the horse dies, or is stolen, or must be sold for food. After that, the traveler has to walk for himself, and by evening he is footsore and limps along with a staff."

She smiled as she leaped from her pedestal to stand beside me. "That's a good reply," she said, "even though you lack the advantage of lameness. I've always thought it was his lameness that gave Swollenfoot his clue." Though she stood on four legs and I upon two, she was so huge that she still looked down into my face, as she had from the pedestal.

I asked whether my answer was a correct one.

Gaea only adjured me to follow her, in order that she might show me the palace. "Poor Mnemosyne's one of my daughters," she said. "She doesn't get a lot of sacrifices."

I asked who Swollenfoot had been.

"A man who was too good. His father maimed his feet when Swollenfoot was a baby; he was always a little lame thereafter. Yet he was a wonderful fighter, like you. Shall I tell you his answer?"

"Please."

"He said it was a mortal, crawling upon hands and knees in the morning of life, soon walking erect, then at last—like your traveler—with a stick. If you ever get to Hill, they'll tell you that in my despair at his response I threw myself from the wall of their fortress and perished on the stones below. You'll observe that I'm winged." She chuckled.

I ventured that the mere solving of a riddle, and a rather easy one, hardly constituted a basis for suicide. All this time we were walking side by side down the avenue of statues, which were of a thousand different kinds, and approaching the doors of the palace. These, as we neared them, loomed higher and higher.

"The truth is that I returned to my element. Doesn't it trouble you to find earth winged? I'm not often considered a deity of the air, like the Lady of Thought."

"No," I said. "The sophists believe that the earth is a sphere." I paused in the hope that she would confirm or deny it, but she did neither. "A sphere is the only perfect shape, or so I've been told, no doubt by Hegesistratus or Simonides. In other lands, people believe that the earth is flat and say that it floats upon an endless sea, or that it's supported on the back of a great turtle, who swims in such a sea."

"Continue," she ordered me.

"I hesitate to speculate in the hearing of one who knows the truth."

Gaea looked at me, and though her face was the face of a woman, her eyes were the eyes of a lioness. "She is eager to hear your speculations."

"As you wish. It is soon seen that such explanations fail to resolve the question. If I slap water with my hand, it does not remain in the air but quickly falls to earth. Thus though the sea exists, it too must be supported in some way. Besides, a man who swims in the sea finds that the earth lies below it. It is true that he comes at last to such a depth that he cannot reach earth; but if another comes, a better diver, this other diver reports earth still. Plainly, then, the sea is held like water in a bowl, deepest at the center, but hardly endless at the center. And in fact a bowl that was endless at any point could never be filled."

"Continue," she said again.

"If I continue, Gaea, will you tell me the significance of your riddle?"

"No, you shall tell me. But continue."

"One who observes the sun at evening sees that it moves no more slowly at the horizon than it did when crossing the sky at noon. Similarly, it rises in full career. Where, then, does it halt? Plainly it does not halt, but circles and recircles the earth without cease, as do the moon and the stars, of which the same things might be said. If the sea proposed by some existed, the sun, the moon, and the stars would plunge into it and their lights would be extinguished; but that doesn't occur. All these things show that the proposed sea, upon which the earth is said to float, doesn't exist. As for the sea on which we sail, it's supported by the earth, and not the contrary.

"I said that water falls to earth. What doesn't? Birds, clearly; otherwise they would be killed. If you startle a bird from a bush, it may perch upon another—but it may not. And anyone may see for himself that eagles and vultures need not alight except to eat and drink, for they remain upon the wing without effort. What supports the earth? What supports these birds? The earth flies; Gaea is winged."

"Well reasoned," she said. She remained silent after that until we reached the stair that led to the entrance arch of the palace; then she asked, "Why do you think I said I devoured all who could not answer my question?"

I ventured to say that the earth devoured all men at last.

"Not those who understand my question, Latro. Isn't your traveler upon the journey of life? Say yes, or I'll devour you at the end of your days."

"Yes," I said as we mounted the stair.

"Explain."

"In the morning of life," I said, "a young man goes forth as though mounted, because he is carried upon the shoulders of his parents. By midday their support has vanished, and he must walk for himself. In the evening of life, he can hold up his head only because he is supported by the memory of what once he was."

As I spoke the final word, Gaea's vast wings roared behind me and I felt a wind as violent as a storm at sea;

by the time I turned, she was already very far above me. Higher she rose, and higher still as I watched open-mouthed, until she was little more than a dark speck against the overarching azure dome, and I felt certain she would soon disappear into the cloudless sky. But at last she settled upon a cornice of the topmost battlement, where she remained motionless and appeared to have become again a mere figure carved from the reddish stone, as she had been when I had first seen her.

Alone and wondering I entered that great palace. Its rooms were spacious indeed, but filled with little more than light and air. While I wandered from one to another, seeing here, perhaps, a single red-glazed urn displaying the capering black figures of satyrs, and there an iridescent enameled beetle rolling a great golden sun toward some corner of an empty chamber, I sought the meaning of Gaea's riddle. Why had she asked it of Swollenfoot? And why of me? Why had she offered to show me this palace of memory, yet deserted me as I was about to enter?

When I had walked through many empty rooms, I came upon a statue of a young woman dancing naked among daggers, her marble limbs so delicately poised that I hesitated to touch her for fear she might fall. At length I did, and she fell, shattering upon the many-figured floor.

I looked up from the ruin of this statue and found that I was staring into the wrinkled face of Simonides. His hand was on my shoulder. He asked if I was well.

I apologized for having nodded, and added, "That was a very strange dream!" The truth was that the desert palace seemed far more real to me than the windy night or the rocky hilltop where we sat about our fire. Hegesistratus and Simonides urged me to recount my dream, which I did.

That is everything I have to write about it, except that this morning a slender young woman Io had not named for me took me aside and told me she had dreamed of me the night before. I was flattered (as no doubt she intended I should be) and asked to hear her dream.

"I was dancing in an empty hall," she said, "watched by no one but you. At the end of my dance, when I stood on one hand surrounded by my daggers, you pushed me, and I fell on one and died." I gave her my word I would never do such a thing. Her name is Anysia.

Today, as we walked, I told Io about my dream—although not about the dancer. Io was excited, most of all (I think) because I still remembered so clearly all that I had seen and said. She asked what Hegesistratus had said about it, but the fact is that he had said next to nothing.

I have not yet told this to Io, and perhaps I will not; but while writing of my dream, I have thought of yet another answer to Gaea's riddle, and perhaps this one is more nearly true (for me, at least) than any of the rest. It is that a young man such as I am undertakes the journey of life as if on horseback, ever hurrying forward. As he grows older he comes to realize that it is but a pilgrimage to the grave and walks more slowly, looking about him. When he is old, he may take up his stylus and begin to write of what he has seen; if so, unlike other men, he is not devoured by the earth in which his body lies when life's journey is done, for though dead he still speaks to the living, just as it seemed the shade of Simonides still spoke to me outside that vast building in the desert.

When he talked with me this morning before Cimon's house, he asked first about the statues. I described that of Gaea to him, but when he asked what it signified, I could not say. He said that by that image, which at any moment might take wing, I was to know that my thoughts would be lost if I failed to give each into the guardianship of some image within or without my memory palace.

* * *

We have stopped here for the second meal, and here we will pass the night. I have taken the opportunity to read all that I wrote during the past three days. Of Cimon's banquet, and our offering to Mnemosyne after it, I recall nothing; yet the memory of the palace remains before my mind's eye, more vivid even than that of the house in which I was born. I see the man-faced lion with *Latro* cut in its foreleg, and the now-empty pedestal where once Gaea crouched, the mighty doorway, the strange, bare rooms, and all the rest. It would be remarkable indeed if a man could remember only his dreams, but the truth is that I can remember no other dream than that.

30

Tower Hill

Adeimantus' city is the finest in all Hellas, according to Io. Simonides confirmed it as we sat over wine with Adeimantus and his sons. Themistocles laughed and told Adeimantus that when Simonides was staying at his house in Thought, he liked nothing better than to rail against the citizens of Tower Hill, seeing only greed in the fine marble, silver, and gold everybody else admires. "And yet," finished Themistocles, "this man who can't bear to see others living in a beautiful city has had his own ugly old face painted by Polygnotos."

Simonides laughed as loudly as anyone. "I've done no more than follow the course of wisdom I profess to teach. All of you will concede, I think, that when other things stand equal, the best-looking man will get the most support from his fellows and the most votes in the Assembly."

Everyone nodded.

"Well, then," Simonides continued, "it must follow that the finest city will get the most support from the rest as well—if other things stand equal. And since Tower Hill's a rival of my friend Themistocles' city, and I can't malign its wide streets and imposing buildings, I criticize the morals of its citizens. That I can do with perfect justice even though I know so little about them—the morals of citizens everywhere being atrocious. As for this face of mine, I can't do a thing about it. But in time to come, I'll be judged not by my face but by my picture, which is perfectly beautiful. Fifty years from now everybody will say I was the leading figure of the age."

Adeimantus commanded the ships of Tower Hill at the Battle of Peace. It was he who opposed the ships from Riverland, which everyone says were the best the Great King had. The walls of his house are adorned with captured shields and weapons, and the figureheads of ships he destroyed. The wrecks washed ashore at a place called Crommyon; he had his men saw off the figureheads there. He presented one to every captain who served under him, he said, and kept the rest for himself.

Because these weapons and figureheads looked familiar to me, I asked Io whether we have ever been to Riverland; she says we have not. Adeimantus said he had never visited that country either, but that people are mistaken to envy the Great King his possession of it, though it is the oldest and most revered in the world. "The men who fought so hard for a foreign king will fight against him harder still," he told us. "The whole nation rose against the Medes after Fennel Field, you remember. And it will rise again."

If the hearts of the men of Riverland are as dark and proud as their crooked weapons and painted shields lead me to believe, I feel sure Adeimantus speaks no more than the truth. The black man confirms this, if I understand his gestures, saying that men like himself—his own nation, in fact—held sway over Riverland for a long while, but eventually its populace drove them back to their own country. He says also that he has been there, but he and I did not know each other then; it is a fine place.

There will be a play tonight. All of us, even Io, are to have seats.

A man with one hand has come to speak with Themistocles.

Io came to warn me of this man—thus I wrote quickly that he had come, then stopped to hear her. His name is Pasicrates. He fought me in the Troad, Io says, and it was I who cut off his hand. I tried to explain to her that war is war. A soldier rarely hates the men he fights, and when the fighting is over, he is happy to sit down and hear how things were on the other side.

Just then the man himself joined us, followed by Simonides and little Polos. I doubt that there is any need to describe him, since I will surely know him by his missing hand, which it seems I cut off somewhat above the wrist. But he is strikingly handsome in the fashion of Hellenes, with darting, intelligent eyes. He is smaller than I by half a head, perhaps; but if he is as quick and strong as he appears, he must have been a very dangerous opponent.

"Good evening, Latro," he said. I had stood when they came into the room, and he embraced me as I might have the black man. "You don't remember me, I know, but we're old friends as well as old foes."

I said I hoped that he, as well as I, could forget any past enmity.

He laughed and held up the stump of his left forearm. "You made it hard for me to forget, but you're going to be one of us, and my life in battle may depend upon your comradeship. So I'd better forgive you, and I do."

I wanted then to hear how we had fought, but I did not ask for fear it would reawaken past resentments.

"You're coming to Rope? You mean to accept Pausanias' offer?"

I know we are on our way to Rope, thus I said, "I'll decide after we get there."

"He wants you for the games, did they tell you about that?" Pasicrates left for a moment and returned carrying stools for Simonides and himself; when the old man was settled, Pasicrates sat down beside him.

Io had shaken her head when he mentioned games, so I said, "I know nothing of games. Does this mean I'm going to have to fight someone?"

"Exactly. Boxing, wrestling, and the pankration—they're the things I told him you'd be good at. You might do for some local meet in the footraces, but you couldn't possibly win at Dolphins, no matter what Pausanias thinks."

"Dolphins?" Io asked. "Is that where we're going?"

Pasicrates nodded. "If your master will agree to do as the regent wants."

"The big games for the Destroyer," Io told me. "They have them every four years. They're always two years after the ones at Olympia, and girls can watch as long as they're not married. Isn't that right, Simonides?"

The old sophist smiled and nodded. "It would be a great honor for you, Latro. One that you might never forget."

"I've never been to Dolphins," Io said. She added firmly, "But I'd really like to go."

"Then we will," I promised her.

Pasicrates and Simonides left us soon after that to prepare themselves to go to the theater. Pasicrates had brought neither clothing nor sandals, and Simonides was going to lend him some, though he warned him that they would not be up to the standards of Tower Hill.

"He seems to be a fine man," I told Io when they had gone, "but I think he hates me."

"He does," Io said. "We'll have to be really careful around him. You, too, Polos. He's the kind who hits boys."

Polos asked, "Did you cut off his hand with your sword?"

I shook my head. "How did it happen, Io?"

"I wasn't there," she told us. "But Pasicrates tried to beat you—I mean with a whip, because you were supposed to be the regent's slave. You wounded one of his real slaves with a javelin, and then you must have fought him, because you split his shield with Falcata, and it went right down through his arm. He yelled something terrible—that was the first I knew anything about it. There were a hundred Rope Makers besides the slaves, and all of them came, but you got away. I didn't see you again after that till I was walking close to the wall with Drakaina—you ran up to us, and all of us got taken into the city, which was what we wanted anyhow."

The Median boy had entered silently as she spoke, and I told him there was no reason he and Polos should not use the stools Pasicrates had brought.

Polos rolled his eyes and shied; Io told him, "It's really there, whatever it is. If Latro touches it, then we'll see it, too."

"I see him a little already," Polos said, "but I don't want to see him any more than I do right now."

I asked Io what they were talking about, but the Median boy spoke—impolitely, I would say—while she did, so that I did not hear her. "There are so many people living in this house. Have you met the others?"

I said I had been introduced to our host and his sons, and seen some of his servants.

"Soldiers from Kemet, and they're very angry." The Median boy turned on his heel and left.

Polos relaxed and took a stool. "He's like Latro—only he can't remember he's dead. I think that his thoughts must always stumble there."

I asked where Kemet lay, but neither knew. I must remember to ask Simonides. I have cut it across the chest of the hawk-headed man.

Polos asked, "Do you *have* to be very strong to fight with a sword?"

I told him it was certainly better to be strong, but better still to be quick.

"If the strongest man's the quickest, too, does he always win?"

Io said, "Or woman, Polos. Remember the Amazons? I've got a sword, too, and I've killed my man."

"No," I said. "Not always."

"Who does? And how could Io kill a man? She's said that before."

I considered the matter, knowing what I needed to say but unsure of how to make my point. The fluting notes of a syrinx floated through the window, and I looked out; three small boys were coming down the street, one tootling the pipes while all three danced. Some dignified-looking men had stopped to laugh and cheer them.

"Look," I told Polos and Io. "Do you see those boys?"

Io said, "They're playing Pan-and-satyrs. We used to do it back in Hill."

"I want you to study them. Pretend that they're men, not boys, and that they're fighting with swords instead of dancing. Can you do that?"

Both nodded.

"See how they move. A sword fight is a kind of dance, even if the fight's on horseback. Look at them carefully—which is going to win?"

Io said, "The one with the pipes," and Polos nodded.

"Why?" I asked them.

Polos said, "Because he dances the best."

"That's right. Why does he dance better than the others?"

They only stared at me, so I sent them off to find three sticks, each a trifle shorter than my arm.

When they returned, I showed them how to hold their sticks like swords instead of axes, with the thumb at the top of the grip. "An ax is a good weapon, but a sword is a better weapon. If you hold your sword like an ax, you'll chop with it like an ax. A sword slashes and thrusts—you must be a butcher boning a carcass, not a woodchopper cutting down a tree. Don't either of you understand yet why the boy with the pipes danced best?"

"I do!" Polos said. "Because he had the pipes."

Io nodded. "He knew in advance what he was going to play, but the others couldn't know till they heard the notes."

I told them, "That's the one who always wins a sword fight. Now each of us ought to have something for the left hand. It's always very unwise to fight without something in your left hand. A shield's best; but if you don't have one, use something else, a knife or even another sword."

Io got her cloak and wound it about her left arm. "You did this sometimes in Thrace, master. A couple of times it got cut, and I had to sew it up for you, but the blade never went through to your arm."

"If you were to lay your arm on the windowsill, any sword would cut through the cloth and bite bone," I told her. "Very few will do that in a battle, however, though possibly Falcata might. It's one good reason for getting the best sword you can and always keeping it sharp. You should let a little more cloth hang down to flutter before your opponent's eyes."

Polos said, "I don't have a cloak. Should I buy one here?"

"Yes, buy one tomorrow—though not for that reason. But you must fight now, not later. What are you going to do?"

He picked up his stool and said, "I'll pretend this is my shield."

I told him, "You don't have to pretend. A stool makes an excellent shield."

Io said, "You used to fight the Thracians with a javelin in your other hand, master. I think they thought you were going to throw it, but you never did."

I nodded. "Because if I had, I would have had nothing for my left hand except my cloak. But you can never be sure such a thing will not be thrown—your opponent may believe it will end the fight, or see something else he can use. If Polos were to throw his stool, for example, he might snatch up this other one.

"But now that you have your swords and shields, you must forget about them for a moment. Do you remember that I said a sword fight was a sort of dance?"

They nodded.

"I said it because you must move your feet in the right way without thinking about them. If one of you were going to teach me a dance I didn't know, I'd have to think about moving my feet—but I wouldn't be a good dancer until I didn't."

Polos performed a little dance to test himself.

I told them, "An untrained sword fighter will nearly always favor one foot. Usually it's the left, because the left hand's got the shield. He'll step forward with that foot and drag his right foot behind it. For people like you two, who're liable to be a lot smaller than those you fight, that's a great advantage. You take a step back and cut at his leg. You don't have to wait to see it—it'll be there. Just make a quick cut that brings your point well in under the edge of his shield."

I had them practice this, tapping my calf with their sticks while I used the other stool as my shield.

"Now that you know how that's done, you know also that you mustn't advance your left leg like that," I told them.

Io added, "And why Acetes' shieldmen wore greaves."

"That's right," I said, though I do not remember who

Acetes is. "And they didn't wear just one, did they? Didn't each man wear two?"

Io and Polos nodded.

"That's because a good fighter uses both his legs, and uses them equally. The next thing you have to learn is never to move one leg only. Whenever you move one leg, you must also move the other; and you mustn't favor the left leg over the right—or the right over the left."

So we passed the time until Simonides came to lecture the children about proper behavior in the theater.

31

From the Tomb

We came up the hillside along a wide white street. Now the men from Riverland have gone, and so has the Median boy. The sky is light enough already for me to write. Soon we will leave, too; Themistocles says our road runs west to Stymphalos, then south through Bearland.

Last night we went to see a play. I do not know whether I have been to a theater before—perhaps to one somewhat different from this. It seemed strange to me, but not entirely so.

Our seats were at the bend (the best place) and well down in front. The long benches are curved like a horse's hoofprint. The acting floor is in the center with the actors' tent behind it. Pasicrates sat next to me until the black man changed his seat to sit between us—I think because Io asked it.

The jokes concerned the doings of the city, yet many amused us just the same. The actors wore masks, contriving to change the expressions of these wooden faces by varying the angles at which they poised their heads and covering certain parts of the masks with their hands, which I thought very fine. These masks are carved in such a way as to make this possible, of course.

It was pleasant to sit in comfort on a warm evening and be thus entertained; but from time to time my gaze left the actors and wandered away to the stars, seeing there the Ram, the Hunter and his Dogs, the Seven Maids toward whom so many temples look, and many other things. The cold moon-virgin appeared to warn me it was to her land we were bound; and as she spoke, Io whispered in my ear, "When we get back I'll have to tell you the story of the White Isle, master. I feel like I've just seen it." Then I could not help wondering what the watching gods thought of us, with our clever masks and our jokes. What we think of crickets, perhaps, whose singing we hear with pleasure, though some of us smash them with our heels when they venture into sight.

After the play, the gaudy litters that had carried them to the theater awaited Adeimantus and his sons, Themistocles, and Simonides. The rest of us trooped after them, but the black man soon drew me aside. There are many wineshops here where one may drink and crack nuts, and trade banter with attractive women if one likes. The rule, as several women told us, is that they may enter only the ones that permit them, and that they must pay the owner (often once such a woman as themselves) one spit each time they leave with a man. Most asked for six, explaining that they could keep only three, having to pay one to the proprietor (as I said), one to the city, and one to the goddess of this place. A skin of unmixed wine was very dear, so the black man and I drank mixed wine by the cup—this so weak in some of the shops that he pretended to drown and once told me with his fingers that he had seen a trireme in the krater.

In the third or fourth, we came upon a slender, dark-haired girl from Babylon who could speak the black man's tongue as well as the one I use among these people. The black man wished to go with her—and for me to come, too, for it is by no means safe to visit such places alone. Here was a difficulty: I liked neither the Babylonian nor the friend to whom she introduced me, while the Babylonian would have to pay double if both of us left with her. It would have been better if I had given her an additional spit, but we soon arranged that they would linger in the street; and I, soon after they had gone, would meet them there.

This settled, they left. I stretched, yawned, and gossiped a few moments longer with the Babylonian's friend, a skinny girl who said she was from Ithaca, drained the last cup and wiped my mouth, and wandered out.

I had drunk enough to heat my face and ears; I still recall how pleasant the night breeze was, and how I wondered why we had chosen to linger so long in the close, smelly wineshop. When I began to walk, I discovered that I was not as steady on my feet as I had expected to be, although I flattered myself that no one else would have observed it.

It appeared that the black man and the Babylonian had gone on without me; but I soon caught sight of them, deep in talk, a few doors off. I waved, and they made their way arm in arm down the street. I hurried after them, then realized that the black man would not relish my company and maintained a distance great enough to allow them some privacy. After a time, they left the narrow, dirty street for another narrower and dirtier still. I recall turning the corner to follow them.

It seemed then that a great wave overwhelmed the city, and I was tossed with many another among rushing waters. I could not breathe this dark water, and indeed I could scarcely breathe the air of the strand on which it left me at last; but it seemed I had no need to. I got to my feet, my body hardly heavier than a child's, and stared about with unbelieving eyes at the immense cavern in which I stood.

Its shadowed ceiling was as remote as the highest mountain peak. Through it here and there streamed vagrant silver light, much as one sometimes sees the sun thrust golden fingers through the chinks of a stormy sky; it did little more than emphasize the general gloom.

If the cavern was lofty, its height was as nothing to its breadth. In desolate plains, barren hills, and sullen meres, it stretched on, mile upon mile, in every direction, until at last all was lost in darkness. During the whole time I spent there, I never so much as glimpsed a bird, or a single bat, or indeed a beast of any kind, though once or twice I crossed their watery tracks, dim prints deeply impressed in the soft clay. Here and there, however, I saw wandering human figures, bent, naked, and alone.

I called to some. When none responded, I set out after the nearest, an elderly man whose painful, shuffling gait gave clear evidence that I would quickly overtake him. "Who are you, wise one?" I inquired, feeling it would be best to make some friendly overture before asking where this cavern was and how I could get out of it.

"I am myself," he grumbled, "just as you are yourself. Go. Leave me in peace."

"But what's your name?" I insisted.

He shook his head and shuffled forward. He would not meet my eye.

"I am . . ." I found that I could not complete the thought. Frantically, I searched my memory. "I'm called the mercenary," I said at last. "There's a statue—a lion with a man's face—that knows my name."

For the first time, he glanced at me. "Give me your hand." He clasped it between his own, which were as cold as snow. "You are not wholly gone," he told me.

I said at once that I would leave if my presence disturbed him.

"No, stay. When I lived, I was called Gortys. That is how we speak here, though it was not truly I that lived. The part of me which lived is now dead, and what you see is the part that never lived, hence cannot die."

I tried to draw my hand away; his freezing grasp had grown painful. "The child called me master," I said, "the one-handed man Latro, as I told you."

"I will come with you." He took my arm.

Some distance from us was a man wrestling a boulder almost as large as himself. I saw him squat, get his fingers under it, and lift it nearly upright before it escaped his grasp and fell. Having nothing better to say, I asked who he was and what he was trying to do.

"He is a king," the old man told me. "Do you see that hill over there?"

I nodded.

"Sisyphus must roll his stone to the summit and leave it there. While it remains in place, he will be released from his torment."

I watched him spit on his hands, wipe them on his thighs, and lift the stone again. "Who'll release him?"

"The god who condemned him."

I led the old man over to him, and it was a long and weary distance indeed, for the floor of that vast cavern was streaked with dark gorges too broad to leap that could not be seen until they gaped at our feet; most held sunken streams and were lined with slimy stones.

When at last we reached the toiling king, it seemed that he had advanced his boulder by no more than three strides. He was as naked as the old man whose icy fingers still clasped my arm, though his body was smeared with the ocher mud of the place; and his cunning face was beaded with sweat and sagging with fatigue.

"Are you permitted to accept help?"

He shook his head impatiently and bent again to his stone. "What would you want for your help?"

"Nothing," I told him, "but perhaps two of us could do it."

My hands were already on the boulder as I spoke. Together we rolled it forward, though it twisted in our grasp as though its center leaped within it. Dirty and wet already, my chiton tore as I heaved away; I tore it off and tossed it aside. In that moment the stone, which we had then rolled nearly halfway up the hill, slid from the king's grip.

I caught it, though I cannot tell how; and in an agony of frustration lifted it clear of the mud. Every joint in my body creaked, and it seemed that every bone was about to snap, but I staggered to the hilltop with it and slammed it down, embedding it in the soft soil around the spring.

For a moment it trembled there, like an egg about to hatch; then it split. The report was deafening, the rush of light from it blinding. I reeled and fell.

As I lay on my side in the half-frozen mud, I saw the faces of the black man and the Babylonian girl within the stone—faces wreathed in flames. The black man shouted something I could not understand and extended his hand to me. I helped the king rise, and together we clambered up and into the narrow, fetid alley I recalled.

The Babylonian had ten thousand questions, none clear to me thanks to my bewilderment and her accent. She and the black man held blazing torches. I took hers from her and dropped it into the hole from which the king and I had clambered.

For a moment I glimpsed age-blackened masonry, bones, a green sword, and armor rotten with verdigris; but soil from the alley was already sliding into the hole. I felt the ground give way beneath my feet and stepped hurriedly back. A crack shot up the wall above the hole. The Babylonian screamed, and the king and the black man pulled me away. With a roar like the storm's, the entire wall fell. We fled, coughing and wiping our eyes to free them from its choking dust.

* * *

The black man and the Babylonian—her name is Bittusilma—came to tell me they are married. When I raised my eyebrows, she explained that she is going with the black man, who wants to return to his home in Nysa. She will leave him when they reach Babylon, or come near it.

The black man spoke to her then, and she said, "He thought the chief man in your party wouldn't let me go with you, but he says he won't refuse now. He says you're his friend. You have to insist that both of us be allowed to come."

I promised to do my best.

"I was married to a captain," she told me. "He was killed here last year—then I couldn't get away. Hepta Leones* wishes me to tell you I'm his third wife."

Proudly the black man held up three fingers.

I questioned her about the pit in the alley. She said she and the black man had lain together for a long time; that was when they agreed to marry. They thought I was waiting outside. When they found me gone, they made torches with which to search the alley. I asked what had happened to me, wishing to hear how she would explain all she had seen. She said that when the king and I had entered the alley, the roof of a vault, "one forgotten perhaps for many years," had given way.

I should say here, too, that I spoke much with the king while we walked back to this house. It was he, he said, who had built the first tower upon the hill, thus founding this city, which he calls Ephyra. He described it.

He asked whether I knew of Asopus the river god; and I, not wishing to appear ignorant, told him I did. This river god, the king said, had ever been his friend. He is

---

*Usually translated, but here in the original Greek, perhaps to indicate Bittusilma's careful pronunciation.—GW

not a great god like the Twelve upon the mountain, and the king himself is—or so he says—a son of the storm king by a nymph whose father is Asopus; thus he and the god are related, and differ less in the respect due them than gods and mortals commonly do.

When the river god's daughter Aegina had been stolen, the king had witnessed it. He told the river god where the girl had been taken, and asked in return for a spring at the foot of his tower so that he and his men might never lack water during a lengthy siege—thus he was punished as he was. He told me that he had always hoped the river god would remember him and find some way to help him. He thought I was the aid the river god had sent. He asked what reward had been promised me, and I was forced to tell him that if I had been sent by the god—or anyone—I was not aware of it.

"I never gave anything away while I was among you," he said sadly, "and anyone who wished my help could have it—at a price. You have seen the riches I gathered by it."

Bittusilma, the Babylonian, happened to overhear this and looked around. The king saluted her, whispering to me, "I know my own breed. If she plays you false, I'll ask them for leave to make her suffer for it." I do not know to whom he referred.

That was when we came to the house and found the soldiers from Riverland terrorizing everyone.

32

For the Second Meal

We have halted here near the lake. Though we did not leave the city early, we put in a hard morning—even the black man rode on the cart before it was done—and ate the first meal long after the usual time. We did not go far after that, and Themistocles has chosen to stop here, where a cool wind blows from the water and there are good facilities for travelers. As we walked, Io talked of the hauntings last night, which seem to have disturbed everyone. I have read about the theater and how I assisted the king, but it seemed I did not write much about them; thus I have been anxious to speak with Pasicrates or Simonides, and when we sat to eat the second meal, I contrived to sit between them. Had Simonides or Themistocles told me to take a lower place, I would have, of course; but if Pasicrates had done it, we would have had words. No one did.

"This is the lake," Simonides remarked, "at which Heracles killed so many monstrous birds."

This interested the black man, who asked (through his wife) whether these were the same birds that visit his own country and war against the small men of the south.

Before Simonides could reply, Pasicrates announced proudly that this Heracles was an ancestor of his. It seems that he is related on his mother's side to the Agid royal family. "But I can recount these family matters for you anytime," he said to the black man's wife. "Ask your husband whether he has seen the creatures himself."

The black man nodded and spoke to his wife, who translated. "He has seen them flying over, and once he saw one some children killed."

Everyone except Pasicrates and the black man laughed loudly at that. Pasicrates was very angry, I think. Through his wife, the black man said seriously, "Sometimes these birds attack our children. We think it's because they think our children are the small men of the south—that's the reason every boy in my land carries his own little spear. The long beaks of the birds are like spears themselves, and their necks are very long, too. They strike like snakes, and because they can fly, they're formidable enemies, though they won't often stay to fight a warrior. They fly very high—far beyond the reach of our arrows. If this man Heracles killed many, he was our friend."

Everyone wanted to talk of something else then, I think, so I asked Pasicrates whether he had been disturbed by the ghosts, as Io had.

He nodded. "I was awakened by someone's screaming—one of Adeimantus' daughters, I think. I sprang from my bed and found myself face-to-face with a tall man who had a barbed spear and a big shield. I remember thinking—even then—that it was exactly like the one on the wall; it had the same horizontal stripe. The man thrust at me. . . ."

Pasicrates fell silent, staring at the stump of his missing hand. Possibly I was mistaken, but it seemed to me that he went pale. At last he muttered, "It isn't much of a ghost story, I'm afraid, but then I didn't make it up. He jabbed at me with his spear, as I was about to say. Then spear and shield dropped to the floor. When I got a light for my lamp, I saw they were the ones that had been hanging on the wall of my room. I won't tell anyone about this back in Rope. They'd laugh at it, just as all of you laughed at the slaughter of the Stymphalian birds, which has occupied so many great poets and artists. But there may be more to it than appears—again, like the birds."

From the foot of our table Io said, "It *was* one of Adeimantus' daughters. It was Callia, and Polos saw them, too. What I don't understand is why they went away all at once."

The black man's wife said, "The man who'd fallen into the tomb with your master took them away. He was what people here call a magus. He asked your master if he wanted them exorcised, and when he said yes, he summoned them and left with them."

Pasicrates asked whether she had been able to see them.

She shook her head. "But as soon as he spoke, the house was quiet."

Io said, "Once when we were in a little place near Thought, there was a farmhouse that was terribly haunted, just all of a sudden. You don't remember wrestling Basias, master, but that was when it happened. The innkeeper told us about it."

Themistocles said, "Adeimantus felt that we brought them, though he was too polite to say so. Tell us about this magus, Latro. Was he actually from Parsa?"

I do not recall the man himself, but I remember what I read of him here; so I said that I had thought him a Hellene.

"That certainly seems more likely. How did you meet him?"

I explained that he had been trying to move a stone, and I had assisted him. "We were both very dirty by the time the job was done," I said, "so I offered to let him wash up at the house where we slept last night. I didn't think anyone would object. Was that Adeimantus'?"

Themistocles nodded.

Simonides told him, "Latro still has great difficulty in remembering anything for more than a day or so, although he's improving. There were earth tremors all over Tower Hill last night, it seems. I didn't feel them myself."

Io said, "That's what probably made the hole that swallowed my master and this magus. Isn't that right, Bittusilma?" To Themistocles she added, "Bittusilma saw it."

The black man's wife said, "It was a tomb. The people of that foolish town had forgotten where it was and built over it."

Simonides shook his head sadly. "A great stone rolled into the sacred spring at the summit of the Acrocorinth and split. It's clearly an omen."

Io sighed. "I wish Hegesistratus were here."

Pasicrates darted a glance at her and said, "Then read it for us, sophist."

Themistocles cleared his throat. "Simonides has favored me with his interpretation already. We'll reserve it, at least for the present, I think."

Pasicrates said, "In that case, O noble Themistocles, I'll favor you with mine. Tower Hill links Hellas—your mainland to the north with our own Redface Island to the south. The spring is the heart of Tower Hill. Its damming by the stone indicates that Tower Hill will be vanquished. The splitting of the stone, which permitted the spring to flow freely once again, indicates that Hellas itself shall be split in two. When that takes place, Tower Hill will flourish as before."

I did not wholly understand this, but I saw that Simonides and Themistocles appeared uncomfortable; so I asked Pasicrates who he believed would vanquish Tower Hill.

"Certainly not Rope—it's our principal ally. If I thought your little slave knew anything about the politics of her city, I'd ask her whether Hill could be the one; but

I've got to admit it doesn't seem likely. It's an inland agricultural center like Rope. Hill wouldn't have much reason to attack a seaport so far away."

Io asked Simonides, "Would it be the Earth Shaker who sent Tower Hill this omen?"

He shrugged. "From a strictly rational point of view, it's alterations in the courses of underground streams that cause the earth to tremble. As far as we know, any god might make use of those tremors to send an omen—certainly the Earth Shaker might. Or any of the chthonic deities."

Io nodded, half to herself. "What about the ghosts?"

Simonides told her, "It's well established that disturbing tombs frequently produces such manifestations; and many tombs must have been disturbed last night"—he nodded toward the black man's wife—"as we have heard."

Pasicrates said, "When I led the contingent sent by my city to the siege of Sestos, I heard that the barbarians had ravaged many tombs, taking not only the offerings left before them, but the grave goods, too. I did not hear that any of them had been punished for it."

"What about the loss of Sestos?" Themistocles asked dryly.

"If you like," Pasicrates conceded. "Certainly it was a very strong city, and it fell very quickly. I'm told that we had not yet boarded the ship that took us home when we received word that the city had surrendered."

Io asked, "What do you mean, you heard?" I could see she was afraid of Pasicrates, yet she spoke up bravely. "You were there. I was there, too, and I remember you."

"I was ill," he told her. "My wound had brought a fever."

Themistocles said, "It was not you, then, who ordered the Rope Makers home. Or was it?"

Pasicrates shook his head.

Polos asked, "You can't hold a shield anymore, can you?"

Pasicrates smiled at him and looked as though he wished to tousle his hair. "I can still use my shield—it was made for me by one of our finest armorers and has straps with buckles. I'll show it to you when we get to Rope."

That, I think, is all that was said at the table that I may need to know tomorrow. After the meal, Io said she was going to walk beside the lake and asked me to come with her. The shore is marshy in spots, and there are lofty reeds, though one sees also where these reeds have been harvested for thatch; there are many frogs. I asked Io whether she was afraid of the birds.

"No, master," she said. "Or maybe yes, a little bit." She had brought her sword.

"They're not here," I told her, "or at least not many, or there wouldn't be so many frogs. Water birds with long, sharp bills always like frogs."

Io nodded and sat down on a fallen tree. "Aren't your feet sore, master? We went a long way today, and you never once rode in the cart."

I admitted they were, but said that if she wanted to walk farther I would go with her.

"The truth is I don't want to walk at all, master. I only wanted to get you away so nobody could hear. I know you still remember what Pasicrates said about the ghost in his room. What do you think he was going to say when he stopped talking?"

I considered the matter for a moment. "That he was afraid. Most men would be afraid of a ghost, I think, and most would not be ashamed to admit it. Pasicrates might be."

Io spat out the hair she had been chewing. "I don't think so. I mean, he'd probably lie about that, like you say, master. But I don't think that was what stopped him. If he'd been going to say he was afraid at all, he would have said it when he told about hearing Callia screaming, or when he first saw the ghost." Io slid from the log and picked up a long stick. "Look, master. I'm the ghost. I have a spear and a big shield, and I'm going to try to kill you."

I snatched at the stick, which snapped between our hands.

"That's right," Io said. "You'd try to grab the shaft." She threw aside the broken stick and resumed her seat beside me on the log. "I think that's what Pasicrates did. He probably caught it, too—he's really quick."

"With his right hand? That would have been very difficult, Io. He would have had to reach across the ghost's shield."

She shook her head. "With his left hand, master. I think that was what he was about to say. He looked at the place where it had been, remember?"

"Do you mean that he was lying? He didn't see the ghost at all?"

"No, master. I mean that when he fought it, he had a left hand." She said nothing more, staring at the sun-bright clouds across the waters of the lake.

"A ghost hand, because the other was a ghost?"

"You don't remember Hegesistratus, do you, master? Did you read about him today?"

I told her I had not.

"He was a mantis, a really good one. He knew a whole lot about ghosts and gods, and right after we met him he said that people who'd been killed with your sword might be particularly likely to come back. It was you that cut off Pasicrates' hand, master. With your sword."

It is very late now, but I do not think Polos is asleep. I cannot sleep either, so I have lit this lamp. Far away, on the mountainside, someone pipes. When I lie down and close my eyes, I seem to see the capering figures that ring the majestic red urn in my memory palace—one of them pipes, too. I think that it is better I remain awake for a time and write more.

I should have written that this Pasicrates was waiting

for Io and me when we returned. He said that he had errands in the town and asked me to tell Polos to obey him; Io shook her head, but after I saw the stump of his arm I did as he wished. When Polos returned tonight, he trembled and would not speak.

I went to the room where Pasicrates sleeps. He swore that he had not struck Polos. I saw that he hates and fears me very much, and that he hates himself, too, for that; I pitied him, though perhaps I should not have. I asked if we were not going to Rope, and if it was not his city—I felt sure it was, because he had said he would show Polos his shield there. When he said that we were, and it was, I told him I would kill him if he hurt Polos, though we stood in the marketplace of Rope. Once more he swore that he had not hurt him.

We woke Themistocles; he said I should not harm Pasicrates (which I knew already in my heart, I think), and sent me back to this room, where Polos and Io and I sleep with the black man and his wife.

The moon is high. I have read many sheets of this scroll—much about Hegesistratus and many times about Pharetra. My eyes burn and weep.

33

Bull Killer

The goat man named him—*Kain-Tauros.* Now I fear him, though he is only a boy, and smaller than Io. I drew her aside and asked her about him. She said he is my slave, at which my jaw fell.

"You forget, master. Do you know that? Usually you do."

I nodded, having found already that I could not recall how we came here.

"You were in a big battle. You were wounded." She guided my fingers to the scar. "Before we came here we were in Thought and then in Tower Hill, and before that we were in Thrace—that was where you got Polos. You got me last summer when we were in Hill."

I promised her I would free them both and let them return to their families; but she said she does not remember hers, and his is very far away.

After that I called him to me. I said that I could see he was not happy, that a slave's lot is never a happy one, and that if it was I who had enslaved him, I regretted it; in any case, I said, I would set him free whenever he wished.

He stared at me. His eyes are big with night, like Io's, and they soon filled with tears. He said that it was better for him to be the slave of a good man who would teach him, and feed and protect him, than for him to run wild and perhaps be caught by a bad one; but that I had not always protected him, that I had lent him to a bad man. He pointed this man out to me; it was Pasicrates, the one-handed man who ran so swiftly before his thigh was torn by the boar. I promised Polos I would never lend him to anyone again, and told him that if I forgot my promise he was to remind me. I asked what Pasicrates had done to him, but he ran away. Io says that she does not know. I think that she suspects, however; and so do I.

I have read what I last wrote in this scroll. There was no lake where we woke this morning; thus I believe I have neglected to write for at least a day.

This house is in Bearland, where no field is ever flat; its mountains rise all around us, many and steep but very green. No one plows here, which seems strange to me. The women work small gardens with wooden spades, and short hoes whose blades are the shoulder bones of sheep. Their men herd sheep and goats, with a few cattle and horses, and hunt. We, too, hunted today; it was then that I saw him. This is how it came about.

This morning, after Io had named those in our party for me, Themistocles instructed me to put on my helmet and mail. I wore my sword as well, and though I have no shield, I carried a pair of javelins. The black man was equipped much as I, with a long sword; but Pasicrates had not so much as a knife—Io says it is because he ran all the way from Rope to meet us.

We had not gone far before we found the road blocked by a landslip, which Pasicrates swore must have taken place since he had passed that way. If we had not had the mule cart, we could have clambered across the mud and stones, perhaps; but to clear them away would have taken many days. There was nothing for it but to turn back and try to find our way south by another route, one that Pasicrates did not know; and before the sun was higher than the mountains we were thoroughly lost.

Then Pasicrates urged that we turn back yet again, because the road seemed to become worse with every stade we walked; but Themistocles and Simonides wanted to press forward until we met a traveler who could advise us. Their words were becoming warm when Tillon noticed a ditcher at work and crossed the fields to him.

The argument stopped; and Bittusilma, by smiling at each in turn, got them to agree that we would take the ditcher's advice, whatever it should be. For a time all of us stood watching him as he spoke with Tillon and Tillon with him, though it was much too far for us to overhear anything they said.

Before long Tillon returned, bringing the ditcher with him. "He was born near here," Tillon explained, "and he says he knows all the roads between here and the Silent Country—he's traveled a great deal. He says he'll guide us for his food and a spit a day."

Themistocles took out an obol and gave it to him. "Here's your first day's wage, to show I mean what I say. As this good man told you, we're on our way to Rope, and we're in a hurry—you'll get two more as soon as we reach the Silent Country."

The ditcher, who was muddied to the hips and still carried his mattock on his shoulder, took the coin and mumbled thanks.

"Now, do we go forward or turn back?"

"You're in a hurry, so you got to push ahead, the main road bein' blocked. There's other ways, but all about as bad as this or worse."

Themistocles and Simonides were triumphant; Pasicrates asked angrily about the road ahead.

"Worse'n this," the ditcher told him. "But we can get that cart through."

Simonides inquired about lodging for tonight, at which the ditcher shook his head. "There's gentry. I can show you where their houses is. Whether they'll take you . . ."

He led the way, and we walked beside him; we were soon well ahead of the rest of the walkers and the cart. "This is Latro, my master," Io told him. "I'm Io, and this is Polos."

He grinned and nodded to all of us. "Aglaus." He has lost several teeth.

Io ventured to ask whether his own master would not be angry with him for leaving his work.

"Happy to be rid of me," he told her.

"Where do you live?"

"You mean a house? Haven't got one."

"We don't either," Io said.

I explained that I was not a Hellene, spoke to him in this tongue, then asked whether he had ever encountered anyone of my nation.

He shook his head. "Not many foreigners comes to Bearland. What comes out's less than that."

"Bandits, you mean?"

He nodded. "The one-handed man, he's a real Rope Maker?"

Io said he was.

"They'll leave you be, then."

Polos asked who these bandits were, but Aglaus pretended he had not heard him. He asked Io, "Do you like that man with the money?"

"Not as much as I do my master and the black man, or Polos. But he seems to be a good man, and he's a friend of Hypereides', our old captain."

Aglaus nodded, absorbing this. "The old man?"

"Themistocles is his master, I think. They don't *say* that, but it seems to me that's how it is. He's not mean, though, and he's really trying to help Latro."

"The lady?"

"I like the black man a lot, and he likes her."

"I'd heered there was people like him, but I never seen one till now." Aglaus chuckled. "I don't suppose it hurts. Wonder how we look to him."

"I don't know," Io admitted. "I never thought about it." She pondered the matter for a hundred steps or so. "I bet we look sick to him. Did you notice the scar on his cheek?"

Aglaus nodded. "Can't not see it."

"That's from a sword, and I was there when he got it. He lost a lot of blood, and he wasn't a whole lot darker then than my arm."

"That fella Tillon seemed all right. Who's t'other one?"

"Diallos. They don't do more than they have to."

Aglaus grunted. "And the Rope Maker with his hand gone?"

"Stay away from him."

"I see. You know any more Rope Makers?"

"Not very well," Io admitted. "Eutaktos and Basias, but they're both dead."

"Was they better'n him?"

"Yes, a little," Io told him. "No, Basias was a whole lot better. Eutaktos—well, Eutaktos was hard, but he wasn't mean. If somebody didn't do what he said, he'd beat them or whatever, but not because he liked it. It was just so they'd be afraid not to obey him the next time. And I think he liked money too much, but there are worse things."

I remarked that he had been a brave soldier.

"Do you remember him, master? Why, that's wonderful!"

I said that I remembered the sacrifice of the girl, and how Eutaktos had encouraged his men until he died.

"I wasn't there," Io said, wondering, "and I don't think you told me about it. Was that after Cerdon was bitten by a snake?"

I confessed I did not know.

"What happened when Eutaktos died?"

I remembered the Great Mother and the promises she had made the slaves, but I thought it best not to speak of it, and I did not. I wondered much, however, to find these things so clear in my mind when I recall only this day, my childhood, and the fight at the temple besides.

Not long afterward we overtook the men carrying the corpse. The dead youth—Lykaon was his name—appeared to have been two or three years younger than Pasicrates. His wound was horrible. All of us expressed our grief as the custom is, and Aglaus bowed very low to Lykaon's father.

"I've heard of you," this man told Themistocles. "I was in the army. So were some of my sons."

There was more such polite talk; I gave it scant attention, watching those who held the corpse instead, and those with them. There were seven in all, and they were studying us—Pasicrates, the black man, and me particularly—with equal intensity. Those whose hands were free fingered their javelins and the hilts of their big hunting knives.

Then the old man, whose son the dead youth was, spread his cloak upon the baggage in our cart and ordered them to lay the body on it. At that, everyone relaxed and smiled, and I found that I was smiling, too. I asked Io where we were going.

"To their house," she said happily. "We'll spend the night there and help out with the funeral tomorrow."

Themistocles had taken off his own cloak. He and the dead youth's father covered the corpse with it.

This house is old and very large; it has a tower, and there are other houses around it and a wall of stones about the whole, more than twice the height of a man. The dead youth's father is Ortygenes; he has eight living sons and a great many daughters. Aglaus says he has outlasted three wives.

One of the young men ran ahead to tell the many women here what had happened. They met us on the road wailing and tearing their hair. Soon afterward, the eldest of Ortygenes' sons told Pasicrates, the black man, and me that he and his brothers, with some other men, intended to kill the boar that had killed Lykaon. All of us were anxious to go with them, and so was Polos; but I reminded him of the dead youth's wound and strictly forbade it.

We were far from the house when at last we heard the hounds—not the song of hounds on the scent, but the barks and sharp yelps by which hounds that have brought their quarry to a stand urge one another forward. Everyone began to run, and Pasicrates and the black man were soon far ahead of the rest of us. Though I ran as fast as I could, I was well behind, with one of Lykaon's brothers close behind me.

It shamed me that Pasicrates had outrun me. I do not like him, and I sense that he hates me—thus I sought some shorter route to the hounds and thought that I had found it. A moment more and I was alone, still in earshot of the chase but unable to see even the slowest of the other hunters. One check after another presented itself: first a tangle of thorn, then a sheer drop too great to jump. Very angry at my own folly and walking instead of running, I made my way slowly to open ground.

Then Fortuna, who had just played me so ugly a trick, chose to smile upon me. Not half a stade away and watching me through one eye stood a most promising bay colt; he trotted over at my whistle as though he had known me all his life. Though much of this countryside is too rough for horses, I saw immediately that here I might ride for two stades at least down the valley, and so be much nearer the boar than I was. I sprang onto the colt, and we skimmed the half-wild fields at a crackling gallop.

Now I must rely upon what the black man has told me about the hunt, with his fingers and speaking through his wife. The boar had taken shelter in an old wolf den, so that the hounds could not get behind it. Someone ran back to fetch fire with which to smoke it out; but as soon as he had gone, Pasicrates crawled into the den. If this is so, the Rope Maker must surely be the boldest man alive—and the most foolish.

The boar charged, as was only to be expected. Pasicrates' javelin caught it in back of the shoulder, leaving a raking cut along its ribs. The tusks that had torn Ortygenes' son made no more than a shallow gash across Pasicrates' thigh. Had the den been smaller, one or both would have died of course.

When the boar burst into the light, the black man was not the first, he says, to cast his javelin; but it was his that remained in the boar's body as it broke the ring of hounds and dashed into the forest.

And out of it, where I upon the bay colt caught sight of it with a score of hounds at its heels.

I cannot say whether the colt answered my hand or charged the boar of his own accord. My cast was lucky, as the sons of Ortygenes said afterward; but I was close when I made it, which is ever the mother of good luck.

At once the boar stumbled, and the hounds swarmed over it like so many ants on a dead beetle. All this was soon sponged from my thoughts by what came afterward; but now, as I write of it, I seem to see the boar again, the great, dark head with its flashing tusks lifted for the last time.

No one could tell me to whom the bay colt belonged, though several of the dead youth's brothers advised me to keep him until another claimed him. I dismounted, however, because I was eager to retrieve my javelin and (in truth) see whether it had pierced the boar's heart, as it had. With no one to watch him, the colt wandered away, though I would have caught and kept him if I had known of the injury to Pasicrates then.

The boar was gutted and its entrails thrown to the hounds, as the custom is. Someone felled a sapling, and we were binding the boar's feet over it when Pasicrates joined us, leaning upon the arm of the black man. He wished to know who had killed the boar—and was not much pleased, I think, to learn it had been I; he congratulated me nevertheless, and offered me his hand. I do not think I can ever have been very fond of him, but I came near to loving him at that moment. "I'll stay with you," I told him, "while they go ahead with the boar. Perhaps someone will bring one of Ortygenes' horses for you."

"No one has to stay with me," Pasicrates replied. "I can find my way back alone."

Then the black man, speaking with his fingers, told me to go with the boar and the men from the house, and to return with Themistocles' cart, if I could reach that spot with it.

I agreed and hurried ahead of those who carried the boar. That was when I glimpsed him trotting through the trees, Polos to the waist.

34

The Feast Is Over

There was much eating, and much wine drunk—far too much of it by me. I slept for a time, and woke to find myself stretched on the earth of the courtyard beside many another. It shamed me, and I rose and left this house and its proud wall behind me, and walked to the ford. There I was ill and washed, taking off my chiton and washing it, too, in the cold mountain water, wringing it out, and letting it dry awhile on a bush before I put it on again.

By then the sun was low, and I thought it best to return to this house. I spoke with Ortygenes, its owner; and afterward by the help of this lamp I read what I wrote yesterday. How I wish now that I had said plainly what it was I saw! Whom did I call "the goat man"? A goatherd? Surely I know the proper word for that!

This day was given over to the funeral rites of Lykaon, who was Ortygenes' son. Io helped the other women wash and perfume his body. There were thirty of them at least, when three might have done everything necessary with ease, but every woman in the place wanted to have a hand in it, and did. When it was complete, Lykaon was attired in his best clothes, with a fine green cloak and new sandals with white lachets.

Meanwhile, some of Ortygenes' male slaves had felled an old olive tree, a very large one already more than half-dead. Its wood was cut up and split, and every bit of living sapwood pared away. While the men were doing this, the children gathered many baskets of olive leaves and wove Lykaon's crown, of green twigs with their leaves still on them.

Ortygenes and his sons, aided by Themistocles and Simonides, the black man and me, and various others, prepared Lykaon's bed, first laying down very carefully a thick layer of pine kindling, then shaping the bed from the olivewood, with a hollow down the center to contain the leaves. (Pasicrates did not assist us in this because his leg pains him too much.) Io, who had left the other women to supervise the weaving of Lykaon's crown, carried it in. It was not until this crown had been fixed on Lykaon's head, she says, that the coin was laid upon his tongue; though small and old and worn almost smooth, the coin was gold, which impressed her greatly.

When everything had been made ready, Lykaon was carried in by his brothers, with his father, his sisters, and all the other women following the body. His father and his brothers preserved a manly silence; but the women wept and wailed aloud, even Io and Bittusilma.

Each brother spoke in turn, recounting some incident which recalled Lykaon's courage, honesty, cleverness, good nature, and so on; most were brief, but two marshaled too many words. His father then described the portents that had accompanied Lykaon's birth, recounted the prophecies he had received concerning him, and explained how each had been fulfilled.

Simonides recited verses he had composed for the occasion, describing the sorrow of Lykaon's noble ancestors at his death as they received him into the Lands of the Dead. (Afterward I asked Io whether she had enjoyed this poem. She said she had, but thought it somewhat inferior to one that she had once heard at the rites of a sailor.)

Ortygenes spoke again after Simonides, explaining to all those present that Simonides was a famous poet from Ceos, and praising Pasicrates and Themistocles.

Pasicrates spoke only briefly, first assuring the people

of Bearland of the friendship of Rope, then explaining that it had been because of his desire to avenge Lykaon that he had entered the den of the boar.

Themistocles began by speaking of the friendship of Thought for both Bearland and Rope. It was in those places, and only in them, he said, that the ancient virtues of the Hellenes had been preserved. Thus, he said, they must become the teachers of the rest of Hellas, reminding the people of the high ideals of their forefathers, ideals exemplified by the noble youth lying before us. There was, Themistocles said, in his train, a man who each day forgot everything that had passed the day before; yet even he did not forget the training he had received in his youth, and thus—though he could not be wise—he was honorable, just, and brave. (I did not know he was speaking about me until I saw the faces of so many others turned toward me and Io thumped my ribs with her sharp little elbow; then my blood rushed to my cheeks and I resolved to commit some unworthy act so that Themistocles would never speak of me in that way again. But in truth I feel already that I have committed many.) So is it with Lykaon, said Themistocles. He has drunk of the waters of forgetting, the last, merciful gift of the kindly gods that spares the dead so much care; but the education he received in this house as a boy remains with him, and because it does he will be received among the dead as a hero.

It was not given to men to escape death, Themistocles said, but to the immortal gods alone; for a man the sole question was whether his death brought good or evil to his fellows. Today the Long Coast, the Silent Country, and the Islands, too, were gathered in friendship with Bearland to mourn her son. If the barbarian was eventually vanquished for good, it might well be because of this.

After Themistocles had spoken, Ortygenes ordered the torch to be brought, and the full mourning of the women began. They keened, wept, tore their hair, and scratched their cheeks until they streamed with blood, mourning not only Lykaon but all their dead, and confided to his ears messages of love, comfort, and longing, to be repeated when he should encounter their lost ones among the shades. His father, Themistocles, and even my Io, had penned letters, and these were put into the bosom of his peplos.

Then the torch was applied to the kindling, which took fire with a crackling that soon became a roar; and Lykaon's final bed was curtained with red fire. The day was hot, clear, and nearly windless. How bravely the towering column of sable smoke rose into the blue heavens! All of us backed away; even so, many a hair was singed on one and another. Through the leaping flames I caught sight of the very face of Death, and quickly turned my eyes away to look instead at the green grass, the lowing cattle, and the gracious olive trees that are mine—though they are in fact Ortygenes'—for a brief while longer. Soon I shall be as Lykaon, perhaps far less mourned, soon remembered only by these scrolls.

The sacrificial beasts were a young bull, three rams, and three black he-goats. They were dedicated in good style to the chthonian gods and roasted upon Lykaon's funeral pyre. The boar we hunted yesterday was roasted, too; there was more than enough meat for everyone present. The black man told me I had killed the boar, which I had already forgotten. He says also that we saw a much larger boar in Thrace. No one succeeded in killing that one, however.

Aglaus stopped to speak with me, and I asked how old he is. He is in his thirty-second year, though he looks so much older—I think because his hair has begun to gray and he has lost some teeth. His father was called Aglaus also. He asked whether the letters I use were pictures. I explained that they are, *A* being the head of an ox and so on; but that I did not intend an ox now when I set down *A*. I showed him how to write his name in my own tongue, scratching the letters in the dirt.

He thought that the goat man was a certain god who lives in the mountains of Bearland. His name is All. I asked how he came to bear this strange name, and Aglaus said that he is the fourth son of Time and Earth, though his brothers do not recognize his claim to the fourth world, which is this one. The other three are the sky, the sea, and the Lands of the Dead, which lie under the earth. It is he who brings terror at noon to those who wake him from his slumber. I asked whether Aglaus had ever seen him. He affirmed that he had. Io, who had come to listen to us, says that this god aided the men of Thought against the barbarians at Fennel Field.

When Aglaus had gone, I asked Io about the letter that she had put into Lykaon's bosom. At first she did not want to tell me, but when I promised I would not tell anyone else, she told me it was to her parents. She does not know whether they are dead, but believes they may be. She said she told them she was well and happy and has a fine man, but that she misses them both very much. I wanted to ask her who this man is, but she was crying, so I comforted her instead.

Now only what I said to Ortygenes remains to be written.

I found him staring into the embers. There were many men around him, all asleep. He had a skin of wine and offered some to me, but I refused it. He asked whether I had ever seen his son alive. I could not remember, and shook my head.

"He wasn't as big as you," he said. "We hardly ever are. But the old blood ran true in him."

I said that everyone had told me what a fine young man he had been.

"Are you a Bundini?" Ortygenes asked. "Some tribe of the Getae?"

I could say only that I did not know; in any case, I do not think he heard my reply.

"Our line fought on the windy plain of Ilion," he told me, "but in his entire life my poor boy never saw anything beyond these mountains.

"'Some marks of honor on my son bestow,
And pay in glory what in life you owe.
Fame is at least by heavenly promise due
To life so short, and now dishonor'd, too.
Till the proud king and all the Achaean race
Shall heap with honors him they now disgrace.'

"Here's a secret—you'll forget it anyhow, what's-his-name says. Know who the Achaeans are?"

I admitted I did not.

"We are," Ortygenes said, "and I'm a king in hiding. You think we'll ever win our country back? We won't. Nations are like men—growing old, never young. My son had the misfortune to be a young man of an old nation. So did I, once. Yours is young still, whatever it is. Give thanks."

This morning we entered the Silent Country. Themistocles gave Aglaus money and dismissed him; but when we halted for the first meal, we discovered that he had been following us, which made the Rope Maker very angry. Themistocles permitted Aglaus to share our food, but told him to return to his own land after he had eaten, that we no longer required a guide and would not pay him anything more. Aglaus was very humble, saying he would serve us without pay, like a slave, and do whatever work Tillon and Diallos thought too hard. Themistocles shook his head and turned away.

Then Bittusilma and Io spoke to the black man and me. The black man has money, it seems, and so do I. (Io is keeping mine for me; it is on the cart.) They proposed that we should employ Aglaus as our servant, each giving him a spit on alternate days. The black man was doubtful, but I said that if he did not wish to do it, I would hire Aglaus myself to wait upon Io, Polos, and me; then the black man agreed to the arrangement Bittusilma and Io had originally suggested. Aglaus rejoiced when we told him, and I think even Themistocles and Simonides were happy, though they tried to appear otherwise. Tillon and Diallos welcome him now as a comrade.

I have said nothing, only nodding when Io explained the new arrangement to him; yet I welcome him, too, as something more. When he arrived, as we sat eating, I recalled a silver chariot. I remember standing in it and holding the reins, though no horses were harnessed to it. Perhaps it is only an imagined object in my memory palace, but I do not think so; it seems to me that it stands among rocks, not walls. If having Aglaus near helps me remember, I would pay him much more than a spit.

Tonight I read about Lykaon's cremation, and what Ortygenes said to me. When I had finished, I asked Pasicrates whether the people of Bearland were called Achaeans. He said that they were not, the Achaeans having been destroyed by the Dorians, his own tribe, who had slaughtered all their men and seized their women. Aglaus confirmed it—but looked (or so it appeared to me) rather too serious.

35

Cyklos of Rope

The judge to whom Cimon gave me a letter has welcomed me, with Io and Polos, into his home. I had forgotten the letter (as I have forgotten the man called Cimon) but Io says I showed it to her before I rolled it into my old scroll, and she told me what it was and gave it to me when I needed it. Cyklos is of middle height; though his hair is as gray as iron, no young man could stand more straight. I have not seen him smile.

I should set down here that the wounded Rope Maker who was with us ran ahead of us when we neared Rope, though it clearly gave him a great deal of pain to run. Nothing of that showed in his expression, and the strides he took with his right leg were as long as those with the left; but when he looked back to wave good-bye to us, his face was white. After seeing it, I watched him closely as he ran, and twice he nearly fell. Themistocles and Simonides had tried to dissuade him, but he said that it was his duty to announce us, and as long as he could do his duty he would do it. I offered to send Polos, who runs very swiftly, in his place; but he would not hear of that.

He must have reached Rope well ahead of us, for we received a magnificent welcome. All five of the judges had marched out of the city to meet us, accompanied by at least two hundred Rope Makers under arms. Their armor gleamed like gold in the bright sunshine. With them was the Women's Chorus, which I am told is very famous, playing and singing, and with the Women's

Chorus, a score of lovely young girls who danced to their music.

The greatest welcome was for Themistocles, who was embraced by all the judges; but when each had greeted him and praised his shrewd leadership during the war (in which Io says the black man and I took part), they inquired about me and greeted me as well. I said that so far as I knew I had done nothing to deserve their goodwill, but that I would attempt to deserve it in the future, at which they appeared pleased. That was when Io passed me the letter, which she had taken from the scroll in my chest. Cyklos had already introduced himself, and I gave it to him.

In Rope we were first brought to the palace of the Agids. We did not see Prince Pausanias, who is said to be the greatest man here, but Simonides says that we will surely see him at the ceremony tomorrow. We were greeted instead by the white-haired Queen Gorgo and her son, King Pleistarchos, a boy about Polos' age. Gorgo told me that she recalled Io and me from our earlier visit to her city, and asked Io what had befallen the beauty who had accompanied us. Io said she had been killed at the siege of Sestos. Gorgo nodded, and said that she had foreseen that death, sudden and violent, awaited her. I must remember to ask Io more about this woman; I place this wish among the shattered fragments of the dancer.

I should write here, too, that the Agid palace is not a great structure like the memory palace in which I attempt to store all the things I may wish to recall, but only a commodious house of stone. This house of Cyklos' is not even stone, however—merely mud brick, and of moderate size.

Now I must write everything I have been told concerning the solemn ceremonies that are to take place tomorrow. Before I go to sleep, I will put this scroll in a prominent place so that I will be certain to read it in the morning; thus, I hope, I will be able to act well tomorrow, even though I must necessarily be separated from Io.

First, that they will begin at the rising of the full moon—that is very important here. Simonides and I spoke at length with Cyklos this afternoon; he told us that there had been great concern here lest we come late, in which case many features of the ceremony would have had to be eliminated. I lay between the paws of the panther: *Everyone must be in place before twilight brings the rising of the moon.*

Second, that about two thousand others will be honored with me, though I am to be their head and chief. In order to ensure that there are no mistakes that might offend the Triple Goddess, each of us is to be accompanied by a sponsor, a young Rope Maker who has already rehearsed the ceremony several times. Mine will be Hippoxleas, one of the youths attending Cyklos; he is as tall as I am, and I would call him handsome (though perhaps somewhat overheavy at the jaw), but Io does not like him. She said that he was of the same mold as Pasicrates, the one-handed Rope Maker who ran ahead to announce us. By this I thought she meant that the two were closely related, so I asked Hippoxleas whether they were brothers. He smiled and told me that they are only distant cousins, but good friends.

"You'll have the most difficult job of all," I warned him, "if I'm to lead the entire group. I forget, as Simonides told you."

He laid his hand on my shoulder in a friendly fashion and grinned. "Not at all, Latro. Think they'd give it to a simpleminded fellow like me if it were going to be too hard? No, it's the rest who drew the tough jobs." And indeed, of all the young men about Cyklos, only Hippoxleas seems to be looking forward to the great events of tomorrow night. I lay his name, *Hippoxleas,* just to the left of the wide door, at the foot of the doorpost.

Third, that our preparations will begin long before sunset. Following the first meal, all of us are to assemble on the bank of the Eurotas, north of the temple. There we and our sponsors will be able to practice by daylight all the things we will have to do in darkness. Io wants to come; Hippoxleas says there is no reason she should not, though she will have to stand among the spectators. That *we must go after the first meal,* I write upon the floor before the golden sun the blue beetle rolls.

Fourth and last, the order of events, because I do not know whether I will have an opportunity to write after the practice. Following songs by the Men's Chorus, there is to be a sacrifice on behalf of the entire Silent Country. It is assumed that the omens will be favorable, because the wishes of the goddess have been consulted upon several occasions during the past few days, and each time she has urged that the ceremony proceed.

After this sacrifice, there will be speeches honoring both Themistocles and those who are to receive residency; I do not know exactly how many, or who will give them. Then Themistocles himself will speak, honoring the Rope Makers, their auxiliaries, and their allies for the great part they played in the war.

Next he will be crowned with trefoil by the two kings. (It seems very odd to me that Rope should have two kings, but Aglaus and Io both confirm it. Polos knows no more of this place than I.) We must cheer very loudly as the wreath is placed upon his head. He will then be presented with gifts; as I understand it, each of the five judges, the kings, Queen Gorgo, and the prince regent will all make him rare and valuable presents, after which Themistocles himself will offer an unblemished white bull to the King of Gods. (This bull is one of the gifts he is to receive.)

Thus far I, at the head of those who will be freed and made residents of Rope, will have been merely an onlooker; but now we are to throw aside our clothing and bathe in the Eurotas. Each sponsor will carry perfumed oil with which to anoint us, as well as a towel and a new white garment. When all of us are freshly attired, we are to form a column, with Hippoxleas and myself in the lead. I am to stand at his right.

We will file past the temple of Orthia, where we will be given torches, and our sponsors offerings, by the priestesses. (The Women's Chorus will perform while these are distributed.) Then we will march to each of the temples of Rope in turn. The dancers are to go first and the Women's Chorus after them; we need only follow. We are to sing the refrains of all the songs—I am told that these refrains are short and easy, and that we will be drilled in them during the practice tomorrow. At each temple, a hundred men will make offerings. (These have already been told off; each group of one hundred will march as a unit.)

When we return to the temple of Orthia, I am to make my own offering together with all the men who have not yet made theirs. The prince regent, the five judges, and both the kings will pass among us, accompanied by priestesses. As each declares each man free, the priestess with him will place a crown of wildflowers upon that man's head. *I will be the first man freed by the prince regent,* who will be assisted by Queen Gorgo. *I must thank each briefly, humbly, loudly, and gratefully.* As soon as I have finished speaking, I am to throw my torch into the river.

By the time the last slave has been freed, the meat of the sacrifices should be done. There will be general feasting, and—as Simonides warns me—a great deal of wine.

In my avenue of statues there stands one of the Hydra; it has seven heads and four feet. I cut an event into each: *the first sacrifices, the speeches, Themistocles' own speech, the presentation of gifts to him, his sacrifice, our cleansing, the distribution of torches and offerings, our march, my offering, the ceremony of manumission, and the drowning of the torches.*

Io asked whether I had seen the black man. We found him at a gymnasium near here, watching Hippoxleas teach Polos the Rope Makers' sword drill. Io showed us a small room without windows, on the other side of the court from the one in which Io, Polos, and I sleep. It holds only a pair of stocks, of oak reinforced with bronze and iron; there are bloodstains on the floor. Io and the black man found a place in the wall where it has been repaired. They say that a man we know was imprisoned here and escaped by breaking through this wall. Both warned me not to speak of it. We left that room without being seen by anyone, though one of those who attend Cyclos saw us as we crossed the court.

Io says she will be very happy to get out of Rope—she does not like it here. Nor do I, though after tomorrow it will be my city. Io asked me to ask Cyklos when we will go to Dolphins for the games.

We ate the second meal at the barracks of the mora to which Hippoxleas belongs. It was a long low shed, bare of everything except tables and benches. Io said on the way over that we had eaten in one of these when we were here previously, warning me not to taste the broth. I soon saw, however, that all the Rope Makers eat it with relish; I tried it, but found it bitter and salty. Hippoxleas told me where it gets its black color, but I do not believe him—there was much teasing of the black man and me, and even a little of Themistocles and Simonides. Bacon, onions, and barley boiled together made up the rest of the meal, though Hippoxleas says they seldom get bacon.

Later I sat listening to Cyklos talk to Hippoxleas and the other young men, although some did not like having me there. I would not call Cyklos a good speaker—his voice is not musical, and he seldom turns phrases—but the young men hung upon every word.

A slave brought wine and dried figs. I wanted to awaken Io and Polos so they could have some, but Cyklos shook his head and I did not. I have saved a fig for each, however.

Though they were couched in so homely a style, some of the things Cyklos told us seemed very striking to me. He talked of Cyrus, a barbarian king who conquered many nations. One of his counselors advised him to shift his capital to a place where the climate was milder and the land more productive. Cyrus refused, saying that soft lands bred soft men. Cyklos then spoke of the fertility of the Silent Country, which abounds in wheat, barley, and every kind of fruit. He asked how it could be that the Rope Makers were not as soft as their soil.

He spoke also of a law which makes a woman a widow as long as her husband remains abroad, asking first whether the law was fair to her husband, and then (when no one replied) whether it was fair to the woman herself. The young men debated the matter and concluded that it was fair to neither: a man should not lose what is his each time he leaves home; nor should a woman forfeit the security of her husband's name because she is separated from him. Cyklos explained the reason for this law; it was made for the benefit of Rope, which must have infants because it requires men. Though he did not say this, I wondered whether it was not made also so that men would not desire to travel.

Cyklos asked, "Would you leave your wife here, Latro, now that you know our law?"

I said that I would not, at which everyone laughed.

"You don't have to worry," he said. "The law applies only to us, not to you." But it seems to me that it has application to me whether these people rule that it applies or not, because I would surely forget a wife as soon as we were separated. And indeed, it is entirely possible I have a wife now, who supposes herself a widow.

"It's we Rope Makers who defend the city, you see," Cyklos said, "and not you neighbors, though we can call on you to fight at need. Did you see our mighty walls today?"

I said that I had not, and that I did not think this city had any.

"It is walled with our shields," he told me.

He yawned and stretched. "We'll have a lot to do tomorrow, I'm afraid—all of us will be up late." I rose with the others, but he motioned for me to sit once more.

When the young men had left, I said, "It's very generous of you to house the children and me as you have, but I'm afraid we must be a burden as well as an inconvenience. Soon, I hope, we should be on our way to Dolphins. I'm sure that you'll be glad to see us go."

He waved that aside, pouring a fresh cup of wine for me and one for himself. "Hippoxleas says you're a master swordsman."

I said I hoped that I had not boasted to him.

Cyklos shook his head. "He's been teaching your boy, and found that you've taught him a great deal already. Pasicrates said you cut off his hand; he thinks there's something uncanny about you. So does the prince regent."

I said, "I think I'm a very ordinary man."

"Then you're not—ordinary men never think of themselves that way. Themistocles tells us you forget. Tomorrow morning will you remember what I tell you now?"

I said that I would write it in this scroll and read it in the morning.

Cyklos opened the chest upon which he had been sitting and produced two wooden swords, tossing one to me. "No thrusting at the face, understand? Everything else is fair. Now try to kill me."

I cut at his hand. He parried very cleverly and sprang at me; I caught his wrist and threw him down, my wooden sword at his throat.

When he had risen and recovered his breath, he asked, "How is it that you don't forget what you know of the sword?"

I explained that knowledge and memory are distinct: "Words written remember, a seed knows."

"Can you drive a chariot? Four horses?"

I do not know whether I can or not, and I told him so.

"In the morning, Prince Pausanias is going to ask you to. In less than a day you'll be declared a resident of Rope, and thus a subject of His Highness. Will you agree?"

I said I would certainly agree to try, if the prince of my new city wished it.

Cyklos turned and paced the courtyard, no longer watching me. "We've lost a great deal of prestige," he said. "First it was Peace, then after Clay, Mycale and Sestos. But we'll soon sweep Themistocles from the board, which should help enormously. Then if we dominate the Pythic Games—we *must* win the chariot race—and move boldly against some city of the Great King's—"

I asked whether he intended to kill Themistocles.

"No, no," he said. "Honor him—heap him with honors and gifts. No one can blame us for that."

36

Bloodstained

Torn and ruined clothing, cloven armor, and the weapons of the heroic king hang in the hall of the prince's house. "These were King Leonidas'," the prince's son explained to us. "My father got them at the Gates when he brought Leonidas' body home. He was my grandfather's brother. Please don't touch anything, sir. My father doesn't permit it."

I took my hand from the dead king's chiton, Themistocles assured the prince's son we would not, and Io whispered, "You want to be a famous warrior? This's the price they pay."

Polos (at whom her whisper was directed) did not appear to hear her, staring at everything with wide, dark eyes.

Pleistoanax said, "All mortals die. Since I must die, I wish to do it as he did, face-to-face with my enemy."

I remarked, "He wasn't actually facing the man who killed him. He was struck from behind by a javelin."

Pleistoanax smiled. "I see you know his glorious history, sir. He had broken the barbarians' line and was charging their king. One of the king's bodyguards killed him, exactly as you say."

Themistocles was eyeing me narrowly. "I don't think Latro can remember Leonidas' history—if he ever heard it—or much of anything else. How did you know about that, Latro?"

"From this chiton. There's a lot of staining near the arms and around the hem, but it's fairly even on both sides; I'd say that someone hacked the arms and legs of the corpse. The wound that killed him left a circular tear in back, about a hand above the waist, and a small hole across from it in front."

Pleistoanax went to look at the chiton as I spoke, and I noticed he did not scruple to touch it. He is a tall boy not yet come to manhood, and rather too handsome for my taste.

"The weapon penetrated his backplate," I continued, "passed through his chest, and was stopped by his breastplate. An arrow wouldn't have pierced the bronze, and would have left a smaller hole. A sword would have left a broad cut in the linen, not a round tear—so would a dagger. A horseman's lance would have made a larger hole, and it would probably have gone through his breastplate as well." I was about to say that the tear left by a shieldman's spear would have been larger, too; but I stopped just in time and substituted, "A king of Rope would never have had his back to the spears.

"So it was probably a javelin," I concluded, "a strong cast by someone not far behind him."

A young Rope Maker with a hand missing had entered while I spoke; from what I read here this morning I knew that this must be Pasicrates. I greeted him by name, and though his face kept his secret, his eyes revealed his surprise. All that he said, however, was, "His Highness will see you, even the children."

"And I?" Pleistoanax raised an eyebrow, determined to show he was no child. I doubt that he is as old as Io.

The prince stood to greet us, in the most gracious possible fashion, embracing Themistocles, Simonides, and me, patting Io's head, and pinching Polos' cheeks. Although Io warned me against him before we came, I liked him at once. His face is rendered hideous by a scar that draws up the right side of his mouth, but no one can be blamed for such accidents.

"This is Tisamenus, my mantis," the prince said, gesturing toward the pudgy little man who had sprung to his feet when the prince rose. Seeing him, I told Io by my glance that she and I would speak about this later. She had described this rabbity little creature as a monster; the monster seemed ready to fawn upon Themistocles whenever he snapped his fingers.

"Sit down, all of you. You, too, Pasicrates. Since you're going with us, there's no reason you shouldn't hear this."

Themistocles cocked his head. "Cimon said something about Your Highness wanting Latro to represent Rope at Dolphins. Will you attend the games in person?"

"Yes, and take you with me if I can—that's why I asked you to come here this morning. It might make a good impression if we could mention it tonight at the ceremony."

Themistocles and the prince had seated themselves by then, so the rest of us sat down, too. Themistocles said, "I haven't seen the great games in quite a while—it's certainly tempting. Simonides here goes every year."

"My trade," the old poet explained modestly. "I celebrate the victors from Thought without asking for a fee, if they wish it; as a foreigner, I feel I owe it to the city that's received me so graciously. And there are rich fees to be picked up from the other winners, now and then."

Prince Pausanias winked at his son. "Suppose *I* won, poet? You wouldn't charge me, would you? Don't you—and Thought—owe us something for my victory at Clay?"

Simonides cleared his throat. "Indeed we do. Why, I'd say that we owe you every bit as much as you'd owe the Long Coast if Themistocles—an example taken at random—had won the Battle of Peace. Who was the fellow you Rope Makers put in charge of the combined fleets? I forget his name. Anyway, between the two of them, I'd have to call Peace your greatest victory, because it was the first."

Pausanias roared with laughter, joined in a moment by his plump little mantis and Pasicrates, and at last by Themistocles himself. Io whispered, "Themistocles was the real commander at Peace."

The prince wiped his streaming eyes. "Poor old Eurybiades! The triumph of a dozen lifetimes, and no one will accord him the least credit. If I win, Simonides, you shall compose my victory ode. Without payment, if you insist—but no one has ever called me ungrateful."

Simonides made him a seated bow.

"Our entry's only nominally mine, however. It's no secret, and you might as well know the facts at the outset. My aunt's the one who bred and trained our team. You've already met her, I understand."

Themistocles and Simonides nodded.

"She's got an eye for horses, and a way with them,

like no one else I've ever seen; but you know the law—no married women, and a widow's accounted a wife still. Once wed, always wed, as far as the gods are concerned. We didn't think it was much of an obstacle at first. She'd give the team to Pleistarchos."

Themistocles said, "Sounds reasonable. What went wrong?"

"Pleistarchos, mostly. He can be just as stubborn as any other Rope Maker, and he insisted that if he was going to enter, he wanted to go to Dolphins and watch the race. I think he was actually hoping to drive himself, although he hadn't got up the nerve to propose that."

Themistocles chuckled.

"As you may imagine, my aunt wouldn't hear of it. Neither would the judges—they get nervous whenever one of our kings is out of the country, and who knows when the barbarians are going to try again?"

Themistocles said smoothly, "The war's over, if you ask me. A king of Rope is more likely to be in danger on Redface Island than away from it."

"My thoughts exactly—everything's getting back to normal. Take a look at this letter. The messenger arrived last night."

Themistocles glanced at the papyrus, then read it out loud: "*'Greetings, most royal Pausanias Kleombrotou, from your devoted servant Agis Korinthou! The spoils of war you entrusted to me I have entrusted to the honest Muslak Byblou upon the following highly favorable terms. Muslak has this very day delivered into my hand a full eight hundred darics for you as surety. Of what your goods bring, he is to retain every tenth coin, and no more. The other nine he shall render in a year, less the eight hundred darics already paid. Shall the gold be sent to you? Or ought I to trade with it? Tin is coming once more and we might do well in that.'*"

Io whispered to Simonides, "I thought they didn't trade."

Overhearing her, the prince said, "We don't, child—that is to say, Pasicrates here doesn't, nor do any of the Equals. But King Leotychides can and does both buy and sell on behalf of our city; and so do I, acting as I do in place of King Pleistarchos. Having heard that letter read, you can understand the dangers inherent in it. I find myself, without my knowledge or consent, dealing with a Crimson Man—in theory at least an adversary."

As we walked to this field, I asked Io whether she thought the prince's agent would really do business with the enemies of her people without his permission; the prince and Themistocles, strolling arm in arm, were too far in advance of us to overhear.

"They aren't the enemies of *my* city," Io said, "and I don't know a lot about them. But I know a lot about Pausanias, and I feel sorry for the Crimson Man." After we had taken a few more steps, she added, "I think he would. He'd know what Pausanias wanted—as much gold as possible, any way he could get it. And he'd know, too, that Pausanias couldn't say it was all right."

I had not thought of that. It made me admire this girl all the more, though I cautioned her against judging a maimed man by his scars—I think it must be his appearance that has turned her against the prince. She wanted to take my hand while we walked, but I pretended I did not notice and kept it closed so that she would not see the blood smeared on my fingers.

When we reached this place (seven stades, Pasicrates says, outside the city) only the chariot I am to drive was waiting for us. I took its reins and gave the team a little light exercise, without letting them reach their full speed or anything close to it. They seem good enough, responding well to the reins and the whip, but rather lacking the mettle I would have liked to see.

Polos told me it was marvelous to listen to me describe in so much detail how King Leonidas had been killed by a javelin. No one was near enough to hear us, so I confided to him that the javelin had not in fact been thrown—that the man who had killed Leonidas had stood above him with the javelin in his hands and driven it through the king's armor and into his back. (I do not understand how I have come to know this, and yet I am absolutely certain it is true.)

Polos looked puzzled. "Wouldn't the point have gone right through his breastplate, too? Couldn't you stick something with a javelin harder than you could throw it?"

"That's true," I said, "if you're only practicing, jabbing your point into a tree or something of that kind. But in a real fight, a thrown weapon always strikes harder. Something makes us hold back, if only a little, when we strike another man. To strike hard at the back of one who has already been knocked down is particularly difficult."

Although the blood appears fresh, it cannot be wiped away, ever on the papyrus.

I should say here that after I read, I carried this scroll with me in order that I could read and write when time allowed it. The queen and her chariot still have not appeared; thus I write. This is a very pleasant spot, a wide expanse of level, open ground, with a few large trees that shade the horses, and us, beside this clear, cool stream. The breeze is soft, the air wonderfully clear.

I thought I heard a shepherd piping and went to see; it was only Io, playing pipes she says Aglaus made for her. I saw that he had cut them from green rushes, cementing them with beeswax and binding them with split willow twigs. Io had named him for me this morning; now I asked whether she was not ashamed of our having a servant so poor and common looking, with many missing teeth, for I know women are often very sensitive concerning such things.

Io laughed and said we were about to get another, because Polos' milk teeth are coming out. Her own are nearly all gone. She grew serious, saying that she liked Aglaus very much though there was something about him that reminded her of Elata. I do not recall Elata; I tried to conceal it, but Io saw that I had forgotten her and told me that she is the wife of Hegesistratus of Zakunthios, another mantis.

"I liked her, too," Io said. "But I was afraid of her."

Polos shouts.

37

The Dead Man's Stare

His face and outstretched hands appear to me whenever I close my eyes. He tries to speak to me, I know, yet I cannot catch his words. I will write instead, though I had to beat Cyklos' slave before he would bring the lamp; I will write until I fall asleep on this stool, my back propped by the wall.

The queen and the boy they call a king came in her chariot. The driver was a slave, short but muscular; a most cunning man, I think, about horses. He wanted to know how much I had driven. When I told him I could not be sure, he winked at me and thumped my shoulder with his fist.

Queen Gorgo spoke with me. There cannot be two such women in the world! She asked whether I recalled our meeting in the temple of Orthia. When I explained that I sometimes forget, she told me gently, "But you must remember our meeting at my house, yesterday."

"Of course," I told her. "No man could ever forget a queen so lovely and so gracious." It was a lie, and I blushed for it even as the words left my lips. As quickly as I could, I turned the talk to her horses, which are all grays, very beautiful and finely bred.

"I think they're probably the best in Hellas," she told me. "We've raced them against my nephew's before, and they've always won easily; but now he says that his can't lose as long as you drive for him. Are you going to cast a spell on my horses? Or on your own?"

I told her I knew nothing of such things.

She nodded slowly, and her eyes were sad. "You remind me of Leonidas; you're a plain fighting man. You've something of his energy, too, I suspect. It's a good thing for Rope that there are such men as you, but not for your wives and mothers."

While I spoke with Gorgo, Polos had been scrutinizing her team. He told me how eager they were to run, and how confident of victory. Of the one I was to drive he said, "They know they aren't going to win. They only want to finish the race and go back to the pasture."

I asked, "How can they know they won't win? Did they tell you that?"

Polos shrugged, and appeared every bit as downcast as if he were one of the horses himself. "They only say that the man who drives always makes them gallop too fast, so that they're winded before the race is over."

I dropped to one knee, bringing our eyes to a level. "Tell them I won't ask them to do their best until the last stretch of the last lap. Nor will I shout until then. When I shout, the race will be practically over. Then they must show their heels, and afterward they'll be walked back to their pasture. Can you do that?"

"I think so. I hope they'll understand and remember."

We raced three times around the field, which was large, as I have said. The finish—and the start—was the great oak under which we had rested. Gorgo stood there to judge the race; she held up fingers to give us the count of laps, although that was not really needed. When her driver saw that I did not force my horses to their utmost, he took a comfortable lead and held it. I permitted him to do it, even though Prince Pausanias shouted for me to drive faster at the end of the first lap, and also at the second.

Perhaps I should not write it, but it was a great joy then to drive as I did—very fast and yet without any straining for more speed—through the clear, warm morning. No dust rose from the soft grass, and the tall trees and low walls of piled stones seemed to spin past us in a sparkling dance.

I do not know whether Polos can actually speak with horses; such things seem impossible to me. But as we swung through the third turn at the far end, I felt all four steady themselves for the final dash. We gained a bit on Gorgo's chariot then.

Half the lap passed . . . two-thirds. *"Now!"* I roared it with every shred of wind my lungs would hold and cracked my whip like lightning over the heads of the team. They bounded forward like four stags.

When we had brought both our teams to a halt, Queen Gorgo's driver spat all the ugly words he could lay tongue to into my face—some of them words I have never learned. Until Pasicrates stepped between us, he pretended that he was about to strike me with his whip. Prince Pausanias paid less heed to him even than I, grinning at Gorgo, who much to my surprise smiled at him in return. As for pretty Io and little Polos, they fairly capered with delight; and even Themistocles and Simonides were wreathed in smiles.

Then Gorgo's driver threw himself at her feet, talking very fast and pointing to her team. I could not understand all that was said, but I knew that he was begging her to propose a second race. It is never good, as I explained to Io, to make a horse run twice in the same day, though it must often be done in war. Indeed, it is best to give a horse several days in which to rest after a hard run.

But the prince readily agreed to hold a second race before the first meal. Their drivers walked both teams until they no longer sweated, examined their feet, and at last permitted them to drink a little. I asked Polos whether our horses understood that they would have to run again. When he nodded, I asked him to explain to them, if he could, that it was not my doing, that when I had promised them they would be returned to pasture after the race, I thought it true.

Polos positively glowed with pleasure, saying, "They don't mind. They want to race again."

I would not have held them back if I could, but I did not urge them forward. Of their own will they thundered around the meadow, keeping pace with Queen Gorgo's until the final turn. Then, as her chariot drew well ahead of mine, it threw a wheel. Her driver fell, and was dragged half the length of the course by the grays. For a moment it seemed we would trample him, but my team answered, swinging right. He was stunned, however, and when I saw Pasicrates cut the reins from his wrist, I thought him dead; but before we left, he stood and walked.

We ate the first meal here. The food was not good, but Io says the food at the barracks is worse. We eat there at times, she says. She wants me to ask the queen to let us dine with her, though I have told her Cyklos would surely be offended, and rightly. Io asked Aglaus where the black man was, but he could only tell us that he had gone out alone shortly after we went to speak with the prince.

As I left with Hippoxleas to go to the practice, I happened to pass the room where the black man sleeps with his wife; and I overheard him addressing her, his voice that in which an officer gives his orders in battle. We had not gone far when both came running after us. Gasping, the black man's wife asked whether I could wear my sword when I was made a resident of Rope; and when Hippoxleas declared that all weapons were absolutely forbidden, she drew me aside almost rudely, while the black man prevented Hippoxleas from going with us.

"There'll be trouble tonight," the black man's wife told me breathlessly. "He wants me to wedge the table against the door, and not open until I hear his voice. He's going to the ceremony—he'll bring your sword with his, wrapped in his cloak. He'll throw it to you if you need it."

I told her to take Io and Polos into the room with her, but she said, "Aglaus can protect them better than I could, and he'd kill me if he found Aglaus with me."

I will say nothing of the practice; it was easy enough, and I cannot recall anything that need be noted here except, perhaps, that Queen Gorgo directed it.

After the second meal we assembled, as before, to await the rising of the moon. We stood in silence, as we had been taught at the practice; and on the rare occasions when anyone dared to speak, he was hushed at once by several young Rope Makers. The slave standing next to me in the darkness (a wiry little rogue from what I could see of him) nudged me once or twice as though to assure himself, as well as me, that this was no dream. I had overheard these slaves talking among themselves at the practice and knew they were those who had fought best in the war, chosen by their fellows.

The full moon rose at last, hailed by the deep tones of the Men's Chorus. There can never have been another so beautiful as that silver shield upon the arm of the goddess!

Hardly had the men's voices fallen silent than we heard the bellowing of the bulls. Trotting they came, one black and one pied, each with two strong men to hold the shining chain through its nostrils. Priestesses cast fresh logs on the fire, and when its flames shot twice the height of a tall man, King Leotychides dispatched both bulls, which knelt in reverence to the goddess as they died. Together, Queen Gorgo and Tisamenus (the prince's mantis) examined them, she announcing each finding in her strong, clear voice.

Afterward each of the judges spoke, praising Themistocles. It was while he was replying, loudly cheered by all of us, that I happened to bump slightly against the young Rope Maker who was to sponsor the wiry slave. It was far from violent, and indeed I doubt that he gave any heed to it; but my arm told me that he had a dagger beneath his cloak. I thought then that he had been warned as I had, and had felt it wise to bring a weapon, though he risked the displeasure of the gods.

Themistocles was crowned by Leotychides and Pleistarchos, and our voices echoed to the heavens. Surely there is no point in listing here all the gifts he received, for there were very many; but I will say that the prince gave him the finest of all, a chariot of silver, set with precious stones and drawn by the horses I drove twice to victory. That was the final gift, and I saw how widely his eyes opened when he received it. There is a certain look that a man wears when he finds he has risen to a height he never dreamed of, and Themistocles of Thought wore it then.

As for me, my face must have made my amazement plain, for Hippoxleas whispered, "Is anything wrong?"

I shook my head, and did not tell him that I recalled that chariot, having seen it elsewhere.

Aglaus touched my arm, and when I turned to stare at him, pointed out the black man among the spectators, with Polos and Io before him. The moon was higher now, and the sacred fire lit the whole scene; I could see the cloth-wrapped bundle the black man held, which he had been too prudent to bring close to the young Rope Makers.

We bathed in the cool waters of the Eurotas, as we

had also at the practice, but this time we did not resume our old clothing; our guides consecrated us with a perfumed unguent and clothed us anew in white.

When this was done—and it did not take long—we formed our double column. There was considerable confusion, though we had practiced it again and again. I wanted to bawl orders as though upon the drill field, and I saw the same wish on the faces of Hippoxleas and a dozen others; still we kept silent, and it may be that the column shaped itself more smoothly because of it.

No doubt the march around the city should have tired us. I cannot speak for the rest, but I was not conscious of the least fatigue. The clear voices of the women, the graceful and ever-changing figures of the dancers, and the solemn scenes at temple after temple buoyed all our spirits, I think. In the flickering torchlight the carven faces of the gods smiled upon us. Lustily our voices answered those of the women as we praised each god in turn.

Sooner than I would have believed possible, our procession was over. Another temple, I thought, and it did not surprise me to find that it was upon the banks of the Eurotas, for the last two we had visited had stood there also. But it was the temple of Orthia, to which we had returned; and there I presented to an ancient image of the goddess the silver figurine Hippoxleas had carried for me, and cast away my guttering torch. Those who had not already made offerings now presented similar figures, though theirs were of lead. Mine depicted the goddess winged; wearing a tall headdress, she stood before her sacred tree. Those of the slaves that I saw were of beasts of the chase or small soldiers bearing bows or slings.

Prince Pausanius himself placed the crown of blossoms on my head, just as I had been promised he would. He seemed even more cordial than he had been in the morning, embracing me and twice instructing Hippoxleas to see that nothing evil befell me during the feast to come; each time Hippoxleas assured him that nothing would. It seemed strange to me that a man such as I, larger and (I believe) stronger than is common, should be cosseted like an infant. I could not but observe how brilliant the eyes of Queen Gorgo appeared; but such was my fatuity, and such the excitement of the moment, that it was not until the wreath was upon my head that I realized they were bright with tears.

When the feast began, Io, the black man, Polos, and Aglaus joined us. There was meat and wine in plenty, fruits and honey, honeyed breads and cakes—everything that anyone could wish for. We ate and drank our fill, and the black man collected figs and grapes, and a skin of good wine to take back to Bittusilma. By that time the scarlet moon rode low in the west. Half or more of the feasters had gone to their homes already, or so it seemed to me. I had forgotten the black man's warning, and so perhaps had he, though the bundle that held our swords lay at his feet. Not far off a hundred hounds or more coursed deer; their baying haunted the night whenever the noises of our feasting slackened.

There came a scream of anguish and despair—I hope I never hear such a sound again—and with it a running man, his chaplet of blossoms half-fallen from his head. He had one of the knives the priestesses had used, and though I could not be sure in the darkness, it appeared to me that he was drenched with blood. At once Hippoxleas rose as though to stop him, received the curved blade in his belly, and snatched away my crown of flowers. All this took place so quickly that I was still staring openmouthed when Hippoxleas lay dead at my feet.

A dozen daggers struck down the man who had killed him; the crowd surged about us, and I lost sight of the black man and the rest.

For what seemed to me whole days, I searched everywhere for them. I never found them, and when I felt that a new day should already have filled the sky, exhausted and more than half drunk, I decided to return to this house. I stumbled a score of times, but fell just once, when I tripped upon the legs of the expiring slave.

He, too, had worn a crown of blossoms; it lay in the dust not an arm's length from where he had fallen. Though his mouth ran with his blood, he struggled to make his speech clear to me, to forgive me, warn me, or tell me I know not what—or perhaps merely to beg my help; all the gods know how gladly I gave it. It was then that I recognized him, for in trying to stanch his blood, I had drawn him out of the shadows and into the moonlight. He was the slave who had driven Queen Gorgo's gray horses, and though I did him no harm, he will not let me sleep.

Since returning, I have learned that the one-armed man and some other Rope Makers had forced the black man, the children, and Aglaus to leave the feast, threatening the black man with the laws of Rope when he would not.

I am in a place besieged.

Part

4

38

The Pythia

The priestess of the god of Dolphins is very young. She appears kind.

I have written it, and do not know what more to write. But Kichesippos and my slave girl stand and stare.

They cannot read these letters, yet they know what letters are. If I make mere marks here, they will remonstrate with me, but what is there to say, and why should it be said? My slave girl slept with me. When we woke, the prince asked whether I had covered her. She said I had, but I know she lied. She fears he will bring me a boy.

Again. Io says I used always to do this, Kichesippos that it will make me well to speak of my disease, whether to him, or to the shining god of healing whose place this is, or merely to this roll of papyrus. When we hear ourselves, says Kichesippos, the gods hear us. That cannot be.

I asked Io what to write. She said I must write all that I remember. What I remember is only this: my mother's kiss before I slept. In my sleep I died and was swept into the Lands of the Dead, the dark kingdoms beneath the mountains. Long I wandered through the caverns where the nights to come are stored. There was much stone there, water, and mud; but nothing more. I heard the neighing of the horse of He Who Gathers, and the roaring of lions. At length I walked once more in the lands of the living, here in the pavilion of the prince; yet I know they come for me.

Io taught me her name; I thought her my sister, but she is my lover. The rest—the prince, Cyklos the judge, Kichesippos, the black man with the scarred cheek, his wife, the angry one-armed Pasicrates, our romping Polos, Amyklos, and Aglaus. There are more whom Io did not name, most of them slaves of the prince; and in the clear sunshine very many, for thousands gather here.

Pausanias and I went to the holy cave again. I write *again* because it seems from what Apollonios told us that we have been there before, though I do not remember it. The priests wear no sandals, and they are not to wash their feet. When I stared at them, the prince explained these things to me; he says, too, that they must sleep upon the ground, but everyone save himself does that here. We sacrificed, mumbled the many prayers, washed, did everything Apollonios instructed us to do. Then we entered the cave.

Its walls are damp and very high. Far above our heads, the narrow wedge of sky was nearly black. From it I knew we were in a place other than the lands of men; for when we had stood upon the mountainside, the sky had been bright with the glorious azure that is the most beautiful color of all. Here, then, the sacred fire of pine and henbane burned. Here, wrapped in preternatural gloom, the child-pythia sat her tripod behind a curtain of gauze.

Apollonios had guided us no farther than the entrance; Anochos, the proxenos of Rope, waited behind him.

The prince spoke: "I have been promised victory, and yet my charioteer is ill, gripped by a dread that neither he nor I understands. What am I to do?"

No one made a sound or moved a finger after that—nor did, nor could, I. The thudding of my heart no longer echoed in my ears, and no breath stirred in my nostrils. Some distant voice drew out a single, melancholy note that neither rose nor fell.

In the depths of the earth the python stirred. I heard it, the rustles of its scales, the hiss of its exhalations soughing so faintly that I believed it far away until its head was thrust from the crevice beneath the lofty tripod. Scarcely to be seen, it wreathed the pythia in phantom coils.

She screamed. We started, for at her scream our breath and life returned to us. Her arms flew out, her head back so that I thought her neck must break; the voice of the prince issued from her throat. As a lancer unhorsed might wrench his eyes from the blade poised to take his life, I glanced toward the man himself; he was not speaking, but stared as astonished as I.

"Thou art royal, royal be."

Afterward Apollonios reminded us that no one but a priest could understand the ravings of the pythia, and recited for us the following verses:

> Not gems nor spears can forge a crown,
> What gods raise up, men drag not down.
> Though queens in rags, they queens remain,
> Gracious in aid, their favor gain.

When we had left that sacred place, the prince said, "You understood the words the pythia spoke, Latro. Tell me."

I was frightened and asked, "How did you know?"

"Because you know the servants of him who stands behind all gods, as I told you last year. And because I saw your look when Apollonios prepared to tell us what she had said. Now, what did she really say?"

I repeated the pythia's words to him.

"Interpret it for me."

I shook my head, and he slapped me hard enough to stagger me. "Be a man! Once you would have tried to kill me for that."

He berated me much more. I do not recall all that he said, and I would not set it down if I did, no matter what Kichesippos and Io may say. Perhaps he would have struck me again, had not Polos ridden up.

Upon seeing the prince, he slipped from his mount's back at once. "Your Highness . . ."

The prince whirled to confront him.

"Your Highness, when we were up north, Latro used to ride all the time. He liked to. I thought maybe—"

As a squall blows off at sea, leaving the rainwashed sun, the anger drained from Pausanias' scarred face; he grinned and ruffled Polos' brown hair. "I suppose it can't hurt, and this certainly isn't helping. Latro, do you want to straddle this bag of bones?"

I shook my head.

"Then you probably ought to. What a nag! Where'd you find him, Polos?"

"He belongs to my uncle, Your Highness. He's a very good horse, really he is."

"To the venerable Amyklos? Then I shouldn't be so hard on him." The prince grasped the horse's jaw and skinned back its lips. "But he's an old horse, Polos—thirty at least. Nearly too old to work. Mount him, Latro!"

Polos dropped to his hands and knees so that I might step on his back, which made me itch to kick him. As soon as I was up he said, "I'll run alongside, Your Highness. I'll keep him out of trouble."

"Good!"

I let the old horse have his head, thinking that he would walk if he chose to move at all; to my astonishment, he darted away like a blooded racer, along the road, then into the trees and headlong down the wild mountainside, so that Polos was left as far behind as the prince. I heaved on the reins; at once the old horse slowed to a walk, and I let them fall to his neck. He whickered, and it seemed to me, almost, that he had spoken.

"You're welcome," I said. After that I sat looking at the pines and laurels through which we passed. It seemed to me that I could see their roots as well, the greedy fingers with which they tear at dead men's bones.

Soon we were joined by a riderless bay colt who appeared to enjoy the company of Amyklos' horse; and before long, our path—which I left entirely to the horses—began to climb; thus I rode up the mountain, always at a slow walk, for what seemed to me a very long time.

At last we reached a small temple of native limestone, in which stood the marble image of a maiden with a bow, and a real woman hardly less lovely. Leaving the shade of the temple, she extended her hands to me. "Dismount, Latro. You and I must talk awhile. Aglaus, will you look to the comfort of our guests, please?"

The gap-toothed servant, whom I had not noticed before, now stepped from behind a column to take the reins of my mount. As soon as I slid from his saddle, he let Aglaus lead him away; the colt trotted after them.

"There's a spring nearby," the pythia of this temple said. "Aglaus will fetch water for you if you wish it—but water, alas, is all we have. You did not bring your book?"

I shook my head.

"A pity. These are high matters we will discuss. I cannot speak of them yet, because all who must be present have not yet arrived. But you must promise, Latro, that you will write down everything. In fact I ought to do it myself—I drink too much, my husband says. But then I drink to forget."

I promised then that I would write as she advised (which I am doing now), for her touch had lifted my spirits a little; and I apologized for having brought no wine.

"We were lovers once," she told me, "lip to lip and lip to cup. Perhaps we will be so again. But not at present; not as you are today."

I nodded my agreement, for I have no desire to lie with any woman.

Soon Aglaus returned, bringing Polos and Polos' uncle, the long-faced old Amyklos. They had drunk at the spring and still wiped their mouths, flinging sparkling drops into the sunshine. I was conscious of my own thirst, but only as I might have been conscious of someone else's—it seemed pointless to satisfy it. The woman made them welcome, and they joined us in the shade of the temple.

"I hope you don't mind our taking you here," Polos said. "We're only trying to help you."

I told him that when he had invited me to step on his back, he had gone too far, that I would be old soon enough.

"What about sitting on my back to ride?" he asked.

I said I would not ask to do that for some while yet.

"But you already have, to steal the horses, and then to kill the boar."

I gave him an angry look, and he said, "I know you don't remember, but it's true! Tell him, Elata—you were there the first time."

The pythia said, "I can show it to you, Latro, if you want. You stole the horses of the sun, with the help of Polos, a lion, and a woman called Pharetra."

Embarrassed, the boy looked away. His old uncle laid a hand upon his shoulder. "You believe great warriors shouldn't weep. Can't you understand that the greatest must?"

When his nephew did not answer, he said, "You think highly of strength, Polos, and there's nothing wrong with that, because you're not strong yourself yet. But Latro can't think highly of it; he's strong, and so he's learned how little strength can do. You see, a boy can look up to a hero—in fact it's only natural at your age. But if that hero were to look up to himself in the same way, he'd be a monster, and not a hero at all."

When I had wiped my eyes, Polos told me, "I'm not ashamed of you, Latro. Really I'm not. You only remembered Pharetra because Aglaus is here."

That surprised me enough to awaken me for a moment from my despair. I feel sure my jaw dropped, and Aglaus himself looked as astonished as I.

Polos asked his uncle, "Is it all right if I tell him?"

"No, I'll tell him. You forget, Latro. We've talked about that before, so I know you know it. Gaea did it, as even young Io understands, and Aglaus is sacred to her."

My gap-toothed servant shook his head. "I don't mean any offense, sir, but nobody never told me that."

"You've been her lover since you were a boy, Aglaus, or so I'd guess. She returns your love, and perhaps loves you all the more because you don't know it."

A memory came to me, as though a singing bird had perched upon my head. "You've seen the god All," I told Aglaus. "You told me once."

"I've seen a few things," Aglaus admitted, looking hard at Polos and Amyklos. "Usually I've got sense enough not to speak about it to them that won't believe me. I told you 'cause you'd seen him yourself."

I nodded. "What are you doing up here, Aglaus? Don't you have work to do?"

"She brought me," Aglaus explained, pointing to the pythia. "She came while I was helping the cooks. Io knows her, and said for me to go with her and do what I was told, which is what I've done."

The pythia said, "This is a sanctuary of my mistress'.

You call her a goddess, and I'm her servant—far more so than Io or Aglaus are yours. I've been sent into this quarrel to represent her interests. Amyklos, Polos, and Aglaus are here for her foe, Gaea, who took away your memory."

"Prince Pausanias asked the oracle," Polos said. "And the god there told him to have me get my uncle to help you. He's a famous healer."

Old Amyklos added, "I haven't been able to accomplish much, I'm afraid. That's why we're here."

"And I'm here," a new voice called, "simply because I'm a friend of Latro's."

The speaker emerged from the pines some way down the slope. He is muscular, of middle size, and has the eyes of a fox. "I doubt you remember me, but Sisyphus is the name. A driver you beat told me about this, and I thought I'd like a hand in it." He hesitated, then roared with mirth. "You won't see the joke, but it *is* funny."

The pythia murmured, "Now we can begin."

Learning from Polos that my long ride had lifted my spirits somewhat, Kichesippos walked with me to the town and back. Now he insists I write of it. The air was fine, the sun bright. A slave in the marketplace called me brother. I was ashamed and pretended I had not heard him. Later I asked Kichesippos. He says I was freed by the prince. They are Crimson Men, and their ship lies at Cyparissa. They will be sold with their goods, said to be rich, when more have come to watch the games. Kichesippos is himself the prince's slave; he says he does not wish freedom. The pythia, he says, is the slave of the god—and that is much the same.

39

Diokles

The gymnastes has begun my training. Prince Pausanias wants me to box, and fight in the pankration, besides driving for him in the chariot race. Diokles talked with him, Cyklos, Tisamenus, Amyklos, and me this morning. Diokles is a head shorter than I. His beard is dark gray and bristling, and he spits often. He is training Pasicrates, too, for the footraces.

"I can see that he's strong," Diokles said. "What's the matter with him?"

The prince looked at Tisamenus, who shrugged. Old Amyklos said, "He's dispirited, and he can't remember, that's all. But exercise appears to help, not harm, him."

Diokles nodded sagely. "That's the way it usually is. What's he downhearted about?"

Tisamenus sighed. "You may leave that to us, sir. As you have been told, he does not remember."

Cyklos cleared his throat, the noise of one who feels that the time has come for him to take charge. "Our prince regent's mantis and this man, who I am informed is a noted physician, are treating these difficulties. It is for you to prepare his body for the contests."

Diokles nodded to show that he understood, though his eyes wanted to argue.

"It is vital to Rope that he do well. He must win at least one event and perform creditably in the rest—no excuses will be accepted. When will you enroll him?"

"Tomorrow, when the lists are opened, if he's got his fee."

The prince smiled. "Tisamenus has it. He'll go with you—there may be some difficulties. You can tell the hellanodikai that Tisamenus speaks for me and for our city. He'll explain to them that Latro qualifies in every way."

"I see." Diokles nodded to himself.

When we were alone, watching Pasicrates jogging around the track, Diokles asked in what way I did not qualify, and I told him I did not know.

"I'll swear you do," he told me. "You don't have to worry about that, see? I'll be behind you all the way. But I've got to know what we're up against. You're not from Redface Island, are you? You don't sound like it."

I said, "I think you're right."

"But you don't know? Huh! Can you wrestle?"

"A little, perhaps."

"That's good. A lot of wrestlers enter the pankration, but they never win. You talk to them and they'll tell you that once they get their grip on their man, it's all over. Fine. Maybe it takes them to the semifinals, see? Then they don't get their grip." He paused as if awaiting my reaction. "You know what it is, don't you? The pankration?"

I said, "I think I can guess from its name."*

"But you've never seen a match?"

"I don't know."

Diokles spat. "This is a great job, this is. All right, it's boxing, wrestling, and kicking. Can you box?"

"I think so."

"We'll find out. How about kicking?"

I said, "I suppose that anybody can kick."

Diokles spat, as before. "Take off those sandals. Don't put them back on till the games is over." He extended a hand at shoulder height. "Kick it, and kick hard. The harder you kick, the better I'll like it."

---

* *All-power*—GW

I kicked as hard as I could, but the end of my foot barely touched his palm.

"Try again!"

The result was scarcely better than before.

"With the other foot!"

This time I could not even touch his palm.

"Now hold out your hand for me."

I did as he said; the tips of my fingers were level with his eyes. His feet pumped like a boxer's fists: right-left-right, each kick higher than his head. At the third, I jerked my hand away.

"There's half a dozen kicks, and you're going to learn them all, with both feet. That's the first thing. I'll show you how you work out on the korykos."

Quite suddenly, he struck at my face. I blocked the blow with a forearm and backed away. He slapped at me with his other hand, and I blocked that as well. Swiftly his right fist jabbed at my waist; I knocked it aside.

"Now let's see you tag me."

When I had pinched his nose and smacked his face, he said, "You *can* box. The prince says he's seen you drive, and you're good. It's the only thing I'd trust him on, but I'd trust him on that—these blue bloods generally know horses even when they don't know anything else. The pankration's the problem."

Pasicrates was passing us just then. Diokles called, "One more lap—as fast as you can go—and then I'll give you a rubdown!"

Seeing Pasicrates sprinting around the track, I would have thought him fresh. He seemed to fly.

"He could win," Diokles mused. "We're going to write him up for stadion, diaulos, and dolichos. By the twins, I believe he's got a chance in all of them. Friend of yours?"

I said that I supposed he was.

"He says the girl's yours, but you and him are partners in the boy."

It seemed safest to nod, so I did.

"You leave them both alone till after, understand? I told him and now I'm telling you. Don't touch them, or anybody!"

Io sits watching me, but I will write no more.

Today, when I was very tired, Io led me to a grove in secret. The woman had wine, and had brought a cloth for us to lie on. I drank, and explained that I had no interest in her and no money. She laughed and rubbed my manhood between her fingers; but after a time we returned here.

Diokles sat down beside me after the second meal. He said, "Latro, I can't quite figure you out," and I told him he had no reason to.

"I've got to earn my fee." He spat. "The old judge, he thinks that if you don't win, they're not going to pay."

I nodded, knowing what he had said was true.

"Well, he's wrong about that. We're all hooked up with the oracle here, see? We've got to be. We have to make an offering every year after the games, and believe me it's a lot. But when somebody don't pay up, the priests go after him. So I'll get my money, and quick, too. Are you listening to me?"

I said that I was.

"But in your case—what's wrong with you, anyhow? Tell me."

I said that I did not know, then that it did not matter.

"Huh! Not to you, maybe, but it does to me. You want to win, don't you?"

"I suppose so."

"All right, then let me tell you something. In any event you can name, the ability a man's born with counts for a lot. That's a gift from the gods. Nobody can change it. Condition counts for a lot, too—it's very important. Then there's all the training he gets, and the tips from somebody like me who's done it here, done it at Olympia, done it at Nemea and Isthmia a dozen times. Things like that can make a big difference. But the most important thing is what's in a man's heart—whether he wants to win so much that he'll do whatever winning takes. You know the story they tell about Heracles and the cart?"

I did not, nor did I care to; yet I will set it down here because I must write something. (I am afraid that if I cease to write, I may throw myself upon my sword. There is a spirit in me that longs for it, and my hand strays to the hilt whenever I lay the stylus down.)

"This farmer," Diokles said, "had been trying to drive his cart along a narrow road, and it had slipped off into the ditch. 'Father Zeus,' he prayed, 'send me help, please! I'll never get this thing out by myself.'

"Just then, who should come along the road but Heracles of Hill, the strongest man in the entire world. 'Praise to Zeus,' said the farmer, 'who's sent you in answer to my prayer. Noble Heracles, won't you hoist this old wreck of a cart out of this ditch for me? You might help my oxen up, too.'

"But Heracles just laughed. 'Father Zeus hasn't heard a word you've said,' he told him, 'and I passed this way by pure chance. Now take your whip in your right hand and the ox goad in your left. Lay your shoulder to that wheel, and shout and curse your oxen with all your might. That's the only way that Father Zeus ever hears a man.'

"And it's a fact," Diokles affirmed. "I've seen men win, and boys, too, that didn't have a chance. Winded and out of it, and nine or ten strides behind, then beating somebody they had no business ever to beat. Some god sees them, see? 'Well,' he says, 'ain't he the plucky little 'un. I think I'll just puff him along a ways.'"

When I said nothing, Diokles finished, "There isn't any god going to do that for you. Not the way you are."

I spoke to him then of my feelings, as I have not spoken to anyone, not even little Io. I do not recall all the many, weary words I used, but what I said was this: that it seems to me that there is nothing to be found upon earth but treachery and hatred and the lust for blood and more blood. Man is a wolf to men, a vile predator that preys upon its own kind. I know that is true of me, however much I detest it. I know, as well, that it is true of everyone else, without exception; and that most of them do not even detest it as I do.

I ceased to write and, fearing my sword, shut it away in my chest; then I sought a lonely road, down which I walked for many stades. At length it seemed to me that another kept me company. At first I could not see him. After some while, there came a shadowy figure there, and at last a man who seemed as solid as I. I asked whether he was a ghost, and he freely acknowledged that it was so.

"You don't have to be afraid of me on that account," the ghost told me. "Most people are dead—you live ones are just sort of taking a holiday, and it'll soon be over. We'll laugh about all this then. Say, remember helping me with that rock?"

I did not, but I said nothing.

"They let me come because you did that. Our queen said it would be all right—they're a queer lot, sometimes. Did I ever tell you why she and our king were so down on me? It's a pretty good story."

The ghost waited for an answer, so I shook my head; he must have seen it in the moonlight.

He chuckled. "Well, back before I died, I decided I wasn't likely to care much for the Lands of the Dead; so I got my wife, Merope, to promise that no matter what anybody said she wouldn't bury my carcass, or burn it, either. Merope's a good girl—not too bright, or she'd never have married me; but once she pledges her word on a thing, that's the end of it. She'll do it if it kills her."

I said, "I see."

"You don't see *her*." He pointed toward a cluster of stars. "She's the one you can't see—the family's never forgiven her. Well, anyway, I died—being a mortal, you know—and Merope laid my body out and left it there, just like she'd promised. Pretty soon it was stinking up the whole palace, but Merope wouldn't let anybody touch it.

"As soon as it got ripe enough that people were kicking up quite a fuss, I went to our king. 'Let me return to the Lands of the Living,' I said, 'and revenge myself upon this faithless wife of mine who won't even give me a decent burial.' You see, I knew how seriously he takes these things.

"Well, to make a long story short, they let me out. I ran off and hid, and had a wonderful time until they finally fetched me back. I'm not going to do that this time, though—they might find me another rock."

His voice grew serious. "What I came to tell you, friend, was that we've been looking into killing Pasicrates."

"If you wish," I said.

The ghost laid a hand on my shoulder, and though it seemed that of a living man, it was as cold as ice. "Most of us agree it's an awfully attractive idea, but our seers tell us that it doesn't look as if it would be of any help to you until you're dead yourself."

"Which will be soon," I said.

"You're right, and that's precisely why you shouldn't rush things, my friend. Anyway, since killing him won't help, we're going to have to force him to let go. That Elata's a nice girl, by the way. She reminds me a lot of Merope, and she's on your side for old times' sake, as well as your having promised the Huntress that you'd fix the race. She got that mantis of hers to look into it for us, and he agrees with Amyklos. Amyklos is on your side because of his nephew, of course."

When I returned here, I found that someone had draped an old cloak across two stools as if to curtain the place where I would sleep. I thought nothing of it; but when I lay down, I found that a woman lay beside me.

"You've been mourning," she explained. "I've come to kiss your tears away."

How sinuous her body was, fragrant and smooth with perfumed oil! Perhaps it was that the ghost had brought me hope, perhaps only that she was somehow different; but though I had been able to do nothing with the woman with the wine, with her I was a man again.

Afterward, we walked hand in hand by moonlight. "I know you," she told me. "No wonder I had that dream! I'm in love with you."

Her name is Anysia.

"Diokles the gymnastes sent me," she said, and pressed some coins into my hand. "Here's what he gave. Return it to him—or keep it yourself if you like."

I slept well after she had gone, but not for long, I think. Now I am awake again; the sun is not yet above the mountaintops.

40

For the Sake of Days Past

Elata is kind to me, partly because I have promised the Huntress that a race will end as she wishes—or so the ghost said. After I read what I had written, I asked who Elata was. Io explained that we met her, and

Hegesistratus her husband, in the north; Io called him a mantis, as the ghost had. Elata, it seems, was the woman with the wine of whom I wrote.

"They're here with a five-tests man from Zakunthios, and to consult the oracle. Zakunthios isn't big enough to have someone in every event, the way Rope does."

She wanted to know whether I recalled meeting with Elata in the grove. I admitted I did not, but said that I had read of it here, at which she blushed. "Elata thought she might be able to cheer you up," she told me, "so I said that if it would make you better it was all right with me. And you really *are* better, but I think it's the special food. Kichesippos had a big fight with Diokles about that, and Amyklos looked like he was getting ready to fight both of them. He says more barley and no meat at all."

I told her that I would eat whatever my physicians wished, if only it would help me remember.

"It isn't that now," Io said. "It's just to help you feel better, and I think it's working, a little. You're writing more in your book, and that's a good sign."

Io said, too, that this Hegesistratus is eager to see me but will not come to our pavilion. He is afraid of the Rope Makers. There is a truce everywhere in Hellas in honor of the games, but he does not trust them even so.

The Huntress is a goddess, Io says. She knows nothing of a promise I made her, but she says I may have taken an oath at her temple in Rope. The black man would not let Io and Polos go to the temple with me.

He and his wife will accompany Pasicrates, Tisamenus, and me this morning, when we go into Dolphins with Diokles to have our names entered in the rolls. Now we are waiting for Diokles.

While waiting I have read about many past days. *"Pharetra, 'bowcase,' is as like it as any word I know, though she laughed at me."* My heart leaped when I read that. What has become of her? Perhaps she died of her wound.

Tisamenus came to speak with the black man and me. I know that Io does not like him, but he seems friendly and polite, and everyone defers to him because he is said to be an illustrious mantis. "Last night I conferred with Trioditis concerning you," he told me. "She will do all that lies in her power to aid you, provided you do all that lies in yours to aid Rope. 'The queen must win,' she said, 'and thus the queen must lose.' Does that convey any meaning to you?"

I shook my head, and so did the black man.

"I feel certain it is Queen Gorgo, her priestess, who must win," Tisamenus told us. "When you drive for our prince regent, sir, you will represent her as well. The rest we must strive to understand.

"By favor of divine Trioditis you are improved," Tisamenus continued. "Your thoughts, I hope, haven't turned to the taking of your own life?"

I did not reply, at which the black man stared at me.

Tisamenus said gently, "When the soul has been overwhelmed by grief, sir, as yours has been, a man does nothing that he is not compelled to do, for then he believes that nothing can help him. At such times, he is no danger to himself or anyone else. But as the claws fall away, hope—the final horror, if I may say it, from that deadly box the gods packed for men—hope returns. It is then that his family and friends must watch a man, because he's apt to think that by putting an end to his life he'll put an end to his sorrows."

I confessed then that such thoughts had sometimes stirred in me.

"Never trust them, sir." Kindly, he laid his hand upon my knee. "Trust me instead. I've trafficked with many ghosts, and they are less happy even than we, and envy us. I've heard that while you crossed the barbarian lands you journeyed for a time in the company of Hegesistratus the Tellidian?"

I nodded, recalling what Io had said about him.

Tisamenus shook his head. "He is a great mantis, sir, and is now counted by some the head of our clan, though he dare not show his face in Elis. But he is consumed with malice, sir. I am his kinsman, and I find those words as bitter as gall in my mouth. Yet they are true. He is the sworn foe of Rope, and has said that he will destroy it, if it does not destroy him."

Here the black man made several quick gestures. I did not understand most of them, but one certainly represented a dagger plunged into his own chest.

"It's true," Tisamenus told us, "that Rope imprisoned him, and that he escaped as you describe." He heaved a sigh. "With what infinite patience the gods labor to teach us! We speak at times of a man who will stop at nothing; I have not infrequently spoken thus myself. And yet it never strikes us, when we must deal with such a man, that he will, in fact, stop at nothing."

Tisamenus pierced me with his eyes. "But he had slandered our city, sir—your own and mine. You forget, hmm? You haven't forgotten, I hope, that you've been proclaimed a resident of the most glorious city in Hellas?"

The truth is that I remember nothing of that, but out of politeness I said, "Certainly not."

"And I"—Tisamenus touched his chest—"I have been granted a like privilege. We're her adopted sons, sir, both of us. You will have heard before this, no doubt, that the noble Pasicrates desires to marry in order that he may adopt the little barbarian called Polos. Tell me, sir, who owes the greater loyalty to his father? Is it the son of his body, or one he has adopted?"

I said that I supposed the adopted son owed more, for his father had been his rescuer as well.

"Nicely reasoned, sir! Consider my position, then, if

you will. I was in Elis, where I still maintain the house that once I shared with my wife, for the Italoan Festival. There, too, was my cousin, leveling the grossest insults and the vilest slanders against the very city that had a short time before honored me by making me her son. What was I to do? Sit silent and appear by my silence to consent? I essayed a response to his defamations, and was shouted down by men I had known—had numbered among my friends, in fact—since boyhood. In desperation, I dispatched a letter to our patron and another to my good friend Cyklos, both carried by the swiftest of my slaves. In them I recounted what I had seen and heard, and urged that they warn my cousin that he was making enemies of many who would greatly have preferred to be his friends. Would you not have done the same?"

I agreed that I would, though I would probably have gone to Rope myself to hurry things along.

"Just so, sir. As it happened, the prince regent had not yet returned to the city, but Cyklos dispatched several trusted officers to reason with my cousin. They came as a delegation, you understand, and not a military force. I believe there were five or six all told. Elis welcomed them, and when they found that nothing they could say would sway my cousin, they invited him to visit Rope, where he might speak with Cyklos in person, pointing out that he had never troubled to see for himself the modest place to which he had imputed so much evil. He demurred; they insisted, and at last, having received permission from the magistrates, placed him under restraint and carried him to Rope by main force. Do you know how criminals are commonly confined, sir, in Rope?"

I did not, nor did the black man.

"They are flung into pits, sir, and afterward their food is thrown down to them. Nothing of the sort, you may be sure, was done to my ill-mannered cousin. Instead

Cyklos himself, one of the most distinguished men in our city, welcomed him as a guest in his own home, though he was later forced to confine him when he insisted upon leaving at once.

"As I was about to say, I think it likely that my cousin is responsible for the sorrow that oppresses you. It is more than possible that he has charmed you in some way. I wished to speak with you now because I have heard that he is here for the games. I trust that you recall his appearance? If not, your friend can point him out to you."

When I wrote that which stands above, I had no notion that we would in fact encounter this man, who seems generally to be called Hegesistratus of Elis, so quickly. Diokles came (which was why I stopped writing), and we went to the place where the judges of the games sit to receive those who wish to take part—we were a great throng, come as I soon learned not only from all parts of Hellas, but from every other place where the Hellenes' tongue is spoken.

In this courtyard in Dolphins many were examined at length, for the rule is that only Hellenes may compete. The black man's wife told me, in fact, that he had been anxious to take part in the stadion and the javelin throwing, but had been told that he could not, though he had offered to pay his own fees. We waited there for some while before we were permitted to address one of the hellanodikai.

This man knew Diokles and greeted him by name. Diokles in turn introduced the rest of us and explained that the black man understood that he would not be allowed to compete, but that he wished to study the way in which the games were conducted with an eye to establishing a similar event among his own countrymen. Pasicrates' name was entered on three rolls as soon as his fees had been paid.

"Are you a Hellene?" the hellanodikas asked after looking long at my face.

I said, "Certainly," and explained as Tisamenus and Diokles had instructed me that I had been made a citizen of Rope.

"That's bronze-bound, Agatharchos," Diokles declared when I had finished. "I got it straight from King Pausanias. I wasn't going to take him on until I did."

"I see." The hellanodikas fingered his beard.

"He will drive His Highness' chariot," Tisamenus told him. "I myself have been made a Rope Maker, as you may know already; I am commonly called Tisamenus of Elis. The noble Pasicrates, a Rope Maker by birth, will vouch for him as well, I feel certain."

All eyes turned toward the one-armed man, who said with the intonation of a serpent, "He is a resident of my city—but he is no Hellene."

At these words, I saw something I would never have thought to see. Tisamenus whirled and raised his fist to the one-armed man, who backed away with fear naked upon his face.

Deftly, Diokles stepped between them. "A little rivalry, Agatharchos. You understand."

The hellanodikas shrugged. "Better than I want to. Latros Spartathen, if you're really a Hellene, let's hear you spout some poetry."

I confessed that I did not remember any.

"Come, now. You must know something. How about this:

> "'For thee, my son, I wept my life away;
> For thee through Hell's eternal dungeons stray;
> Nor came my fate by lingering pains and slow,
> Nor bent the silver-shafted queen her bow;
> No dire disease bereaved me of my breath;
> Thou, thou, my son, wert my disease and death;
> Unkindly with my love my son conspired,
> For thee I lived, for absent thee expired.'"

Sorrow swept me away—a moaning wind. My eyes filled with tears; I could only shake my head.

"Sir," Tisamenus whispered, "you must speak now, and speak poetry, or—Cyklos does not regard you kindly."

The palace rose before me, tier upon tier. Frantically I hurried from image to image—a man with the head of a crocodile, another with that of a hawk.

"Well?" the hellanodikas inquired.

I tried to repeat what he had said about the silver-shafted queen, though I did not know then—and do not know now—what it meant. For an instant, I seemed to glimpse her behind him, her smooth, fair face aglow above his black hair. From somewhere or noplace the half-remembered rhymes rose to my lips:

"You golden lyre, Apollo's and the muses',
Your tune commands the dance, your tone he uses,
When master of the warbling choir,
He lifts the crystal voices higher."

Faintly I heard someone shout, "What . . . ? *Latro!*"

"You quench the bolt, the lightning's fearful fire,
The eagle rests his wings, that never tire;
To hear you shaken by your song,
Fell Ares quits the spear-proud throng."

"Latro, it's me, Pindaros!" Though he is older than I by ten years at least, and smaller, too, he wrapped me in a bear's embrace and lifted me off my feet.

"Will drive for His Highness in the chariot race," muttered the hellanodikas as he wrote. "Boxer. Pankratiast."

Pindaros and the black man danced, swinging each other like stones in a sling.

41

The God Himself Shall Rule

Thus it was decided after much argument. Pharetra is going tomorrow, with her queen, Themistocles, Hegesistratus, and the rest. Meanwhile, a score of travelers arrive each time I draw breath; and it is the talk of the town—still more so of the great camp beyond it that spreads ever wider. When Pindaros invited us to join him over wine, I doubted that there was a drop left in Dolphins, or a single place to sit; but he guided us to the inn where he stays whenever he comes here.

"Which is every four years," he told us, "each time they hold the games. I haven't won as yet, but I have high hopes—very high—for this year. And it's good publicity."

Thinking him too old for the footraces, I asked whether he boxed. He and Diokles laughed about that. (Pasicrates and the mantis were not with us, though Pindaros had invited them both. Pasicrates would not stay, while Tisamenus, I would guess, did not wish him to speak with the prince alone.)

Over our wine, Diokles and Pindaros explained the structure of the games to me. There are to be trials of music as well as strength and swiftness. For a time I ceased this writing to ask Diokles about their order again, which Kichesippos allowed; this is to be relied upon.

- Singing to the lyre. Pindaros was set down for this when we finished the wine. The verses must be contestant's own, ones never heard before.
- Flute-playing.
- Stadion—a single circuit of the track. Pasicrates will run.
- Diaulos—two circuits. Pasicrates entered this as well.
- Dolichos—twenty-four turns. Pasicrates entered.
- Five trials—they are running, throwing a diskos, jumping, casting a javelin, and wrestling.
- Wrestling.
- Boxing—I will do this.
- Pankration—this also.
- Horseracing—the prince entered Argas; Ladas will ride him.
- Stadion for boys.
- Five trials for boys.
- Boxing for boys.
- Dolichos for boys.
- Diaulos for boys.
- Chariot race—I will drive for the prince.
- Lyre-playing—Simonides will do it.
- Running in armor—the last event.

On certain days there will be several events. For example, on the first Pindaros and the rest will sing in the morning, the flute-playing will begin after the first meal, and the stadion before sunset. All the boys' events (except the horserace) will be held on the same day, and on the last, the lyre-playing will be followed by the race in armor.

Io found us while we sat over wine, bringing the news that Themistocles of Thought had come, riding in a silver chariot. I do not remember this man, but Io and the black man say that we traveled with him to the prince's city; the Amazons will use his chariot if they compete.

I should write that I believed Bittusilma the black

man's wife, but both swear there is nothing between them. Polos says this is because married women may not watch.

When we had drunk the wine, we went back to the courtyard where names are set down upon the rolls so that Pindaros might enter. There we met Themistocles, a burly, jovial man in fine clothes, and Simonides, an old man. He had come to enter the lyre-playing. Themistocles told Pindaros he had come only to see the sights, and explained how the black man and I had been freed, as Bittusilma had before. It was much the same. Then Pindaros told everyone how he had gone to Hill to get the money to buy our freedom—though we were never truly slaves. When he returned to Thought, we were gone. He left money with a woman there and went back to Hill, where he asked the wardens of the city to make Thought free us.

As I heard all this, I thought better and better of him. I know that not everyone who shouts a greeting is in fact a friend, but I think Pindaros one. I asked if he would play and sing for me, to lift my sorrow from me. I know music has that power. He said he would if I would come to him this evening. Now I do not believe it will help, though Kichesippos says that it may.

There is much more to write; I will strive to be brief.

The Amazons arrived like stones through a window, stilling all babble. Heads turned; then we saw them, five, gaunt and far taller than most men, clad in grace and ragged skins but bearing beautiful weapons. My jaw fell with the rest—but that was as nothing, for the tallest turned aside to embrace me. We kissed, and a thousand throats laughed and cheered. My cheeks burn now as I write of it. This Pharetra was my lover in Thrace. When I learned of that, I went to speak to the judges with her and the other women; but the judges ran to get others, and we were left to wait.

That was when I saw the prize for the chariot race, which I had not noticed before. It is a tall red urn, the work of some excellent artist, filled they say with the finest oil and sealed with wax. But it is more: it is the urn from my memory palace, although when I walk into the palace in my mind, it stands there also—this seems very strange to me. Black dancers with beards, and the ears and tails of horses, caper around it.

The hellanodikai returned, a dozen at least, all of them shaking their heads. No woman, they insisted, could compete. That the queen is unmarried made no difference—no women at all. Nor could anyone compete unless he was a Hellene, and none of the Amazons can speak as the Hellenes do—or only a few words.

I had not observed that Io had left us, but now she darted through the crowd to us, bringing with her a handsome, limping man with a curly beard. Themistocles greeted him as a friend, the hellanodikai hailed him, and the Amazon queen embraced him. While he was speaking with one and another, Io told me that he is a great mantis—more famous even than Tisamenus. He was with Pharetra, Io, and me in the north.

He speaks the tongue of Amazons, and he assured the judges that a very great god, the god of war, had sent these women; but the judges still refused.

When he had heard them out, he turned to Themistocles and the old lyre-player. These three spoke together very rapidly, but their voices were too low for us to overhear them.

When all had nodded together, Themistocles stepped forward to address the judges—or rather, to address everyone present while pretending to address them. His booming voice filled the whole courtyard.

"You must pardon my ignorance, friends," he began. "It's been many years now since I attended these games."

The hellanodikai and several others assured him that

they were delighted he had come this year, for it seems he is a very great man indeed.

"I have been informed that my dear friend Prince Pausanias of Rope has entered the chariot race," Themistocles continued. "Tell me, does he intend to drive his chariot himself? Will the reins be in his own hands?"

At this several of the judges pointed to me and explained that I was to drive on behalf of the prince.

"And that's the prize, that fine red jar there? Will Latro get it if he wins? He's a fortunate man!"

The hellanodikai hastened to explain that I would not—that it was actually the prince who was competing, not I.

"Oh," said Themistocles. "That explains it. I know Latro, and he's no Hellene—"

They hastened to say that they had ruled I was a Hellene, and that I had been permitted to enter two events.

"But not the chariot race," said Themistocles. "Clearly, it is the prince who is the contestant in that. Tell me, is it lawful for a woman *not* to enter?"

At this the judges looked perplexed indeed. They whispered among themselves, then said that since women could not enter, it was of course implied by the rules that they need not enter.

"Wonderful!" Themistocles rubbed his big hands together and smiled broadly. "But I might enter? I am both a man and a Hellene, and I have a fine chariot."

The judges said that they would be delighted to have him enter; there was no question of his qualifications.

"Then I'll do it," he told them. "Put down my name, please. I'm Themistocles Athanaios, and this woman is to drive for me." Here he pointed to Pharetra.

Afterward I kicked the korykos, instructed by Dikles. It is a pigskin filled with meal, suspended by a rope. Agatharchos the hellanodikas came to watch me because my name is upon three rolls now. He told me that many who have been set down will be struck off when the judges have seen them practice, but I will not be. Diokles says that I am better, that he still does not approve of love in advance of the games, but that he made a good investment. I did not follow him; and though Io watches me as I write, I hesitate to ask her. I feel I— There are cliffs here from which a man might throw himself onto rocks or into the sea.

I have had a strange evening and a very strange dream. I will write here of what actually happened first; then if there is time, recount the dream; then if there is still time, how I feel now. That is most important of all, but I do not think it apt to change again, so I may write of it whenever I choose.

Io and I went to the inn where we had drunk with the poet. He welcomed us and, seeing how fatigued I was, suggested that I stretch myself upon his bed while he sang. I did, thinking all the while: thus it is for the dead—a rest from which they need not rise. It was then that I dreamed my dream.

The poet said, *"I'm afraid that's all for tonight. I don't dare strain my voice."*

At these words I sat up.

Io was crying. She hugged and kissed the poet, saying over and over how lovely his music and verses had been. As for me, I recalled not a single line. But I felt myself a hero who might raze cities or raise new ones; and so I grinned like an idiot as I embraced him, pounding his back while he pounded mine.

"I knew hearing me would help," he said. "If you hadn't an ear for poetry—yes, and a heart for it, too—you wouldn't have remembered that scrap of mine I heard you recite for the judges this morning. Not you of all men, because you forget everything; but the Shining God heals, Parnassos is his place, and he's our patron."

It was pitch dark when Io and I left the poet's inn for the streets of Dolphins; we had a long walk ahead of us, and I found myself wishing I had brought my sword.

"Pindaros must be the greatest poet in the world," Io told me. "And just think—he's our friend!"

I asked whether I had snored.

"Did you nod off? Master, you couldn't have—it was too wonderful. Besides, your eyes were open the whole time."

I said, "I was afraid I had, just for a moment. It seemed I'd missed a verse or two."

Io shook her head. "Well, you certainly didn't snore—I would have shaken you right away. And you're so much better! Even Diokles says so. It was not seeing Pharetra, wasn't it? You've been pining for her, but now that she's here you're all right again."

A new voice announced, "She is closer than you think," and the lame man hobbled through an archway, followed by the Amazon queen, Pharetra herself, and a slender woman whose floating hair did not even reach Pharetra's shoulder.

Io said, "Hegesistratus! Oh, I'm so happy! Latro's so much better now."

"And so he ought to be," Hegesistratus agreed. Pharetra slipped her hand into mine.

The queen spoke using the tongue of Amazons, which I do not understand; and Hegesistratus said, "We are going out to have a look at the horses. Would you like to see them, too? They will be racing against yours."

We went to the Amazons' camp, where the other three guarded their horses. They held up brands so we might see them. Surely there have never been better ones! They gleamed like flames in the torchlight, snorting and stamping. Io said how good it was of Themistocles to help the women as he has, and of the lame man to enlist

Themistocles' help for them. The lame man only shook his head and spat into the fire. "He has become a friend of the Rope Makers," he told her. "For the good of the world, he must be discredited, and they destroyed." Afterward, he cautioned us to say nothing of this.

The lame man remained behind with the queen and the other women when we left, but Pharetra came with Io and me. A woman was in my bed; when she saw Pharetra, she attacked her with a little dagger. It woke the prince—Cyklos—everyone, but they were not angry and cheered the women as they fought. Pharetra knocked the dagger from the smaller woman's hand, caught her at last, and threw her into a ditch.

When everyone had gone back to sleep, Pharetra lay beside me, and though she is as large as a large man, her kisses were a woman's. I loved her very much. She speaks a few words of the Hellenes' tongue, and she told me that once she and I tended the white horses in a cave. She wanted to know whether I remembered Hippostizein, who died in the north. (I do not.) Late at night, she told me, fear comes upon her. If she loses when we race our chariots, her queen will surely offer her to appease their god. I held her very tightly after that. She woke me when she left, and thus I write here as I do, having carried this lamp outside and lit it from the embers.

This was my dream.

A boy stood beside the bed. When I turned my head to look, I saw he was younger than Polos. His feet tapped the floor, for they were those of a kid; horns budded from his forehead. "Come with me," he told me, and we went out into the mountain town, up a crooked street, then climbed steep slopes.

"You're a faun," I said. "Fauns bring dreams." Someone had told me that—I do not recall who.

He nodded, "I bring you." His kid feet climbed the rocks better than my human ones.

We reached a little temple where a fire blazed on the altar. Here is something very strange—a lovely woman made me welcome, and later I was to meet her waking. No doubt I had met her this morning, and she had lingered in my thoughts. Polos and Amyklos were there, both horses from the waist down. Polos frolicked between the temple and the trees. "Don't be afraid," he said. I told him that I wished to die, thus nothing held terrors for me. But the last was a lie.

Tisamenus and Pasicrates came, attended by my servant and conducted by a strange, sly man who grinned when he caught sight of me. Hounds bayed. Later, when we admired the Amazons' white horses, the lame man asked whether I heard hounds. I did not, as I told him. I did not tell him I had heard them earlier in my dream.

"Take back your hand," the woman said to Pasicrates. "Take it back, if ever you hope for rest."

The one-armed man snapped, "He took it from me; let him keep it." Tisamenus murmured, "It's you, then. You're doing this. Now that I know it, I may break the charm."

"There is no charm," Amyklos told him. "Only hate."

"In that case he must die, sir." Tisamenus nodded his own confirmation. "Cyklos is weighing that already, because of—" He jerked his head toward Polos. "He's not one of them. Such loves are dangerous."

Aglaus said, "If you're harming my master—"

Pasicrates struck him in the throat. Aglaus fell, and did not rise again. At once Amyklos was upon Pasicrates, stallion and rider, too, knocking him off his feet and planting both front hooves upon his chest. Pasicrates stared up, pop-eyed, as Amyklos mocked him. "You preen yourself upon strength, swiftness, and courage. Look at me! Old, but stronger and faster than you are—or will ever be. And braver, too. What are all your boasted qualities compared to any charger's?"

Grim, the woman crouched beside Pasicrates. "Don't

deceive yourself. Do you think this only a dream? Death here is death, and Amyklos could kill you easily. Those you call friends will find you dead where you slept. Your prince will have forgotten you long before the sun breeds worms in your corpse."

I helped Aglaus stand, then asked Pasicrates what he had done that had roused such wrath against us in these people; but he would neither look at me nor reply. Polos begged his uncle to allow Pasicrates to sit up. "You want me to love you," Polos told Pasicrates, "and I *want* to. Truly I do."

Something stirred in me, like a spider on its web.

"I *would* love you," Polos said. "I promise I will."

Standing next to the woman, I had bent over Pasicrates to speak to him. Now he reached toward me with his stump of arm; when he withdrew it, it was a whole one like my own. Far away, someone said, *"That's all for tonight. I don't dare strain my voice."*

I have watched the sun rise. I forget, I know, but I have not forgotten the night that crushed me like the horse-Amyklos of my nightmare; thus I write as I do, hoping that if it returns I will read this.

A man's life is indeed short, ending in death. If it were long, his days would be of small value. If there were no death, of none. Let him fill each day with honor and joy. Let him not condemn himself or another, for he does not know the laws of his existence or theirs. If he sleeps in death, let him sleep. If while sleeping he should meet a god, he must let the god decide how well or ill he lived.

The god he meets must rule upon a man's life, never the man himself.

42

Pausanias Rages

Io says that when Kichesippos came to speak about me, the prince struck him. I think it shameful to strike so aged and learned a man. So does Pausanias—I saw it in his face—but he struck him nonetheless.

"The gods toy with me." Thus he spoke to Tisamenus when he summoned us. "They give me the greatest victory in history and tear its fruits from my hands."

"The Hellenes should restore your goods to you," Tisamenus told him. "They're deeply in your debt."

"I can't ask that!"

"Of course not, Your Highness." Tisamenus rubbed his plump chin and rolled his eyes to heaven. "Yet some others might urge such gratitude—without so much as a hint from Your Highness, to be sure. Themistocles is here; and Simonides, the poet, is with him."

Here is what happened. I learned of it bit by bit, and the last only by going to the agora and speaking to the Crimson Men held there under guard. Pausanias entrusted the spoils of his victory to their ship; they had been promised a safe passage by Tower Hill, but they were overtaken and boarded by a ship from Hundred-Eyed, and towed to a port at the foot of the mountain. By this he has lost a fortune.

Their captain knows me. Muslak is his name. Not wishing him to see how I forget, I hailed him in return when he hailed me. *Lewqys,* he called me, and perhaps that is my name; surely no man is really named Latro.

He said, "I knew you'd come back when you could

come alone. You didn't want the old man to know we're friends, did you? But we hoped you'd come sooner."

I told him I had seen no point in returning until I learned their situation, though the truth was that I had no notion how I might help them. When one understands nothing yet must speak, it is best to question. I asked a great many. When I wanted to know whether he would return me to my home if I were to free him and his crew, and return their ship to them, his eyes flew wide. He swore he would. He assured me he knew the place, pointing to the west. *Luhitu* was the word he used. We spoke as the Crimson Men do, so that their guards would not understand.

I still do not know what can be done, but I know that for gold these Hellenes will connive at anything. Io has some, as I saw when she got out the coin I gave Aglaus.

The prince watched me box with Diokles. We wear himantes to protect our hands and do not strike hard. Diokles is quick and wary; as I explained to the prince, that is what is needed in practice.

"You seem cheerful enough today," he told me.

I showed him how Diokles tricks me with his left hand, and explained how much trouble that had given me. "So I've learned something new, Your Highness. I will forget where I learned it, I know. But I think not what I have learned."

He grinned and slapped my shoulder. His scars give him an evil face, but I do not believe an evil heart beats beneath it. "It was you that cured him, wasn't it, Diokles?"

Diokles spat. "He cured himself, Highness, by doing what I told him. I might have helped a little."

"I feel sure you did. I've been keeping track of Latro's physicians, or trying to. He's been cured by Kichesippos and Tisamenus (who had a wondrous vision last night, by the way). And by Amyklos, I'm sure, although he hasn't come around yet to claim the credit for it. Yes, and by his slippery little wench Io. That's four. And now by himself and you, which makes six. Is there anybody else? How about Polos?"

Recalling the dream of which I wrote at sunup, I told him, "Yes, Highness, by Polos and Pasicrates. But by Polos most of all."

"That brings my total to eight—I shall win the laurels for certain. But I wanted to ask both of you something about Polos. Latro, can you recall what Tisamenus told me concerning him this morning?"

"Certainly. That he should ride Argas for you."

"You have the ear of the gods, Latro, as I've said before—whether you know it or not. So do you agree?"

I shrugged. "Does Polos want to?"

"I haven't asked him."

Diokles spat again. "'Course he does. He's asked me about the boys' events, wanting to get into everything. I had to tell him he couldn't, and those big boys would thresh him anyhow. But he's lighter than Ladas. That's always good. Besides, you never saw such a hand with horses."

Aglaus rubbed me while Diokles did the same for Pasicrates. "What a dream I had! You knocked me down, then helped me up."

I have forgotten my own dream, but I had read of it here. I asked whether he was certain it had been I.

"Sure, because I thought you'd hit me again when you lifted me. My neck's sore—that brought on the dream, I suppose."

Pasicrates remarked that such a dream seemed a good omen for a boxer.

"No more boxing for Latro," Diokles told him. He counted on his fingers. "He's only got four days till the real thing, and he mustn't carry bruises into it."

I should say here that no boxer would hit a man again

after helping him rise—when a man has been knocked down, the fight is over. It is only in the pankration that a man knocked down may continue to fight.

Afterward, Pasicrates spoke with me in private. "I had a dream, too," he said, "but in mine it was I who struck Aglaus." I said nothing, and he continued, "When you saw how angry I was, you asked whether I wanted my hand back. I was angry at you—I suppose I struck Aglaus because he's your servant—and I said that since you had taken it you might keep it. I felt that if you returned it, I would have to end our quarrel, you see."

I said that if that was the case, I certainly hoped I had given it back to him.

"You did. We rode to your quarters, and you got it out of your chest. Your sword lay on top; under it were chitons and so on. You kept pulling things out and putting them on the ground. My hand was at the very bottom. I took it out and stuck it on my arm somehow."

He laughed, and I laughed with him. "I hope you helped me repack my clothes."

"I don't remember. But the truly odd part is that all day I've felt as if I really had it back: like a complete man again. I can do anything that anybody with two hands can, after all—except play the lyre, perhaps."

Tisamenus took me to the prince, and the three of us called upon Orsippos. Tisamenus says he is a warden of Hundred-Eyed and its richest citizen. At first, I could not understand why I had been brought to be stared at by Orsippos, who is fat and has lost hair at the crown. Later I realized that it is because the prince has bet with him and he wished to see me. Their bet on the chariots was doubled.

Though it made some other Rope Makers angry, Pasicrates and I marched side by side at the opening of the games; the ceremony was extremely impressive. Afterward, the Babylonian, the black man, and the children found us; and we remained with them in the stadium to hear a poet from Cowland. Pasicrates ridiculed his twanging accent at first, but soon acknowledged him the best of all. The hellanodikai were of the same opinion, awarding him the laurels. He is certainly a friend, as Io says he is, for he talked with us for a time though a hundred at least were waiting to speak with him.

The stadium is very fine; its lower seats are stone, though the upper ones are wooden. It is open at each end so that those who please the god may come and go. The oval track is exactly a stade in length—we marched around this. All the poets brought stools; they sat in the center, with their stools on the grass. The listeners left their seats to gather around their favorites. By the time the contest was over, the crowd around our poet was very large indeed.

I have begun to read this from the beginning. Today I read about Artaÿctes and his son, but learned little of use. I have told Aglaus that he must speak to me each day, privately, about the slaves in the market; and I have told him what he must say.

Pasicrates ran well but did not win; the prince was angry. At his command, Tisamenus and Diokles sought to have my name set down in the wrestlers' roll, but the judges would not permit it, saying it is too late.

This has been an unquiet night—laughter, I find, can be as hard to bear as any blow. Pharetra lay with me, and for a time we talked of bows and the like, she having visited the house of a man who deals in such things. His swords, she says, are fine, his bows not bad. I told her to find out whether he would sell her bows, arrows, and swords without asking why she required them. When she said she had nothing to trade, I explained that I would supply her with money. She has learned enough of Io's tongue to make herself understood.

The other woman came. She did not dare enter the

pavilion but screamed at Pharetra, calling her a wild cow and many other names; she roused everyone. Pharetra chased her away, but even Polos laughed at us. I could not remain. I write this by the fire of a knowing man with a wooden foot. He has consulted the gods for me, and says I will do well in the games, and score my greatest triumph in the chariot race. I have been considering what I must do, and feel sure he is correct.

Today was the day of the diaulos, the most popular of all the footraces. Elimination heats were held in the morning, the great event at evening. Pasicrates ran so well that it seemed to all of us that he had won, but the judges ruled in favor of another. The distance between them cannot have been more than the width of a man's thumb.

Diokles taught me wrestling. He calls it the least useful part of the pankration, but says that I should know it as well as the rest. He taught me several valuable holds, but when we actually wrestled, I beat him easily.

The poet with many rings is composing an ode to honor the winner of the stadion; the man's city will pay.

A man from the Isle of Roses has won the dolichos. It was terrible to hear the blows and see Pasicrates' face afterward; I should have knocked the mantis and the old physician aside and stopped it. When it was over, he called Polos to him and kissed him, and embraced me as a brother. He limps, as I noticed after the race, when he thinks himself unobserved. Now the prince has sent him to Tower Hill, telling him not to return without gold.

This was the day of the five trials. I did not go to the stadium with the others but into the town, hoping to buy a stall for Aglaus. The market was empty, however, because everyone had gone to the games. I was ready to leave when Anysia invited me to share the first meal with her; thinking she would want money, I told her I would not lie with a woman until after the chariot race. She took my arm and said I need not, that she wished to speak with me. When everyone returned to eat, we ate, too; I found an old woman (cast in eye, south side of the agora) very ready to sell her little fruit stall. Later Anysia and I went to the stadium with the rest.

Here is everything Anysia told me before the first meal; it is certainly important if it is true, and perhaps even if it is not. She is from Thespiae, west of Hill, and lives by dancing. Tonight I watched her in the red glare of the torches—how like a goddess she appeared!

"I'm your true love," she said. "You forget, and so you can't really know love, but I love you and I'll never forget you. I'm as true a love as you will ever have. Do you think you love Pharetra?"

"I must," I told her. "My heart leaped when you spoke her name."

Anysia seemed to study me. "You probably won't believe me, but the Amazon you think is your Pharetra isn't. Your Pharetra died in Thrace."

I felt then that I had heard my own death sentence.

"There's a certain Amazon," Anysia continued, "who others may tell you is Pharetra. She's very tall and strong, and has brown hair. Do you know the one I mean?"

Io had described such a woman when we woke, calling her Pharetra.

"Her name's really Hippostizein. She was a comrade of your Pharetra, who was quite a bit shorter and had red hair. Seeing how you grieved and knowing you forget, your slave told you this woman was Pharetra, after she volunteered to play the part."

I said nothing.

"They laugh about it behind your back, no doubt, and think themselves extremely clever; but your slave girl, at least, has exchanged her happiness for yours. Or so I'm told."

I nodded, for I feel that I understand.

"As a favor to me, who've told you the plain truth, please don't beat her too severely—I've been beaten myself, a time or two. You can kill the tall one for all I care."

I shook my head, knowing that I would harm neither Io nor the tall woman. "How did you learn all this?"

"From someone I met last night. I'd danced a long time and was tired, but music woke me. I've never heard music like that. I followed it, hoping that I could get the piper to join us, and since I was thinking about how I'd dance to his music, I started to dance as I turned over the steps. When I spun around, this woman—Elata's her name—was dancing, too, following me. She's beautiful, and a wonderful dancer, by the way.

"When the music stopped, she asked why I'd been crying. I told her about you and all the awful things the Amazon had done to me, calling her Pharetra, which was what somebody told me her name was. And she—this Elata—explained that she'd known both of them in the north, and that Pharetra was dead. Your slave had talked to her husband about it, and he had the Amazon kiss you."

We spoke a good deal more, she telling me much concerning a dancer's life that I will not set down here. She said that she loved me. I told her I could not marry her, or anyone, until I found my home; and that even after I found it, I might be in no position to marry. She said she wanted my love, not my property—this is a new idea for me, I think. At first she assumed that I forgot with every cup, and when I had proved that I remembered everything we had said in the market, that I recalled much that I do not—how the tall Amazon she calls Hippostizein had pushed her into some water, for example.

I, too, will call her Hippostizein, for I think that Anysia spoke the truth. But I need her if I am to free the friends who know where my home lies, and thus I must say nothing to her. I did not speak with them today for fear their guards would become suspicious.

Polos came to watch me exercise the horses. As Diokles and I rubbed them down, he asked me to explain *arete*. "I know Ares is the war god here," he said, "like Pleistorus. But this isn't war. How can anybody say that the man who runs fastest shows his *arete*?"

"It isn't the man who runs best who runs from the enemy," I told him, "and sometimes you want your men to run. When they do, you'd like to see them escape so they can fight again, on better terms or from a better position."

Diokles spat. "War isn't all blood and death, lad. And it isn't always the biggest army that wins. Pretty often it's the one that drills the best, and keeps its armor clean, and stands up best to long marches on short rations. Old Ares isn't some kind of monster, see? Think of him as a plain man that wants to win the war and get back home to Aphrodite. He's for training, discipline, and fair play with the men. And he whistles when he loses just like he whistles when he wins."

I asked Diokles then whether other events are to be held on the day of the chariot race; he said not. Thus my friends will be left in the market, perhaps, to wait the return of the crowd—at least I must hope so. Wrestling tomorrow, but I must go to Cyparissa to see the ship. I have ordered Aglaus to remind me of it. I should not have mentioned the ship to the dancer, but she cannot have guessed what I plan.

The road to the coast is steep, and narrow in many places. All that is good, but I could wish it not so long. It will be dark, or twilight at least. The ship is unguarded, moored with a single cable. It will be hard to conceal my sword—perhaps it can be tied beneath the chariot. I must try this.

* * *

There are marble seats above the wooden ones. I saw them and the watchers there, when I stunned the last man; but when I pointed them out to Io, she could not see them, though a woman there waved to us.

The prize was a beautiful dish full of the finest figs. I gave them to everyone who wanted one and presented the dish to Prince Pausanias, who was very pleased. He put his arm about my shoulders—a signal honor. He won a large sum by betting on me.

The judge has drawn up a deed for me by which I give the children to the poet from Hill. I signed it and left it with him; thus Io at least will return to her city. The all-power fighting is tomorrow.

They say the Amazon will drive the horses of the sun, but it is I who will drive like the sun himself. When I cut the harness, we will have four riders; the rest must fight on foot.

43

Pindaros of Thebes

Makes this offering to the Shining God, his patron, ever the patron of letters, whom he dares call his friend. The pythia has asked him to do this so that it may be known how the god worked his will.

A queen out of the north brought to the god's games his own flashing horses, deep-chested and headed like bulls, with fiery eyes. About the track they thundered, behind them the brightest gift of the merciful Lacedaemonians, lent by Neocles' son, ship-commanding Themistocles. A second turn. Lo, the Dorian chariot holds the pace stride for stride. Crowned still with the sacred boughs of Daphne—fairest daughter of the river—the conquering pankratiast guides it, Latros of Sparta (whom once I conducted as the god directed me) smiling upon the god's virgin handmaid. Five others are crusted with the showering dust. At the sight the cheers of the Hellenes ring loud, like the beating of bright shields.

As a skillful hand strokes the strings, the god's servant, the dark spearman's daughter, restrains her eight-reined team, forewarned of the fast-approaching turn. By a head—a neck—half a length, the mighty four, speechless slaves of Heracles' heir, best in battle, outreach them. So Latros drives. So drove Diomedes, when heroes mourned the son of Menoetius—but drove a straight road.

Before Latros a thousand scatter as quail, war-tried heroes who crushed the barbarian upon the Boeotian Plain, frightened as children, fleeing like the sad Asteria before the earthshaking steed of Poseidon, parting as the wave before the prow of *Argo*. None pursue the flying Latros, for none can.

Now what need of speed or dust? What envious hopes strain after the argent chariot of the gray-eyed Athena? This lordly urn, the gift of the god, her servant receives, presents in his turn to the virgin queen—thus is peace forged between Theseus' foes and Theseus' city. Hippephode receives it glorying, joyful in duty done, speaks by the lamed son of Elis, great in counsel, of the road home. Advised by him and royal in bearing as in deed, she dedicates it, emptied of rich oil, to the Shining God upon his holy mountain—the god's forever.

Scarcely has the daughter of war spoken than the voice of war sounds. Dull is he whose lips malign the line of

Heracles, whose strength lingers even in fostered sons. Like his mighty club, speeding Latros has struck the sacred city. In freezing Colchis, Jason sowed the dragon's teeth, brought forth from the furrow hundreds armed and fierce for battle. So was it with him who was once my charge. He from tumbled apples and pomegranates in the marketplace brought forth sharp swords, loud-voiced bows, and quivers rich in arrows. And from the slaves of the Argives, soldiers.

At once the Argives, sworn foes of Lacedaemon, call for the aid of Lacedaemon's manly sons, mighty in brazen battle, against the defilers of the sacred peace. Declaring he has no guilt in the matter and credited because of the gold he lost on the race, the Lacedaemonian prince musters his dreaded guards and marches in tardy pursuit.

No man dare say the immortal gods have had no hand in this. Io, my slave, wise beyond her years and full payment for all the good I sought to do Latros, led me to the limping Hegesistratus, the tongue of the Amazon queen, where he sat grieving his lost wife. "I have failed Cynthia." Thus he groaned in my hearing. "Before you, you see a corpse, foul already with the stench of death. The silver chariot would be overheavy, and Latros bore the victory always. Nor would the woman who had desired him so long dare to defeat him, now that she had his love. Bribed, I swore to serve the deity of my enemies, but could not serve her well. My end I foresaw in distant Thrace—her slaves shall wrest me from my island home, and five swords send me down to death."

Mantic Tisamenus, Iamus' child, gave me this scroll and the other, this as he said for the wide-shouldered pankratiast. "He implores the mercy of the Shining God, ever generous. In these the ill-starred Latros gives the offended god his life—all that he has had." The queen of the one-breasted daughters of war has urged that these be added to the urn she has given. His priests consent.

Tomorrow she will sacrifice before setting out for her own land, well content.

Themistocles of Athens will not be welcomed when he returns to his violet-crowned city, so many of his fellow citizens say, alleging that he has sold himself to Lacedaemon, however hotly he denies it. His cup-fellow Simonides grinds away at the rhyming mill as before.

The Spartan regent is cried up for his sagacity everywhere, and talks of marching against the Sons of Perseus. All know now that the ship Latros took carried his cargo, and it is said that at his command his Lacedaemonians shunned the Phoenician steel, by their well-considered hesitancy obstructing the narrow way so that others could not join the battle. In this way, so runs the tale, the shrewd prince gained ten times over what he lost. But some to whom I spoke in Cyparissa report that as the vessel bore Latros and the slaves away, a slender woman with a bow stood at his side. These do not scruple to name her Artemis, the argent twin; that it was a chariot of silver that triumphed no one can deny. Whether this be truth or empty fable, it is certain that Pausanias the son of Cleombrotus is accounted twice a hero among the stratagem-loving Greeks.

As for this poor servant of the Shining One, the patron of the muses, he and his slave will return to their own seven-gated city—or perhaps journey to far-distant Sicily, rich in flocks, as the grave emissaries of glorious Hieron, splendid in victory, importune. If that be so, he prays the blessing of Ino, white keeper of the chambers of the sea among the daughters of Nereus. Permit us to voyage in safety, O lovely Ino, to that great city, Syracuse, the precinct of Ares.

Glossary

See *Soldier of the Mist* for the following terms: Acetes, Aram, Artaÿctes, Asopus, Basias, Bearland, Budini, Cerdon, Chersonese, Clay, Cowland, Dolphins, Drakaina, Eurotas, Eutaktos, Falcata, Fennel Field, Gaea, Gorgo, Helle's Sea, Hill, Hypereides, Iamus, Ino, Io, Ister, Kalleos, Kichesippos, Kore, Latro, Leonidas, Leotychides, Lyson, Mardonius, Medes, Nysa, Parsa, Pasicrates, Pausanias, Pindaros, Pleistarchos, Pleistoanax, Riverland, Rope, Sestos, Simonides, Susa, Themistocles, Thought, Tisamenus, Triple Goddess, and Xanthippos.

Achaeans—An ancient tribe, displaced by the Dorians.
Achilles—A leader of the Achaeans at the siege of Ilion.
Adeimantus—A magnate of Tower Hill.
Aegospotami—A small city on the eastern coast of the Chersonese, near its midpoint.
Aeolians—A tribe of Hellenes inhabiting the northern coast of Asia Minor.

Agatharchos—An official of the Pythic Games.

Aglaus—The poor laborer employed as a guide by Themistocles in Bearland and later as a servant by the black man and Latro.

Ahura Mazda—The supreme god of Parsa.

Amazons—Barbarian priestesses of the War God.

Amyklos—A centaur famous as a healer.

Anochos—A citizen of Dolphins employed by Rope to represent its interests there.

Anysia—An acrobatic dancer in the troupe engaged by Cimon.

Apollonios—A priest of the oracle at Dolphins.

Apsinthia—The barbarian kingdom just west of the Chersonese.

Ares—The god of war.

arete—The virtues of a soldier, ranging from cleanliness and love of order to courage in the face of death.

Argas—Prince Pausanias' racehorse.

Artembares—The young son of the governor of Sestos under the Great King.

Artemisia—The warrior queen of Halicarnassos.

Asopodorus—The commander of the cavalry of Hill at the Battle of Clay.

Athena Ilias—A goddess who aided the Hellenes during the siege of Ilion.

Badizoe—An Amazon; her name means "slow march," or "walk" when applied to cavalry.

Bittusilma—The Babylonian who attaches herself to the black man; her name means "house of perfection."

black man—Seven Lions, the soldier from Nysa who cared for Latro after the Battle of Clay.

boiled leather—Cuir-bouilli; leather hardened by immersion in very hot wax.

Byblos—The sacred city of the Crimson Men, said to be the oldest city in the world; it lies north of Sidon.

Cape Mastursia—The tip of the Chersonese.

Ceos—A small island off the southeastern end of the Long Coast.

Cimon—An aristocratic young politician famous for hospitality; pronounced *Keé-mone.*

Cleombrotus—An Agid prince, son of Anaxandridas and brother to Cleomenes and Leonidas.

Cleton—A merchant from Hundred-Eyed long resident at Cobrys.

Clytias—The founder of the pro-Laconian branch of the Iamidae.

Cobrys—A port on the Thracian coast; the capital of Apsinthia.

Crimson Men—Traders from the eastern shore of the Great Sea, from the color of their robes and the dyed cloth they sell.

Cybele—A name under which Gaea is worshiped in the east.

Cyklos—One of the five judges of Rope.

Cynthia—The Huntress, born in a cave on Mt. Cynthus.

Cyparissa—A small port at the foot of Mt. Parnassos.

Cyrus—The first Great King, founder of the Empire.

Damon—Pericles' tutor, once a famous singer.

Deloptes—A Thracian nobleman.

Diallos—A slave of Themistocles'.

Diokles—The professional employed to train Latro and Pasicrates.

Elata—A dryad of the Chersonese; her name means "pine."

Elis—A small city near the western tip of Redface Island.

Europa, the—The trireme commanded by Hypereides.

Fortuna—The goddess of chance, now commonly called Lady Luck.

Getae—Barbarians of the northern forests; the Budini are a tribe belonging to this group.

Hebrus—A river of Thrace.

Hegesistratus—Mardonius' seer and sorcerer.

Hellas—The country of the Hellenes, a peninsula extending south into the sea.

Hellenes—The sons and daughters of Hellen, linked by a common language.

Hieron—The tyrant of Syracuse.

Hippephode—The queen of the Amazons; her name means "cavalry charge."

Hippostizein—The tallest Amazon; her name means "trooper."

Hippoxleas—A Silent One, reporting to Cyklos.

Hubrias—A merchant captain of Hundred-Eyed.

Huntress—An aspect of the Triple Goddess.

Iamidae—A clan of prophets, descended from Iamus.

Ilion—A ruined city of the Troad; it lies on the Asian coast south of Sestos, near the southern outlet of Helle's Sea.

Kemet—Riverland; the black land.

Kotys—The name of numerous Thracian kings.

Kotytto—A name under which Gaea is worshiped in Thrace.

Kronos—The king of the old gods; he prevented the heavens from further influencing the development of life on earth.

kybernetes—Sailing master.

Lacedaemon—That portion of the Silent Country anciently governed by Rope; the lambda on the Rope Makers' hoplons derives from this name.

Lewqys—*Lucius,* as pronounced by a Crimson Man.

Luhitu—Possibly a garbling of *Latium.*

Melas—A river of Thrace.

Miltiades—The victorious commander at the Battle of Fennel Field and the builder of the wall across the Chersonese.

Mnemosyne—A titaness; her nine daughters are the goddesses of astronomy, comedy, dance, geometry, history, poetry, rhetoric, song, and tragedy.

Molossis—The region between the Acheron and the Arethon; it is famous for its huge dogs, which are widely exported.

Muslak—A merchant captain of Byblos.

Nereus—Among the old gods, the sea god.

Nessibur—A Thracian nobleman.

Oeobazus—The Median engineer who built the bridge of boats across Helle's Sea.

Orpheus—A shaman killed by the Thracian women; his head was cast into the Hebrus, still pronouncing the name of his lost wife.

Orsippos—A magnate of Hundred-Eyed.

Pactye—The northernmost city of the Chersonese, just south of Miltiades' Wall.

Paetians—The Thracian tribe north of the Apsinthians.

Pandion—An ancient king of Thought.

Parnassos—A lofty mountain north of the Gulf; Dolphins is on this mountain.

peltast—A foot soldier armed with a pair of javelins and a pelta.

Pericles—Xanthippos' teenage son.

Perseus—The father of Perses, and thus the founder of the nation of the Great King.

Pharetra—The Amazon loved by Latro.

Philomela—A princess of ancient Thought; her name means "lover of song."

Pleistorus—A name under which the War God is worshiped in Thrace.

Polos—The young centaur sent to Latro by Gaea.

Polygnotos—A famous painter of Thought; Cimon's sister Elpinice is rumored to be his mistress.

Priam—The last king of Ilion.

Procne—A princess of ancient Thought; her name means "firstborn."

Protesilaos—The first hero to die at the siege of Ilion.

pythia—The Destroyer's virgin prophetess, probably about fifteen.

Pythic Games—Contests held at Dolphins every four years in honor of the Destroyer; they include competitions in music and poetry as well as footraces, boxing, etc.

python—Gaea's sacred serpent, slain by the Destroyer; it haunts the oracle he wrested from her.

Raskos—A peltast killed by Latro.

Rhea—The mother of the gods. A name under which Cybele is worshiped in the west; it means "earth."

Seven Lions—The black man.

Sicily—A large island west of the Gulf.

Sidon—The capital of the Crimson Men; the king of Sidon is the commander of the Great King's navy.

Sisyphus—The first king of Tower Hill.

Swollenfoot—A king of ancient Hill.

Syracuse—A great city established by colonists from Tower Hill.

Tegea—A small city in Bearland.

Tellias—The founder of the anti-Laconian branch of the Iamidae.

Tereus—The name of numerous Thracian kings.

Thamyris—A Thracian prince; King Kotys' chief adviser.

Thespiae—A small city in Cowland.

Thrace—A vast barbarian country stretching from the eastern bank of the Nestos to the western shore of the Euxine.

Tillon—A slave of Themistocles'.

Troad—The area once controlled by Ilion, including the Thracian Chersonese, Mysia, and Phrygia Minor.

Xerxes—Khshayarsha, the Great King, ruler of the Empire.

Zakunthios—An island west of Elis.

Zalmoxis—A shape-changing shaman deified; his name is presumably derived from the Thracian word *zalmo,* "skin."

Zeus—The king of the gods.

Zihrun—The alias adopted by Oeobazus.